Perfectly Candid
J.S. Jasper

Copyright © 2024 by J.S.Jasper

All rights reserved.

No part of this publication may be reproduced, distributed, or transmitted in any form or by any means, including photocopying, recording, or other electronic or mechanical methods, without the prior written permission of the publisher, except as permitted by U.S. copyright law. For permission requests, contact jsjsprwrts@hotmail.com

The story, all names, characters, and incidents portrayed in this production are fictitious. No identification with actual persons (living or deceased), places, buildings, and products is intended or should be inferred.

Book Cover by Yenthe Jolie

Map Illustrations by George Outhwaite

Edited by Rachelle of R. A. Wright Editing

BLURB

Aliyah Giorgia Juliet Panimiro was never meant to be queen. It's not in her blood. Yet, after a family tragedy, the duty to wear the crown was thrust upon her. Now, she spends her time alone, dreaming of a day she won't have to attend balls with the dreaded goal of finding a husband, as though she's living in a doomed fairytale and not the twenty-first century. Aliyah knows the pressure to marry is high, but is it too much to ask to fall in love first?

Elliot despises the royal family and everything they stand for. So, he's not quite sure how he ended up working for them this summer. There's nothing he wants from Galineria Palace apart from a glowing recommendation and to make his family proud. He has no intention of leaving with anything else. And then he meets a girl under the plum tree, and he wonders how bad it would be if, just this once, he talked to her...

Contains discussions of body negativity from parents, abusive parents, disordered eating, waterboarding, and an attempted sexual assault.

For Deni x

"I was made and meant to look for you and wait for you and become yours forever." – Robert Browning

PROLOGUE

Cold, sharp steel presses against Elliot's throat. Usually, that would bother him. On any other day, he might think about asking why it's a knife and not something easier, perhaps pepper spray or a taser. Today, though—his first day on the Galineria grounds—he can't find it in himself to mind all that much. Not when the perpetrator looks like a daydream.

He wonders if the woman in front of him likes coffee or tea with breakfast. Perhaps it's neither. She's close enough that if she had a drink this morning, he'd be able to smell it on her breath, but he can't smell anything but fresh linen and strawberries.

Elliot wonders whether she prefers walks by Lake Dalinko, which he hasn't had the chance to visit yet, or strolls in the Giorgian Gardens. Whether she shares the same disdain for the monarchy as him—the monarchy they both find themselves working for. A lifetime's worth of questions flit through his head so quickly he can barely hold on to them, and with what he thinks might be the last moments of his life, nothing but her flashes through his mind. There are no childhood memories, no regrets, no lost loves. Only her.

The way her ebony hair twists over her shoulder in braids. The rogue curls that blow against her sharp cheekbone with the faint breeze in the air. His gaze flies over her face, noticing the tremble of her lips. The deep blush he can see on her cheeks, even with her brown skin. In another lifetime, he would have spent an upsetting amount of time trying to get her attention. She'd have ignored him, of course, because people who look like her don't want people like him.

"You're magnificent," he says, on a breath. It's a struggle because the hilt of her knife is pressing against his larynx, but it's worth the effort when her brow furrows. No, she might not want him in this lifetime, but he's about to go into his next one anyway, so he figures, *what's the harm?*

She takes a deep breath, but it does nothing to stop her manicured hands from shaking. (Elliot always notices someone's hands because he likes to figure out if they work outside, like him. But he chances a glance at her polished nails and assumes she works indoors.) Interesting, though, that she seems more nervous about this encounter than he does, and she's the one wielding the weapon. If she's nervous, at least the likeliness of her burying him next to the plum tree they stand under is lessened. Even if he hadn't noticed her hands, her doe-eyed, deep-brown eyes give her away. Along with being the most delightful thing he's seen in his entire lifetime, she looks utterly terrified to have found herself in this situation. She swallows, and he watches the movement like his life depends on it.

She blinks rapidly. He knows she's about to say something, and it's going to change his life.

"I beg your pardon?"

Elliot would laugh. He would do anything to lessen the fear on her face, but as his luck would have it, the blade still rests against his throat, shaking a few millimeters every second. He would rather it didn't, because he's pretty sure—despite the aforementioned knife to his neck—the woman in front of him doesn't *want* to behead him in the middle of the woods. It would be just his luck that due to the way her knuckles tremble, she might not have a choice.

"I'm just saying," he says quietly, with a slow, exaggerated shrug.

Her eyes drop to the knife against his skin, and she pulls it back a touch. Barely noticeable, he thinks, but enough for him to know she's not going to kill him. So now, instead of being in a deathly situation with a woman who will certainly haunt his sleepless nights, he's simply under a plum tree in the chilly early spring morning with the girl of his dreams. So, it's not his fault when, instead of fleeing, he says, "You're beautiful."

She blinks, what looks like pure surprise covering her face. It's as if no one has ever said that to her before. Elliot would bet his life savings (barely enough for a car from the nineties with no power steering) on the fact that people must fall over their feet to talk to her. Her face is poetry. Then she frowns, her lips pouting, clearly forcing herself to respond in a way she thinks is suitable, and if he wasn't a gentleman, he'd be leaning in already. He wonders if it's possible to live in this moment—a moment when she doesn't have control over her reaction—forever.

"Are you flirting with me?" she asks, her voice like velvet. Her hand drops, and she seems to have forgotten she was threatening him mere moments ago. "I am trying to kill you, am I not?"

Elliot chuckles. He wonders how she can't tell he would die to flirt with her. Alas, his mom would be furious if he croaked on his first day. So, even with his awful hand-eye coordination (he was a swimmer, but all he ever had to do was not swim into the side of the pool, which is less than helpful for getting out of a would-be murder), he manages to spin and disarm her entirely.

He pries the knife from her hand, his head cocked to the side as he asks, "Are you?"

He's careful with the blade, his fingertips against the sharp edge so if anything went wrong, he'd be the one to get hurt. He doesn't touch her at all. He thinks if his skin touched hers, that might be more lethal than a blade slicing his palm. He spins as she turns, and it's as smooth as a practiced dance. He wonders if, in another lifetime, they would be more than strangers in the woods. If maybe they would waltz across walnut floors beneath a hundred glistening chandeliers. He wonders if, at another time, it would have been them in the palace that sits hidden behind the trees under which they stand.

Elliot thinks maybe it's only him who feels that way, because as he turns with the knife he has no intention of ever pointing anywhere near her, the woman in front of him backs up against the tree. Her eyes frantically look around her and yet have him pinned to the ground. He wants to tell her she can go; he won't chase her. That he has no intention of doing anything other than whatever will make her happiest. But it's too late. He's caught in the deep brown of her eyes, the sharp line of her jaw, the furrow of her brow, and he misses the way her foot sweeps the ground. In the end, a ridiculously small log takes him out at the ankles, and he watches her disappear into the bushes from where he lies.

Usually, he (and his parents, which is how he finds himself working on the grounds of Galineria) would say that he found himself in difficult situations because of his behavior. But as the knife sits in his hand, his head throbbing from hitting the ground, he still can't be all too sure how he ended up here.

CHAPTER ONE

FORCING HER HEAD BETWEEN her satin pillows, Aliyah sighs, willing her daydream about *him* to come back. That or the overwhelming scent of strawberry detergent to render her unconscious. It's useless, of course. The ominous presence at her bedroom door lingers even as she tries to remember what position she dreamt herself into. So, she spins and throws her forearm over her eyes as she attempts to tune out the scathing rant of the woman pacing on the other side of the threshold. Queen Grace Laurel Panimiro—or, as Aliyah so often calls her, Mother.

Whenever the Queen makes the journey to this side of the palace, Aliyah knows she's done something wrong. *Biblically* wrong, if the Queen has made her way to Aliyah's bedroom rather than meeting in one of the sitting rooms. Aliyah can practically hear the anger seeping through her mother's words as they fly around the room like carefully designed throwing stars—never meant to be seen, only used to inflict maximum damage.

Often when her mother is listing off scathing insults, Aliyah isn't sure what the problem is. There's no use in her guessing, because that would take her years and would tear down the only self-worth she has managed to conjure up for herself. It's normally something against the royal code. A reason as utterly terrible as throwing up a peace sign as the paparazzi follow her home from another ball she never wanted to go to in the first place. (Classic.) Or when she donates large sums of money to causes the palace would never usually advocate for. (Necessary.) Or when she wanders off and almost gets herself assassinated on a royal outing. (Not entirely her fault.) Usually, Aliyah would be guessing what the issue is the moment she hears the guards down her hallway shuffle back into place and the Queen's heels hitting the floor maddeningly.

This time, Aliyah need not guess. She already knows.

Of course, it was never her intention to threaten a man in the middle of the woods—nor did she expect anyone to catch the altercation on camera—but if there's something she's learned from being thrust into the limelight at four years old, it's that everything can be seen in some way. Usually, not at all the truth, but once the version the press wants is out, it's too late to say anything. In her defense—one she does think she deserves, seeing as he walked away unscathed—he *was* creeping after her in the woods. What was she supposed to do? *Not* defend herself, when everything about palace life has taught her different?

Aliyah is to be on guard from the moment she wakes up until the moment she goes to sleep. *Of course,* a strange man stalking her through the woods would require a knife to the throat. What Aliyah wasn't expecting was for him to look like he did—beautiful, and utterly shocked they were in that position. The moment she pinned him to the tree, she knew he wasn't there to cause her harm, but she couldn't leave. And she still doesn't know why, even though she's thought about nothing else for days.

"Princess," her mother sighs, disdain dripping from her tongue. "Have you seen the news?"

Aliyah swallows. She could plead ignorance. It wouldn't be a total lie. (Aliyah refuses to entertain the news because most of the time it's entirely unflattering, and worse than that, it's hardly ever true.) Or she could admit that she did almost slice a man's throat. (A stunningly beautiful man whom she's thought about at length ever since, but a man nonetheless.) But, honestly and truly, she was never going to go through with it. Besides, she only had her knife on her because whenever she's by herself, she finds herself needing it. And she was only in that garden because no one has let her beyond the palace walls in *years*.

Aliyah has thought about upgrading her defense to something more modern. A taser, or mace, perhaps. But then she would have no second chance, if she pressed the button, they would already be hurt. A knife is a threat only, and one she never plans on acting upon, because she never wants to hurt anyone. It's supposed to be the whole point to the royal family. A point both her mother and father don't care for – especially when it comes to her.

Her mother seems to be in a fouler mood than usual today, which probably means she's scowling, the vein on her forehead throbbing with annoyance. Aliyah daren't look at her—ever since she was a child, Aliyah had found that pulsing vein hilarious. But when she was a child, laughing about it was something she was allowed to do. Her sister and she would giggle at state dinners when their family didn't get the alliance they wanted, and her mother was furious. Now, Aliyah barely walks out of turn without fear of being punished.

And yet.

"The price of bread has risen thirty-four percent in the past six months," Aliyah drawls, sitting up on her bed. Her arm hits the mattress with a thud, and she scowls, trying to get some feeling back into her fingers. "We should intervene and offer the farmers an initiative to lower the price of wheat before families cannot afford basic groceries."

Aliyah chances a look over at her mother. Her answer did nothing but make the Queen's face redder, her gleaming blue eyes staring her down. Though she finally stopped pacing, it's worse, somehow, when she's still.

"Amusing."

Sometimes, Aliyah thinks her parents don't care about their status as the heads of this kingdom. The idea of people suffering does nothing to alter the way they sleep at night. She wonders if she would think the same as them if she was biologically theirs. She shakes those thoughts from her mind. She *is* their child, even if they don't want her to be. Aliyah is theirs. Although, as her twenty-fifth birthday looms, Aliyah's feeling out of place here has gotten increasingly worse. The King and Queen have dropped all pretense that they care for her beyond the need for her to carry on their royal lineage. They've made it clear Aliyah will be married by her twenty-fifth birthday or *else*. Else *what*, she's never been too sure, but her parents aren't people to be messed with. Not when it threatens their legacy.

The Queen unfolds the newspaper and drops it on the floor in front of Aliyah's bedroom with a thud. Aliyah sighs, heaves herself off the bed, and walks over to pick it up. She'd make a big deal about her mother throwing it at her, but she likes that no one ever comes in her room.

It takes her a moment to scour the page looking for the words "murderer." Thankfully, they're not there. Chancing a look up at her mother, Aliyah realizes she's still kneeling on the ground, and stands.

By the time she sits on the chaise lounge in front of her bed, the only thing on the front page of the paper is still a picture of her running across the gardens. Her face isn't entirely visible, but anyone in the kingdom would know it was her. She's the only one within the grounds with braids, after all. Aliyah scrunches the paper in her hands, frantically reading the words to find out exactly what about this front-page news is news at all, let alone why her mother is shaking with disappointment and rage.

"You know how I love how we close we are, Mother?" Aliyah asks.

Her mother gives her a look that suggests she might throw her in the dungeons if she says one more smart-mouthed word. (She hasn't been in the dungeons for a few months now. It's usually no longer than a few hours, at worst—maybe a day if her mother is in a particularly bad mood—but since she hasn't found a husband yet, the threats have started to become more frequent. Although, Aliyah did practically live in the dungeons during her teenage years because she snuck out to see a concert. Still worth it, in her opinion, but that doesn't mean it's something she wishes to do again.) So, she swallows a sigh.

"Would you mind letting me know what the problem is?"

She places the newspaper on the chair, wondering if the slightly new angle will show her flipping off the paparazzi. Her mother sighs like she's been asked to go down the mines and not simply vocalize why she's upset, but Aliyah doesn't push it, not this time.

PERFECTLY CANDID

"Your dress is *filthy*. We took you *out* of the orphanage to come live in a palace, so I do not know why you continue to act like you roam the streets." Well. It's true. She was adopted by the King and Queen twenty years ago, and anyone would think it would have stopped being brought up by now, but her mother likes to remind Aliyah how she was *saved* by them.

"Graham is close to the family, is he not?" her mother asks. He's not. If he was a close family friend, then she'd know more about him than the fact his name isn't *actually* Graham, it's Nathan, and she'd see him at birthday parties and for Sunday dinner, if they had such things. And he'd know more about her than her measurements and that she bloats ever so slightly when she eats bread.

Beyond the occasional state dinner and over-the-top event because her father managed to survive another year (while doing nothing at all), guests are not invited to the palace. The only reason there are ever people within the grounds at all is because Aliyah announced a fully funded program for underprivileged children while she was live on air at eighteen, and her parents couldn't take it back without losing face. Aliyah saw the inside of the dungeons for a *while* for that one, and, shockingly, she's not been allowed on live television since. The only reason the kingdom has seen her at all since then is because the people seem to love her, but she may as well have her jaw wired shut for all she's allowed to speak.

"I see," Aliyah replies. There's no point in telling her mother the reason she was running across the grass despite the "keep off the grass" sign at the bottom of the photo. At one point in her life—probably between the ages of five and eight—Aliyah had wanted to tell her mother everything. What she dreamt about, what she would like for dinner, the flowers she liked in the garden. It took her far too many years to realize her mother never cared. That if Aliyah simply didn't speak, the Queen's life wouldn't be any different (possibly easier). And maybe, given the heartbreak her parents endured, Aliyah should give them a pass. But she knows that even if her sister, Lydia, were still alive, Aliyah still wouldn't be "theirs." She never really was "theirs" in their eyes.

"Try to remember we are expecting you to obtain a husband *before* you are dead and buried. Traipsing around the palace like you live in the slums will not help with your limited suitors."

Aliyah wants to point out that she's not allowed to leave palace grounds, and the men they bring around for her are vile, but she said that the other night at dinner, so she daren't repeat it now. Plus, Aliyah knows her mother and father have had someone lined up to marry her since she came here; she's not entirely sure why they pretend she has any say in the matter at all.

Her mother, with her porcelain skin, sweeps her hand across the front of her gown as if she's trying to rid this conversation from the delicate fabric. Aliyah wonders how she can be bothered to be in a silk dress this early in the morning, but she doesn't ask, and she doesn't bring it up lest she's forced to match for breakfast in the dining hall. The crown perched upon her mother's perfectly straightened blonde hair glints in the sunlight, taunting Aliyah that she'll have to wear something similar for the rest of her life.

Unless...

Aliyah swallows her laugh. She'd never actually abdicate. She used to think it was because she owed her parents too much, but now she knows the difference she could make if she were given the power. Still, it's a nice thought to have when she has trouble falling asleep.

Aliyah pulls her knees to her chest. "I am twenty-four, am I not? Or do you believe me to be one foot in the grave already?"

Her mother ignores her quip as she eyes Aliyah's outfit with disdain. Aliyah is well aware her mother disapproves of her shorts and T-shirt combination, but in her defense (again), she is in her room, and it's barely seven thirty in the morning. She hasn't even had breakfast yet. The thought of having this entire conversation again with her father, in front of the myriad of staff, makes her want to skip the meal altogether.

"We have a guest at breakfast," her mother says, instead of anything about her attire, but Aliyah knows better than to let her guard down while her mother is on this side of the door. "Do try to make an effort to look less like you have been dragged through a hedge backward." And there it is.

PERFECTLY CANDID

The door slams closed, and once again, Aliyah is alone. It's how she likes to be. There's no one within the palace grounds she trusts enough to be in her room with her. Apart from Anna, of course. Anna basically raised her, and still, she hasn't been in this room before. Not since Anna was banished to the outskirts of the palace grounds, and Aliyah had to move rooms because a new library was being installed and they wanted her stained-glass windows. Now, this is the one room where Aliyah can do what she wants, and be who she wants, without the threat of it becoming front-page news. It's how she gets away with putting up colored curtains (they're a light orange linen at the moment), and how the watercolor sunset sky she has painted on the ceiling hasn't been covered.

Aliyah drags her feet across the plush rug she had snuck in through the back door of the palace, digging her toes in as she stretches. She looks around at the ornate picture frames she's slapped posters over because she thinks it's creepy to sleep in a room with paintings of a four-hundred-year-old white man she doesn't know. Her father thinks it's incredibly disrespectful, but he's never understood why she feels out of place here. She stopped trying to explain her feelings back in her teenage years. Perhaps it *is* disrespectful, verging on childish, to cover portraits of those who have come before her, but Aliyah is allowed to be both of those things in her own bedroom. If there were anything else to cover the portraits with—photos of her family or friends—she would have used those. Unfortunately, for that to occur, she would need to have either.

Outside of paparazzi snaps and official painted portraits, there has never been a photograph of her and her family that she has seen. Aliyah has always loved candid photos. The images when someone's about to smile, the way it tells someone they were happy even if the smile never comes to fruition. The occasions that are just *so* magical they need to be photographed. The only pictures Aliyah has of her family, or herself, are professional portraits in gowns that are more money than should ever be reasonable and a fake smile. She sighs. She doesn't have time to dwell on what could have been. There's an oppressive breakfast and more lecturing to get to.

J.S. JASPER

Aliyah opens her bedroom curtains slightly. It's nearing eight a.m., but with the spring season, the mornings are still ever so slightly dark. It's not quite late enough in the year for the sun to be high enough in the sky that it reaches the southern gardens this early, but in a couple of weeks, she will be able to sit on the balcony and read, and she won't need a dressing gown at all.

For now, she wraps her fluffy robe around her and ties it at the waist, covering her bare legs in case someone has snuck a camera in the bushes while she slept. Somehow, despite that being a hideous invasion of privacy, it would still be her fault.

Despite the feeling that she is a princess trapped in an ivory tower (her tower is made from stone and covered in wisteria and roses, and she is technically allowed to leave it, but still, the helpless feeling remains), Aliyah loves looking out over the palace grounds. Her palms hit the limestone balcony, and she's about to close her eyes and let the morning air hit her face when she sees *him*. The back of him, but she knows it's him all the same. The shoulder-to-waist ratio is unreasonably attractive, and she's thought about it at every given chance since she first saw him—the guy she didn't kill a few days ago. The man whom she'd fallen asleep thinking about for the past three days. There was something about the sparkle in his eye, and the way he didn't look terrified, even as she held a blade to his throat. Something about the way he smiled when she threw him to the floor. Something about the way he called her magnificent.

Aliyah has been taught to be calm and collected under pressure. She barely broke a sweat the last time she was almost kidnapped. (Though calling it that is dramatic—he didn't even manage to get the pillow over her head before she'd taken his toe clean off with her heel.) Now, as she watches, the guy turns his head, and she drops to the floor.

In the end, he doesn't even look her way. She watches him though. He walks away, his unfairly large thighs taut under the slacks he has on. She has wondered why he was here. Part of her hoped he would be the mystery guest at breakfast. Maybe, in another life, he would have been the person the King and Queen were trying to set her up with. Perhaps then she wouldn't fight them so hard on it.

He's got a green overcoat clasped in his hand, one she knows is standard uniform. Another person she'll never get to speak to again. It would be easy to find him under the palace directory... if she wanted to know his name. It would make her daydreams feel all the more real when she could whisper his name as her hand glides across her chest.

Aliyah doesn't think he's working right now, but she watches him all the same. The ground under her knees is uncomfortable, and she has to shuffle so the gravel doesn't take up residence in her shins, but it's worth it when his fingertips brush over the Camilla flowers in bloom. She wishes there was a memory of his touch on her skin.

He looks around the gardens, and she wants to know what he's thinking about. If he likes the rose bushes more in spring or summertime. If he hopes the sound of birds chirping infiltrates his daily life as much as she does. If he's looking over his shoulder because he thinks he might get attacked again. If he's thought about her.

Aliyah wants to know what his name is, if he likes it, if he's happy. She'll never get to ask, of course. A princess doesn't have friends. Instead, she watches him unlock the greenhouse, and as the door creaks open, she knows she'll spend the rest of the day thinking about this moment.

CHAPTER TWO

ELLIOT LETS THE SUN warm his back as he strolls through the palace grounds. The rays hit different in the kingdom of Iledale. Elliot's mom, Tinisha, always used to say the phrase "the grass is always greener" was a lie made by people to ensure everyone was always striving for more—a new car, a new job, a new house—something that meant they were never satisfied with what they had. Now Elliot is here, he sees it's not everyone else that was wrong. It's his mom.

(He'll never tell her that, though, because he loves her, and he's too tall to dodge her flying slipper very well.)

The grass *is* greener here. The sun is warmer, the sky brighter. He's unsure why. His home country of Loven is not that far—barely a twenty-minute ferry crossing, and still governed by Iledale—and yet, he can feel the sun healing the deep bruises he has under his eyes from lack of sleep. (He's never been diagnosed with insomnia, but he spends at least sixty percent of his days utterly knackered.) He wants to be annoyed about nature clearly having a socioeconomic bias, but the sound of birds and the scent of freshly cut grass makes it difficult.

Usually, Elliot would never be somewhere like this. Galineria Palace is not somewhere Elliot has ever thought about without disdain. It used to be an argument he would have with his much, *much* older (by twelve whole minutes) sister, Melody. While she shares his general dislike for the royal family, she has a keen liking for the Princess. Aliyah, Elliot thinks she's called, but he's spent his entire life making sure he knows nothing about them, so he's not sure he'd be able to pick her out of a lineup. Though the royal family is everything he isn't—white, powerful, and rich—so he'd likely recognize the Princess immediately because she'd be dripping in privilege.

As he wanders the grounds he's due to start working soon, Elliot understands it's hypocritical to hate it so much. But, in his defense, his mom made him apply for the position here. Yes, he's twenty-six, but he's not above listening to his parents. He never will be, not really. Elliot still hears his father's advice in his ear, even though he passed away eight years ago. Ever since, Elliot's mom has been getting tired of his behavior. It wasn't *all* that bad. He wasn't selling drugs, or out making trouble. He just wasn't doing... anything.

Elliot and his father had been the closest of friends. His friends always thought it was strange—their fathers were either absent or strict beyond belief. Dominik wasn't like that, though. He was strict, sure, but never physically. He had a way about him so that you knew if you let him down, it would devastate him more than his sickness ever did.

All Elliot really remembers about him is the outward way he loved them all. There's not a time he can think of when his mom ever opened her own car door or made herself a cup of tea. He was never absent from Melody's choir performances. He always waved the team flag at Elliot's football matches, even though, at the time, Elliot was a chubby eight-year-old who spent most of his time on the bench. Then, when he found his way to swimming, his father was there with orange wedges at every single practice and competition.

His mom was always there as well. She was quieter with her love, but it was obvious all the same. In the way she braided his hair late at night when he decided he didn't want to go to school with an afro. The way every one of his and Melody's school photos is in the living room of their childhood home, both of them shining with the amount of Vaseline on their faces. All Elliot ever wanted to do was make them happy. Maybe retire them early, if he could figure out what to focus on. Something to do with the garden—he always knew that much. But then his father passed, and his entire life turned upside down. It shouldn't have. Not really.

His father had been sick since before Elliot knew what a healthy father should look like. He assumed every dad had an oxygen tank and struggled to walk down stairs. He just never expected him to actually go.

Elliot had prepared for the inevitable funeral—for the crowds of people turning up with unseasoned chicken casserole and well-wishes. He'd prepared for the weeks after—who to call, how to manage his father's will, how to send the oxygen tanks back. He had never prepared for *after* that. For what happens when the fanfare dies down and the days go back to normal. The nine-to-five of life started again, after the weeks of compassionate leave for his mother and the holidays ended at college, and he was supposed to carry on, without his father. He had no idea how.

He spent years barely getting through life, because what was the point? But he had seen the light go out in his mom's eyes once, and he decided he wouldn't be the reason it happened a second time. So, he's here. Working as an apprentice at the ripe old age of twenty-six. He passed his environmental degree thanks to his mother's stern words and a healthy number of extenuating circumstances, but still, a four-year absence is nothing employers take lightly. Melody told him about the palace initiative for "young" (she said this with a wide smirk because she believes he's forty-five years old when she is in fact still older than him) Black men, and she didn't stop talking until he applied. It's just for the summer, so what's the harm? He only needs to get the certification, avoid the royals like the plague while he's here, and get out. But now here he is, walking under the plum trees and around the trickling streams, and he can't help but feel a *little* excited.

Melody thinks it's his win. Elliot thinks it's hers.

J.S. JASPER

Aliyah always welcomes newcomers. It's one of the only main roles she has at the palace. One of the only ones her parents let her get away with, anyway, because how could she possibly corrupt someone who has only just stepped foot on the grounds? Aliyah thinks her parents give her too much credit—she's not planning on overthrowing them anytime soon. She has no power, no alliances, and no backup. She's *maybe* thought about it a little, but it's never something she would put into place.

However, she misses the first dinner, and it's all his fault—the man she doesn't know from Adam. The man that's messing up her mind, because Aliyah does not do *anything* for a man, least of all miss an event she's meticulously planned for months. And yet, she sits in her bedroom, hearing the dinner music floating up from the dining hall.

It's stupid—utterly ridiculous—that she's here instead of there because she didn't want to see him. Not because she thought he might say anything about her almost beheading him, but because then he'd know who she was, and he'd either feel too intimidated to talk to her again, or he'd act different around her. She'd never know the real side of him, the side people hide from her. It's a ludicrous thought anyway because she has no intention of ever seeing him again regardless.

But no one ever talks to her normally. No one ever asks how her day is or what her favorite color is or if she's alright. For a while, Aliyah assumed the dresses, the jewelry, and the tiara scared people off, but even when she strolled around the palace grounds in leggings and a sweatshirt, no one said a word. Aliyah guesses he didn't actually talk to her, either—nor will he ever be able to again, even if he *did* want to—but she doesn't want to lose the illusion that someone might want that. Still, he did more than anyone else has in two months and seven days, since a delivery man mistook her for staff because it was six a.m. and she refuses to be in silk before midday.

Aliyah wonders if he likes her. The Princess. If he's part of the fan club she appears to have with younger men and he just didn't recognize her under the tree. Or maybe he did, and every daydream she's had about him since is a lie because he knows *exactly* who she is. She wonders if that would be better or worse than him being indifferent. *Ugh.* She hates thinking about things she has no control over, even though those things take up most of her life. She needs to breathe.

Aliyah slides her balcony doors open, then walks out into the cold night air. Usually, she'd be nervous someone would see her, and she'd cover up a little more, but she knows everyone will be in the dining hall. The welcome mixer usually lasts well into the early morning, people finding *their* people on the first night. So, she doesn't mind standing here in her shorts and a tank top. No one ever looks up here anyway—at least, no one looking for her.

Aliyah closes her eyes, lifting her face to the moon. She takes a deep breath, and her mind settles a little.

"Hey."

With a shriek, Aliyah jumps, searching the dark night for whoever called to her. It doesn't take long. She finds him sitting on the raised beds below her bedroom. She wants to say "Hi." She wants to invite him up. She wants to go and sit with him and ask him why he's not inside. She wants to ask him if he was just thinking about her. But princesses don't have friends. So she turns around, heads back into her room, and slams the door that leads to her balcony.

Now she's annoyed because she's missed an event she cares about over a boy she doesn't know and never will, *and* she's cold to the bone even though she was sure it wasn't all that cold tonight. *Ugh*.

CHAPTER THREE

As E<small>LLIOT</small> <small>LOOKS</small> <small>AROUND</small> his room, he thinks, *could be worse.* The walls are bare, but it's not unwelcome. It feels homier than his halls at college ever did, and besides, he has his own bathroom here. It's a little chilly, but it's spacious enough. It's bigger than his room at home, but, to be fair, he could barely afford a studio apartment. So far, the palace has not let him down. But he wasn't hoping for it to. It's not like he walks around looking for justification for his hatred of the monarchy. He doesn't need it. He knows their views on people that aren't like them, and they have a tracklist the length of his arm of shitty decisions. He's here to get what he needs, and to go.

Still, while he is here, he'll try and enjoy it. There are a few cute people here, as he found out last night at the mixer, and if they're anywhere near as flirtatious as they were then, at least he'll have someone to talk to. Elliot's not looking for anything serious (he's leaving in six months, after all), but he doesn't mind the idea of having someone to spend the evenings with. Elliot is a romantic at heart, and he can't wait to fall in love for real, but for right now, he's content to get his qualification, and get out.

There's a part of him that was hoping to spot the would-be murderer at dinner last night, if only so he could put a name to the face of the girl he jerked off to in the shower. He guesses she's been here too long to go to welcome evenings. But then he did see her, all long-legged on the balcony, and she looked like heaven. He said "Hi," and she said "No thank you"—except without the decency of even saying thank you. He took it on the chin, of course, and didn't moan her name when he touched himself in bed last night, because he is a gentleman (who doesn't know her name).

There were rumors that the Princess was supposed to attend last night. Elliot didn't care, obviously, which is good because she never turned up anyway. Beyond the glances at new people and the few conversations he wasn't too tired to partake in, the evening was fine. There were thankfully no tours, but the goody bag did come with a map of the palace grounds. (Suncream and condoms too, which was bizarre but welcome.) It's mainly forests, the palace itself, and some outbuildings and stables, and Elliot knew his first port of call would be finding somewhere hidden in the forest, just for him, where he can hang out and avoid the royals.

So, he shakes all thought of the Princess from his mind as he walks through the forest, his phone in his hand, camera open and ready to capture the next magical thing he sees. He'll pretend it's all for Melody, but he can't deny this place is picturesque, with its stone archways draped in almost-budding rose bushes, and buttercups and crocus flowers circling the tree stumps. And the dangerously gorgeous woman that sinks below the bright blue lake. The— *Wait*. He double-takes, holding onto the tree trunk for support before his knees give way entirely.

She's in the lake to her neck, her head tipped back so far only her face is visible. It's her. That much he knows, even if he can only see the line of her jaw and the sharp lines of her collarbone. He'd always know the woman he'd spent the entire last few days thinking about. She lifts her head, and her body moves through the low ripples of the lake. With every slow movement she takes, he's transfixed on her. On the way water droplets stick to her arms; the way they drip from the curls that have evaded the braids on her head.

Elliot could stay here forever, watching her dip under the water only to emerge elsewhere, like she's playing chase by herself. She starts to walk out on the side of the lake opposite him, and he sees her shoulder blades, a trickle of water down her spine, the way her hair sticks to her skin. The thought of running his hands over her body is like an obsession. It's not until moments later that he remembers *he wasn't invited here*. He's disturbing her peace in a way he doesn't think she'd thank him for. So, he turns and goes to leave. There's a splash of water, and he smiles at the thought of her diving back in, but he won't turn to look. He'll leave... if only he had any idea where he was going.

Elliot never believed in maps. His family always just knew the way, and he thought it was the most magical thing when he was younger. Now he knows they knew where they were going because that's the town they lived in. They never left the limits of the town, not really. Every summer, they'd go to the beach, but beyond Loven is something Elliot has never seen often. Or without a direct train. And he's lost.

He could walk around. Presumably, at some point, he'd find a path. But it's possible he'd walk right in on her again, and there's a fear in the back of his mind that she would think he was chasing her. The idea that she might think he was creepy for, once again, finding her alone in the woods, in what he assumes is nothing but underwear, keeps him glued to the spot. There should be no real reason he would care what she thinks, but he does. Elliot sighs as he carefully sits against the tree trunk. He'll just wait for her to leave, and then he'll find his way back.

The sun begins to set, and Elliot regrets not bringing a sandwich. He's hungry, and when he's hungry, his entire personality changes. "Hangry," Melody calls it, but she usually says it while throwing a bag of chips at his face. Now, Elliot has lost count of the number of times he's tried counting to a hundred to take his mind off the gnawing in his stomach. (It's only been since breakfast, not since birth, but still, he's prone to dramatics when he's peckish.) The background noise has been comforting though. She's been in water for hours, the splashing noise making him smile every few minutes.

Still, his thighs are burning from swapping between squatting to avoid squashing the flowers and sitting on bare ground, when he hears rustling. He's never looked at the wildlife of Iledale. It could be a bear. It's *unlikely* to be a bear, he thinks, because this palace has the tallest walls he's ever seen, but he's tired and he's hungry, and he might be talking himself into some delusion that something terrifying is about to catch him in its claws.

Then she walks around from behind a tree. Her cloak floats over the ground like water. It looks like velvet, but he wouldn't know for sure unless he reached his hand out. He thinks about it, but before he knows it, there's a knife inches from his face. Her hand doesn't shake like it did previously, but he believes she intends to kill him about as much as he did last time. Honestly, from this angle, she's just giving him more to think about in the shower. She towers over him, her face blocking out the last of the light as she looks at him with a frown, and she's utterly radiant.

"Must we always meet like this?" he asks. She doesn't roll her eyes, nor does she let up. Maybe she will kill him this time. Huh.

"You tell me," she replies, her voice deathly calm. In his memories, her voice is always softer, breathier, calling his name. "*You* are the one watching me from behind this tree." Fuck, she's posh. Far posher than he remembers her being, and far posher than she's been when he's thought about her late at night. It's annoyingly hot.

"I didn't," he starts, clambering up from his spot on the ground. Her knife follows the point on his throat she's clearly looking at. "I wasn't even facing the right way." Elliot is taller than her like this, maybe an entire head taller. Somehow, she's looking up at him, but he feels like she's got the upper hand. It might be the determination in her stare, or the way she carries herself. It might also be the knife. Elliot thinks it's just her.

"So, you were not watching me earlier?"

"Well..."

"See!" Her knife inches closer to his skin.

"Woah." He laughs, swinging a little on his feet. If it takes him a step farther away, he won't call himself a coward. "If I tell you, are you going to attack me?"

"Are you going to do something that means I will need to defend myself?"

Elliot frowns. "Did I last time?"

"You followed me through the forest, did you not?"

Elliot's frown deepens. Is the palace so corrupt that women can't be alone without threats from other people? Is there no safety here at all? He'll need to wait a few weeks before he invites Melody to visit. If he survives that long, obviously.

"I didn't know you were there," he replies. "I swear. Until I had a knife against my throat, of course."

"Oh." She lowers the knife, and her gaze. He only misses one of those things.

"But I am sorry. I never meant to scare you."

She spins a ring on her pinky finger and looks back up at him with a frown. "No. It was my mistake. Please, accept my apologies, for…"

"Attempted murder?" he asks, sitting down again. She doesn't look particularly sorry.

The daisies are out, and somehow, he missed them, but now he's looking for something to look at that's not her lips. The daisies are ridiculously cute, and when they were kids, he and Melody would have spent weeks here in summer, making chains. Their entire childhood was full of daisies stuck through his locs and sitting on top of Melody's afro. (It became harder when she started wearing wigs, but they made it work). The woman in front of him chews on her lip as she looks out at the forest. Elliot wonders if she's been here long enough to know how to get back in the dark.

She turns back to look at him. "I was never going to…" Her brow is furrowed, and her plump lip taking the brunt of her teeth. Elliot wonders if she thinks he'll tell the palace about her, but he's content to keep them a secret under the trees. She pushes a strand of hair behind her ear, and she looks more terrified at the thought of him thinking she would hurt him than anything else, though he notices she never actually finishes her sentence. It's possible she gets away with anything she wants—even holding a knife to someone's throat with just half an explanation here and there—because people look at her and want to give her anything. Everything she might hint at.

Elliot reaches his hand up to rest against hers, something everyone in his family does. Physical touch is something that comes so naturally to him he forgets others don't like it as much. She flinches and holds her knife high again, closer to his cheek than he appreciates. He shouldn't have sat back down when she still had a weapon on show just because she's got a nice face.

"Sorry," he says, raising his hands in surrender. "I just wanted you to know I know you were never going to kill me."

She swallows. "You do?"

"Of course. I knew it at the time."

She squints. "You did not."

"I did," he replies. She can't think he genuinely fears for his life as he sits here, resting against a tree? Though he is a bit bored of having a knife shoved in his face. This is a classy establishment, not the back alley of the dodgy street his family lived in when they were younger. "Can you lower your knife, please?"

"I do not know why I would."

He scoffs. "You're beautiful, but my God, you might be the most frustrating person in this forest." She raises her eyebrows, a hint of amusement on her face, if he had to guess. "You don't even know me, yet you act as though I want to skin you alive—when, in fact, *you* are the one waving the knife at every opportunity!" he says, his voice louder than he would like. "While I've just been sitting here like a lemon, looking in another direction, so you didn't get creeped out by me." He swallows and takes a deep breath. "I saw you earlier, by accident, and I *swear*, I saw your shoulders at most, and I turned around."

His eyes drop to her shoulders now, and it's frustrating that she's covered in a thick cloak, yet he can still see the droplets of water, clear as day. It probably doesn't help that he spent the entire afternoon imagining dipping his tongue into the dip of her collarbone. Maybe he does deserve the knife. She looks at him, and he feels warmer than he ever has.

"Then why did you not leave?" she asks.

He groans. He may look creepier than he would ever intend, because this excuse always sounds like exactly that. "I'm lost."

"Excuse me?" she says, though he notes that her knife lowers just slightly. He wonders how many she has seeing as he has her other one on his bedside table.

"This place is a fucking jungle, my phone has no signal, and I don't know how to get back. And I'm tired and hungry," he says, feeling like he's dangerously close to having an actual tantrum.

"Are you going to stamp your foot?" she asks. There's a whisper of a smirk on her face, and he thinks he'd do it if it would make her laugh.

"Maybe."

She smiles, just a small one, but it takes his breath away all the same. He takes the moment to hit the bottom of her knife with the heel of his hand. It spins in the air, and he thanks every God that he manages to catch it instead of impaling himself in the stomach.

She sighs, but there's no surprise on her face. Elliot wonders if she already knows everything he's going to do before he does. "Are you planning on giving that one back?" she asks.

"I would have given you the other one if you hadn't run off. Though it is frighteningly easy to disarm you, so maybe you shouldn't have it back at all."

She laughs, folding her arms as she looks down. She's outlandishly attractive, with her full lips and her bright teeth. If this were any other place, any other lifetime, he would have never had the courage to talk to her. If Elliot saw her in the street, he wouldn't even look her way through fear she might look back. "If I wanted you dead, you would not have seen my face."

Elliot gasps, his hand against his chest. He's not anywhere else, he's right here, and he thinks maybe talking to her is worth the risk.

"What a tragic life that would have been, to have never seen you."

The woman blinks, and a light blush comes to her cheeks. He was expecting an eye roll at best, an "obviously you think I'm attractive" at worst. He wasn't expecting this—an expression of slight shock over her face. *Interesting*. She pulls it back as quickly as she has every other facial expression she clearly didn't want to show.

She clenches her jaw and asks, "How were you planning on getting back?"

Elliot sighs, running his hand over his face. "I was hoping someone would notice I was missing, but then I remembered I haven't really spoken to anyone since I've been here—well, apart from you, and that barely counts, because you've had a knife at my throat longer than we've actually spoken."

She doesn't respond to his thoughts on the knife, but she does smile as she looks at the floor and then back up at him, like he's not allowed to see it. It's now his life's mission to get her to smile at him. Because she *wants* to show him.

"And how would I alert the palace that you were missing?" she asks.

Elliot stands. She doesn't back up like he's expecting, so there's barely thirty centimeters between them. It feels like there are sparks, a dangerous no-man's-land in the space between his chest and her folded arms. That if he dared to inch forward, he might explode on the spot. Being this close does mean he towers over her, and there's a thrill running through his veins at the way she looks up at him. It takes him a moment to remember she asked him a question.

"You'd find the first guard and tell them a ridiculously handsome man is stranded in the forest."

She laughs—really, truly laughs—and Elliot can't find it in himself to care if it's because she thinks his statement is hilarious. Her entire face lights up, and it illuminates the forest more than the moon and the stars ever could. There's a chance he'll be looking for a high like this for the rest of his life.

When she refocuses, it takes her longer than usual to settle into her nonchalant face. The giggles force their way up her throat anyway, and she looks a little ridiculous trying to pretend she doesn't think he's the funniest guy in all the land. Like a child playing at being posh. It's adorable.

She clears her throat. "I am not saying that."

Elliot sighs dramatically and leans against the tree.

"I can't believe you won't admit you think I'm stupid pretty," he says with a groan, and she smiles, looking away from him. "You could show me the way."

She hums, her fingers tapping against her arms. He wonders if she'd flinch if he tried to touch her again. (He won't. He'll wait for her, if that were to ever happen.)

"What if I do not want to take you back?" she asks.

"I would never force you to do anything. Not that I'm sure I'd ever be able to make *you* do anything you didn't want to," he says, with a light laugh. "If you don't feel comfortable alone with me in the forest, I understand, even if you probably do have another knife, and I wouldn't use this one on you anyway."

She narrows her eyes at him, and he laughs lightly.

"If you could inform the palace..." he says, leaning toward her only slightly. She doesn't flinch back, but her eyes do dip to his mouth, and he takes it as a victory. "...I would be ever so grateful to be saved by a hero on horseback."

She hums, and Elliot thinks she might take pity on him, which wasn't entirely his intention, but he'll take it if it means getting out of here.

She takes a step closer. Her beauty is almost overwhelming when she's this close, and he wants her to get closer still. A story plays in the back of his mind—something about flying too close to the sun and burning to death, *etcetera, etcetera*. But when the sun has a smattering of freckles on her nose, he finds it difficult to not do whatever she wants. Then, she slides the knife from his hand without so much as grazing his skin, and he wishes she managed to touch him at all, but he assumes it was on purpose. He wonders if being stabbed would be worth it to feel the weight of her hand on his chest.

"I will let them know," she says, moving to walk away.

He takes the blow like his father always taught him—head high like a champ. Then, he bows his head dramatically, his hand sweeping out in front of his body, and when he lifts his head again, he catches the end of her eye roll and a smile she doesn't try to hide from him, and he wonders if he lost anything at all.

"I appreciate it. Be safe, please."

CHAPTER FOUR

ALIYAH HAS SPENT HER entire life walking alone through this forest. Every season, it looks different, from bare branches to full color. She's not allowed a phone, so she's never captured a photo of the way the sun shines through the leaves, but she's been around long enough to have the image imprinted on her mind. She's seen every tree and bush in every light. She's sat by the lake at sunrise, alone. She's run under the canopy of the trees with too many thoughts in her head as the sun set, alone. And now, she has the chance to not be alone. Someone else can see the trees with her, if she wants.

It's a terrifying thought. He could be anyone. There's a chance he's the paparazzi and he's trying to trick her into a quote that will be misconstrued. He could be sent by Feathermore house as a mole, to find out her weaknesses and make it all the easier to overthrow her. Aliyah has never been lucky in life. The tabloids—and many of the kingdom, she's sure—would think she was the luckiest person alive. Plucked from an orphanage to live in the Galineria Palace is a fate most would dream of. All it's ever done for her is make her lonelier than she ever thought possible.

There's something about the man sitting beneath the trees, leaving her to walk alone because she told him that's what she wanted. Something about the way his brow furrowed when she suggested he was there to harm her. He looks *nice*. Like he grew up wearing matching pajamas for the holidays and his family were there for all his school events. Aliyah knows better than anyone that looks mean nothing. That the crease between his brows doesn't mean he'll be kind; that the small dimple he has on his cheek that rendered her mute for a few moments doesn't mean he wants the best for her. So, she walks away.

Aliyah barely makes it to the makeshift turn in the forest she made for herself on all the lonely walks she's completed in her life before she groans. It's not as if she feels guilty for leaving him behind. He's barely a fifteen-minute walk from the path; he'd find it. She just... well, she doesn't want him to be sad. Would he be if she left him here? Probably not. He's a grown man, and people don't get upset over trivial things. Maybe he'd be disappointed. Maybe he'd forget all about it when she sent a guard to collect him. But there's a part of her that doesn't want him to be disappointed with her. It's a frustrating thought. She doesn't know him, he doesn't know her, and there's an entire kingdom of people disappointed in her on a daily basis, but that's different. They're disappointed in the Princess. He'd be disappointed in *her*. When she turns back to face him, she finds him sitting on the floor, entirely unfazed that she was about to leave him there. She said no, and he didn't argue it.

He looks up at her, a boyish grin on his unfairly attractive face, and waves.

"Come on, then." Aliyah sighs and turns back around before he has a chance to say anything.

His footsteps are loud behind her, and the nerves start in her stomach. God, it's so stupid. She's not at a state dinner with hundreds of men vying for her hand. She's just walking in a forest with a guy. He's just a *guy*. She's not affected by this.

She tilts her chin up when he catches up to her. Aliyah almost stops to ask him why he's daring to walk next to her when she remembers he doesn't know who she is. No one has walked any closer than five steps behind her for years. She almost doesn't know how to walk in a straight line with someone this near. Maybe it's the way she's never had to be aware of someone else's presence. Maybe it's the way he smells—like coconut and something she thinks might just be him, the only reason she stayed so close under the trees. Maybe it's the way his arm brushes against her cloak like he has no idea he's almost touching her. Like the thought of touching her doesn't make his chest flip-flop like sandals on the beach. Like being this close doesn't make him feel like he's burning from the inside out.

"I knew you'd change your mind," he says, practically skipping next to her. His strides are much longer than hers, and his thighs tense with every step he takes. It takes her an embarrassing amount of strength to look away. The only reason she does is because the way back doesn't have a real path, and she doesn't want to trip on a tree root just because he has thighs she wants to take a bite out of. (It has very little to do with the thought of a trip being embarrassing, and more to do with the way she thinks he'd catch her, and if he so much as touched her, she might go up in flames.)

Instead, she scoffs lightly. "Is that right?"

"Mm-hmm."

He doesn't follow up, and she doesn't push it in case he says something utterly charming as if it's nothing. As if he's reading a grocery list and not calling her beautiful. As if he's rambling about ingredients off the back of a cereal box instead of telling her she's magnificent. His charm disarmed her the first time she saw him, and she lost her upper hand and her favorite knife in the process. She swore it wouldn't happen again, and then she spotted him at the side of the lake, and she had to throw her head back so he wouldn't see the smile on her face. Now she has wet braids that she's going to have to rinse and dry tonight, and she wants to do neither of those things. She should hate him right now. He's an utter nuisance.

"Would you like to walk in silence, or can I talk?" he asks.

Aliyah thinks maybe she doesn't hate him at all.

"If I say the former, how long would you last?"

"I can last a long time." He laughs, then says, "maybe not with you."

Aliyah swallows, her jaw clenched as she looks at the ground. There was nothing in his tone that suggested he meant *anything* that wasn't simply answering her question, yet her mind is already rolling around the gutter. Thoughts of his thighs and his hands and how long he can last make the back of her neck sweat. It's embarrassing, really, how hot she feels with a few words that weren't intentional, when she's never been touched by anyone but herself.

"But," he replies, and she flinches at the sound of his voice. In her mind, his voice was soft, closer to her ear. "If you want a silent walk, I can do that."

Aliyah doesn't say anything. She fears her voice may shake. But, to his credit, he just walks next to her. Occasionally, he slows down to admire a plant on the side of the makeshift path she's created by her daily walks through the forest. He crouches down, then turns to look up at her, a smile on his face as he shows her a primrose. They're one of her favorite wildflowers because they signal the start of spring—the start of something new. When he stands, pulling his T-shirt back down from where it's gathered under his arms, she realizes if she wants to hear his voice again, she has to talk. There's nothing in her mind that isn't laced with desire. So, she searches her mind for anything she might ask someone new if she'd gone to the welcome party last night.

She swallows, counts to three in her head, then asks, "How are you finding palace life?"

He laughs, a deep, hearty sound she feels in her bones. "That's your first question?" She frowns, but he answers it all the same. "I haven't been here long."

"I know."

"Oh, you do?" he says, his eyebrows wiggling. Aliyah rolls her eyes. Silly. This is why she doesn't talk. He's a little ridiculous though. As if he doesn't know he looks like *that*—all wide and attention-taking in a somehow subtle way. She'd recognize his face if she'd seen him before. "Palace life is okay," he continues. "Are the dorms better in the palace than at Alfred House?"

Aliyah frowns. There are no dorms in the palace, but he wouldn't know that.

"What is the issue?" she asks.

No one has ever told her about an issue before, though she supposes no one would come up to her in the middle of the gardens and tell her something in their living quarters is unsatisfactory. But she does have aides that people are supposed to talk to if they want.

He shrugs. "You can't control the heating, but I suppose I do run colder than a lot of people."

Aliyah grabs her notepad and pen out of the pocket of her cloak. It's unreasonable how her heart constricts at the thought of people being cold. She knows what it's like from her stints in the dungeons. They have so little protection from the elements she's surprised she's not got the flu permanently.

"What else?" she asks, noting down the heating issue. The radiators are supposed to be free to use. It's not like the palace can complain about heating bills when the twelve fountains they have run with warm water in case they dare splash her mother on her weekly walk.

He laughs, running his hand over his face. "It's not that big a deal. I wouldn't bother the royal family with this."

Aliyah's frown deepens, and she comes to a stop. "Why ever not?"

He turns to face her. "Well, they'd have to give a shit about people for this to matter."

Oh. He's anti-monarchy. She thought he might be too good to be true. People can dislike the monarchy, obviously, but his obvious hatred is for the person right in front of him. She'll just have to not see him again. That would be fine... probably.

"They house the people in their employ," she says, choosing her words carefully so he doesn't immediately figure her out. "It is their duty to make sure they are warm—one of the most basic human rights."

"Because they care about human rights," he replies, with a scoff that Aliyah feels in her chest. She knows people dislike the monarchy—she barely likes them, and she *is* the monarchy—but there's an ache in her chest all the same. Aliyah doesn't have friends, and this is a stark reminder of why.

"Can you tell me everything you would change?" she asks.

He runs his tongue along his lower lip as he looks at anything but her. He's the only person who's ever given her anything, the only person who's ever suggested anything was wrong. Aliyah isn't naive enough to think everyone is happy here, but there's not much she can do without the information. She's had such a ridiculously sheltered life; she'd have no idea what people need.

He groans. "I can't believe I'm going to lose my job before I've even started."

"I will not say it was you," she promises. "I swear it. I will do an inspection. The royals need not know. I just... I do not know what to look for."

He looks at her, his gaze across her face like he's trying to figure out if she's lying. He sighs, and she waits for him to walk away.

"The heating," he starts, his hand out as he lists the issues. Aliyah writes down everything he has an issue with. "Food and dinner provisions." Specifically, the strict timings that don't align with the working schedule. "Un-authorized breaks." Aliyah wasn't aware that the staff were watched so closely. Especially not when they're on lunch. The palace only employs adults, much to her parent's dismay, so Aliyah knows the staff can figure out when they need a break themselves. (She doesn't list down that he thinks he should get a private pool, because he was laughing when he said it, but she does make a note to ask him if he's a swimmer at some point.)

"Thank you," he says, when they get back to the main path. Aliyah needs to leave him here, because if anyone else sees her, his hatred for her will start before she's figured out if he's happy with the changes she's going to implement.

"Now that we are not far from your bedroom," she says, fighting the images that come to mind at the thought of him in there, "may I have my knife back?"

He laughs, his hands deep in his trouser pockets. "You already have one in your possession. You think I would give you another?"

Aliyah pouts. She barely resists the urge to smile when his jaw drops slightly at the motion.

"I cannot believe," she says, "I was your hero, and yet you are stealing from me."

He smiles, a blindingly bright smile that challenges the moon for the prettiest thing she's ever seen. He wins, but she won't tell him that.

"Can I walk you back?" he asks, and she blinks, the reminder that they are not friends searing into her mind. She turns away.

"I am sorry," she replies, her back to him. "I do not fraternize with petty thieves."

His laughter penetrates the dark night sky. The glow from the palace and the obnoxious need to have so many lights on despite the fact most people are asleep keeps the stars at bay, but Aliyah has his face in her mind regardless. She walks across the grass, even though she knows there's a sign that tells her not to in sixteen languages. She misses his voice already.

"Will I see you again?" he calls after her. She turns her head, and his eyes are wide, as though the answer might hurt him. Aliyah thinks she might regret her next words if she tells him she can't see him again, so she doesn't.

"We both work here, do we not?"

He smiles, and she turns before she smiles back. It's not successful. She finds herself smiling at the daisies instead.

"Good night," he calls. She holds her hand up in a wave. She can't turn, of course, because he'll see her smiling, *again.*

"Sweet dreams!" he shouts, and she almost turns to throw something at him. She doesn't, though—there's no way he knows they shouldn't be seen together. So she pulls her lower lip between her teeth, and she knows she'll dream of him, but they may not be sweet.

CHAPTER FIVE

THERE'S A PIT OF *something* Elliot doesn't like swirling around his stomach, and it has nothing to do with the cheese sandwich he's eating. Melody called, and so far, he has spent the entire time shoving food in his mouth so he doesn't tell her about this girl that's on his mind twenty-four-seven.

Elliot tells Melody *everything*. When they were in seventh grade, she knew he had a crush on Belinda Taylor, and when they were in eighth grade, she was the one who told him Belinda Taylor was gay. Elliot told her when he was struggling in college after their dad died. She already knew, of course, because she knows everything, which is why he's trying not to give anything away. It's why he's eating his third sandwich since she called seven minutes ago. It's why the *something* is so devastating.

It's not as if he doesn't want to tell her. Elliot has told Melody the most useless information before. When his trousers are uncomfortable during his college lectures. When he's hungry even though he just ate. When he had his first stint as a lifeguard during high school, he sent her thirty-three texts before she'd even got out of bed. None of them said anything at all. But he's not sure what he'd tell her now. There's a girl whose name he doesn't know because he's too scared to ask her in case she doesn't want him to know, and his life is shattered? There's a girl who haunts his dreams, and he's barely known her a week; really, he barely knows her at all? There's a girl?

"It's pretty decent, you know," Elliot says, swallowing a mouthful of food as he watches Melody on his phone. Her face is scrunched, and he takes a sip of his drink. "Sorry," he says, covering his mouth with the back of his hand.

"As you should be, you animal. So the food isn't bad, and it's pretty there? I can't even hide my jealousy."

"It was a bit shit the first few days, but it's much better today," he says.

Maybe *she* mentioned it to someone in the palace. She seems like she might have influence among the staff, even if he thinks she doesn't quite suit that role. Someone as striking as she is needs to be—he doesn't even know. Somewhere. On stamps or something. Elliot wishes he knew her name. Calling her *she* in his head doesn't seem appropriate. He will ask, if he ever sees her again.

"Well, I'm glad it got better," Melody replies, typing on her laptop. "When can I visit?"

He shrugs. "Whenever you want."

"I think there's an open day in a couple of weeks. You can show me around the hidden parts without getting kicked out, and I'll be able to get the day off work."

"Tight. How's Mom?"

Melody sighs. "She's fine. Worried about you, but she's gone back to the knitting girls."

"Oh," Elliot says, genuinely excited with this news. Their mom had the hardest time with their father's passing. It was expected, but neither he nor Melody had any idea how to help. Elliot wonders if she would have been back at knitting if he'd managed to get out of bed earlier.

"Not everything has to be about you," Melody says, looking right at him. He hadn't even noticed she stopped typing.

"Why not?" he jokes, badly. "I'm amazing."

"You're a mouth! But I'll let you get away with it because I have an interview for more funding in a minute," Melody states, throwing some paper away. She runs a semi-successful (depending on who you ask) nonprofit for inner-city kids. (If anyone asked him, or any of the people that benefit, they'd say it was a thundering success. If anyone asked Melody, she'd say she's minutes away from financial collapse.) "I can't believe I missed the Juliet deadline."

Elliot's never known Melody to miss a deadline, and he knows the Juliet funding was significantly more than anything else she's tried for before. "Want me to see if I can get you in now I work here?"

Melody laughs. "You and what connections?"

Elliot sticks his tongue out. Does he think *she* would help him? Would she even be able to? Does he even know what he'd need to ask?

"Have a good day, brother bear," Melody says, with a wave.

"Bye, Mel."

"Oh!" She stands up, and he knows she's about to close the laptop with a dramatic thud. "Next time we chat, I want to know about the girl."

"What girl?!" he asks, but she's already gone.

The sun turns her eyelids orange, and still, Aliyah can barely hold her eyes open for longer than four seconds. There was no reason for her to have been awake at five a.m. for a photoshoot that didn't even start until nine and is within palace grounds. Washing her hair and drying it in a way that suggests she hadn't been lake swimming took her way too long last night. So, by the time she lay down on her bed, she only had a few hours to sleep, and she spent an embarrassing amount of them thinking about Elliot. (She looked him up in the palace directory and then spent an upsetting amount of time wondering whether or not she regretted it.)

But now, as she is prodded and maneuvered until she sits flawlessly, his name is the only thing keeping her sane. Instead of wearing a corset that might snap her ribs before her mother, who sits annoyingly present just behind her, thinks her waist is small enough, Aliyah can imagine his hands lightly tracing the embroidered pattern. He'd be gentle, she thinks, unless she asked him not to be. Every time someone utters the word "ugly" or "disgusting," she swaps it out for "magnificent." She closes her eyes and remembers the way he looked at her. Like there was no way she was real. Like if he touched her, as he clearly wanted to, she might disappear.

Aliyah can't remember a time when anyone looked at her with such admiration. There are looks, of course. It comes with the status. The way eyes linger as she enters a state dinner, or the gazes from people as she walks around the palace grounds. Some are fond. Some people smile. Some are predatory. There are always looks, apart from her father, he avoids her gaze like if he dared look at her, he might turn to stone.

None match the way Elliot looks at her.

When she was younger, Aliyah placed so much of her self-worth on her face. Her body. The way people wanted her to look. Her hair was straightened daily, the natural curls subdued until her hair was flat against her face. She never understood why someone would want a Black child only to then try and hide the aspects of her that were different. Straight hair and an overly contoured nose didn't change her skin color. Not allowing her to go out in summer lest her skin darken even more didn't stop her from being Black. It was difficult to feel beautiful in a world where those words were only ever given to girls who looked nothing like her.

So, she poured her self-worth into her mind. She studied, and she followed online courses under a fake name. She never got to graduate, of course, there were too many instances where she couldn't be on camera. But it was worth it all the same.

It wasn't until Aliyah was a teenager that she started to see people that looked like her. Anna, her nanny, had always tried to get her to appreciate the beauty in her natural features. Aliyah always fought her on it. It wasn't worth the criticism just because she liked what she saw in the mirror. Then, Anna started smuggling in magazines and books. There, Aliyah read about people like her—the way their hair was described, and the way their skin shone under the moonlight. She tried a few hair styles in the safety of her bedroom, but they always looked a little off because she hadn't practiced, and her hair pattern was so desperate to be straight after years of a hot iron. There were months when she transitioned back to her natural curls, months she was a frizzy mess. It's all the papers talked about. She was barely allowed out of her bedroom.

Then, when Aliyah turned eighteen, they held a ball—a coming-of-age type thing she never wanted nor planned to attend. It was basically a parade to say she'd start looking for a husband. As if she'd ever spoken to a boy outside of her father's friends before. She was under the strictest of rules for how to dress, how to act. Her hair was to be perfectly straight, flowing down her back. She'd agreed, of course, the threat of punishment too great for her to rebel, but as she was getting dressed, she'd had a breakdown. Just a small one. A mini one barely worth thinking about. But something snapped. She didn't ask to be here. She was just taken from an orphanage and forced to dress and act like a different person.

She'd done it for fourteen years, and the thought of doing it for the rest of her life made her want to climb to the top of the tower and throw herself off. The only reason she hadn't thus far was because of the small changes she was able to make—the programs she created for inner-city children, the funds she was allowed to donate because her parents wouldn't know if she was off creating a new identity if it didn't negatively affect them. She realized she made a difference; she *could* make a difference. So, she got Anna to smuggle in a hairdresser. They had two hours and an entire royal party to piss off.

It worked. A little too well. She'd seen the anger on her mother's face as Aliyah had descended into the party, her twists swinging to the middle of her back. Aliyah saw the inside of the dungeons for the better part of a month. Her hair still looked great when she was let out, so she thought it was a win, and it was, sort of. The public reaction to her hair was overwhelming positive, even the palace couldn't deny it. And now, she never has to change her hair unless she wants to. But she lost Anna in the process. They'd banished her, knowing that she must have helped. It took Aliyah weeks to get her back from the hole she was forced to live in, and even then, she was only permitted to live at the edge of the grounds in a house that has everything she could ever want. The catch is that she can't leave.

Aliyah has told her to go—to travel to the coast under the cover of night. She wouldn't be chased; Aliyah would make sure of it. But she never left. Anna would say she had no reason to leave. That she liked her life, consisting of the house and her garden. But Aliyah knows it's for her sake that Anna doesn't leave.

Now, Aliyah sighs, looking out of the stained-glass windows of the library that used to be her bedroom. Her reflection looks back at her. It took Aliyah a long time, but she doesn't hate what she sees anymore. That is, until she sees Elliot below her, and she knows the main reason they can never be anything beyond two people who shared an evening and a handful of sentences together is because of who she is. Elliot walks along the path, his wide shoulders tensed beneath his shirt. She thinks, if he were here, she'd tell him all about Anna. She thinks he might listen.

But he is down there, and she is up here, and there is no world in which she would ever be able to have him in any way she may want. In a way she can't figure out, because there's no way that could end well. Sure, she could tell him who she was, and she'd be able to be seen with him in public, but he wouldn't want that. The only way she'd be able to know him, to talk to him, is if he barely knew her at all. She's trapped in a too-tight corset and locked behind stained-glass windows while he frolics between patches of wildflowers. And that's all they ever will be.

CHAPTER SIX

ELLIOT CAN PRETEND ALL he likes that he's wandering around the forests, looking for places to show Melody, but really, he's on the hunt. Not a *hunt* hunt, because then everything she said about him when she had a knife against his throat will be true. But on a small hunt. He just wants to see her. It's been *days*. He regrets not following up their walk home with the question of *when* they would see each other again, because he's been under trees and winding through paths, getting completely and utterly lost in the hopes of seeing her, yet she's been nowhere.

It's easy to get distracted here, though, and the sight of lizards scurrying through the grass takes his mind off her face for a moment. Elliot takes his phone out, ready to take a photo to send to Melody (she loves reptiles), when there's a rustle in the bushes. He wonders if it truly is a fairytale land and a rabbit is about to jump out, but instead, he turns on the path, and there she is—his twice would-be murderer—leaning over, her head bent, against the very same plum tree she almost decapitated him against weeks ago.

Elliot had been hoping to find her. Now, here she is, and he has no idea what to say. He has no idea how to act, because she's so unreasonably beautiful, her arms against the tree and her legs stretched out, that he wonders if she is really there. He thinks maybe he's made her up in his mind, but he's never been that creative. She's panting, and he think she's mid-run, if the headphones and the water bottle on the ground are anything to go by. He could think about her for the next millennium and still not come close to describing how the freckles scatter across the brown skin of her nose, nor the way her back arches and small tendrils of hair fall in front of her face.

She looks up at him. Her eyes widen, and he's transported back to his favorite place. Then they settle back into a nonchalant look before he's had a second to figure out if she's shocked or scared. There's no knife in her hand this time, and Elliot can't figure out if he's disappointed or not.

"No attempted murder today?" he asks, shoving his hands into his pockets. The woman rolls her eyes, and he swallows the sigh that threatens to escape. He wonders if there will be a time they see each other when she doesn't have her guard up. He wonders how long it will take for it to fall.

She moves her headphones down to her neck. "Not today," she replies, her chest heaving as she wipes the back of her hand over her forehead. She makes no attempt to stop her body contouring in the middle of the forest, and he wonders if she's lying—if she's out here looking utterly delightful in skintight leggings just to entrap foolish people like him and then stab them. One reason he thinks that isn't true is because her knife sits on his bedside table. The other is because he's never gotten the best of her, so if she's casually standing here, she knew he was coming.

"Why not?"

He doesn't take a step forward. Outrageously pretty girls make him nervous, and even though he was looking for her, the nerves simmer through him anyway. When he was a teenager, it took him far too long to grow into his ears, and he spent most of his time wondering if any of the girls would ever like him over the tanned, blond boys in his friendship group. From here, she won't be able to see the tremble of his fingers through the thick material of his pants.

She cocks her head, and her ponytail falls over her shoulder. He thinks there's a whisper of a smirk on her face, but he finds it difficult to look directly at her, so it might be wishful thinking. He takes a deep breath.

"Do you wish for me to *attempt* to murder you, Elliot?" she asks. He wonders how long she's worked here. He wonders if she wants to be his friend for real. He wonders if she ever wants a running partner. And, *oh*—she knows his name. He never told her his name... he thinks. It's possible he whispered it to her days ago in the hopes she'd remember at least one thing about him. It's also possible she looked him up all on her own.

He shrugs. "At least then I won't have to work here with the leeches."

She chews on her lip, her breathing still heavy, and he wants to know her name.

"The leeches?"

"I think they're called the Panimiros, but you'd know better than me. You're friendly enough with them to get me extra blankets."

She huffs out a laugh, and he wonders if being rude about her friends is the best way to go. Probably not. Best tone it down.

"If you do not wish to work here, why are you working here?" she asks.

Ah, so she's been here long enough to forget that people actually *need* jobs. That not every family sits on generational wealth paid by the people of this kingdom. He wants to be annoyed about it, but she lifts her tight zipped jumper up to wipe the sweat from her face, and her toned stomach is *right there*, tensing with every breath she makes.

He swallows. "Oh, you know, I like to buy things. Food, clothes, shelter. Basic necessities." She looks as sheepish as he thinks her face would allow. He's beyond feeling guilty for upsetting pretty, posh girls—he dealt with that his entire academic career. But still, he sighs as her blush deepens. "I'm here on the Juliet scheme."

Her entire face lights up, and Elliot wonders how he's supposed to keep standing when she smiles that wide, cheek-dimpling smile at him that he wants to take a photo of. He won't, because he doesn't know her at all, and the things he does know suggest she'd have a knife to his throat before the camera shutter clicked, but if it ever made its way onto his phone, he wouldn't be mad.

"You are? For which branch? Did you find the application reasonable?"

He wonders how she knows his name but not the rest of his information. Maybe she can only access certain things.

J.S. JASPER

He sits down, patting the ground next to him. Not too close, because she's still terrifying, even if there's no knife to be seen. His fingers find the daisies with practiced ease. They ground him. Remind him of home.

"Are you going to get your notepad out again?" he asks. She rolls her eyes at him, and he finds the ridiculously easy motion of splitting daisy stems harder than he should. It's possible she won't sit with him anyway; she's clearly on a run. He wants her to stay though. To interrupt her plans just for him. "Though now you know my name, maybe I should be worried you *are* here to find out everything about me and then take me down."

"Oh," she whispers, a blush creeping back to her cheeks. It's barely noticeable, but he can tell she's flustered from the way her neck pulses just below her ear. "I just—"

"Is it part of your role here?" he asks, suddenly desperate for her to say anything other than disregarding why she wanted to know his name.

"I suppose," she replies. She looks like she's about to run away, and he wants her to stay, so he lets it go.

"I missed you."

He sighs, dramatically throwing his arm over his face because he thinks it might make her laugh. It does, and he wants to take a notepad out himself, to write down that being ridiculous makes her smile. She also clearly likes his shoulders and his arms, if the way her eyes linger means anything. They would be his next notes.

"It has been three days."

"Ah," he replies as his smile grows. "You were counting?"

She pulls her bottom lip between her teeth, the blush on her cheeks glowing like watercolor on a canvas.

"Your blush is the color of the tulips I just planted," he says, his voice soft as he watches the color deepen.

"I do not blush," she replies. His eyes flick up to hers, and she's clearly trying so hard not to laugh that he lets her get away with it. He doesn't even point out that once the tulips grow, he would have made the two most beautiful things on the planet come to life all by himself. (Not entirely. The tulips needs soil, water, and sunshine, but it appears she only needs him.)

Elliot holds his hands up. "My mistake."

She hums, leaning against the tree. She still hasn't sat down, but he doesn't mind when she stretches some more. She pulls her foot up, resting it on the tree, above her head, and there's no way she isn't here just to torture him.

Elliot can't pull his eyes away from the vision. Her legs are long—so much longer than he thought they were when he'd only seen her in cloaks. He wonders how long she's staying. If she was hoping to see him. He sits in silence while she drinks some water, and as he pulls the last daisy from the ground, he misses her voice.

"What would you like to know about my application process?" he asks. He wonders if it's one of her jobs—fixing the ideas the Princess supposedly had. Before she has a moment to respond, he follows up with, "of course, you'll have to answer some of my questions about the palace too."

She pouts slightly, and Elliot has to focus on the task at hand: threading daisy stems together to stop himself from telling her she's glorious. Again. He wonders if she'll challenge him on it. If she doesn't need to do anything he says. It's true, of course—both that she's glorious and that he'd answer anything she asked without giving him anything back.

He threads the last daisy in the chain. It's too small to go on his wrist, but that's okay. It was never for him. With delicate hands, he places it in front of her on the grass. She bends down to handle it like it's a newly born rabbit, her fingers light against the petals.

"I think this counts as a bribe," she whispers, trailing her fingertip along the makeshift bracelet.

"Did it work?"

She looks at him, and he's not sure what she's looking for, but he wants her to find it. If she tells him, he'll make sure it's there. But then she smiles—a smaller one than before, but just as terrifyingly beautiful—as she carefully rolls the bracelet onto her wrist. Thankfully, she sits down.

"Yes."

CHAPTER SEVEN

ALIYAH SPENDS HER LIFE hiding from people. Creepy men with cameras, people that want something from her, her parents. It's usually pretty easy. All she needs to do is wear something neutral (her riding gear, a coat, and a cap), throw her hair into the most natural style she can think of (she still has braids in, so she has her hair in a ponytail), and walk around the castle grounds like she knows where she's going. It's gotten her out of many awkward interviews and state dinners.

Now, as she winds her way through the limestone paths and under the newly green rose bushes, she's hiding from something much less sinister. A boy. Well, a man, she supposes. An outrageously attractive man that she's thought about at length when she's going to bed. The man that plagues her thoughts when her hand slips down the front of her sleep shorts. The man she shouldn't be thinking about because it's abundantly clear he doesn't like her. A *leech*. It's something she's been called before, she's sure, but it's different now. He appears to have no idea who she is, so she's not sure how it's reasonable that he has such a distinct opinion of her.

Maybe she's upset that she cares about it at all.

Aliyah has been called many things, hurtful things that she lets brush straight over her. It's something she grew up with. At first, she remembers everyone being overjoyed that she was adopted. The Princess from the slums (as if she hadn't lived mere miles away from the palace grounds) that the King and Queen *saved*. It took her too long to realize she was a charity case. Too long to realize she was pitied more than wanted.

It was difficult to deal with as a child, and then her sister, Lydia, died, and it was intolerable. Beyond losing a sibling, it became apparent that her parents' worst nightmares had come true. Their child had died, and Aliyah was the only heir to the crown. Aliyah watched as her parents desperately tried to have another child, then tried to change laws to say biological children were the only rightful heir, but their dreams never came to fruition. They said the kingdom wasn't ready for a Black person in the royal family, let alone as queen, but she knows it's her family that weren't ready. Yet she never had a choice, and people acted like her sixteen-year-old self was a master manipulator who had planned this entire life for herself. There were months when the tabloids ran with the news that she murdered her sister, and she's had constant threats upon her life ever since.

Aliyah has some haters, that's true—she has the assassination attempts to prove it—but she's overwhelmingly loved by the public. She was never sure why her parents adopted her. She's never been more aware of the fact they never wanted her, that she was nothing more than a prop to get Black people to invest in the royals. So, no, Aliyah doesn't care about what people think about her. Especially if she doesn't care about them.

That's the main issue here. She thinks she might care what Elliot thinks.

There's a part of her that wants to fix the hatred he has for her, but she spent the entirety of the last time she saw him talking about anything other than the monarchy. There's a part of her that doesn't want to give him a reason to dislike her right now, even as she hides from him. She wonders if it counts as hideously mortifying if she's the only person that knows she's hiding who she is so a guy she doesn't know continues to like her. *Yes* is the answer, but she's ignoring that right now because she's hiding from him anyway.

She wonders if it would be worse if he decided he didn't like her before he found out she was the Princess. She has all the same qualities as one would expect from a royal; he must see that. Maybe that's why he hasn't sought her out. Maybe he doesn't spend as long thinking about her as she does him. Maybe, just maybe, he's a sane person and not placing all their desperate friendship needs on a pretty person he met by chance under a plum tree.

Aliyah skips over the stepping stones as she walks toward one of many stone arches on the castle grounds (this one covered in honeysuckle that is *so* close to budding again), and she tries to ignore the way Elliot kept writing things she said in a notepad. She should assume he's a journalist, sent to destroy her with his outrageous smile and addictive laughter. There's just something about him that she thinks wouldn't hurt anyone. Not on purpose. But she can't be sure, and she doesn't want to see the light look on his face turn dark when he finds out who she is. When he realizes she's been lying to him this whole time. Not now she thinks there might be a chance she has a friend. The loneliness Aliyah felt throughout her life, which she kept so far under wraps it just felt normal, is attempting to peer its ugly head back out from the pits of her heart, but she'll dampen it down with the smell of spring.

"Hi."

Aliyah spins on the spot, and her padded coat catches on the rose thorns climbing the stone wall. Elliot pulls the material away lightly, all while she avoids looking at him lest he figures out she was just thinking about him.

She looks at the daisies on the ground instead. They match the chain she's still wearing. She takes it off to bathe and to sleep, but every morning, she wakes up with him opening the greenhouse doors, and she puts it back on. And now, here he is. The object of all her desires. She could make him go away with one announcement, but she's not sure she wants to.

"I've been looking for you," Elliot says. Maybe she's never been that good at hiding, it's just that no one cared to seek her out.

"You have?"

"Yeah," he replies, smoothing down her coat. She doesn't care if there's any damage right now.

He holds out a container with strawberries inside. Poisoned? It seems unlikely as it's sealed with the crown symbol on the top, so he probably grabbed it at breakfast, but still, she's been taught not to accept things from strange men.

"Good morning," she replies, taking it from him with a wary glance. As always, she's careful not to touch him.

"Morning," he says with a smile. "I have a free day before I need to start work properly, and I wondered if you wanted to give me a tour?"

"A tour?"

"Mm-hmm," he replies, leaning against the brick archway. "Just the grounds, of course. Places that look as ridiculously picturesque as this."

Aliyah looks around, and he is right. On a sunny day, it looks like someone painted the entire scene.

"It is beautiful," she says, with a light sigh.

"It is," he replies, and when she turns to look at him, he's looking right at her. She pulls on her lower lip with her teeth, looking at anything other than the small smile on his face. "But you can say no, of course, and I'll leave with no fuss at all. You won't need to get your knife back out."

Aliyah turns to glare at him, and he's smiling so blindingly bright at her that she feels lightheaded. "How would I possibly get my knife out when you have yet to return it?"

Elliot laughs, leaning his head back. God, he's pretty. "Is that the law around here?"

"Maybe."

Elliot hums, his hands in his pockets. His gaze drops to the pot of fruit he brought her. "Do you think the strawberries are poisoned?"

Aliyah shrugs. "Fifty-fifty."

Elliot laughs, and it's quickly becoming her favorite sound. He holds his hand out, and it takes her at least two seconds to realize he's not asking for her hand. She lets the disappointment linger for a moment too long, then drops the fruit back in his palm. Elliot peels the film back, placing the rubbish in his pocket. There's a small wooden fork in with the fruit, and he looks at her the entire time he spears one and pops it into his mouth. She thinks it's unreasonable for a motion to be so attractive.

PERFECTLY CANDID

"I guess I'll die alone," he says with a sigh, then eats another.

"You are so dramatic," she replies. There's probably enough to show him without being seen by anyone, she thinks. Even then, it wouldn't be the worst thing in the world if someone caught them together. Unlike most of the royals, she speaks to the people who work here. There are a few she would not employ if it were her choice, but that's neither here nor there. And the chances of paparazzi being on the grounds today are low. They usually only come here when there's an event on. Aliyah wonders if being with him for longer, showing him some of her favorite places before he figures out who she is, is worth it. He's just a *guy*.

She takes the fork from the pot, strawberry already on it like he knew she was going to fall for his velvet-like voice and dark eyes. Aliyah eats it, the taste of poison not on her tongue.

"Alright," she says, turning around to walk to another hidden small garden. "A tour. But I am *not* showing you my hiding places."

Elliot catches up to her and pries the fork from her fingers. With how hot she is just from his presence, she wonders if she'll combust if he ever actually touches her.

"I'll find you anyway," he replies. He walks next to her again, and again, she jolts slightly.

"Sorry," he says, taking a small step to the left.

She didn't realize that she missed the closeness of a person, even if they never touched at all. His arm brushes the cloth of her coat, and she wonders if he'd be as close if she took it off.

Every branch she's about to duck below is pulled out of the way by Elliot. Every low stone wall is checked by him. She wonders what he'd do if it were the slightest bit wobbly, as if she would hurt herself from falling off a one-foot wall. Aliyah feels hypocritical, because the rage is oppressive when she goes to an event and someone opens the door for her, moves her chair, and opens her water. There's never a time when she gets to do anything for herself. But it's different here.

Maybe it's because she's distracted every time she comes face to face with a thorny branch because she's trying to look at his face without him noticing. Maybe it's because he seems to do it like he's not even thinking about it. Like it wouldn't matter who she was, he'd hold the thorns out of the way for her regardless.

"That is ridiculous," she says.

"It's true! Fish are *scared* of me!"

Aliyah spins to face him... and to take a breather, because they've been walking the end of the wildflower meadow for what feels like hours. There's a sheen of sweat sitting behind her braids. She shouldn't have worn them up, because now he's going to know she's a sweaty mess when they've only walked across a flat field. She's sure the sweat has nothing to do with walking across flat ground and everything to do with how his gaze is always on her. Aliyah runs every time she's stressed out or feels the need to talk to someone, so she runs almost every day, and now she's sweating because a cute boy keeps almost touching her. Pathetic.

"You mean to tell me you are so proficient at fishing that fish fear your very shadow?"

He shrugs, a smile still on his face. She wonders if there's ever a time when he's not smiling.

"You will have to show me," she replies, before she can stop herself. Did she ask him out? No, not really. Would she be upset if he thought she had? That remains to be seen.

"I am free tomorrow," he replies.

"You have work tomorrow."

"Oh." He frowns, and she likes his pouting face just as much as his happy one. Figures. The sun is ever so slightly in her eyes from this angle, and before the squint can fully form on her face, Elliot has adjusted.

"Better?" he asks. She relaxes her eyebrows, waiting for the blinding brightness to disappear.

She nods. "Thank you."

"You know," he says, "fishing is something you want to do in the early morning."

Aliyah squints again. "How early?"

"How early can it be before you say no?"

Aliyah groans and turns to walk through the trees before she tells him she'll do whatever he asks. She knows there's somewhere they can sit, they just might get a little muddy.

"You know," Elliot says, walking through the trees into the clearing. He takes his jacket off and spreads it onto the ground. "I'm not sure we can continue this friendship."

Oh. Aliyah has trained for disappointment—how to hide her feelings when her heart is breaking—and yet, she fears her jaw might be slack.

"Without you telling me your name," he continues, bending down just slightly like he's desperate to catch her eyeline. She's not sure when she started looking at the floor. He stands up straight, and she follows his gaze. "If you want to be friends, of course."

He's smiling at her, and she always wants him to be smiling at her, even if she's known him for less time than she's had these braids in (fifteen days, and they're still a little tight), but he won't be smiling when she tells him her name. Because Aliyah Giorgia Juliet Panimiro isn't subtle. Maybe she could go with her middle name, but that feels too much like a lie, and she doesn't want to lie to him.

Lying is second nature to her, as much as she used to despise it. If someone asks her something, they have an ulterior motive. No one wants to know who she's wearing to a ball; they want a story out of it. No one wants to know her favorite dish; they want to find a way to make it a scandal. So, she lies. With ease. Without guilt. No one knows anything true about her.

But here he is. The only person who's ever wanted to talk to her first. The only person who asks how she is. The only person who's ever come back. And she's suddenly terrified to lose him. She will, of course, when he finds out she's part of the family he can't talk about without convulsing. But for right now, can't she keep him, for just a little longer?

"Lia," she says. It's not a *lie* lie. The people she is very fond of call her Lia. She doesn't feel good about it though.

"Lia," he repeats, and it sounds like a dream coming from his mouth. "Pretty."

She smiles and takes off her coat, as the midday sun is giving off just the slightest heat. Elliot's eyes are wide, unabashedly watching her move like she's not only taking her coat off. Usually, when someone looks at her, they're waiting to find a complaint, desperate to tell her she shouldn't have eaten bread four days ago, or that her outfit does nothing to help her figure. Elliot looks at her like he couldn't find anything wrong if she gave him a decade.

"Mm-hmm," she says, sitting on the edge of his coat, her hand against the ground to prop her up. He follows, and she feels his hand near her more than she sees it. There's the distinct possibility she'll dream about his hands tonight.

"So, Lia..."

"Elliot," she replies.

"How do you feel about four a.m.?"

CHAPTER EIGHT

"Ouch," Elliot whispers, as he trips over another high tree root. Walking through the castle grounds in the dark without his cute tour guide was not his best move. Lia said she wanted to meet him there, and it's possible she doesn't want to be left alone at nighttime with him. Or she's not turning up at all, because he's been walking toward one of the lakes for the past twenty-five minutes and he's not seen a single sign of her.

He misses her, and it's *stupid*. It's unhinged to want someone this much. To crave their presence. The thought of touching her is on his mind constantly, but it has nothing on how badly he wants to know her thoughts. Does she think his favorite TV show is funny? What's her favorite color, and is there a reason behind it? What's her comfort food? Does she feel as torn up about him as he does about her?

He guesses not, because he finally sees the black water in front of him. The lake ripples under the light night wind, and the sting of her rejection is only slightly lessened by the sight ahead. It's difficult to make anything out other than the moonlight reflecting on the small waves against the shore. The millions of stars take his attention for just a moment, and out of his peripheral vision, he sees movement. Elliot's smiling before his eyes have even fallen on her. He knows it's her because his heart settled ever so slightly.

"Stalker," he says, his voice low. He doesn't think anyone would hear him even if he started screaming, but the atmosphere suggests he should be quiet.

"You begged me to be here," she replies, moving from where she's leaning against a tree. Her face lights up when he frowns. She walks closer to him, and she's so achingly beautiful in this light that he thinks he might struggle to catch anything at all. She mimics his voice, hers deeper than before. "What about four thirty, Lia? We could do five."

"I'm leaving," he says, turning on the spot when she reaches him. She giggles, and it warms him to his core. Lia reaches out, her hand falling just shy of his coat because he moves, and it's the closest they've gotten to touching at all, so obviously, he stops.

"Stay. Please." And it's not like he was ever planning on denying her anything anyway, so he turns back around.

"I will, but only because I think every lady should know how to fish," he replies. It's a lame response, and she agrees, if her pitiful attempt at hiding her laughter is anything to go by.

"Of course," she says, nodding her head seriously. And then she's gone, practically skipping into the rowboat with an elegance that shouldn't exist when someone steps onto a boat on shallow water. "Is now a bad time to tell you *I* am proficient in fishing?"

Elliot groans, throwing his head back as he walks toward the boat. He steps in, praying to someone he barely believes in that his balance is still good. He used to stand on his tiptoes on a twenty-meter-high diving board; he'd better not stack it into four inches of water.

"Would you like a hand?" Lia asks, and he almost says yes just to hold her, but as he looks up, she's got a smirk on her face that is going to play in his mind for the rest of the night. He hops in and gives her a smile right back, even as every single one of his muscles is tensed to keep him upright. He thanks the twenty-five years of attending church every Sunday for the fact he didn't go head over heels in the water.

The oars are, thankfully, easy to locate, and after Lia has sat down, he pushes them away from the shore. His legs don't tremble while he stands, but he'll sit down the moment they're far enough for the boat to rest gracefully.

"If you are so great at fishing, why did you agree to get up with me at four a.m.?" Elliot asks. He knows the answer, he thinks, but it'll make him feel like he will live forever if she tells him anyway.

She shrugs. "I thought your sleepy face would be cute."

He's much taller than her at this angle, and he has to blink the thoughts from his mind. "You think I'm cute?"

"I wondered if your *sleepy* face was cute," she corrects.

Elliot grunts, and she laughs, and he wants those two sounds to dance around together for the longest time. Elliot sits down and moves the oars across his lap so he can start paddling out into the middle of the lake. His stance is wide, and Lia moves her feet until they're between his. He wonders if it's ridiculous to feel like a schoolboy with a crush just by feeling her touching him through two pairs of Wellington boots.

"I think you're cute," he says nonchalantly.

"I know," she replies.

Elliot barks out a laugh that startles sleeping birds at the edge of the lake to flying above them. "Oh, you know, do you?"

"It is obvious," she says with a smile. "But perhaps only because I have been looking."

"At my face?"

"Well, that too." She tucks a curl behind her ear. Her hair is piled into a bun on top of her head, with some stray curls by the side of her face. He wonders if she leaves them out on purpose so he's always thinking about leaning over to move them for her. She looks out onto the lake as he pulls the oars together to stabilize them. Her next words make him feel like he's about to tip over. "But I was hoping you thought I was cute."

He looks at her, waiting for her to look back at him. When she does, he says, "I think you are otherworldly, Lia."

She smiles. Not as wide as usual—a little sleepy, if he had to guess—but it might be his favorite yet.

"That too."

J.S. JASPER

He groans as his hook comes up empty once more. "You're ruining my life."

Lia had told him there was a ripple. A catch. She'd been *so* sure. Just as she had been sure before, and he'd pulled up his line with the excitement of chasing his sister across the beach when they were kids, and yet, it came up empty, and Lia all but rolled around laughing. He knew she was hiding the truth again beneath her deep-brown eyes, but the sunrise was crawling up behind her, framing the wisps of curls and braids that had fallen around her face in a warm orange glow. He would have done anything for her.

"You are so cute," she says, wiping her face. Her shoulders shake, and for the second time, he wonders if it's the effects of laughter, or if she's cold. "I wish I could photograph your face right now." His face is probably a mixture of a pout and wonderment at the fact this delightful woman in front of him dared to call him cute like it wouldn't make his stomach flip.

"Why can't you?" he asks, propping his fishing rod up so he can dig around in his bag. "Aside from the fact I won't let you because you're being mean."

Lia laughs again, and he misses the way her cheeks are full when she smiles, but he finds the jumper he's looking for all the same.

"I do not have a camera," she replies.

He shakes his jumper out. No need to sniff test it. (He washed it purposely in case he had the opportunity to give it to her. He liked the thought of her wearing it more than the thought of him wearing it.) "What about your phone?"

"Oh," she replies, and he catches her looking sheepish. "I do not have one."

"No?" She shakes her head, and he grabs his phone from his bag. "You can use mine." Elliot unlocks it and asks if she knows how to use a phone, and she glares at him... but then asks where the camera is.

"Also, here," he says, holding out his jumper. She takes a photo of him, both of her hands clasped to his phone and her face so close to the screen he'll be surprised if she can see at all. God, she's so fucking cute. Elliot closes his eyes and smiles, and when she laughs, he thinks he might be on top of the world.

She takes the jumper from him. "What is this for?"

"You're shivering."

"Oh." Lia blushes again, and he wonders if that's something she does often, if there are other people around the palace who get to see her like this. A spike of jealousy roars up his spine, and he feels ridiculous about it.

"Can we take one together?" he asks. "So I can remember the night you tried to ruin my fishing trip, of course."

"Will you show anyone?"

Elliot shakes his head. "Not if you don't want me to."

It's a strange question, he thinks—one he'll ask her about in a few weeks, if she stills wants him around. Lia smiles, and he takes that as an invitation to move closer, even if he doesn't touch her. He spins around, and the boat rocks.

"Elliot, if I drown..." Lia warns him, her hands tight against the edge of the boat. He wonders if it would be worth rocking the boat once more just to hear her say his name like that again. Instead, Elliot holds the phone high above them and clicks. He won't look now to see if they're perfectly in frame or smiling correctly. He likes the excitement of looking at them later.

"I spent three summers being a lifeguard and am excellent at swimming," he replies. He feels her hand behind him, and he almost drops his phone in the lake.

"As *proficient* as you are at fishing?"

Elliot laughs, turning to face her, and she's already looking at him, even though she's supposed to be looking at the camera.

"My father would have adored you," he says.

Lia's eyes widen. "You think?"

"Mm-hmm." He moves back to his side of the boat lest he do something like kiss her and end up overboard. "He always used to trick me into thinking I had a catch just to take a photo of my excited face. He'd always let me reel his big ones in though."

Lia smiles. "What happened?" The question is obvious, but it hurts in his chest all the same.

"He'd always been sick."

"Sorry," she says, but he shakes his head.

"Don't be. I love talking about him. He would have loved it here too."

"Even with the monarchy?" she asks, something in her tone he can't quite place.

"He didn't hate anyone," Elliot says with a smile. "Even when I was pushed into the pool at our last swim meet, he still didn't shout."

"Oh, the swimming thing wasn't as fabricated as the fishing?"

Elliot gasps, but she's fallen for his trap all the same, hook, line and sinker, so maybe he is as fabulous at fishing as he claims. He takes his phone back out of his pocket, digging through his old photos until he finds a photo from last summer when he was at the pool. It's before he cut his dreadlocks, and most importantly, he's topless.

"Here I am with my medal, thank you very much," he says, spinning his phone in his hand.

Lia's eyes widen slightly, and she gulps. *Oh*. Very interesting. Elliot hasn't asked her anything particularly personal because he wants her to offer up information she's comfortable sharing, but he'd ask if she had a boyfriend so fast. He thinks she doesn't. She can't, right? Are they flirting? Is she just nice and he wants her to be flirting?

"Massive," she says, with a huff. "Right." She blinks furiously, and he almost feels bad for how flustered she is, but he doesn't.

"Believe me now?" he asks.

She looks at his chest as if he's topless. God, her blush is delightful. She clears her throat. "Yes."

Elliot hums as he turns his phone back. Lia is still watching him as he scrolls through photos. He glances up every now and then to see her eyes trained on his shoulders, his chest, his thighs.

"I thought it was going to be a baby photo," she says, her breath choppy. It's the first time she looks up at his face since he showed her the photo. She's as red as he thinks she could get with her darker complexion, and he almost throws a fist in the air. He feels like the boat is tipping, even as it lies flat against the surface of the lake. "I bet you had chubby thighs." Her eyes drop to his thighs again.

He laughs. "I did. I was a chunker until I was like thirteen."

She smiles, and it soothes something in his childhood brain. A pretty girl smiled at him, something thirteen-year-old Elliot would have killed for. "Did you have dreads then, too?"

"Oh yeah," Elliot replies. He was obsessed with them. "I basically had them from birth. I only got rid of them for this job."

"Excuse me?" she asks, her face gloriously thunderous. "Was that a requirement? Did someone make you?"

"Oh," he replies, his hands up before she goes hunting for a random person who said something about his hair. "No! No, it was for me."

"Oh. Okay. Good."

Lia looks out over the lake, and he wonders if she's embarrassed about her outburst. He wants to tell her she needn't be, but he's not sure he's supposed to know what she's thinking most of the time. A few minutes later, she looks up at him again.

"What about you?" he asks. "Have you been a braids girl since birth?"

Lia looks away. "I was made to have straight hair for a long time. Now it varies. My hair is the only real rebellion I have."

"Well," Elliot says, "rebellion looks marvelous on you."

She smiles, a small thing that he tucks into the folds of his heart. Even on a lake before sunrise, she feels like sunshine.

"Do you *have* any baby photos?" she asks, her eyebrows high.

"Of course," he replies, spinning his phone in his hand as if he wasn't just watching her. "Not on my phone." He clicks back on a photograph from this morning. Just one. He'll look at the others later. The ones he took of her when she was looking at the fish and the glint of the morning light. "But I'll get Mel to send me—"

Elliot gasps as the photo flicks up on his phone. He's there, looking like he always looks, though happier than he's ever seen himself, but he doesn't matter right now. The lake is shining like it might start moving any moment, the morning sunshine barely peeking above the trees. It's picturesque, as with everything here—he could probably submit it for some kind of award. But that's not what has his attention. It's her. It's only ever going to be her.

"What?" she asks.

"Look at your face," he whispers, his finger lightly against his phone. Lia is smiling like she's mid-laugh, even though he doesn't remember saying anything funny. She's looking right at him, and he thinks he might just die—straight up cease to exist—because he's never seen someone so flawless in all his life.

"Is that one no good? Do you want to take another?" Lia asks. He looks over at her, and there's a frown on her face that should never be there, as if there would ever be a time when he talks about her face that would be negative. She's spinning the ring on her pinkie finger, and he turns the phone around.

"Lia."

She looks at the photo, scrutinizing it more. "I could—"

"No," he huffs out, utterly perplexed that she can't see how utterly divine she is. "Look at how pretty you are."

"Oh."

"You know that, right?" His gaze roams her body so she knows he's serious. "You know you're the most strikingly attractive person alive?"

"Shhh." She laughs, his favorite blush coming back.

"Lia." He groans, tilting his head back. "This is like a Shakespearean tragedy. You know, right? You must."

She laughs, an awkward thing that sits in the tension of her shoulders. "I guess."

"You *guess*?"

Lia laughs again. "*Shhh*."

Elliot mimes locking his lips, but the quiet look on her face shows him he's never going to stop telling her how beautiful she is.

"In my dreams, you know how lovely you are." He leans his elbows against his thighs, if only to be closer to her.

She drops her eyes to his lips. He knows she won't lean forward. She's spent most of the trip looking at his lips—as subtle as a bull in a china shop—but something always takes her away. Him and his barely beating heart will wait patiently though.

"You dream about me?" she asks. Her eyes are trained on his lips, but he gives her a moment. He's only known her a little while, and he's spent more time without her than with her, yet he feels like he knows her better than most people in his life, and she's not ready to kiss him. But he never wants her to think it's something he doesn't want. Something he wouldn't move mountains for. Lia swallows. "We should get back."

He sighs, though he puts the oars back in the water all the same. "But what shall I do when I miss you?"

She laughs. "I thought you were going to dream about me."

Elliot smiles, his heart racing as he realizes she's already looking at him. "Perhaps."

CHAPTER NINE

ALIYAH CAN ALMOST HEAR her mother's voice in her head. *"Princesses do not hide behind trees to avoid the guards."* She should also not be darting between bushes and frolicking through the tall grass that, thankfully, has not been cut yet. She definitely should not be making her way to the stables just to see Elliot again, because there's no way this can end well.

Even if he *did* like her as the Princess, there would be nothing she could do about it. Aliyah doesn't have friends. And yet, when she had to leave the lake, she wanted a reason to see him other than just randomly seeing him under the trees, so she asked him if he wanted to go riding with her this evening. It's the perfect time—no one else would be out, and the evenings have been lighter lately, so they'd have at least two hours. But nothing good can come from this friendship. Yet she wanders past the back entrance of the palace and disappears under the shade of the trees all the same.

The forget-me-nots are starting to bloom below the tree canopy, blending in beneath the purples and pinks of the crocus flowers. Spring has always been Aliyah's favorite time of year, and it's even better this time around. It feels like it's been so long since Elliot turned up and flipped her life upside down, when realistically, it's barely been a month. She's not sure how to remember life before he was here. Did she truly just wake up, see and get ignored by her parents, and then see no one else all day? There are the children of her program, of course, but they have been on break for the winter. She wonders how she coped at all.

By the time she gets to the stables, she doesn't have time to do anything like check her face or hair, because Elliot is looking right at her, with his broad nose and his heavy brow and his unwavering smile. He might be the most attractive person she's ever seen in her life. Every time she sees him, she wonders if he's finally looked up the family he despises and he's here to tell her to go to hell. She knows she needs to tell him, and she always has every intention to. And then he talks, and she realizes how much she'd lose if he found out.

His smile softens. "Evening."

"Good evening," she replies. He's in different clothing today. Every time she's seen him before, he's been wearing black trousers and a standard white top, but today, he's in his uniform—dungarees with a white, slightly baggy long-sleeved top underneath. Beige cotton, if she had to guess, but she'd need to feel it to confirm. It's unreasonable that he manages to look this good in clothes she's only ever seen a toddler wear.

"You don't like my uniform?" he asks.

Aliyah sees the smirk on his face as he spreads his arms and takes a spin. She laughs as he comes to a stop in front of her. She thinks the spin brought him a touch closer, but she might have moved also. His movements are the only thing stopping her from pouting, because he's in work clothes, which means he's not coming horse riding with her.

"I do like it."

Elliot smiles like she's told him she hung the stars just to watch his dark skin turn blue under the moonlight, and not that he looks nice in work-approved clothes.

It's a damp day, and the air clings to the back of Aliyah's neck like a bad idea, but she finds herself smiling at him as she tries to figure out how to ask him if he's still going with her. She thinks it's sad that she's this drawn to him already. That the thought of not seeing him today makes her good mood sink to her feet with the heavy wet air. Elliot doesn't know her name yet, not really, and she's unsure if they can continue to be people that sit under the trees together without him figuring out she's a princess... or a *leech*, she assumes is a better way to describe it. There's no need for Aliyah to be here. She could have taken his disdain and run with it. She could be sitting in her bedroom with a book, and in a few weeks, she'd have forgotten all about him. Probably. Maybe.

But there's something about him. Something she likes.

Maybe it's because he's the only person who knows her beyond the Princess title. Usually, no one talks to her without having been spoken to first. No one seeks her out for her advice. No one wants anything from her unless they can have something in return. Maybe she's so lonely that being friends with someone—even when she knows it can't end well—is something she has no choice in.

Elliot isn't like that. She thinks. It's entirely possible that she's a fool and he's waiting to run off to the newspapers because he's always known who she was.

Elliot takes his coat off, and she frowns. It's not raining, per se, but the air is wet enough to leave droplets over the front of his jacket. He hands it to her, and she takes it without thinking. Even with her strategic hand placement, her fingers don't brush his like she wished they would. He looks at her with a strange expression. She wants to know what it means. She wants to know what he looks like when he's hungry, or tired, or bored. She wants to know how to fix it.

"Lia," he says with a smile. "Put it on."

"Oh. But you will get wet, will you not?"

"I won't die from getting a bit wet, will I not?" He frowns. "Wait, that's not right."

Aliyah laughs. "Teasing people for the way they talk will make you look like a fool, will it not?"

"I will always be a fool if it makes you laugh," he replies. Aliyah is suddenly jealous of a bunch of people she's never known—girls and boys Elliot may have dated. If he's this open with casual flirting, he's probably just as open with want. With need. With love.

"I have a feeling I will be laughing at you on a horse soon." She says it before she can think. Before she remembers he's working today and he'll tell her he can't go.

"Oh, I don't doubt it," he says with a laugh, pulling the hood of his coat over her hair. She swallows as his gaze lingers, and she wonders if on the lake, he wanted to kiss her too. "Let's go before I chicken out."

Aliyah has laughed before. She knows that she has, because laughing is as common as smiling, and they're both things that normal people do. But now her chest aches, and her stomach hurts with the amount of laughing she's done in the past thirty minutes, and she wonders if she's ever been this happy.

"I'm not giving you my phone," Elliot says with a small squeak, holding the reins on his horse like his life depends on it. (It doesn't—they've barely moved faster than a trot.)

Aliyah wipes the tears from her face with the back of her hand as she looks for somewhere for them to sit. She dismounts and goes to help Elliot off his horse, but he's on the ground before she can get there. There's no way to know if he fell or if getting off the horse was easier than getting on.

"Are you okay?" she asks, her smile tucked between her teeth. Elliot huffs, but she doesn't think he's all that annoyed. He wipes his brow, strokes Ford—his horse—and thanks him for not killing him.

"I think my thighs are broken," he replies, and she barely resists the urge to look. She finds it frustratingly difficult to tear her eyes from his body once she starts looking. "And to think I brought you cake," he huffs, striding right past her with his backpack.

"Cake?" she asks, tying his horse up properly.

When she turns around, Elliot is setting down a blanket and some food. She didn't even think about bringing anything, but as he ushers her to sit, she doesn't think she needed to. Aliyah chooses the chocolate cake, cheese sandwich, and water, and Elliot makes a note in his pad that he refuses to show her.

The palace grounds are so much prettier when Elliot is around. His entire face lights up when he sees a firefly. His eyebrows fly to the top of his head when he hears something move in the bushes and she tells him there are wild deer. Mainly, Aliyah just likes to be around anything that might seem mundane with Elliot. She wants to do anything as long as he's right there.

"You have any siblings?" he asks. He does this sometimes—asking personal questions out of the blue that any reasonable person might be fine answering. Most of the time, she takes her time pondering and figures something will come to her. But now, as she thinks about the funeral she attended, the shrine in the back room, the way her father's eyes never regained their sparkle, she's conflicted for more reasons than just him finding out who she is. Now, she wants to tell him. Now, she thinks he might comfort her in a way no one has dared try before. But then he might touch her, and so far, she's been careful not to get too close. Shockingly to no one, Aliyah has been touched by her maids, designers, and, on at least three occasions, her mother, but no one has ever touched her because they wanted to. Because she *needed* it. And she doesn't want him to when she's not being truthfully her.

"I have one," he carries on. He does that sometimes too—realizing that things are hard to share with strangers. He never calls her out on it. "She's achingly old, *the* most annoying person in the entire world, and possibly the best person I know."

Aliyah laughs, even as the unease sits in her chest. "Exactly what do you class as achingly old?"

Elliot smiles and looks up at the sky. It's getting dark, and she's already thinking of a reason to see him again. "Twelve minutes older than me."

She gasps, spinning slightly on her bum to face him. "You are a twin?!"

"I am."

"Is she cooler than you?"

"Undoubtedly," he says, with a laugh. "God, she'd love it here."

"Oh? The hatred of the monarchy does not stretch through your bloodline?" Elliot laughs again, and it's simply her favorite sound, even as it harmonizes with the bird song. "She'd ignore the King and Queen like a pro if she saw them on the street." Aliyah can't even complain; she'd do the same if she could. "But the Princess," he says, looking right at her. She wonders if he knows. "She *loves* the Princess."

"She does?"

"She does, and she sometimes has fabulous taste. It's why I'm here." He pauses, frowning at his sandwich. "What's she like?" he asks.

"I think you would know what your sister is like better than I," Aliyah says with a laugh, but she's avoiding the obvious question.

"I mean the Princess," he replies. He takes a bite out of his sandwich while she holds hers uselessly in her hands. "I don't even know her name. Isn't that crazy? I claim to dislike someone I don't even know."

"Uh..." Aliyah starts, trying to get ahead of outing herself as they sit in the meadow. Would he leave her here? Even if she is the better rider than he is, he could leave all the same. Aliyah has spent every waking moment since Elliot arrived in her life thinking about him—his face, his hands, the way he speaks—and it all pales in comparison to how much she dreams about him liking her for real. She takes a small bite just to stall. When she swallows, she replies, "She is nice."

"Are you friends?"

"It is difficult for a princess to have friends, I imagine," she replies, squeezing the bread between her fingers. "I think most people just work for her."

"That's... sad. Does she *want* friends?"

Yes. Desperately. For her entire teenage years, Aliyah yearned for friends. Now, she just wants him.

"I do not think she has much of a choice," Aliyah replies. She pulls her bottom lip between her teeth and catches him staring at the movement. "I think she would like a friend, but it would be difficult to find someone who could see past the things she cannot control."

Elliot looks down at the floor, and she wonders if she's made it too obvious who she is. He takes another bite out of his sandwich.

"She can come and join us, if she likes."

"Maybe," Aliyah replies. "It might be nice to be around people that look like her, being the only Black person in the royal family."

He winces. "God. I bet that's awful. I was one of two Black people in my school, and it still makes me shudder just thinking about it."

"Was it a bad experience?" she asks.

Elliot shakes his head. "Nah. It was just obvious sometimes. It's nice to be around people like you so you're not the only one people stare at when slavery is mentioned in class, if you know what I mean. They act like I was there in the fields myself, y'know?"

"I am afraid not. I was homeschooled."

"Oh, you're *rich* rich," he says.

Aliyah's laugh barely conceals her wince. She's richer than that, but at least they're off the topic of the Princess. She places her sandwich back on the paper.

"Is there a second princess?" Elliot asks. The question hits her in the chest. She's not sure there was ever two; not sure she's ever *actually* been a princess.

"There was," she replies, pulling at the daisies below her. She wishes they could go back to when he was making her bracelets, and not now, when it feels like she's barreling toward the end. "She died."

"Oh," Elliot whispers. "Sorry."

"It is not your fault."

"I should have looked it up myself instead of asking you out of nowhere. That was insensitive."

"Do not worry. It is in the media, of course, but the Princess has never spoken about it all that much, because then there has to be a conversation about whether or not she was ever supposed to be in her position." Before he can reply, she says, "But enough about her for today."

She wonders if it would be worse if he found out who she was on his own. Probably. But at least she wouldn't see the fallout.

"Mm-kay," he replies, rubbing his hands together. "Are you going to show me more of the grounds?"

Aliyah laughs, but it doesn't feel as light as usual with him. "What else is there to see?"

J.S. JASPER

"Everything! I haven't seen inside the palace yet. I need to see everything in the next five months."

"Do you think the palace will cease to exist in five months?" Aliyah asks, though she wonders if their friendship would have come to its expiration date by then. She wonders if in five months he'll like her enough for her being a princess to not matter at all—then she could show him anywhere.

"I'm only here for the summer," he replies, and Aliyah almost falls over, even though she's sitting on the ground.

"Pardon?"

He shrugs as if her heart hasn't fallen to the floor. "The scheme I'm on is only for six months."

"Oh," she replies. Is it? That seems ridiculous, and like something she wouldn't have implemented. Aliyah has always thought you should give someone the best chance at success. A six-month apprenticeship is barely enough to get through basic training, let alone anything else.

"I thought it went on to full-time employment," she says, trying to hide the immediate panic that settled in her bones at the thought of him leaving. He will. It makes sense for him to do whatever he wants, which clearly isn't working here. He hates it, and she's going to lose him. One way or another, she's going to lose him.

"There wasn't anything on the application."

"I can look into it," she says, trying to look as nonchalant as possible. It probably looks like she's pleading for him to let her fix it. "If you want to stay."

Elliot gasps, a wide smile on his face. "We *are* friends."

Aliyah rolls her eyes, but she doesn't tell him he's wrong. He's not, not really. But in her dreams, they are more than that.

"Because we are the best of friends," he says, and she groans fondly. "Will you tell me something?"

She wants to tell him anything he wants the answer to, but she knows better than to say that out loud. "What do you want to know?"

Elliot shrugs. "Anything you want to tell me. What's your favorite color?"

Aliyah laughs, though it comes out shyer than she intended, and she pulls her knees to her chest. The sun is setting, and it's chillier than she thought it would be. Maybe she should have brought Elliot's jumper, but she wasn't sure of the protocol. Would he want it back? It's quickly become her favorite thing to wear. She couldn't bear to part with it now.

"Is that what you want to know?"

It's a dangerous question because it's easy to answer, and she wants him to know the difficult things. The things she's never told anyone.

"I want to know anything you want to tell me."

Aliyah thinks about it. There are things she likes: the pink of the edges of daisy petals, the red of new rosebuds, the blue of the lake. Then there are things she dreams about, things that invade her thoughts without her saying so. The brown of his eyes, the lighter pink of the center of his lips, the darker skin on his knuckles. "I do not have a favorite color," she says. "I like many."

"What's your favorite food?" Elliot replies quickly, like he had a backup ready.

Aliyah laughs and turns to face him. "Breakfast cereal."

"You're so unhinged," he replies, though he looks at her fondly.

She takes a moment to come up with her rebuttal because he's looking up at her from where he's lying on the picnic blanket, only held up with his elbow against the ground. She wants to lie against him, even if everything about his body suggests he'll be rock hard. The evening light bathes his skin in a light glow. He's so beautiful. She wants to trace the length of his face, but she doesn't. She won't. She swallows.

"Cereal is easy," she says, listing the reasons on her fingers, "it takes no time, and it requires little washing up." She doesn't tell him she can also do it all from the safety of her bedroom without having to see anyone, without anyone judging her for how much she's eating. There's a look on his face, like he cares about what she's saying, even if it's the most basic of questions that you could ask anyone.

"What about food from your childhood?" he asks, then, as his face lights up, she gets an insight into how he grew up. "You know, like your mom's roasts she does every Sunday, or the meal your sister makes when she's had a good week, or—"

"I am adopted," she blurts out, interrupting his clear daydream of a favorite time of his life.

"Oh."

"And there has never been a time where my parents have wanted me," she continues, her hands shaking slightly. She's never said it out loud before. "So I do not have those meals. But they sound nice."

"Your childhood wasn't good?" he asks, his brow furrowed, like the answer might physically pain him. As if he ever knew her beyond a few weeks ago.

There should be no reason he would care if she had a bad childhood. No one else did. And yet here he is, the guy she's known for less time than her current braiding cycle, who looks like he might try and give her the world if she mentions her childhood was anything less than perfect. Aliyah has never had someone care in that kind of way. Sure, Anna was here, and she protected her in a way Aliyah would never be able to thank her for, but it was never really a choice. She *had* to be here regardless. Aliyah has never dared think about what would have happened if Anna had a choice right at the start.

"We don't have to talk about it," Elliot says, his hand close to hers but not touching. He never touches her. His hand is always nearby, but he never commits to it. Usually, she's frustrated, because she wants to know what his hand feels like in hers, but right now, she feels awful. Here he is, giving her insight into his life, his mind, his kindness, and she's telling him half-truths.

The guilt swirls in her stomach, settling beside the loneliness that she knows is about to lie heavy in the pit of her stomach for the rest of time when she loses him. She tries to keep the panic off her face. How badly will he hate her when he finds out? But, by the concern sitting between Elliot's eyebrows, she assumes she's wide-eyed.

His voice is frantic. "What about your favorite—"

"I have to go," she says, scrambling to get up from her spot on the ground.

"Lia," Elliot says. His tone is understanding yet firm. It's clear he doesn't want her to leave, but he won't tell her that, not if she tells him she needs to go. All she wants to do is scream that's not her name. But she's a coward, and so, she turns and leaves.

CHAPTER TEN

ALIYAH SPENDS THE BETTER part of the next few days doing a number of things: avoiding Elliot, feeling intensely guilty for running away and forgetting that they rode horses there, and finding any reason why he's not already locked into a lifetime employment contract, apart from the obvious human rights implications. (Something he'd probably say the royals had no desire to protect.) The latter was relatively easy to solve once she knew where to look. "Cost-saving measures," better known as her parents and their inability to need less than an entire kingdom's fortune resting in their coffers. They changed the terms and conditions on her more recent scholarship opportunities to save money they wouldn't even look twice at.

It was a simple fix, in the end. She threatened to leak it to the press. "King and Queen hinder employment opportunities for vulnerable youth." She's now not allowed out of her bedroom, which is usually fine. But she wants to spend her time hiding with Elliot. She wants to tell him she's not avoiding him (she was, but she doesn't want to now), but she has a ridiculous life, and at the grand age of twenty-four, she's confined to her bedroom. Grounded.

Fixing the program does nothing to sort the thumping in her chest at the thought of Elliot leaving, but that pales in comparison to how she feels about continuing to lie to him. She wants to tell him who she is so terribly that it keeps her up at night. Before her grounding, Aliyah had run more in three days than she had the entire time Elliot has been here, but now she's trapped, and her thoughts have nowhere to go but circling about in her bedroom. He helps sort out the mess in her head, and he doesn't even need to do anything beyond look at her.

There has never been a time in Aliyah's life when she's wanted to keep someone as badly as she wants to keep Elliot. Whether he wants to stay in her life is not up to her as much as she wishes it were. There's a part of her—deep down, beneath the childhood heartache and the dark summer days—that thinks he might just forgive her for not telling him. That she might tell him she's a princess and that she's sorry for not telling him, and he'll like her as much as she likes him, and he'll say "Don't worry about it. What's your favorite crown?" But Aliyah knows it's a pipe dream, something so unlikely that she can't bring herself to sneak out of her room, go over to the greenhouse she's watching him work in, and tell him the truth. Because there is simply too much to lose.

He writes her thoughts on paper, he watches her walk away, he keeps her in his mind. She missed him before she even knew who he was, and she thinks even if he left now, even if he said he never wanted to talk to her again, he's changed her life. She wants him to climb the trellis and come see her, but then she'd have to tell him why she's not allowed out, why he can't come in, and then she'll have to have the conversation she's desperately avoiding.

Aliyah has never been sure what will happen when she turns twenty-five. She's always been too scared to ask. Banishment? Death? The law states she can marry whomever she likes, commoner or not. But in all her life, there's never been a single person who wanted to talk to her because they thought she was interesting, or they wanted to know about her favorite book, or they wanted to learn something from her. She hasn't known Elliot long enough to know if she'd ever want to marry him. She's barely known him long enough to know if she would ever like him as more than a friend (if she lied to herself, which she will). But she has had him in her life long enough to know she wants more than a marriage to someone who hates her. Someone that wants her for nothing beyond the crown.

There was a time when Aliyah would have accepted an arranged marriage. It works for millions of people every year, and if she truly believed the people involved wanted the best for her, she would have said yes. But she can't convince herself that her parents didn't try to have her assassinated the moment they thought they were pregnant for a second time. If Elliot had a say in who she was to marry, she'd trust his judgment. It's all his fault she cares about it anyway.

But she can't hide from him forever. Mainly because she misses him, and she knows she won't make it another day before she sneaks out of her room and underneath the plum trees just for the possibility of bumping into him. She already has to apologize for making him walk back with two horses (he barely had the confidence to ride one, let alone lead another while on horseback), but she doesn't want to see him without having a plan in place. Because he could look at her with his wide eyes and his nice teeth, and she'll blurt it out so catastrophically that she'll never be able to look at him again.

So, she writes it down. Her thoughts on it all. Why she hasn't told him yet. How she hopes they can get past it. How he makes her feel like everything might be okay, even if he never speaks to her again. It's the most vulnerable she's been with anyone since she told Elliot she was adopted and then ran away. Aliyah wants to give it to him right now. She could figure out where he lived by looking him up in the directory. She could figure out everything she wanted about him, if she so desired. She's the Princess; it would barely take a phone call to find out everything about him. She won't, of course. She only wants to know what he wants to give her.

Aliyah seals the letter with her wax and sighs. He's still in the greenhouse. Why is he still working? It's late, and she knows he missed dinner. She's made changes to the structure of when food is available, but it's not fully implemented yet because she needed them to hire more staff, so she knows he's missed dinner. It's not her problem, though. Is it? Can she turn up with food because she knows he might be hungry, or is that ridiculous? Is that something a friend would do, or will he look at her weirdly because she might be falling in love with him? She wishes there were a guide on how to be a princess and have friends, because it's been twenty-four years and she has no idea what she's doing. She's just going to go to bed lest she shoves the letter in his face before she's had a day to ruminate on the contents. He'll be fine.

Elliot is *starving*. He hasn't been this hungry since he started working here because, despite his reservations about the state of the catering, the food has been pretty good. (Melody had to post him some hot sauce, but he won't blame the royals for that. His mom makes the best one anyway.) Today, it's his fault. He's trying to get the nigella seeds in the ground so Lia can see the flowers early in the season. He has no idea if she'd like them, but anytime they've been walking around, she seems to gravitate to taller, more colorful plants, so he's trying it out. Of course, it doesn't hurt that nigellas are also called *love-in-a-mist*. He was supposed to do it yesterday, but he didn't, because he spent the entire day wondering where she was. The day before that, he had to put the order of stock in for the summer programs the Princess runs on the lawn, and of course, it took him twice as long as it should have as he was wondering where Lia was.

It's not lost on Elliot that he's initiated every event. He finds her in the woods; he asks her to the lake; he seeks her out. She invited him horse riding, but then abandoned him with two horses, so he doesn't think it should count. Elliot is at least forty-percent sure she wants to be his friend, but that's not enough. He spent the entirety of high school chasing girls that didn't actually want him, girls that never did anything he needed. There's no part of Elliot that isn't a lover of love. He wants the mixtapes and the "I just thought about you" gifts and the random messages. He wants to wait for her to come looking for him... he's just not sure he'll last.

It's not in his nature to wait for something he wants, and he wants her presence so badly. It's not even her face. She's beyond beautiful, that's true. But she's funny, and he likes the way she starts laughing before she's finished her ridiculous joke. He likes the way she looks at him with a stony expression when he says something sarcastic and he cracks up. He wants to know why she always has a barrier up. He wants to know what it would take for her to let him see her without it. He wants her, however she wants him. It's taking its toll on him that maybe she doesn't want him at all.

Now, it's nine in the evening, and he knows he has missed dinner entirely because—of course—he was thinking about Lia. Desperately wanting her to be thinking about him too. Maybe. Hopefully. Probably not. There's a chance she's at dinner, talking to a handful of people that already know her as well as he would like to.

As Elliot places the last seed in the ground, he walks to get the watering can. Tomorrow, he'll go into town and grab some snacks to shove in his bedroom cabinet so the threat of being hungry overnight won't linger in his mind. He wonders if Lia might like something too—something he won't be able to give her until he seeks her out in the forest.

The door knocks just as he turns the tap on the rain barrel.

"Come in," he shouts, waiting for the can to fill. Before he can waste the rainwater, he switches it off, turning to greet his first ever greenhouse visitor.

Lia stands in front of him. She looks utterly radiant, her hair piled high on top of her head. It exposes the long expanse of her neck, and he's suddenly aware of his muddy hands and the fact he's probably sweating from garden work. She's in a dress. He's never seen her in a dress before, and she looks entirely too ethereal to be working here. It's not too extravagant, but he's not sure it's uniform either.

She smiles, and all other thoughts leave his head. "Good evening."

"Hi—hello," he stutters. It's been a few days, and he's reduced to a stammering mess again, even though he was just hoping she would come and see him. He bows dramatically, his hand out to the side because she rolled her eyes last time he did it and he finds it charming.

She scoffs. "For that gesture only, I am banishing you from the kingdom."

Elliot is yet to ask how close she is to the Princess. If the Princess even has the power to banish someone, and if they're close enough friends that she would. He thinks they must be if her work clothes consist of flowing dresses. Instead, he smiles when he sees the blush creep up her neck. She *likes* him. His smile widens, and she rolls her eyes, but it's not long until she's looking at him again. Lia sighs, her hands fidgeting behind her back. *Peculiar.* He moves to look at what she might be holding, but her eyes widen, and she takes a step to the opposite side.

"Lia?"

"May I help you?" she asks, moving away from him. "Why are you moving closer?"

At this point, they're basically dancing in a circle. He figures if it will never be him and her under the chandeliers with the harps in the palace, it can be them under the moonlight with the faint sound of his radio in the background.

"What are you hiding?"

"Nothing," she says too fast. She won't look at him, and he *loves* it. She stops, looking up at the glass ceiling, and then she looks at him, her lips pouting. He can see a dangerous avenue ahead of him that leads to falling completely and utterly in love with her. What a ridiculous man he is that he'll barrel down it headfirst. "You were not at dinner," she says.

"Oh," he replies. He didn't know she was going to be there, otherwise he would have been. She's never been in the dining hall with them—not since he started working at the palace, at least—so he thought she always ate elsewhere. If he had the chance, he'd eat with her for every meal. He won't tell her that, but he thinks she might already know. (Maybe he'll tell her later anyway.) "I was trying to get the seeds in the ground."

"And?" she asks, her eyes lighting up. She spins on the spot like she's trying to find them despite the fact it's just bare ground right now. That's when he sees a brown paper bag clutched in her fingers.

"What did you bring?"

PERFECTLY CANDID

Lia spins back, her eyes wide like she forgot she would get caught. She huffs, holding the brown paper bag in front of her. Elliot reaches out slowly and takes it from her with a wary glance.

"Am I about to be murdered?" he asks. Lia rolls her eyes again, and it's fast becoming his favorite expression of hers.

"I have told you so many times," she says with a sigh, "if I wanted you dead..."

Elliot laughs. "I know." He wonders if maybe she's secretly the Princess's bodyguard. It would make sense—she's brilliant, there's no way she couldn't take anyone down, and yet no one would suspect it of her. "I would be dead, which really means you adore me."

"Eat your dinner," she replies, but he sees the pink hue of her cheeks. Elliot smiles, opening the bag. It's *stacked* with food.

"Sandwiches?" he asks, going to lean against the workbench. There's only one chair in here, and he gestures at Lia to take it. She shrugs, moving to lean against the workbench next to him. "I thought tonight was pie and mash."

He tears the edge of the bag to make a makeshift tray. He much prefers sandwiches. There's something delicious about the different concoctions that can be made. Besides, he had the gravy from the dining hall the other day, and he's not about to run for that watery, tasteless liquid again. The fear of pie day has been on his mind.

"It was," she replies.

Elliot raises his eyebrows and offers Lia one of the sandwiches, but she shakes her head.

"Oh, are these from lunch?" he asks. "They're so fresh."

"Mm-hmm," she replies, but she won't look at him—a telltale sign that she's not telling the truth. He knows because she did it three times on the lake when he asked her if she liked his hair long. Three times means it goes in the notebook. It's supposed to be all about gardening—what went right and wrong with the plants that month—but mainly it reads like a grocery list of things Lia likes.

- *Lupines like colder weather*

- *Lia doesn't like cilantro*

- *She does like my shoulders—wear the long-sleeved black top*
- *She frowns when I mention the monarchy*
- *Don't ask about her parents unless she brings it up*
- *Plant nigella seeds and water well*

"Lia," he starts, and she frowns while looking at the floor. "Did you make these?"

"Maybe."

He smiles so widely it hurts his cheeks a little. "Why?"

She sighs, clearly hoping he was just going to eat them and leave her alone. "Well, you said the food was unsatisfactory, and I have been putting things in place for it to be better, but you seem intent on starving to death anyway."

He smiles, a softer one this time. "Lia." But she's on a rampage. He could write in his notebook that when she's flustered, she won't stop talking. Maybe he should call her out more often, because she's his favorite thing, down to his bones.

"And we both know without food every twenty minutes you are at dangerous risk of throwing a strop, so I just—I wanted you to eat, you know." She swallows. "For the safety of the palace." She chews on her lip, but eventually, she looks up at him.

"You didn't want me to be hungry."

She *cares* about him. It's not mixtapes and random messages, but sandwiches wrapped in beeswax paper is now at the very top of his list, something he'll wish for forever more.

"Yes," she says.

He takes a bite, chews, and swallows. "Thank you."

She smiles at him, a small thing she doesn't try to hide, even as her brows stay low.

"You are welcome."

"I never saw any of the photos you took the other day," she replies, rolling her neck. Elliot has asked if she wants to sit more times than he's asked if she wants half these sandwiches, but her reply remains the same. He doesn't mind, even if she does look uncomfortable to be standing so long, because she follows him around whenever he moves to do another task.

"From lake day? The worst day of my life?"

Lia laughs, a loud thing that rings around the edges of the greenhouse. "Was it truly?"

"Perhaps."

Her laughter settles into a low chuckle, and he wants to stay here, with her and that sound, until the birds wake.

"Will you show me?" she asks.

"Yes. Despite the betrayal, I will show you."

Lia smiles. It reaches her eyes, but it takes some time.

When Elliot pulls out his phone, he realizes it's eleven in the evening, which explains why her blinks are slow. She's tired. It reminds him of being a teenager, when he got his first crush and stayed up far too late just so he could text her even though he was going to see her at school the next day. This feels the same, if not exponentially more frightening.

"It's late," he starts, but she barrels into the conversation so quickly he barely has a moment to frown.

"I did not mean to tell you about my parents and then run." Lia says it like she's got to get rid of the information before she tries to backtrack.

"That's alright." He shrugs. "I only want to know what you want to tell me."

Lia sighs. "I want to tell you everything, it is just..."

"Scary?" he asks, leaning against the workbench once more.

"Terrifying," she replies. She looks up at him, and he wants to tell her not to be scared, that there's nothing she could tell him that would make him look at her any differently. She could be the Queen of Iledale and he wouldn't bat an eye. Maybe. He'd have some thoughts, that's for sure.

"I am not used to having people that care about me," she says, her voice barely above a whisper. Elliot isn't a violent man. He'd rather leave a fight than take a punch just for the sake of it. But he'll defend those he loves like his life depends on it, and with the way his stomach sinks at her words, Lia has worked her way onto that list with startling ease. She chews on her lip, spinning her ring again. "You make it a little better."

"A little?" he asks, scandalized. It does what he wants, though—she smiles. "I guess I need to up my game."

"Your game is just fine," she replies. He smiles at her, not sure what else to say without acting like he's hiding the topic from conversation. He'll take whatever she gives him. It was foolish for him to act like he wouldn't follow her to the ends of the earth if only she turned to look at him one more time.

"I'm sorry you have shitty parents," he says, but she just smiles. He leans toward her, as if he's telling her a secret, even if his words should be screamed from the rooftops. "Sucks to be them. I have it on good authority that you're fantastic."

"Is the good authority you?" she asks, a smirk on her face that he knows means she's about to be mean to him. "Because I still have four carp catches to your one log."

"Ha!" he replies, and she smiles brightly, like he thought she would. "No. Little Jamie told me you were his best friend."

"Jamie is back from break?" she says, half happy, half something he can't place—panicked, if he had to guess. "What did he say?"

Elliot shrugs. "The confidentiality of my client is of the upmost importance to me." Lia pouts, and he sighs, ready to give up his information. He wonders if she already knows all the ways to kill him. "He said, and I quote, 'Lia is my *bestest* best friend because she lets me be Superman.'"

Lia smiles. "He's a very cute Superman."

"I asked if he thought you would be my best friend too, but he wasn't keen."

She gasps, a hand against her chest. "We are not already best friends? But I brought you sandwiches."

Elliot laughs, throwing his head back slightly. When he looks back at her, her eyes are glued to his neck. "My love, I would die to be best friends with you."

Lia takes a step closer. "Dying would be unnecessary," she whispers. Her eyes travel from his neck to his lips and stay there. He needs to get her to stop, because she's not about to lean in, and he's so desperate to feel her lips on his, but he is a gentleman, so he'll wait for her to be ready.

"I'm glad we met here," he says, and it works—she looks up at him.

"At the palace?" she asks, her brows knitted.

"Yeah," he replies. "There's no other world where you would look twice at me. Have you seen how beautiful you are?"

She sucks in a breath, but the smile is all over her face, even if she refuses to show it to him. Lia laughs, and it turns into a yawn that she covers with the back of her hand. "You are ridiculous."

"I'm serious! But now, it's time for bed," he says, and she screws up her nose. Her blinks are slow, and he wants her to rest well, so he asks, "Will I see you tomorrow? We could have lunch on the grass."

"Um... I have a meeting tomorrow about an event in a few weeks' time, and, uh... I am kind of... grounded?"

It's the first time Elliot has got an inkling of her daily life. Meetings, events... for what? He wonders if he'll ever get to see her out in the open—a thought he's trying to avoid.

"Grounded?" he asks, then says, "I know you're not meant to ask a lady how old she is, but God, Lia, please don't be a teenager." The panicked look on her face is back—the one she had when he mentioned Jamie. Elliot wonders how much he's supposed to wait for her to tell him, and what he's allowed to request. At the very least he should make sure he's not breaking the law. Fuck. *Fuck*.

"I am twenty-four, I just... my home life is difficult sometimes, and, well, I am grounded," she says.

Elliot sighs a breath of relief. "Thank God, Lia."

She frowns. "You are glad I am banished to my bedroom?"

He laughs because she's cute, and maybe because she's snuck out here just to see him. "Yet here you are."

Lia blushes, blinking rapidly as she looks anywhere but at him. Elliot shoves down the thought that maybe she's been trying to hide him. He had an upsetting two-year relationship where he wasn't allowed to meet her family. She always thought it was too soon, or they lived too far. He never thought it was because she was embarrassed of him. Perhaps Lia is embarrassed too. Maybe if she told him she couldn't be seen with him because he's so funny everyone would want to be with him and she'd be jealous, then he could abide that. Honestly, there's not much she could say that wouldn't have him hiding in the forest with her.

Her brow furrows, and there's nothing on her face he doesn't want to trust. "I am sorry," she says.

Elliot frowns, folding his apron. "Why?"

"I think it might be strange to be locked in your room at twenty-four," she says, pulling on her bottom lip with her teeth. What he would give to set it free.

Elliot shrugs, leaning against the worktop again. "Everyone has a different life." He smiles. It doesn't quite hit his eyes, but he wouldn't expect her to figure out why.

"Yeah," she says, letting out a breath. "I suppose I will see you in a few days?"

"What is outside your room? Maybe I could come and see you?"

She blinks, a flash of something across her face, then stands straighter. "No one comes in my room."

"I don't have to come in. I can sit on the balcony."

She frowns. "You would sit on the balcony, in the cold, just to see me?"

"You would sneak out of your bedroom to see me, would you not?"

She bites her lip again, but it's to hide her smile. It doesn't work.

"Tomorrow?" she says.

"After work. I expect snacks."

"...snacks?" She pulls a notepad out, and God, he thinks she might be his favorite thing of all time. "What snacks? Do you have allergies?"

"I'm allergic to wheat," he says, waiting. She writes it down, her pen moving furiously while he waits with a smile on his face.

"Wheat, and—" She stops, her eyes wide with panic when she looks up at him. He feels a little guilty. "I—the—where is your pen?" she asks, her hands flailing. "*El*, why did you just eat—oh my *God*, how—"

He laughs, but she's already moving. "Lia..." His heart thumps over the way she shortened his name, and he feels stupid about it, but it thumps harder all the same.

"We need to take you to the matron."

He doesn't move, though the smile is still on his face, just a little. "Lia."

"Darling, please."

Oh. That's new. His stomach slips like a seesaw.

"I was joking," he says, swallowing around how the word *darling* feels like it's lodged in his throat. Her face drops, but she's not sad. She really might kill him though. She stalks toward him, and he wonders if now she might touch him, but the end of her pen pushes against his chest.

"You are *not* funny."

He smiles, but it's hard when she's this close, looking up at him. Her eyes shine in the low candlelight. "Not even a little?"

Her gaze drops to his mouth. She breathes in, licking her lips as she moves slowly, and he can't breathe, can't think, because all he can smell is strawberries. Her eyes flutter closed, and he holds onto the counter as he mirrors her and waits. Lia's nose brushes against his.

"El," she whispers, and he leans down, but he never so much as tastes her lips. He frowns, opening his eyes, and she's a step away from him. "I am funny too, am I not?"

He huffs out a laugh and runs his hand over his hair. Elliot wants to be annoyed. He wants to be frustrated (and with the way his dick pulses in his trousers, he probably will be later), but he can't be. Not when she looks like she's as wrecked as he is, and her lips never even touched him. She got him back, but it cost her as badly as it did him.

"Most amusing," he replies, and she smiles at him. In that moment, it hits him in the gut that he'll wait forever for her.

"Goodnight, Elliot."

"See you tomorrow, Lia."

"Sleep well," she replies.

Elliot watches her walk away, of course. Maybe one day she'll let him walk her home, or he'll know why not. Either or. She reaches the door, her hand lingering on the doorknob.

"Elliot," she says, turning to look at him. He's already looking right at her; she needn't have called his name. "You would always turn my head. In any room, in any lifetime, I would have looked at you."

CHAPTER ELEVEN

Aliyah barely makes it through the night without knocking on Elliot's bedroom door. The only reason she stayed in her room was because she wasn't sure she wouldn't try and kiss him if she saw him in sleep trousers with messy hair, instead of giving him the letter, like she should do. But soon, a small child who likes to jump from planters and pretend he's Superman is going to give her away, and she's not sure there will be a time she can come back from that. She wouldn't even be able to blame him. Children are blameless; it's like their whole thing.

Still, she's restless during her meeting with the heads of Loven regarding the environmental initiative she wants to set up. It always made sense to her—giving the people of the kingdom the tools and the means to grow their own food if they so desire. However, Aliyah usually sets up the funds, the process, and the outline from the safety of her own room. There hasn't been a time since she was eighteen when she was allowed to go to the opening of centers or the charity galas. Now, she's so distracted by the fact Elliot might find out who she is from an overtalkative child that she's agreed to go on a tour of the new museum.

There's a slight excitement sitting in the back of her mind. Aliyah loves getting out of the palace grounds, but she also likes the safety of knowing no one will ask her anything untoward. There's the risk of assassination, of course. Aliyah has experienced more failed attempts on her life than one would like (though better failed than the alternative), but she assumes most of those hits came from her parents themselves, so the fear of being alone in the back of a car is not one she bears.

Perhaps, in some sort of perfect world, Aliyah could tell Elliot who she was. She could hand him the letter and watch as he understood the deepest, darkest pits of her mind and wanted to stay anyway. Maybe then he would be able to go with her. They'd sit together in the back of the car, instead of how she sits alone, to one side, looking at the empty seats. (There was a time she thought the idea of being driven in a limousine was the fanciest thing a person could do. Now she's not so sure it is not a ploy to show her how alone she is, to preclude the notion that she could do this life alone. To usher her into a marriage with a man she detests just so her trips were not lonely.) Maybe Elliot would bring snacks and point out the animals they see on the way. Maybe he'd bring her a blanket even though she didn't ask him too. Maybe they'd hold hands and she'd fall asleep on his shoulder to the sound of his thoughts.

Aliyah walks from the meeting with too many thoughts in her mind. How will her parents react when she tells them she needs to leave? Will Elliot like the way she's done her hair? Is the dungeons a fitting punishment for her doing her job? Will Elliot want to ride with her again? Why did he look so upset when he mentioned lunch on the grass? Elliot, Elliot, Elliot.

She shakes him from her mind, but it does nothing to stop him from invading her bedroom. Her door closes behind her, and she slips his sweater on over the top of her dress. It smells like him. Then the panic sets in.

The way she sees it, she tells him, and it goes one of two ways: either he runs away and she dies (though her track record so far suggests she won't), or he stays and he dies. Because that's what will happen. She'll let him in, and he'll get what she's always gotten—death threats, and attempts on his life. Elliot is clearly a love-out-loud kind of man. It's a love she craves, even if it'll never be given to her. He's shown her enough of what she wants her life to look like. But she'd always need that behind closed doors. He'd want it out in the open, as he would deserve. Aliyah feels like she's known him her whole life, and it's been weeks at best. He wants true love—a shout from the rooftops love—and she can't give him that.

She sighs. She wants to run. Away from here, away from him. Away. But she can't. She's got snacks to find.

***

Elliot is beyond tired. He hasn't been sleeping all that well since he moved here, and his ability to sleep before wasn't good anyway. It always takes his body a while to regulate to a new environment. He's used to falling asleep with the sound of traffic, the buzz of the old refrigerator from the corner shop down the street, the dip in his mattress. Now, Elliot has nothing but the sounds of trees and water, and it's messing with his ability to sleep longer than three hours at a time. There's not exactly white noise compared to the sounds of the inner city.

Still, he looks at the trellis he's about to climb in the dark. He's exhausted, but he can climb two stories to see Lia. It's not like he would be able to sleep if he was in his bedroom anyway. If anything, he just gets frustrated, and he'll pout on his bed. Or, if nothing else works (and honestly, just if the thought of her swings through his mind), he'll get off to the memory of her nose softly brushing against his. He'll fuck his fist to the mental image of what she'd look like on top of him.

After looking around to check no one else is out here, Elliot shakes the trellis. It's stable—wrought iron, he thinks—so it's unlikely to fall away from the wall when he's halfway up. He can't be sure, of course, that it would get him safely there, but he couldn't bring a ladder without looking like he's breaking into the palace. Besides, he's climbed higher than this to dive off, so this should be a breeze.

He takes a deep breath, closes his eyes, and climbs. (He opens them again after two steps because he realizes trying to climb a trellis covered in flower stems is something he might need his sight for.) When he finally climbs onto the balcony, he takes in the view. The greenhouse is clearly visible here, and he wonders if Lia ever watches him working. He can see the tops of trees for what seems like miles, and the light glint of the lake in the foreground. God, what he'd do to live here.

"Hi," she says, and Elliot spins around. He didn't even hear the doors open, but he guesses that's because it slides almost the entire length of the balcony. Lia stands in front of the thick curtains, but he doesn't mind what she's hiding from him. He only came for her. She's in his sweater and some leggings, and he wonders if anyone has ever looked better in all their life.

"Hi." His hands swing by his sides. He wants to hug her, to pull her close and look at the stars with her. But he'll stand here until she wants that too.

She plays with her fingers. "Thank you for coming."

Elliot laughs. Lia frowns, and all is right with the world. She's *nervous*.

"Thank you for having me," he says with a bow, and her frown intensifies. He might be in love with her. As he stands again, he notices the floor. It's tiled—a fancy, colored pattern that his mother would die for—and there are blankets, piles and piles of blankets.

"You can sit, if you like," she says, tucking her hair behind her ear. It falls loose tonight, framing her face, and his fingers itch to touch her. "Or there are chairs too." The chairs are in the corner with a mosaic table, and Elliot imagines her sitting here at breakfast with her bad cereal and a juice. The table is cute, but too far away, so he plops himself on the floor of the balcony. Lia laughs lightly, the nerves radiating off her in waves, but she mirrors his action on the other side of the threshold, within the safety of her bedroom. Then she gets up.

"Wait! I got snacks."

Elliot ate dinner, but he left space for donuts and crisps, so imagine his surprise when Lia comes back with a platter of carrot sticks, cucumber, and something he thinks might be zucchini. *Cold* zucchini. He tries to keep the horror from his face because she's laid it all out neatly, and his chest constricts at how she snuck out of her room to get this for him. She places it, along with a jug of water, on a small table she drags out of her room.

"Thank you," he replies with a smile, and her face drops.

"Do you not like it?"

"What?" he asks, his voice high. He clears his throat. "Yes."

"You are lying," she says with a frown, and it's ridiculous how his heart breaks at the sight. It's just food. Nothing more than a few snacks.

He huffs. "I'm not! I'm sorry, my love, I do like cucumber. I was just... these aren't the kind of snacks I'm used to."

"Oh. I can get you something else?" she asks, her eyebrows high. "There is hummus too, but if there is something else I can get for you..."

"Lia," he whispers, and she swallows as she looks at him. She told him no one has ever been in her room, so maybe she's never had a sleepover either. "Have you ever had a slumber party?"

She frowns. Maybe not.

"What about a standard sleepover, with no snacks?"

Her frown deepens.

"Not even with the Princess?" he asks, and she doesn't look at him.

He sighs. He's not sure what kind of person he'd be today without prank calls and staying up till three a.m. on a sugar high with his best friends, then bringing duvets to the front room just to sleep in a pile on the floor.

"Where's the hummus?" he asks.

"You do not need to," she says, looking sadder than he can deal with. "Please, just tell me what you would like. You can have anything. Whatever you want, I can get it for you."

"Anything?" he asks, and she nods frantically.

"Hummus, please," he says, and the way her hopeful eyes drop into a frown should be studied.

"Eli."

"Lia," he replies, his tone matching hers. She sighs but pulls out a bowl of hummus with a little unnecessarily detailed spoon. He hides a yawn as he dips the cucumber in the bowl. The dip hits his tongue, and his eyes widen. Who knew hummus could be that tasty?

"That's divine," he says, getting another cucumber stick.

"You do not—"

He swipes a healthy amount of hummus onto his stick. "I'm not lying to you, my love. I never was. I just wasn't expecting it. But I wasn't expecting an evening with you either, and I'm very glad to have both."

"What were you expecting?" she asks, and he watches her hands slyly go for her notepad.

He laughs. "Don't even think about it," he says, grabbing a carrot this time. "We'll take it in turns." He holds the carrot out for her. "You *need* to try this." She leans forward, her tongue darting out just slightly and Elliot almost shortcircuits as he pops the carrot into her mouth.

"I made it," she replies, licking her lips.

Elliot pretends to faint, his legs flying up in the air. His shoulder hits the floor hard but Lia cackles, so it was all worth it. The exhaustion in his body makes it more difficult to get back up than usual, but when he does, he's ready to start listing off achievements on his fingers.

"So, let me get this right. You can cook—"

"Hummus requires no actual cooking."

"You can cook," he repeats, and she rolls her eyes, but her face falls into a smile. "You can fish, you can *definitely* wield a knife, and you look like that..."

"Like what?" she asks, a light blush on her cheeks. It would be difficult to see if the moon weren't bright, turning her skin a shade of blue.

"Like I am jealous of the moon because it gets to see you every night," he says, his voice low. "Like I cannot breathe when you look directly at me for too long. Like I would read every poem on earth just to figure out the correct way to tell you that you are breathtaking morning, noon, and night. Like I wander around this kingdom and see you in everything beautiful thing I see. Like if we were in sixth grade, I would be writing your name next to mine in my notebook."

"Oh."

"Yeah." He smiles, then says, "Like that."

She clears her throat, and he wonders if he's made her uncomfortable, but then she frowns. "You do not write my name in your notebook now?"

She's flirting with him. He thinks. Maybe.

"You forget that I don't know your full name." He laughs, and her eyes widen, but he's too tired to figure that out now. "But if you're there under Lia Harper, then that's my own business."

"What is Harper?" she asks, then says, "Are you tired?"

"A little," he replies. "I have insomnia. I haven't gotten used to the new place yet, but I don't know, this evening feels comfortable. Like home. And, apparently, it's about to knock me out. I should go." She hands him a pillow, moving the tables and snacks out the way. Elliot stretches his legs out. He'll just lie down for a moment, and then, when he wakes up in twenty minutes, he'll go.

"And if you must know," he whispers, his eyes heavy even as they close, "Harper is my last name."

There's a light breeze against Elliot's cheek, but his arms feel too heavy to move, as if he's been in the same position for hours. The back of his eyelids are bright orange, and he frowns. His alarm didn't go off, and the mornings aren't that bright yet. He's used to getting up in the dark. Elliot manages to roll his neck slowly, blinking his eyes open. There's no ceiling, no soft mattress under his back. The bright morning sky is right there, the sounds of birds slowly infiltrating his groggy mind. Did he sleepwalk? He lifts the top of his body, resting his hands against the hard tiled floor.

Oh. He fell asleep. Hours ago. He fell asleep *hours* ago. His blinking becomes more rapid, and he rubs the heels of his hands against his eyes. God, he passed out while with Lia. His hands fall against a plush, soft duvet, nothing like the piles of blankets he had haphazardly across his legs. He looks over, and the doors are still wide open, the curtains blowing in the breeze. Elliot can see in the room just slightly—picture frames perhaps—but then his eyes fall on her.

Lia's not in her bed, as he thought she might be. She's right next to him, albeit on her side of the threshold, but under the same duvet as him. He smiles at the thought of her going to get her bedding so she could stay with him. She's got no makeup on, and he's never seen her like this before. There's not a large difference, obviously—she's flawless either way—but she looks younger now. More carefree, with the freckles on her nose visible and her cheeks puffy from sleep. She's tied her hair in one thick braid, and he wishes he had been awake to see her do it. Elliot wants to lie back down and just rest here with her. But he has no idea what the time is—middle morning, if he had to guess—and the children will show up for gardening soon. He stretches, feeling the pull in the back of his shoulders.

"Morning," Lia says, rubbing her hands over her face. Her voice is low, deeper than he's ever heard before, and he's immediately turned on. Immediately harder than he was in his sleep.

"Hi, my love."

She shuffles until she's fully on her side and tucks her hands under her head. "You have to go, right?" she asks, and he wants to ask her to recite the dictionary just so he can hear her voice like this forever.

"Yeah," he whispers, though he lies back down until they're almost nose to nose. "Do you want to go riding with me this evening?"

She screws up her nose, and he almost gets up just to get down on one knee. "Yes," she says.

"Six?"

"Mm-hmm," she replies, wiggling her legs. The duvet moves, obscuring his view of her face, and he frowns until her hand pushes the air back down. "This time, you are on snack duty."

Elliot laughs. "I'm going to bring something so good you'll write my name in your notepad with a heart."

"How do you know I have not already?" she asks, and he groans.

"You're not allowed to flirt with me when you're like this," he says, and she laughs.

Sleepily, she says, "Go to work, or I will never be able to let you go."

"Good," he replies as he gets up. "I'm going to get a blow-up bed, and then you'll never be rid of me."

CHAPTER TWELVE

Aliyah spends her morning researching blow-up beds. She orders four because she has no idea what a blow-up bed is, and she wants Elliot to be comfortable should he ever want to come back. She also now knows that sleepover snacks usually consist of donuts and sweets, not the salad vegetables she currently eats for dinner. It's bland and underwhelming, and everyone else is served a different meal, but Aliyah doesn't fight it. There's no point.

She ignores her mother and father discussing the upcoming visit from Lord Lucian Feathermore. She's going to see Elliot soon, and she doesn't want him to ask her what's wrong. Aliyah hates Lucian. He's racist and rude, and one of the worst people she's ever met. He's also the man her parents want her to marry. So she ignores the conversations of his visit, the discussions of the balls they have planned in the coming months, and the fact that her birthday is dangerously close.

Lia ignores it all until she's allowed to leave the table, and then she sneaks out the side door, finding the riding gear she stashed this morning. She rids all thoughts of Lucian from her mind as she holds her letter in her pocket and follows the longer, hidden route to the stables.

It's not difficult to find Elliot. He's in the stables doing *something* that looks a lot like nothing. He jumps when he turns around and she's there, and it makes her smile for the first time that day since seeing the flowers he left on her balcony. Lia wastes no time, jumping on her horse, Atticus, as he begrudgingly gets on Ford again.

The ride isn't full of laughter like it was last time, and she feels Elliot watching her carefully, as if he shouldn't be watching the path. He doesn't question her, which is good. She fears she might cry if he tries, and Aliyah *doesn't* cry. She can't remember the last time she did, but as he looks at her with his worried eyes, her throat burns.

As Elliot lays out another picnic blanket, Aliyah wonders if he just has a secret stash of these and food ready to go, and if this ride will still be a common occurrence once she tells him who she is. In about five minutes. Or ten. She's been putting it off.

"The Princess is due to come for a welcome dinner," Elliot says, and Aliyah barely bites down that she already knows. That she did it on purpose because she missed him, but she thinks that's too embarrassing to say out loud. That she put it in place so if he hates her after she gives him the letter, he might forgive her if he sees her again.

"Oh, right... Will you talk to her?"

Elliot sighs, and she watches the side of his face like she might be able to figure out what he's truly thinking. But he tells her, and she wishes she'd never tried to figure it out at all.

"Nah. I try not to think about her. I'm stubborn, and then I'll have to feel guilty for hating someone that had no choice in being here."

"Do you think there is a chance you might come to like the monarchy?"

It's a foolish question, but she's desperate for his answer all the same. She should have kept it to herself, though. Then she could dream of a day when he'd come to like her for who she is. Instead, he shakes his head, and her heart falls to the floor with the rest of her sandwich. Aliyah's not sure she could eat now anyway, photoshoot or not.

"I don't think it's in me. You like them, right?"

"Not always," she replies, then, "and not often now."

"There must be something redeemable about them if they're on your good side," Elliot says, and there's something in his tone she can't place. Something that sounds a little like regret, but it might

PERFECTLY CANDID

be wishful thinking. "Do you think I'll meet her and be enchanted, like everyone else?"

Aliyah wonders if he has any idea of the hatred she's gone through to get to a place where only some people like the idea of her, and it has nothing to do with her morals or her thoughts. The hatred is entirely due to things she can't control.

She sighs, crinkling the letter in her pocket. "Not everyone is enchanted with her."

"Is that why she's not married?" Elliot asks, and it hits her square in the chest. "I've only been here a short while and it's the talk of the common room most of the time. They were discussing the balls at breakfast."

Aliyah's throat drops to the pit of her stomach. She wonders if everyone knows the men she's being set up with want nothing more than to destroy her, body, mind, and soul. That there's only ever been one man she thought would be worthy of being her husband, and he hates her too.

"You all have nothing better to discuss than whether the Princess is married?"

Elliot shrugs. "I wouldn't know. I'm barely around enough to entertain those thoughts. I spend most of my time hidden with someone who might spend every evening telling the Princess to banish me." He laughs, looking right at her.

She smiles back at him, but it's forced. Aliyah knows people talk about her; she just tries to avoid it if she can. There's a special kind of heartache whirling around in her chest at the thought of Elliot joining in. Maybe it's all her fault. But if she had just told him who she was, she never would have found out that he makes her laugh. She never would have known what it's like for someone to bring you fruit in the mornings. She never would have known what it felt like to have someone think about her. Now she knows, and she's not sure how she's going to get over it.

"It's none of my business who she wants to marry, but if she has as many suitors flying from around the world to meet her as is suggested, you have to wonder if it's her that's the problem."

Aliyah wonders if she should tell him now. Tell him how the people flying to meet her don't want her. They never want her, or her thoughts, or her mind. They want her power. They want her on their arm. They want her body. She wonders if she should tell him there's a man the Princess has been destined to marry since before she was even here. A man meant for her sister. A man who would ruin her.

"And what would she need to be, for you?" Aliyah asks, her tone dripping with anger. Elliot notices, of course. It's the most outwardly cold she's been toward him since she held a knife to his throat.

"Lia," he starts, his hands high, like he never imagined he'd be able to hurt her. "I know she is your friend, and I'm sorry. That was unkind."

"It is unfair," she replies, her heart tensing behind her ribs, as if there's any way it will survive the realization Elliot will never want her for who she is. "You do not know her."

"I know. I know, my love, you're right."

She stands up and brushes the grass off her trousers. She could tell him now, but the letter remains close to her heart. "So?"

He stumbles up, his eyebrows high and his eyes wide, and she wants to hug him so badly she might just die. "So, what?"

"What would she need to be to be good enough for you?"

"Lia."

"Maybe she should be submissive," she suggests. "Agreeable. Ready to do whatever he wants."

"No," he replies, shaking his head. "That's not—"

"Or perhaps she does not deserve to be happy because she was brought into this family, not born into it. Perhaps a lifetime with someone who hates her as much as you do is all she deserves."

"Lia, please. It's not like that."

She scoffs. Too little, too late, but she won't blame him. He never had a choice, after all.

"Do not worry, Elliot. You will not be banished. Your hatred of the monarchy is safe with me."

In the end, it's Aliyah that goes first, but as she rides through the trees, she can't help but feel like she left something behind.

CHAPTER THIRTEEN

ELLIOT WALKS THROUGH THE forest with Ford at his side. He could barely ride when Lia was here giving him pointers; he wasn't going to risk falling flat on his face once she'd left him. Again. Somehow, despite their various trips together, he's always watching her and not the path, so, once again, he has absolutely no idea where he's going.

It makes sense. He was unnecessarily rude about her friend, and she let it slide so many times. Why couldn't he just say he'd like them? Is it a lie? If Lia was the royal, then everything he'd ever thought about them would be false. His dislike of the King and Queen wouldn't matter to him at all; it would barely be a thought he possessed once upon a time. Why would he care about them if she were there? If it were Lia, he'd move mountains before he ever hated her.

He sighs as he comes to the end of the path. Left, or right? Maybe it's just his luck he'd be stuck out here in the cold, with a horse that won't stop making him jump by neighing loudly every five minutes.

Then he sees it—a corner of the sandwich he brought, very clearly on the left side of the path. He follows it, perhaps foolishly thinking that Lia would lead him back home after how he acted. But, as he moves that way, he sees another piece. He didn't deserve her this morning, and he certainly doesn't deserve her now. Hopefully, he'll find her tomorrow, and he can apologize and make an effort with a princess he's not sure he'll ever meet, whatever he has to do to make sure Lia doesn't look as disappointed as she did this evening.

Elliot wonders if he's being too harsh on the monarchy, even if he takes Lia's disappointment out of it. He struggles with thinking he might ever have admiration for the King and Queen. Even with how little he cares to get involved with celebrity happenings, he knows they've never done anything decent a day in their lives. But the Princess? She can't be much older than him. Perhaps he should afford her the same grace he would give anyone else.

As soon as Elliot decides to think she might be a worthwhile person, he sees her everywhere. There are notices about scholarships and business opportunities on every hard surface when he gets Ford back to the stables. Melody has told him about a few funds she's applying for. He was sure they couldn't just be the Princess's idea—he always thought she didn't have that much power here. Maybe he was lying to himself to justify the hate he had for someone he doesn't know. If you have the favor of the Iledalian people, you have the most control, whoever you are. He knows the Princess is wildly popular with younger people, and that her popularity sometimes stretches to the older generation. He wonders if maybe she does do all this without her parents' help, or anybody's. He wonders if he's allowed to dislike her either way. He wonders if he even wants to.

Elliot's bedroom door closes behind him, finally, and he leans against it. He wishes he knew where Lia was. He went to the balcony and knocked lightly on her door, but he doesn't know who else might stay there with her, and she didn't answer. He thinks that's fair. He's never wanted to see her more than he does now.

His bed looks so unfairly tempting, but he knows he's got the shame of his walk home to wash off first. It's not like he's going to be able to sleep anyway. He throws the pile of mail he almost stepped on onto his bedside table. There's nothing from Mel, so he'll read it later, when he lies his bed, more awake than he's ever been before, replaying the hurt look on Lia's face before she left him.

As the water runs over his body, he thinks about the things he could research. Googling "Is the Princess nice?" seems redundant, and he's not sure how he'll feel when the articles say no. Would he feel as defensive as he suddenly feels now just at the thought? Lia likes her. That's enough for him. Maybe his research would mean his lifetime of hatred was fully founded. Can he dislike people because they refuse to talk to people of a lesser class than they would like? Yes, probably. Can he be bothered to when they are friends with a girl he desperately wants to keep around? Maybe not.

Elliot sighs as he shuts the water off, wraps a towel around his hips, and grabs his phone. He's going to figure out who the Princess is and what she does, and then maybe she can come to lunch with Lia and him, and it'll be fine.

That's what he's supposed to do. But then he opens his phone, and the photo he took of Lia this evening is right there. She's smiling, blissfully unaware that he's capturing the moment, and, un-shockingly, all he can think about is her. The way she pulls her lip between her teeth. The way she blushes when he says something ridiculous. The way she looks at his lips when she thinks he can't tell.

So far, Elliot has been a gentleman. He's kept his hands to himself, whether she's been there or just on his mind. Ever since they started spending more time together, he hasn't touched himself. Now, he's frustrated, and he feels his dick twitch under his towel. He scoffs. She's mad at him. She might never talk to him again. He lies back on his bed, and his hand slowly strokes his rapidly hardening cock.

Touching himself to the thought of her when they've barely even touched has always felt devious. So he's not sure why his pace quickens. Why his brow furrows as he thinks of the way she laughs, or the way her hips move in her riding gear. The way she watches his arms when he moves. Elliot thought he'd struggle to sleep tonight because he'd be too worried thinking about her, but it turns out he's the worst person alive, and the reason he's awake and thinking about her is completely different.

J.S. JASPER

The workbench isn't the comfiest place for Elliot to rest his forehead, but he finds it's too difficult to keep his head up. He's used to being awake most of the night—something his undiagnosed insomnia helps with—but it turns out not being able to sleep while lying in bed and not being able to sleep due to a hard-on with the image in his head of the woman he thinks about morning, noon, and night are not the same. And it doesn't get easier when he hasn't seen her for three days. All he has are the memories of her, and usually, it helps when he's doing mundane tasks in the greenhouse, just hoping she drops by. He spends all his time either here or walking around the plum trees, then placing flowers on her balcony. He's ignoring dinner calls, opting to eat while he's out. He missed the dinner with the Princess, but not on purpose. He was lounging around the common room and heard people talking about her. Nothing too scandalous. Marriage, what she was doing next, how attractive she is... and Elliot felt protective. He thinks so, anyway.

He doesn't know her beyond anything Lia has ever told him, but he stayed to listen to how these people think she might marry Lucian (Elliot doesn't care who she marries, but the thought that it might be someone that hates her weighs heavy on his heart), and how they wonder when she'll next be allowed on television. So, he missed the dinner, and he's avoiding the pile of letters that he has on his desk. It's only some welcome letter that came the other day, and a pile of coupons. He found he couldn't bear to read something he knows would be from the Princess when he was already feeling so guilty about her.

Still, despite the heaviness in his chest, Elliot smiles to himself as his eyes remain closed in the greenhouse. The thought of the way Lia squealed when something caught on her line while they fished is something he'll replay over and over. The smile she gave him when she realized he brought food for her. The blush that spreads across her cheeks when he writes anything down in his notebook. Elliot has never felt this way about someone so quickly before. He's always fallen first; it's in his blood. His father asked Elliot's grandfather for his mother's hand in marriage after about eight hours. Elliot was never destined to fall slowly. But this is different. She's different. Not in a "not like other girls" way, because other girls are great too, but in a life-altering way. In a terrifying way.

Their differences are clear. It would be ridiculous of him to pretend they weren't on different playing fields, even given how little he knows about her childhood beyond the fact she's adopted. She's clearly smart, smarter than he would ever hope to be, but he's got the practical side down. (Maybe not more than her, because she out-fished him like a pro, but it was never a competition.)

Elliot knows he should give the Princess the same grace he gives Lia, and he will. It's not her fault she grew up in a silver-spoon family. It's not her fault she had the world at her fingertips. It's not her fault. He wants to tell Lia that. He wants to tell her he's sorry for his preconceived ideas, and if she wants them all to be friends, then that's what he'll do. But he hasn't been able to find her anywhere. Elliot sighs, lifting his head from the bench. He brushes away the soil that's embedded into his skin because he couldn't be bothered to move anything before he took his impromptu nap.

He grabs his phone, ready to ask the new group chat he's been forced to be a part of (not really; Elliot loves a gossip and makes friends easier than anyone he knows—a group chat is like crack to him) if anyone knows where he might find Lia. When he opens it, his photo app stares back at him—a collage of photos he's taken recently that he's trying not to look through every second of the day.

There's one in particular he's resisting looking at too many times because he wonders if it's wrong that he has it at all. The sky is still dark, thousands of stars twinkling in the background—something he's always wished to see. Stars aren't something that is easily accessible in the city. There's always lights on: a promotional sign, or the lights on shops that think they're more important than the night sky is to a young child. It's something else out in the countryside. He always knew it, but he'd never seen it. It's like rich people have a monopoly on things that shouldn't be monetized. Elliot wishes it was easier for inner-city kids to enjoy things that naturally occur. It's one of the reasons he loves Melody's nonprofit so much—she lets children enjoy things just to enjoy them.

But in front of a backdrop of stars was the real masterpiece. Lia sat on his gearbox, her head almost turned toward him. He knows when she faced him, she was smiling, but every time he looks at the photos, he waits for her blinding smile. It never comes, but it's his favorite photo all the same.

He decides he'll look at it as a reward for finishing sorting the greenhouse out. It's not a mess, per se, but it's obvious someone hasn't been working here for some time. A shame, because the greenhouse is a feat in architectural design, with its brick-lined, waist-height foundation, two double-story high windows, and the peaks in the center. The place is bigger than his childhood home. It's got so much charm he's surprised it's not being utilized for a farm shop, a café, or something else that sells necessities for quadruple the price.

As he moves workbenches and squeals at the size of some of the spiders he's disturbed, he thinks about the way the moonlight danced off Lia's cheekbone when he found her by the edge of the lake. Part of him was expecting her not to turn up—that she didn't want to see him as much as he wanted to see her—but there she was, blanket in hand, with more fishing knowledge than him, ready to step onto the rowboat he'd spent the entire evening before trying to find. She'd invited him to her room—or her balcony, at least—showing him parts of her he's not sure many people have seen before. And now, he misses her.

It's three-oh-eight in the afternoon, and he realizes he'd follow her anywhere. There's a part of him that thinks she might follow him too, if he ever manages to see her again. She might want to come here again and sit with him while he's working. He looks around, and there's nowhere for her to sit that isn't stained with dirt or covered in things he'd have to move for her (and he's not about to let her hear him squeal over a spider). He grabs some wood from the woodstore. It's what he would call "vintage" in color, but he finds some sturdy pieces that he thinks will work. He clicks the music on and gets to work, ignoring the things he actually has to do.

CHAPTER FOURTEEN

Sunlight streams through Aliyah's curtains. Normally, it would be the thing that woke her up, but lately, she's been awake the moment she hears footsteps on the cobblestones below her balcony. If she sleeps with her window open now so she can hear the movement, that's no one's business but her own. She slides out of her satin sheets and finds the jumper Elliot gave her on the lake, eagerly awaiting the time of year when she can stroll around her room in nothing but her shorts and vest. Right now, though, she takes comfort in the fluffy material as she slowly opens her bedroom window.

Her room has always looked over the gardens to the south of the grounds, and Aliyah has never taken the view for granted. The moment the sun rises, she can see it peeking around the edge of the palace towers, and she only has to wait until mid-morning to see it turning the leaves around her a bright green. Soon, the roses that are weaved through the trellis attached to the side of the wall and above her room will bloom, and Aliyah will have a hard time ever looking away. For now, though, her eyes fall on something else.

Aliyah has always thought of the greenhouse as a magical place. The pearlescent glass and the dark-stained wood have always had a mystical air about them. She could see the large double doors from her bedroom window even before she was tall enough to look over the balcony—she could only peek her head through the gaps. There was never a reason for her to go in, but Lia always wondered what they were like inside. Her mother used to say it's no place for a princess. Aliyah used to think it was dangerous—that there was a wizard brewing potions and poisoning apples for her to eat—but she came to learn that her mother just refused to let her get "filthy." She knows now, of course, that there's nothing in there but a man who likes to garden. She sighs, but it does nothing to help the ache in her chest. Elliot never liked her. Not really. Not in the way she liked him.

Still, she knows that when the doors creak open, he'll be there. It's not something she had noticed before; the allure of the greenhouse took a backseat when she knew she would never get inside. She's inevitably heard the sounds before, but it didn't bother her at ten a.m., when the birds were chirping and people awake. The sounds of morning coffee and chitter-chatter obscured the noise. But today, yesterday, and tomorrow, Aliyah knows *he'll* be there early, and she likes his morning face. So, that's how she finds herself sitting on the chair, partially hidden by the balcony, watching Elliot as he potters around the garden. She lets herself watch him for longer than usual because she's going to get over him tomorrow.

He'd made it clear from the start that the monarchy isn't a thing he agrees with, and she tricked him into spending time with her anyway. There was some small part of her that thought he'd like her enough that the royal status wouldn't mean anything. But she left him in the woods, and she left him a letter explaining everything. Who she is, why she didn't tell him, how she hopes it wouldn't mean anything, how very sorry she is. And then she waited. Every night, she waits at the first tree she ever met him under, but he hasn't appeared. He didn't come to the dinner she set up specifically for him, but that's not his fault—he didn't know. Or maybe he did. Maybe he read her letter and figured out it was all for him and stayed away anyway.

It's his right, of course. She always knew there was a chance her being the Princess was too much for him. She's just not sure how she's supposed to go about life now. He's here, for only a few more months. Can she just avoid him? Probably. She's been doing it for days. And the ache in her chest will lessen, right? That's what the books say. That's what the films say. Everything ends and everything stops hurting. That's the whole point.

Aliyah was always going to tell him at some point. Perhaps he deserved to know at the start—when he asked her name, or when she started falling for him, or when she caught him looking at her for too long to be considered friendly. Maybe she should have told him then. It wasn't going to be long, even if her running off did exacerbate it a little. The thought of spending more time with him without telling him the truth made it feel like there were worms under her skin. Aliyah has been trained to deal with hostile environments, and yet, she has no idea how to navigate this.

There's a knock at her bedroom door, and she sighs. The past few weeks with Elliot, she managed to forget how lonely being a princess was. Now, as she's plummeting back into the world she was happy to escape, she remembers they have guests. Guests that hate her, naturally. Guests that want to marry her, obviously.

Lucian. The worst man in the world. Well, second worst, because in a few weeks, he'll bring his son. No one that Aliyah speaks to in the palace seems to find it weird that both a father *and* his son want her hand in marriage. No one seems to think they're only after the crown. Or maybe they do know that and they simply don't care.

"Coming," Aliyah replies. She puts her teacup down, glances at Elliot once more, and then leaves.

Aliyah wanders around the courtyard, everyone else five steps behind. As per her mother's request, she's in a ridiculous gown that pushes her chest up and leaves her barely any room to breathe. Lucian is here, with guards following him around like he'll be attacked in broad daylight by anyone but her. Lucian's been trying to get a meeting with her alone, but she's managed to avoid it thus far. Nothing about his snide smirk nor the dangerous look in his eye suggests she should ever trust him alone. She knows he's here before his son so he can try and win her hand in marriage. As if she'd ever marry either of them. The laws state she can marry whomever she wants, commoner or not. Gardener or not. Aliyah always thought the issue would be finding someone she wanted to spend her life with. It never occurred to her that maybe she would, and they simply wouldn't be interested back.

As she climbs the stairs to walk back inside, Lucian catches up to her. He's a foul man, but he'll admire land he wants for himself like it's going out of fashion. He stands with his arms behind his back, and she just knows that in his head, he's wearing the crown already.

Lia sighs as she looks around the garden, and her eyes fall on Elliot by the greenhouses. She can't tell if he can see her, even as he looks this way. Has he seen her the entire time she's been missing him? He runs into the greenhouse, and she blows out a deep breath as Lucian talks about how he'd take the flower beds down. For what, she's not sure, nor is she letting it take up any headspace, because he's not going to get a choice anyway. If she has any say, of course. She turns twenty-five soon; it's entirely possible her family will force her to the altar with a gun to her head.

Elliot comes back out, though he was on her mind anyway. How many times has he read her letter? Maybe he saw her opening remarks and threw it on the fire. Maybe he's in the process of selling it to the highest bidder. The tabloids would have a field day with the heartbroken princess. Elliot would never, though. Even if he hates her, he's not cruel.

He runs across the field with tulips in his hand—the reddish-pink ones he said look like the blush on her cheeks. Her heart drops. He's coming to see her. He must be. They're his favorite flower, and she had hoped she would have more time to figure out his other favorite things. There's a moment when she looks right at him. His eyes are kind, his smile is hopeful, he is bolting her way, and she realizes... he hasn't seen her letter. There's no daisy chain on his wrist, no betrayal in his eyes. He's coming over here to see Lia. Not the Princess.

Oh no. *Oh no.* There's no way the guards or Lucian will let him get close. Aliyah panics as he gets closer, his brow furrowed as he walks toward her and takes in her outfit. She watches his jaw drop as his eyes glance at her tiara, then back to her face. There's a clang, and she could swear her heart falls out of her chest. Elliot's hand drops to his side. He looks more betrayed than she ever thought he'd be.

"Shall we get tea?" Aliyah asks, her voice unnaturally high. Then again, the only person who would notice would be Elliot, and he probably has no thoughts about her right now that aren't negative.

"What do you want, boy?" Lucian spits out, clicking his fingers until the guards have his arms behind his back, the flowers discarded on the floor.

"It was a m-mistake." One of the guards kicks the back of his leg, and Lia flinches as Elliot is brought harshly to his knees. "I'm sorry. I thought she was someone else." He looks up at her like he can't believe she's done this, though she has as much control over this situation as she does at any other time—very little.

Aliyah can't breathe. She thinks her throat might close up entirely. There's nothing she can do. Nothing she can say that will make any difference; it will only make it worse. She makes everything worse. There's no lifetime where she should have sought Elliot out, no lifetime in which he'd deserve to be in the position he's in right now. Lucian is spitting feathers at the thought of someone disrespecting the ground near him. Elliot didn't, of course—Aliyah knows he would never. Not when she was around. Even if she deserved to be.

The bells are ringing in her ears, and she can't *think*. It's not until Elliot speaks again that she realizes an entire conversation is taking place.

"Excuse me?" he says.

"The dungeons," Lucian replies, a wide, cruel smile across his face. Elliot frowns, but she knows he won't put up a fight. She also knows Lucian's guards are unnecessarily physical with whoever they can get away with hurting. The thought of Elliot being hurt makes her take a step back. She blinks, clenching her jaw. *Fuck.*

The dungeons are a medieval punishment, and she's the only one that's ever in there. She swallows the bile in her throat at the thought of Elliot being subject to his cruel mistreatment. The only way she knows to get Lucian to back down is to pander to him.

"My lord," she says, her voice as sweet as she can make it. "Shall we head to tea? I am so looking forward to spending some time together."

He looks at her, his eyes squinting. Almost... She needs something else to take his mind off Elliot and toward the humiliation he could be granting someone else. She swallows. There's only one thing she thinks will get him to move, and she knows the dire consequences she'll face from offering him something she'll deny later down the line, but she'd rather she were in the dungeons than Elliot.

"I could show you the set of undergarments I kindly received from your son," she says, her voice low as she rests her hand against his forearm. "It is in my bedroom."

The words aren't said, but the intention is so clear that her heart constricts in her chest. Elliot recoils as if she's slapped him, but she'll ignore that for now if it means he'll be let go. Lucian has forgotten all about him, his predatory gaze fixed on her. His eyes drop down her body, and she resists the urge to turn away. She won't let his hands so much as brush against her the moment Elliot is across the field, but until then, she needs to play along. She feels disgusted either way.

Lucian waits as she stands in front of him, and she knows it's about the power. It always is. She knows if they ever did marry, he'd force her to sleep with him, and he'd humiliate her in every single part of the process.

"Yes," he replies. Elliot grunts like he's moments away from tackling him. She needs to leave, but before she does, Lucian gives the guards a dismissive wave and says, "Dungeons." *No.*

Aliyah looks from Lucian to Elliot, the furrow of Elliot's brow still placed on his perfect face. She steels herself. He hates her anyway; she may as well take another beating to save him. So, she curls her lip slightly.

"Do not waste your energy on some dirty commoner," she replies, watching as Elliot's face falls entirely. "I'm sure the cost of guarding him could be put to *much* better use, my lord."

Aliyah hoped Elliot knew her well enough to know she'd always protect him. If he hasn't seen her letter, maybe he thinks she's been avoiding him too. As the guards let him go with a shove, it looks like she may never find out. He gets up, looking at her just once, then he's gone.

Aliyah turns, the burn in her throat intensifying. The bottom of her dress drags the petals of the flowers Elliot brought her along the ground. They don't make it far, though, instead ending up crumpled just beyond the staircase while she turns the corner. She looks over at the gardens, but he's not looking at her. Not this time.

"Lead the way," Lucian says.

Aliyah scoffs, pulling her arm away from him. "Get your hands off me." She walks away, her jaw clenched, and she knows she'll be dragged away soon enough. For now, she just needs to be alone.

CHAPTER FIFTEEN

ELLIOT HEAVES BAGS OF compost over his shoulder. It's finally time to sort out the storeroom in the greenhouse. He's been letting it get cluttered because he's been too busy sitting under trees with a woman who didn't respect him enough to tell him who she was. There are moments when he wonders if everything was just an experiment to her. How much information could she get out of the poor boy for her initiatives before he realized she was the Princess? How many times did she go back to her aides and laugh that he would be foolish enough to think she'd ever want him? He's just waiting for his face to be plastered over the front pages calling him a ridiculous man for ever thinking she might like him.

There's a part of him—a ridiculous part—that thinks maybe she's not like that. The biggest part of him wants to believe she's everything he ever thought she was, everything she showed him under the trees. That part that wants to give her the benefit of the doubt because he's fallen too, far too fast. Maybe it's unreasonable for him to think she should have told him everything simply because her eyes lingered on his lips a couple of times. He could make that make sense to his broken heart, but her name? *That* he deserved.

He wants to forgive her. He wants to hug her and tell her he's not mad. That he likes her and if she likes him, he'll hide with her until she doesn't anymore. But he can't say that because she's still not here. She hasn't been to apologize; she hasn't been to explain. Somehow, in the time he's been working at the palace, he's managed to find her every time he wanted to, and yet, when he needs her to find him back, she can't find him in the most obvious of places.

That's when the smaller, louder, more embarrassed part of him remembers the hatred he has for the monarchy. For the way they treat people as though they are disposable. She was with another man before she had even told him who she was... but he can't be mad, can he? They were never *anything*. They were barely friends. Is he even allowed to be upset she's part of the establishment? Probably not. It's not her fault. But she could have told him weeks ago, before he memorized the way her hair swung when she turned to smile at him. Before he had a notepad of information about her. Her favorite color, the way she doesn't like cilantro, the way lilies make her sneeze. Maybe if she told him then, he wouldn't be in this mess. Maybe he wouldn't have continued to talk to her. Maybe they would have gotten past it. Maybe they'll never know.

Elliot is a reasonable person most of the time. So, deep down, he knows she would have been nervous about how he would react, because he made it clear from the get-go that the royals are not people he cares for. She was just worried about how he'd react. He wouldn't know, of course, because as much as he wished things were different, she never told him. And maybe that's unfair to her. They barely know each other. Well, she knows about his father, about his family, about his life. She told him half of her name. Maybe it's unreasonable to be this hurt over a relationship that was mainly all in his head. She made it clear she didn't trust him, running away when personal questions came up, and changing the topic whenever *she* came up. He was so blinded by her smile and her laugh that he never questioned it. Maybe he's just hurt that even in his wildest dreams, he'll never be good enough for her. Not for her hand, not for her friendship... not for her heart.

Elliot sighs as he leans against the worktop. It's been days since the humiliation of being accosted in front of her and some lord he can't remember the name of, but it still hurts all the same. He walks around the bench he made for her, blissfully unaware she'd never use it. Elliot wonders if he'd be this upset about it if she'd come to see him that first night, or the day after, or the day after that. He would have forgiven her if only she'd looked at him, he thinks, but she hasn't bothered to come around at all.

It's day three now, and he's tired of wallowing in self-pity. He misses her, and it feels like he's drowning in it. A knock on the greenhouse door barely gives him enough to keep treading water.

"Open," he shouts, rinsing his hands. When he shuts off the water, he feels the atmosphere change, just barely. It's calmer. Sweeter. "Lia," he whispers.

"Good evening," she replies. He takes a moment before he turns. What is he expecting? A tiara and a ballgown? Can he call her Lia? Will she ever be Aliyah to him? Does she want to be? He turns, and she looks... exactly like the woman who's been on his mind every day since he started here. It catches him off guard; he almost stumbles with the ferocity of it all. She looks exhausted, maybe as tired as him, but utterly glorious all the same. Her chin is raised, a look on her face that he can't place, like she doesn't want to be here. Like this is just a formality.

"Why are you here?" he asks.

He means to add that she's late—days late—but he finds he can barely speak around her for fear he might tell her he forgives her when she's giving him nothing but her presence. Elliot takes a quick breath, settling his heart for a moment. He would be more prepared for this if he'd spoken to his sister about it, but now that he knows she's royalty, he has no idea what he's allowed to say. Are the phone lines tapped? Will the guards storm his room if he so much as utters Aliyah's name in conversation?

She swallows, though her face remains passive. Trained. She's closed off, as if he's the one that's done something wrong. If she wanted him to be hidden, then she should have given him the rules in the first place. She must know he would have done anything she asked.

"I wanted to see you," she replies, but her face doesn't move at all. He has no idea if she's telling the truth. His eyes flick across her quickly, desperate to find something that tells him she's still the same person as before. That she's not just here to do damage control for the palace. He feels a sense of dread. It makes him act impulsively.

"Did you not get enough entertainment from me under the canopy?" he asks, his tone laced with a jealousy he's not sure he hides all that well. Is he allowed to be jealous she's going to end up with someone that's not him? Has she even made any suggestion that she wants to be with him in any way that's not hidden under the cover of the plum trees?

"I wanted to apologize," she says. She looks like his Lia, but like a stranger all the same. "It is not what it looked like."

"Are you sure?" he asks, leaning against the garden bench. "Because it looked like you didn't know me at all. In fact, it looked like you were going to fuck what's-his-face. So, if you were looking for someone to miss, why not go by his guest wing in the castle? I am sure he would be glad to entertain you for the night."

Deep down, somewhere below the heartache and the embarrassment, Elliot knows there's nothing else she could have done. Was he expecting her to hug him in the courtyard? Once he realized who she was, he should have turned around and gone to his room. He knew nothing good would come from confronting her. People like him don't belong in places like this. But he spent too long in uncomfortable situations based on things he couldn't control, and his body reacted before he could think of the consequences.

She tilts her head slightly. "Why are you speaking to me like that?"

He scoffs, a watery sound that makes him feel too close to the edge. "What, because you are the Princess?"

Lia recoils slightly, like she's never heard anyone say anything with such disdain before. "No. Because you are my best friend," she replies, spinning the ring on her pinky finger. "I want to be your friend, and—"

Elliot scoffs again, something more substantial this time. "We aren't friends, Lia. I'm just someone that works for you."

Her face doesn't betray her emotions. If he didn't know her, he'd think she was truly unbothered by his words. But, luckily for him, he's spent days with her. Not the confident version of her—the persona she puts on with a camera in her face, nor her flawless acting when she's surrounded by other people. Just her.

The one who can't look at him for too long without blushing. Who has her lip between her teeth more often than not. Who frowns like that's how her face is most comfortable. And that's how he sees the tension in her neck.

Elliot sighs. He never wanted her to be hurt in all of this. He's merely confused as to whether he's reasonably allowed to dislike the royals as much as he does if he's still going to think about her all day. If he were a better man—one who deserved anything from her—he would say it out loud.

"Well," she says, her eyebrows shooting up quickly. She huffs out a breath like it's the only thing she can do. Like his words physically hurt. "I suppose I should have expected that."

"Why didn't you tell me?" he asks. Lia—*the Princess*—laughs, though there's no humor behind it.

"What was I to say? Good evening," she starts, her hand waving, perfectly practiced. "I am part of the establishment you have a deep hatred for. I surely hope I make it out of this forest alive."

Elliot laughs. "You were the one with the knife, Lia."

"You may call me Princess, or Your Highness," she replies quickly, efficiently. He barely sees her hands tense at her sides.

He shakes his head. "Don't do that." Elliot wonders if anyone has told her not to do something before. He wonders if he's the first. He wonders if she'll listen.

"Do what?"

"Treat me like I'm someone else."

Aliyah looks at him, *truly* looks at him. There's no blush on her cheeks now. This isn't a stolen glance while he watches the light shine through the leaves of the trees. Back then, mere days ago, he thought she was looking at something she liked. Now it's like she's looking to see if there's anything redeemable about him. He's about three seconds away from tearing his chest open and giving her a better view. She takes a step closer, barely noticeable.

"We are not friends," she whispers. Her eyes flick across his face, and he can't tell if her eyes have always been that wet. "That is what you said, is it not?" And it is. It makes no sense for him to try and be friends with her, yet he can't bring himself to repeat the words, not when he was so cruel in the first place.

"Lia," he breathes, but the motion causes her to blink, and she's taken a step back before he can reach out. She smiles. Something small, something practiced. Something not meant for him.

"If you have any complaints about the grounds or the housing, I would still like to hear them. There is a suggestions box close to the back door."

"Ali—"

"And if you would be so kind as to not frequent the plum trees in the mornings," she says, taking a deep breath, "it would be greatly appreciated. I feel safe there, and I... I do not think I can see you."

She's just as frustrating as she was in the forest. He likes her all the same.

"Princess."

"I am leaving now," she says, as if this trip was a colossal waste of her time. As if she has tried at all to fix what shouldn't have been broken. He never lied to her. "You have to bow," she whispers.

Elliot scoffs. "You're leaving?"

"I am a very busy person," she replies, flicking nothing off her dress. He squints, thinking maybe it's the same one as the other day, but he wasn't taking in her outfit at the time.

"As if I wanted you here," Elliot mocks. She looks at him like she knows he does. Like she's well aware he's been so desperate to see her this entire time that he's barely slept. "As if I've been begging you to come back after you fucked me over."

Aliyah frowns. "You cannot speak to me like that. I am a Princess." And Elliot wants to shout from the rooftops that it isn't the only reason people should be polite to her. It's not the thing that means she should get respect.

"Not to me," he says instead. "You spent the entire time making sure you weren't a Princess to me."

"Elliot -"

"But you are right," he says, his voice low. "I should not have spoken to you that way, and I apologize. I am sorry. You should never be spoken to like that. Even if you did, in fact, mess me around."

"It was never intended like that," she rushes out. It's the only outward suggestion she's made that this conversation is affecting her.

Elliot feels like he doesn't know her here. Maybe it's unfair because he's barely given her time to explain anything, but he would have expected her to try a little harder. He's barely able to remain standing, but he'd be here for as long as it takes as long as the endgame is that she wants to be in his life. She may have been trained not to react to difficult conversations, but he needs her to. He needs her to show him he's different to everyone else. That she feels differently about him than everyone else.

"Of course not," he replies, listing things off on his fingers. "I suppose you always flirt with people under the plum trees, hide your identity from them as they tell you all about their life, and then humiliate them in front of your soon-to-be husband, or is it your soon-to-be father-in-law? Maybe if I were part of the aristocracy, I wouldn't have been kicked to my knees simply because I wanted to say hello to my *friend*. Perhaps if my hair were a different texture, or if I spoke in a more convoluted way, the situation may have been better. Would it not?"

"I do not want you to change for me," she replies, her eyes flicking over his face. She looks conflicted, and he wants to fix it, but he'll never know how. He just... He wants her to smile again. He is always waiting for her smile. "I did not ask that of you."

"It's what you do for people you care about," he replies, his jaw tight. "You wouldn't understand—you've never had to kneel for anyone. Except for your *Lord*, of course." He bows deeply. "Your Highness."

Aliyah looks murderous. Like she might kill him, knife or not. Her hair is frizzed around her face, her tiara sparkling from where it sits at a wonky angle on her head. Elliot almost frowns. Lia has always been prim and proper, even when all they were doing was going horse riding. Now it looks like she hasn't seen a washcloth in days. He doesn't ask though. Earlier, before she came to see him, he could pretend there would ever be a time that they would be friends. Now it looks like she couldn't hate him more. That he's shown himself to be nothing but a petty, jealous nuisance. That she is the Princess, and he is nothing more than a gardener. She doesn't say anything, but her nostrils flare.

"I thought you were leaving," he states, folding a pair of gardening gloves just to give him something to do.

Her jaw tenses. "You are extremely aggravating."

"Don't be kind, Princess," he replies. "You used to like that about me. You know, when you wanted a poor friend to lift ideas from, because God forbid your privileged life doesn't give you what you need."

She scoffs. It's unfair, of course—she's the only reason he was able to get a job here in the first place. If she were being as petty as him, she would throw that in his face.

"You know nothing about my life," she replies, taking a step closer to him. Somehow, she's had a knife in her hand this close before, and yet, he thinks this might be the time she takes him down. "I tried to explain, if you would just listen—"

"So," he says, and she clenches her jaw when he interrupts her. "Feeling lonely and trapped with no one who cares about you and parents who never wanted you, forced to marry a man who only wants your body—they were just made-up things?" The regret seeps into him like a dagger before he's even finished speaking. It's the worst thing he's ever said, and her hurt is evident on every part of her face. Like she never would have expected him to do that to her. He sees the deep breath rock through her body.

"I didn't— I shouldn't have—" He wipes his face as he steps toward her, but she jolts back, shaking her head. It's all he deserves. "I'm sorry."

A pained noise leaves her throat, and he knows she tried everything she could to keep it from him. God, she had been so nervous to tell him that, and he threw it back in her face. Lia's brow furrows slowly, like she's trying to hide her emotions. She shakes her head, and when she looks back at him, the Princess is back, though he can tell it takes all her energy. Her voice shakes as she speaks.

"It was truly not my intention to hurt you like this. I am sorry. I hope one day you may forgive me."

She smiles at him. It's supposed to be supportive, he knows, but she looks so devastated that he thinks his heart breaks in half.

Before she turns, he catches a glimpse of *something* on her face. The glimpse lasts barely a second, and he wants to ask her not to go because the look threatens to take him out at the knees, but she's halfway to the door by the time he can react. Then he sees movement outside, and he knows that just means worse for her, so he rushes past her. He presses his hand against the door, and she sighs, not looking at him.

"There's people outside," he whispers. Aliyah folds her arms, taking deep, steadying breaths as she makes sure she's hidden behind the thick frame of the greenhouse. He wants to ask her if she wants to hide *with* him. Probably not now, not after how cruel he's been. It would have been different, he thinks, if he knew that she wanted to be with him from the start and it is only politics that means she has to hide like she did on the stairs. He knows it, of course, but he wants her to tell him that. But not now, not now he's spent the last ten minutes discounting himself from ever having a part of her life. Not now that he's hurt her.

"Lia," he whispers, and she looks up at him. "I didn't mean that. I'm sorry. I'm so sorry, I... I didn't mean it."

She smiles, but it goes nowhere. "Okay."

She doesn't believe him. He closes his eyes as he holds the door closed.

The guards stand under the canopy of the greenhouse, and Elliot curses that they're stuck here. He drops his head, and when he chances a look at Aliyah, she's already looking right at him. He sees the moment her gaze drops to his lips. It's fleeting. Barely a passing glance, just like the times he's caught her before. To anyone else, it wouldn't be noticeable, but he's spent the past few weeks overanalyzing her movements. He knows she looks at him when he's busy at work. He knows she likes his shoulders, because her eyes linger there when she pretends to be looking outside. There was a time when he was so sure she wanted to kiss him, even though she only looked at him for a second. Now, she's got nowhere to look but at him.

They're too close. Her blinking is rapid, and she lets out a slow breath as he leans in just slightly. He never wants to see her flinch again, so he'll always be slow. His hand leaves the bench next to her, his fingertips lingering against the wood as he checks for any discomfort on her face. He'll forgive her for anything and everything if she so much as brushes his lips with hers. He's about to lean forward even more, to press their bodies together finally, when the door handle rattles.

It shakes beneath Elliot's palm, and he presses his whole body against it. He realizes now how catastrophic it would be if he was caught here, with the Princess. She doesn't look as worried as he feels. If they got caught, would she blame it all on him?

"I wonder if they have locked the Princess in here this time," a guard from outside says. The other lets out a bellowing, gluttonous laugh that makes Elliot feel ill. He frowns. Why would the Princess ever be trapped anywhere in her own home?

"No," the other says between laughs. "This is too nice for her. She deserves the dungeons."

Elliot turns to her. In what world would Aliyah ever deserve to be in a dungeon? He lets his hand go slack and opens his mouth, ready to argue, but she stops him in his tracks.

"Elliot," she whispers, her voice hidden beneath the laughter at her expense. He turns to look at her, and she shakes her head. Her tiara wobbles on her braids. She's right, of course. So he holds the door closed, though they've stopped trying to get in.

"Did you hear why she got herself put in there?" *In there?*

"Nah," the other guard replies. "Who gives a fuck. If it were me, I'd never let her out."

Elliot's rage vibrates through his palm. Lia looks utterly unfazed at their words. If she's been in the dungeons while he's been stomping around, wondering where she is, he might break this door down.

"They used the water, though." The guard cackles as they walk away. Lia flinches, and Elliot swallows down the bile at the thought of whether it's over the word "water," or if it was his hate-laced tone. At least if the guards leave, Elliot won't become a murderer in the next five seconds, he supposes. Everything but his concern for her leaves his body. He's surprised he managed to be upset with her for longer than a tea break.

"I'm sorry?" Elliot asks. She blinks, looking around like she has no idea why he's shaking with anger. "What do they mean you were in the dungeons?"

"Oh," she starts, looking embarrassed. She wipes her hand over her dress, and he sees it now. It *is* the one she wore days ago. The one she wore when he convinced himself she never wanted him, that she truly wanted to be cruel, that she was ever anything other than the delightful person he was falling in love with. And it hits him all at once: this is the first place she came when she was let out.

"Uh, there was an altercation... with Lucian."

His hand shakes as much as his voice when he asks, "And who is that?"

"The man you saw me with the other day."

Elliot thinks back to the way her hand lingered. As if he's thought about much else for the last few days—probably while she was being thrown in the dungeons and sequestered there, and he feels sick for being so narrow-minded. The entire time he's known her, she's done nothing to suggest she's anything other than the lovely person she's been while with him. If he could have seen past his own hurt and humiliation for longer than three seconds, he could have figured out why she didn't run to meet him on the stairs. Why she didn't immediately tell him who she was when he spent the first few days making sure she would have no comeback. Lia looks away, and he realizes he never followed up. There's a burning sensation in his throat he thinks might make a home there.

"Did he hurt you?" he asks, though he doesn't know why. He's not sure there's a way he could hear that she was hurt without immediately getting himself killed by taking the guy out. Aliyah rolls her eyes.

"Uh, no. It is a power play that my parents will always go for." She's lying. She won't look at him, but he can't test his three-time theory because he thinks he doesn't deserve to ask her again. He doesn't deserve for her to tell him her pain anymore.

"Power play?"

J.S. JASPER

Lia looks up at him, her lip caught between her teeth again. "I was never going to show him my room," she replies, looking away. "I knew it was the only way to get him to leave you alone."

"You knew you'd go to the dungeons for that? Lia," Elliot says, his voice unknown even to him as he pinches the bridge of his nose. He feels sick to his stomach that she protected him like that. He should be protecting her. Every time. "You should have... I would have been *fine*."

"What was I supposed to do?" she asks, her brow furrowed. "I could not leave you—"

"Yes! Yes, you can!" he replies, his hands tight in his hair. "You should *always* leave me, Aliyah. Always. You do not protect me. You don't need—"

"You would have never forgiven me."

Elliot stops in his tracks, looking at every small thing that happens on her face. She looks like she truly believes he would prefer for her to be in the dungeons than him. That he would ever want her to be hurt.

"Lia."

She shakes her head. "You would not."

"Lia," he repeats, stepping closer until she looks at him. "I never want you to be hurt. I would never want you to—"

She scoffs, a watery sound that threatens to take him out more than the look on her face.

"What?"

"You would *never* forgive me," she repeats. She shakes her head again. He thinks she's dangerously close to crying, and he's not sure what to do about it. "I can barely live in a world where you hate me for something I cannot control; I am not about to have you hate me for something I could."

Elliot frowns. "I would never hate you."

"I may not have told you who I was, but I told you enough, and you *just* said—" She looks up at him, the pain so evident on her face he barely stays standing. She swallows, trying to clear her emotions. "Do you know that if I were on my knees for Lucian, as you so clearly think I am desperate to be—"

"Ali," he begs. "I'm sorry. I'm sorry."

"It would never be because I wanted to be," she says, her eyes glistening with unshed tears. And Elliot knows he'll spend the rest of his days making sure she only ever does what she wants.

Aliyah clears her throat. "Anyway. You should not care what those men say about me. I do not. They will hate me either way, and I only..." In an instant, her face changes. Her jaw drops, the mask gone, nothing portrayed on her face that isn't hurt. It feels like his chest is in a blender, and he has no idea how to fix it. He'd let himself bleed out, let himself be cut into pieces if it meant she never looked like that again.

"Only what? Lia, what? What's going on, my love."

She rubs her hand over her heart, her voice nothing but a whisper as her face drops. "God, *no.*"

"Lia, please."

"It is my own doing," she says, her breath getting caught in her throat. "I knew. I always knew it would end like this."

"Lia."

"I—I need to go," she says, but he doesn't move. "I swear to God, El, I will have you banished if you do not move."

"Talk to me," he pleads. "Just tell me, please."

There's a panic in her voice he'll never forget as she says, "Let me out."

Elliot moves the moment her voice cracks, and she's out the door before he can stop her.

"Princess," he whispers, and she turns around, but he wonders, were he given the chance again, would he be selfish and let her go so he doesn't have to watch the first tear fall. She bats it away, but he knows the truth.

"You *hate* me," she says simply, a shuddering breath following, like she was just saying it before, and now she believes it. He's said the one thing that would make her believe he could ever hate her, and it's his fault. "Not *annoyance* hate. You hate me like they hate me. *Put me in a dungeon* hate me."

Elliot shakes his head violently. "No, never. Never."

She takes a deep breath and looks skyward, though her eyes are closed. He wants nothing more than to reach forward, to bridge the gap between them and tell her it wouldn't matter who she is, as long as she is everything she's shown him she is. But he's not sure he's allowed to touch her now. He never was, not really. Lia looks back at him, her face wiped entirely, and gives him a small smile.

"Goodnight, Master Harper."

Elliot barely bites back a groan. She waits, and he's not sure for what—maybe she's hoping to find something redeemable about him—but all too slowly, again, he realizes she's *the Princess*.

"Please, don't go," he says, but he bows his head, and she does exactly that, and he lets her. Elliot wonders why he ever wanted her to show she was affected. Now, he fears he'll hear her pained gasp of breath for the rest of his life.

CHAPTER SIXTEEN

THE MORNINGS TURN TO nights then to mornings again before Aliyah can gather a single thought in her mind. Somehow, she manages to lie in bed, the image of Elliot next to her clear in her mind though he's never stepped foot in here. She's never seen him anywhere near her things, and yet, it feels like a piece of her is missing as she looks at the watercolor clouds on her ceiling. Heartbreak is something Aliyah knew about. She'd read about it; she'd felt it for most of her life. But here, now, *weeks* after she last spoke to him, it's the worst pain she's ever known. She feels pathetic down to her bones. Her heartache goes almost as deep as the love she has for him.

There's a part of her mind that is screaming at her to get up. To do something. Talk to him. Redecorate her bedroom. Start a new initiative. *Anything.* Yet even the helpless feeling simmering beneath her skin along with the bright sunshine don't make her get out of her room for longer than a dinner break she'd be thrown in the dungeons for missing. Sometimes, she wonders if it would be worth it. The cold from the floor would eat away at her. At least it might take her mind off how he hates her; how the only person she's ever liked, trusted, wanted more from, hates her like everyone else does.

The only reason her parents haven't called her out on being rude to their various dinner guests is because she's barely eating. They've always appreciated her making efforts to be thinner, even if it was detrimental to her health. It used to be something Aliyah did without realizing. She'd eat less and less, hoping her parents would call her out on it and show her they cared. That they thought about her at all. But with every day, she'd get hungrier and hungrier, and no one ever said a thing. But they never wanted her anyway. The words uttered from her favorite person in the world's mouth.

It's true, so she's not sure why she's so upset by it. It's not as though he was lying. But it's been weeks without anything but dinner. One meal a day, and a measly portion at that. She should be hungry. She should be eating and setting a good example for the children in the kingdom so they don't have to see article after article talking about her body weight. Talking about how gorgeous the Princess looks in her runway-size designer gown. But all she feels is empty.

There's a corner of her mind that wonders if she's allowed to be this hurt over a man she barely knows. She tries to convince herself it's a petty crush and it only hurts this much because she's never had one before. So, it's pent-up teenage hurt more than feeling like she might actually dissolve into nothing if he never speaks to her again. She wonders if there's something she's supposed to ask, if turning to religion would help her in this instance. But she doesn't get on her knees and beg. Aside from dinner, the few minutes of watching him she allows herself every morning, and her nightly run, she doesn't get out of bed at all.

Her days are spent wondering if anything could have changed what happened, and she *hates* it. She hates how he's making her feel and that he's probably fine. She hates how, the day after she cried herself to sleep, he went to work like nothing happened. She hates how he's managed to get out of bed at all. It's pathetic and the worst she's ever felt, and there's nothing she can do to stop it.

His eyes still fly through her mind the moment she closes hers. His touch still ghosts over her skin when she shakily rinses in the shower, and he never even touched her. She's basically hallucinating over something that never happened. She's tragic. Every thought she has of him is made up. He's never looked at her lips in the way she thinks. He's never thought about climbing the trellis to reach her room just to say hi. He's never spent hours thinking about how she'd make him feel if they ever ended up in the same bed. It's not lost on her that she somehow got him and lost him before she ever had the chance to touch his skin.

Aliyah sighs as the greenhouse doors creak open. She heaves herself out of bed with the same effort it would take someone who is actually dying and not someone who misses a boy. God, she's embarrassing. Yet she wanders over to her window, as she always does in the morning, and she hides behind her curtains, avoiding the way he looks up toward her balcony.

Elliot still takes her breath away. It's infuriating. Why can't he look like a depressed mess? Why does he have to wear a long-sleeved T-shirt that allows her to see the outline of muscles she'll never *actually* see? It's embarrassing to want to sit here and watch him work because she only ever feels safe when he's around, and yet, she pours a tea and settles into her chair all the same.

Every day that Aliyah refuses to leave her room, she hears Elliot laughing with the children from the summer program. They're back, which means Elliot only has a few months left before he's gone completely. There's a part of Aliyah that wants to avoid him until then. It would be possible; she's just not sure if it will actually help. Will not seeing him for months make any difference when she knows she'll never see him again? The application process is fixed, so whoever wants to apply for his position after him can stay, if they so choose. She's fixed it for him too, so there would never be a need for anyone else. But she doubts he wants to stay now.

Aliyah wonders if he's read her letter yet. Sometimes she thinks about creeping into his room and stealing it back. There's a pit in her stomach that grows with each day that she thinks about him reading her most vulnerable words and doing nothing about it. Did he care about her at all? Or was it all about how she looked? The moment he realized she was someone else, would he have disregarded her completely? More laughter floats from the bottom of her trellis, and she peers over. Elliot is with the children from her Giorgia Gardening Center. God, she misses him. She's desperate for him to look up, to see her, but she's not sure what for. Is she so desperate for him to remember she exists that she wants him to see her at her worst?

But he doesn't look up. He laughs, and he dances, and he sends out high fives. He's not affected at all. And she's conflicted. Does she *want* him to be sad? No. Does she want to know that he might have liked her at all? Yes.

The thoughts are swirling in her mind. Was any of it real, or did she imagine herself in an impossible life? Was he playing her this entire time, or playing a game he didn't have the rules to in the first place? Can she be this hurt when she never gave him enough of herself to make a decision? Does it hurt more or less that the moment he found out she was the Princess, he disappeared? The thoughts pull her under, as though she's been treading water all this time and it's all too late. She pulls her trainers on, throws his sweater over her head again, and runs.

Every day at five, Elliot watches Aliyah run. She's not running toward him. She twists behind the trees to the east, and they've never been there together. There's a high chance she's not supposed to be seen at all, but he'd find her anywhere. It's been weeks, and she still won't let him see her. He waits under the trees, and he walks by the lake, but she hasn't been to either since. He's thought about climbing up on her balcony again, but the first few nights she ignored him entirely and he's not about to be a man who ignores her wishes. It might be slowly killing him. If the bags under his eyes are anything to go by, it's not all that long until he stops breathing all together.

The past few days, Elliot thought he'd just try and get over her. She doesn't want to see him, and that's her right. He was cruel and unkind and everything she never deserved. If he were reading this scenario in a book, he'd be rooting for her to stand her ground. He'd be cheering every time she ignored him completely. But this isn't a story, and his heart pounds with every step she takes away from him. It doesn't mean he deserves for her to hear him out, to tell her he's never had a bad thought about her, and that's why the only thing he could say was something she so kindly told him. But God, does he spend his nights wishing she'd stroll over to his greenhouse again.

The way he thinks about her is messing with his life. His simple daily tasks are harder when he hasn't slept because the thought of her being in the dungeons again makes him feral. He stalks the palace grounds at three a.m., trying to find a way to check she's not there. He's been muddy and bruised, finding ways in and out of the palace for if, God forbid, he ever hears she's there again. Elliot isn't foolish enough to think he could stroll into the palace, meander down to the dungeons and get her out, especially with his distinct lack of weapons, so he needs a backup. And now he has two. Three, if he counts the iron saw he had overnighted.

It's not just the way he sleeps, because he was already used to not sleeping that well. It's in the way his day functions, in the way he's slacking at his job. The only thing that gives him joy at the moment is the Giorgia Gardening program. The children who spend their days running around, getting dirty, playing with watering cans, and maybe planting one seed. The children who tell him jokes about the Princess, how she likes to spin them under the sweet-pea frames. The children who keep asking when Princess Lia is coming to see them, and he doesn't know what to tell them. They wouldn't understand if he told them anything true, so he smiles and tells them *soon*. He hopes it's soon.

In the midst of Elliot doing a borderline-awful job in the gardens, he found that his job listing has been changed. There is simply a checkbox he has to tick if he wants to stay. He wonders if it would be against her wishes now to say yes, he would like to stay, when she so clearly doesn't want him to. He sighs. He's too caught up in it all. He needs another opinion, even if he can't tell them everything.

He grabs his phone and dials without looking. It only rings for a moment, and he smiles as he hears a familiar voice.

"What's up, girlfriend?"

"Hey, Mel."

"Oh God," she replies, and Elliot can hear the wind behind her words. She's never just at home. His sister is always *doing* something. He's usually always doing something too. Elliot doesn't like to waste days doing nothing—which is why he's in a hidden staircase waiting to hear Lucian's schedule when he comes back to the palace. Elliot has heard enough in the common room about what a man Lucian is. The guards share the same block as him, and he's not about to have Lucian coming back here with no escape plan in place for Lia.

"Is this about the girl? Guy? Enbie?"

Elliot rolls his eyes. "What are you talking about?"

"Ellie, you haven't missed a 'hey, girlfriend' since you lost your teddy bear in, like, the eighth grade." (Elliot would like to point out he didn't get the bear in eighth grade. He'd had it since birth and happened to lose it in eighth grade, and those are very different things.) He laughs despite her figuring him out in seconds.

"I don't know why I call you."

"I'm great," she replies, then mutters a thank-you to someone on the other end of the phone.

"Are you busy?" he asks, knowing the answer.

"Nope, and you haven't answered my calls in weeks, so tell me what's going on or I'll turn up."

Elliot sighs. "There's a person—"

"I know," Melody replies effortlessly. Elliot groans. "Show me your face."

Elliot moves the phone in front of his face, his sister now on his screen. She's eating a pineapple and *something*. The food here has gotten better since Lia kindly fixed it for him, but it's not the same as home.

"What's that?" he asks, peering into the phone at a different angle, as if that means he's going to see what is off screen.

"Hot honey and Tajín."

He groans. Maybe he should just go home. The food is better, and the scenery is nice, but it sinks into his chest... he doesn't want to leave her here.

"So," she replies, taking another bite. "What happened?"

"Uh...."

"Wait, where are you?" she asks, frowning as she looks at his bricked backdrop.

"Library," he lies. He can't tell her he found a secret underground tunnel and he's spying on the royal guards. Well, he could, and all she'd do is think it was dope, but he won't.

"Ohhh, she's well read?"

He laughs. "They might be."

"Ellie, I love you—you know I do—but I have another proposal meeting in twelve minutes. If things were good, you'd have already sent me three photos of their face and an essay about what to tell Mom when they visit. So, what's the issue?"

Elliot frowns. Melody is upsettingly good at reading him. But she's also the one person he'll always turn to for advice. If she tells him to let it go, then it's the right thing to do. Even if it might kill him. But then he realizes he can't tell her enough. How is he meant to tell her the person he loves didn't tell him she was a princess... without telling Melody she's the Princess? Melody would tell him it's not wise to fall for a princess, so he can't tell her. So, it boils down to the basic question—what is he most apologetic for?

"They told me something in confidence, and I threw it in their face when I was upset."

"Ahhh," Melody replies. "The *Elliot is upset and doesn't know how to handle it* reaction."

"Yeah." He sighs. "It was cruel."

"And what have they said since?"

"Nothing."

"How long?"

"It's been, like, three weeks," Elliot replies, his chest constricting at the look on Melody's face. Situation unsalvageable. He knows it is.

"And what have you said?" she asks.

Elliot frowns. "Nothing." Before she can curse him out, he adds, "They, uh, work in the palace, and I can't get in there. It's... Well, I can't talk to them unless they let me. They used to sneak past guards and things to come see me, so it's not like I can just stroll in."

Melody hums. "And have you seen them since?"

Elliot sighs and rubs his hand over his face. "They run every day, but they—"

"Every day? Same route?"

Elliot nods, and Melody acts as though she's a detective on a prime-time TV show.

"So, this person you like—who evades palace guards to see your ashy ass—is running in a place you can see every day?"

Elliot nods, though he doesn't get her point.

"They *want* you to see them."

He frowns. "I do see them."

Melody sighs, rolling her eyes to the heavens. "They want you to *see* them. They're putting themselves in your space on purpose. So... you need a gesture," Melody says casually.

A *gesture*? For the Princess of Iledale? Usually, Melody has great advice. Today, she's unhinged. It may be because she doesn't know who he's talking about, but that's neither here nor there. But a gesture is not going to cut it. Aliyah trusted him with her thoughts and her feelings, and he disregarded them like they were nothing because he couldn't see past his petty hurt.

Of course she was nervous to tell him who she was when he spent all his time telling her why she wasn't a good person, when everything she's done since he arrived suggests otherwise. Now he knows why he has four extra blankets in his room—because he mentioned it would be cold and the palace wouldn't care. Now he knows why the scholarships are efficiently run when every other scheme the palace has that doesn't have her name attached is barely afloat. Because she made it so.

"Ellie," Melody practically shouts. She's the oldest and the most dramatic. Elliot looks at her through his phone screen. He wants to laugh because she looks like an old librarian with her "take me seriously and offer me money" wig she often wears for fundraising meetings, but she'll probably hang up on him. "I've never seen you like this. It's been like two months, so I will need you to get a grip."

Elliot laughs and leans back against the wall. He thinks about it. Truly, he thinks about getting a grip and just... getting over it. But then he thinks about how he's spent the entire time thinking of ways to run into her. If he got impaled by his garden fork, would she come and see him? That seems like something a princess might do. It seems like something she might do... for him. So, it seems unlikely he'll be able to get over it when he thinks he'd risk death just to die in a place that she'd have the chance to see him.

"Oh my God," Melody gasps. "You're *pouting*."

"I am not!"

"Ellie's in love," she sing-songs, like falling in love isn't the worst thing that could happen to him right now. He rolls his eyes. His sister would tell him falling for a princess is a bad idea.

"What kind of gesture?" he asks.

CHAPTER SEVENTEEN

ELLIOT STANDS UNCOMFORTABLY STILL at the side of the dining room, his hands down by his sides. He has no idea what he is expected to do in this situation apart from looking ahead and not moving... he thinks. There's probably extensive training he's supposed to go through, but it turns out, just turning up in the right clothes (he *borrowed* them from storage) and being in the right place means he's right where he needs to be. Also, some man who looks a bit like a child chastised him when he first turned up, telling him to stand in line properly and that he's told him before. Elliot did as he was told instead of telling him he's never seen him in his life because he doesn't even work *in* the palace. Apparently, working within palace walls gives everyone a high horse to sit on the moment they walk in.

Melody had no actual ideas of gestures beyond him running alongside her. Elliot isn't sure she'd like that, and he's not sure he'd make it a hundred meters. So, he thought the only other way to get in her orbit was to put himself somewhere he knows she'll be.

The dining hall is disgustingly ornate. Marble floors clash with decadent wallpaper and outrageously high detailed ceilings. Elliot always wondered if it's a deal the wealthy have to make—they can have all the money in the world so long as they have absolutely no taste. (He thinks the large sash windows are gorgeous, but he's not about to compliment the royals, even if it is in his head.)

He allows only his eyes to move, to look at the portraits on the walls. The King and Queen sitting in their gold frames. Separately, of course. There's another portrait of a younger girl. She's wearing a crown, so Elliot assumes she's royal, but he hasn't seen her since he's been here. Aliyah hasn't mentioned her either, but she has spoken so infrequently about her family that he's not surprised. But then he remembers the small facts Aliyah did give him about herself. Her... and her dead sister. How she was hounded for it. He can't believe he's never held her—told her it's not her fault, that it would never be her fault. A pang of guilt flows through him, settling along the pit of despair that's sat in his heart ever since she left the greenhouse, about how she's had to hide parts of herself from him. It makes the itchiness of this ridiculous navy blazer all the more apt.

There's a portrait of Aliyah too. She's stunning, because of course she is, but her portrait doesn't match the others, and not only because she's the only one with brown skin. He feels foolish to not have realized now, but he spent so little time thinking about anyone but her. Still, it's not her skin color or the fact she has straight hair in the portrait that doesn't quite match. It's as if it was painted separately. There's an air of disdain to her portrayal. Maybe it's the way she looks—furious and glamorous all at once. Maybe it's the paint strokes; maybe the royal painter didn't take too fondly to her. He supposes it could be both. He feels a rage simmering in his stomach, and it has nothing to do with how much money is sitting in this one room. It's about how he can tell from a single portrait how hard her childhood must have been, and how he's done nothing but make her life worse.

The first arrival for dinner is announced in a booming voice. Everyone else here must have been expecting it—no one jumped in their skin quite like Elliot. The announcement at least makes him remember where he is and snap his eyes away from the portrait Princess's frown to look straight ahead.

Lord Lucian Feathermore III struts into the room with a cane. The air of superiority is rife with him, his gaze disgusted as he waits for his chair to be tucked in behind him. When he sits down, snarling at the staff, Elliot recognizes him as the man from under the canopy—the man Aliyah pretended to want just to get him out of trouble.

PERFECTLY CANDID

Elliot knows Lucian won't recognize him. Why would he care who he is? Regardless, the fury that flows through Elliot is palpable. It comes off him in waves, and he wonders if this is the reason Aliyah didn't tell him who she was. Beyond his obvious dislike for the monarchy, was she protecting him? What would he be able to do now, if Aliyah came in here and someone hurt her? Nothing that wouldn't get him killed, and he'd do it anyway.

There's another announcement, and despite the fact Elliot knew it was coming, his shoulders jolt all the same. He watches as the Queen is seated, and moments later, the King arrives. Elliot thinks it's bizarre that they wouldn't just walk in together, but he gathers there's protocols he doesn't know about. There's a simmer of *something* sitting uncomfortably under the suit that doesn't quite fit him (he's worried the seams might split on his thighs), because he's not quite qualified to work in the palace. He could get thrown out before Aliyah even enters the room. She might not even turn up. She might watch him get thrown out on his ass, but at least she'll see him.

So, here he stands, at the edge of the room, his fingers tapping against his thighs. He wonders when she'll get here. He wants to see her face; he wants to know she's alright. There's nothing Lia could do if she does see him here anyway. It's not like he's expecting her to run over and hug him. She's been avoiding him for weeks so he's not even expecting her to look at him. But God, he still misses her. It's not like he can expect anything from her in these circumstances. She is royalty. Royalty does not interact with the staff. He knows that. He knew that before he even took a job here. Everyone knows that—it's practically written into kingdom law. But over the past weeks, Elliot has realized he doesn't care if she doesn't speak to him in public, if he gets her in secret. As long as they have moments when it's just them.

While he waits, tapping his fingers lightly against his side because *gosh* this is dull, he eavesdrops on the conversation at the dinner table. They aren't talking quietly, so he assumes it's fair game. The Queen talks to Lucian as if they are old friends (Elliot knows he is the King's friend because he stalked him online), though her voice remains unkind, even if her words are not sharp. He wonders if she ever smiles. The King says nothing at all.

"Lord Feathermore, when you were last here, did you manage to speak with the Princess in private?" she asks as her water glass is filled. She dismisses the waiter with a flick of her fingers.

"No, Your Majesty," Lucian answers. "We were chaperoned by His Majesty's aid. I have been hoping to have a more *intimate* meeting with her for some time. I think both sides would benefit from an engagement between our distinguished families."

Elliot scoffs under his breath, and it echoes lightly around the room. His stomach roils with disgust. The man is seventy-five if he's a day! His hair is entirely gray. What is Elliot missing?

"There is much to think about," Queen Panimiro replies. "For how long have you been trying to speak with her privately?"

Elliot realizes no one ever calls Aliyah by her name. There's no fondness with the way the Princess is spoken about.

"For some time," he repeats. That could mean anything, seeing as the man is at least forty years her senior. "She is not the easiest person to get a hold of." He huffs like he's doing her a favor by being here. "I do hope she is more amenable now, especially after her time in the dungeons."

Elliot almost breaks his fingers trying to keep his hands still. How dare he come into her home and disrespect her like that? She's not even here to defend herself. He feels a pit at the bottom of his stomach. This is what she thinks he wants for her? All because he would not open his eyes for one moment and see what she was begging him to figure out? The Princess is kind. She's thoughtful. She's quickly becoming his favorite thing in the world, and she hasn't even spoken to him properly in weeks. He can't believe he had the audacity to suggest this is all she deserved.

The Queen laughs, a sinister snarl that makes the dead look in her eyes glow. "Well, you will be the one to train her, Lucian. I assume the water method was used this time?"

Lucian nods, a hideous smirk over his face. The water again. Elliot takes the deepest breath he can, settling any thoughts that there's a goddamn room in this place where she is *hurt*. The Queen is supposed to protect her above all else. The idea Aliyah has had to live with parents that not only don't care about her, but actively put her in harm's way, is criminal. They should see the inside of a jail cell for the rest of their miserable lives.

The Queen hums. "That will work, eventually. We have not tried that before. We've always known she is stubborn. There is a reason she has not married, after all, is there not? And if you fail, then I guess your son can have what is left of her."

"Forgive me," Aliyah replies, and Elliot almost snaps his neck to look at her. She's radiant, of course, in a light pink silk gown that pools at her feet even as she graciously glides into the room. He feels a little lightheaded. Material falls gracefully over her arms, and her shoulders are entirely bare. What he would do to touch her there, to show her how wanted she is in this room. Elliot realizes a moment too late that he is the only person who acknowledged her entrance beyond a curtsey, so he forces himself to look forward and bow his head. Lia speaks again, and he smiles before she's reached the end of her sentence.

"I assume many in my position would object to marrying your sixty-five-year-old friends who have never spoken to a Black person in their lives."

She reaches her seat and gives a small smile at the member of staff who moves her chair for her. Her hand hovers against the seat like she's not used to this treatment, or maybe she just doesn't like it. When she's seated, her mother is the brightest shade of red Elliot has ever seen, and it's *glorious*.

"Lucian. It is a pleasure to make your acquaintance, again," Aliyah says. Her hands are in front of her, and if Elliot had to guess, she'd be spinning the ring on her pinkie finger under the table.

Lucian side-eyes her. "You may call me 'my lord.'"

She laughs lightly. "I doubt formal terms are necessary. You are in my home, are you not?"

"I suppose I am, Aliyah," he replies. Elliot is surprised he's still a living being and hasn't spontaneously combusted with how livid he looks. It's greatly amusing.

Aliyah smiles. "You may call me 'Your Highness.'"

Lord Lucian almost chokes on nothing at all, and Elliot barely stifles a laugh. Elliot wonders if he's been missing this part of her the whole time. She's so confident, even if Elliot is the only one in this room who can see she's pretending. She's utterly fabulous. He misses her so much.

Aliyah looks around, her tiara glistening underneath the chandelier. Elliot can't believe he hasn't had the good fortune of seeing her under every light possible. He knows she'd be breathtaking at golden hour. When she wanted to see him before, the sunset before golden hour wasn't even a thing. Now, it's weeks later, and he wants nothing more than to walk through the forest under the golden leaves with her.

Elliot's fingers tap against the side of his thighs as he thinks about moving the braid that has fallen in front of her eyes. Then, because she's never needed him—or anyone, he gathers—to help her, she flips her hair over her shoulder. It's practically in slow motion. Her lips part slightly, the sheen on them catching in the light of the room. She looks around the space like she's never been here before, and Elliot thinks watching her do anything at all might be his favorite thing to do. The ache in his legs from standing stock-still after a day at work disappears as she smiles at *something*. The want to touch her never disappears though, especially as she plays with her jewelry like she's not entirely comfortable here. In her own home.

The food is placed down in front of her, and she looks at it with disdain. She moves her food around her plate, occasionally piercing a small piece with the tines of her fork and eating it. No one says a thing as the starters are cleared, her plate still full. No one bats an eye when the same thing happens with the main course. She's not eating. He swallows. Tomorrow, he'll figure out a way to get her to eat. Maybe he'll stand next to her until she does. He'll figure it out.

For now, he watches as Aliyah rolls her neck, and Elliot almost walks over to ask if she's alright. To just be close to her. He's always known he wants to touch her, but the need now is almost animalistic. His fingers itch to trace her collarbone to see if she's as soft as she looks. He can't believe he's known her for longer than three seconds and he hasn't come up with all the reasons to touch her yet. Would it be too strange to ask just to hold her hand?

He feels like he might go insane at the thought of not holding her a moment longer.

He doesn't move though. She'd hate that considering what happened last time. She might hate him now. He'd probably get banished for daring to look at her, and he'd lose her all over again. So, he'll stand here.

She looks around the room again, and Elliot has missed the entirety of the dinner conversation because she hasn't said another word and he's been watching the way she chews her lip. Her gaze sweeps over him, and he can't even be annoyed; he's still glad he came. But then she looks back, and her eyes are wide, and she's *smiling.* Truly smiling. Not the smile she gives waiters, and not the one reserved for photographers. The one for him. The one he sees under the plum tree. The one his dramatic heart never thought he'd see again.

She either remembers where she is or remembers she doesn't like him at all and blinks, then looks down at her plate. From then on, the only time she looks at him is when he's not looking at her. It's agony. The way he misses her seeps into his soul. It's affecting everything from his breathing to his sleeping, and he doesn't know how to fix it, or if he even deserves for it to be fixed. All he knows is that everything feels better when she looks at him, even if it hurts all the same.

He spends half the time looking at her, but then he looks at the portraits because he likes when he feels her gaze on him. Elliot listens in and out of the conversation at the dinner table. He's only focused when Aliyah is speaking, which isn't often at all. He thinks there is talk of a ball. Usually, he'd scoff, but now he thinks about Aliyah in a ballgown, and all that's running through his mind is how he could sneak his way in there too.

Finally, the King speaks, and it makes Elliot pay attention. "We shall make an announcement then."

Elliot's gaze falls back on Aliyah with practiced ease. She looks uncomfortable, more so than she has this entire night.

"I will not marry him."

Lucian sneers. "And I suppose when I have removed all of your *teeth*, you will be attractive to anyone else?"

Before he can think, Elliot's feet move one step in front of the other until Aliyah holds her hand up subtly. It's just a slight movement, but he catches it all the same. She doesn't need him. She never did. He steps back, and her hand softly touches the table again. No one else seems to have noticed she moved at all; they're too busy fizzing with anger that she dared say she didn't want to date a man whose shadow is basically the crypt keeper.

She looks at Elliot again, and he's been so desperate for her gaze that he's looking right at her. Aliyah takes a deep breath.

Her mother leans across the table to get closer to her, as if she couldn't be heard by everyone in the kingdom. "You have no more time. You are going to ruin this family because you want to *choose* who you marry. Beggars don't have the luxury of choice. You are an orphan, Aliyah. Nobody wanted you then, and nobody wants you now."

"I suppose not," Lia replies quietly, looking anywhere but at him. He'd marry her in a heartbeat. If anyone but her dared to look at him, they'd know he's five seconds from dropping down to one knee. Elliot bows his head and takes a deep breath. "But I will not marry him all the same."

Elliot raises his gaze in time to see her quickly looking away from his face, and he realizes that he'll be here, every day, as long as she'll have him.

His sister would tell him it's not wise to fall for a princess, but now, it's too late.

CHAPTER EIGHTEEN

The sweat drips down the back of Aliyah's neck as she runs the same route. She's late to breakfast, and it's Elliot's fault. Her run is muscle memory now, even though it's not the same track she's run for the past twenty years. There's a slight detour she's added since she started running more. For the first few days, every time she ran under the plum trees instead of around the back of the stables, she frowned. It makes no sense for her to go that way, but she found herself there all the same. Then, she saw Elliot through the greenhouse windows, and he didn't see her. Suddenly, she knew why she'd taken that route.

Now, she runs earlier, because Elliot is in the greenhouse earlier. The first day threw her off completely, but now she knows it's because he's working the catering shifts. Elliot's motives are lost on her. She thought maybe he was working during the dinner shift for extra income, but then he appeared at breakfast as well. Aliyah knows he's still working in the gardens because she's all but stalking him.

The frustrating thing now is that she can't just ask him. They haven't spoken since the greenhouse debacle, and that wasn't even a conversation. It was the single worst thing that's happened to her in a long time. He told her to leave, then asked her to stay, but she couldn't because he only asked out of pity. And now, he hasn't said anything at all. All she wants is for him to come back, even though she knows she'll spend the time pushing him away, just to see if he tries to stay. Aliyah is used to everyone leaving, whether she asks them to or not. There's no way for him to know that—he's known her for mere moments—but she wants him to play the game without the rules. She wants him to win.

She wants him to stay.

For a moment, she thought he was there for her. His glances are always for her. Sometimes, when she dares to look over, he doesn't immediately turn away. Sometimes, in blissful agony, they look at each other until something makes them stop. The end of dinner, her parents barking a command at her. But then nothing ever comes from it. He looks at her, and it makes her want to sink to the floor, but if she turns to look at him, he glances away. Is he there to hurt her? To make her want something he so clearly doesn't want to give? Elliot doesn't seem the type, but the last time he told her anything about himself was so long ago she barely remembers the sound of his voice.

It's possible that his motives have nothing to do with her. Elliot might just be looking to move from the gardens and into the house. Maybe he's tired of the early mornings and the cold weather. If only he'd tell her, she'd make it happen. And now, she's late to breakfast.

Yesterday, it would have been fine because she dined by herself morning, noon, and night. Elliot was there, of course, his eyes on her the entire time. She assumes he'll be here today too, and she regrets her tardy timing because she's still in her gym gear when she gets to the palace. She wonders which would be worse to her parents: showing up to dine in leggings and a sweaty jumper, or being late. Then she remembers whose jumper she has on, and how he hasn't spoken to her at all, and she's mortified. And still late. So, Aliyah jogs into the dining hall, wiping her forehead with the back of her hand. She tries to swallow down her pants, but everyone turns to look at her when she enters. God forbid someone walks into the dining hall without being announced with fanfare akin to gunfire. When she's queen, she's going to make them stop. She wants to walk down the halls without her presence being shouted every hundred steps.

"You are late," her mother says, without looking up from the book in front of her. She's not reading; it's the same book in front of her every day. Aliyah finds Elliot at the edge of the room, and the venom coming from the Queen's words affects her less.

"I am."

"And you are dressed like a common street rat."

Aliyah rolls her eyes as she goes to sit down, but she's beaten to the chair by a guard, who pulls it out for her. She suppresses a shudder as she remembers the last time she was in the dungeon. The same man had held her down while Lucian tried to *convince* her marrying into his family would be in her best interests. Three times her size, yet he had used his entire weight on her shoulders all the same. She was bruised for days. He pulls her chair out, and she smiles as sweetly as she can, ignoring her pounding heart. His face is so livid she's surprised he hasn't hit her.

"I thought you would be glad I was exercising," Aliyah starts, folding her hands in her lap. "You are always wanting me to look better, are you not?"

"Your Grace," the guard says from behind her. Lia jumps slightly. She thought he'd moved away. She swallows, her jaw clenched as she scans the room for the only thing that makes her calm. Her eyes fall on Elliot, and for the first time, he's not looking at her. He's looking at the guard, his brows furrowed and jaw clenched. Aliyah has never seen him look so furious.

"The dungeons have been cleaned."

"Ah," her mother says, closing her book with a thud. "Excellent work. I have the feeling they will be needed soon, will they not?"

Her mother has been on a warpath ever since Aliyah said she wasn't marrying Lucian. There have been traps every time she dares leave her bedroom, desperate attempts to get her in the dungeons. Her parents could throw her in there for no reason at all—that's what most of their 'reasons' are anyway—but her mother likes to pretend they are *fair*, so there's always some reason she's down there, embarrassing Lucian being the most recent. Usually, Aliyah accepts her fate. The dungeons are grimy and cold, but it's not *hell*.

And then the water was introduced, and she thinks it's pretty close. Aliyah has never betrayed a kingdom; she's never committed treason. Her worst crime is being an unwanted child in a position of power, and yet the water is poured over a cloth held over her face all the same. She holds her hands in front of her, trying to stop the panic from rising. She's in the dining room. She's not there. But she remembers how she couldn't breathe; couldn't scream. She couldn't do anything but take it, and she is terrified to go back.

Elliot looks like he's about to burst something from holding in his rage, and Aliyah never wanted this for him. She knows how that feels—the panic between protecting someone you care about, and the realization there's nothing you can do. So, she does something she never does.

"I apologize," she says, her breath still choppy. "For being late, and underdressed. I apologize. It was inappropriate of me."

Her mother looks enraged, like she was never expecting her to back down. There will be another reason soon, and Aliyah will have to face the fact once again that showering will be too difficult a task for her to do properly for another week.

Aliyah swallows as her mother looks away, her father barely looking up from his newspaper. The waiters move around the room silently, and she refuses to look over at Elliot again lest she tells him everything from her place at the table. How everything has gotten worse for her this year, but he's the best thing to ever exist. That there's not a timeline where she would ever want to be without him, even if they don't talk. She misses him—truly and to her core misses him.

Even with the way her hands shake with the desire to stay calm, to just get through breakfast alive, she only lasts a moment before she needs him again. She looks over, and he's not there. A soft, pained noise leaves her throat before she can force it back down. No one notices, of course. There's the possibility she could be set aflame and no one would move. They'd know, because her mother most likely would have lit the match.

Aliyah should have figured out why Elliot was working here and not in the gardens. She should have found a way to get him out of it, because now, she needs him. Now, she's not sure how to get through the breakfast without looking behind her to see if the guard is still there, watching her with a predatory gaze. Now, she can barely breathe in her own home, the sound of water cascading over her face so prominent in her mind that she feels like she might fall to the ground.

Then Elliot's hand arrives next to hers, and her heart settles as he places her bowl down. He's close—closer than any other staff member ever gets to her—and she keeps her head perfectly still and forward as she breathes him in. There's no salmon and cucumber in front of her. No quail eggs and rocket. In front of her, Elliot has placed a bowl of cereal. *He remembered.* He made sure he remembered. He wrote every good thought she ever had down. She wonders if he reads it now.

"Lia," he whispers, then, after a quick glance to make sure no one else is watching, says, "*Please*. Eat."

It's embarrassing how her entire body shudders at the sound of his voice. God, she misses him. His hand lingers against her spoon, and he only moves it when she places hers lightly underneath his. The heat from his skin makes her eyes close, even if they never actually touch. Aliyah knows he'll walk away; he has to. There's no reason at all for him to stop and talk to her, to touch her in the way her body aches for. It's a little pathetic how badly she wants him to. How she wants Elliot to claim her in front of the guards, to bend down and kiss her in all the ways she's dreamt of. It would do nothing but cause a scandal. It would even possibly get her (and him) killed in the process. But she can't help the way her heart flutters at the thought, and if the small sigh that leaves Elliot's mouth is anything to go by, he might feel it too.

Aliyah would tell anyone else not to get so invested in something so dangerous. To keep their dignity intact, because once you become foolish over a man in public, there's no going back. But her thoughts do nothing to stop the way her eyes follow in his direction as he walks away. They do nothing to stop the way her fingers flex against the spoon he just held as he passes without a word. The only solace she has is that when he stands back in line, he looks right at her.

His fingers tap against his thighs as his eyes flick between her and the bowl. Aliyah rolls her eyes, though she picks up her spoon and eats anyway, if only to stop the worried look on his face. A braid falls from the shoulder, brushing the back of her neck. She wonders if anyone has ever touched her there. Or perhaps the hollow of her throat, or the inside of her ankle. She wonders what it would feel like if Elliot touched her with the long fingers he drums against his own legs.

Worked up in her thoughts, she eats the entire bowl and finds that she's hungry still, her spoon clattering against the china with a clang as she sets it down.

"What are you doing eating? You have a ball at the weekend," her mother says, as if she knows she's contemplating eating more. Aliyah has never controlled her eating before simply because her mother asked her too. If she told her she was too chubby, or that there was an event coming up, she just ate in her room later. Her need to decide when, what, and how much she was eating was for her and her only. Now, she frowns, the scoff she wants to make shoved down her throat.

Elliot is already on his way over to clear her plate, but she supposes she can eat later.

"Would you like another bowl, Your Highness?" he asks, his voice low as he bends closer than necessary.

Aliyah swallows, nervous her voice may shake when she talks to him for the first time.

"Yes," she mutters, "But—"

"As you wish," he says, getting ahead of her refusal. She doesn't want Elliot to think she's pathetic for hiding how she eats from her parents. But she deals with so much hatred from the inside of this dining room, and she's not sure she can add food on top of the reasons for it. Not today. She already feels like she's about to fall over. She wonders if he'll offer to bring her something under the trees, or if that's just wishful thinking. He's not been outwardly rude to her. That's the only difference between him and anyone else in this room. It's not his fault she's in love with him.

"I... I will leave it in the kitchen for you, Princess."

She deflates, though she's surprised she could hear him over the thumping of her heart in her ears. And then he's gone.

CHAPTER NINETEEN

Elliot sweeps the greenhouse floor and makes sure the pots are stacked neatly. Melody comes to visit tomorrow, and he wants everything to look as orderly as possible. He's nervous to see her. Mainly because she'll see right through his cheery texts, and there's a high possibility she'll figure out who he's in love with. Maybe. There's probably clues everywhere in this greenhouse, even if Aliyah was only in here once when he knew who she was—and that meeting didn't go all too well. Melody will know he's got seed trays full of colorful, tall flowers just for her. She'll know that the bench was made just for her. She'll know his notepad is full of thoughts about her, dates that he's checked the dungeons and nothing has changed, badly drawn maps that look like he's plotting to kill the King. She'll know.

Maybe he should tell her, because he's not sure how many more dinners he can get through before he hits someone, and she'll have advice. Elliot has never thought of himself as a violent person, but every day, someone tests his patience. Aliyah is a saint, and the best person he's ever met, because she never rises to their petty rudeness but shuts them down all the same. Everyone that ever tries to talk down to her or embarrass her has to sit in the awkwardness she forces them into. Elliot almost cheers every time it happens. He just wishes she had to defend herself less.

Sometimes, like tonight, someone mentions who Aliyah is marrying. Apparently, there's two options now, though the common room hasn't given him information about the latest addition yet. Lucian—the grim reaper—or his son, Dorian. No one apart from

J.S. JASPER

Elliot seemed to think it bizarre that two men from the same family were claiming to be helplessly in love with the same woman. Elliot would understand it, of course—she's fantastic. But beyond the fact he knows Lucian threw her in the dungeons weeks ago, it's clear from the way everyone talks about Dorian that he also doesn't like her at all. Lia flinched every time either of them were mentioned.

It was worse whenever someone mentioned water—always either her mother, or the tall guard who hovers near her (who *looks* like a guard but must have more authority for how he gets away with talking to her)—and it was always said with a warning tone. She's a fucking princess, for God's sake. It took every single ounce of control he had to not walk over to her, to tell her to get her stuff and they'll go. Wherever she wants to go, he'll take her. And then the Queen mentioned the wedding night, and Elliot almost popped his jaw. Aliyah looked over at him then. He thinks she might be trying to kill him. He wondered, at first, if she thought of him whenever the idea of sleeping with someone came into her mind, and then all thoughts left his mind when the King and Queen discussed what would happen like she wasn't even there.

Elliot's never heard the King speak before the first day Elliot conned his way into the dining room, and hardly ever since, yet His Majesty piped up to tell Lia—well, not tell her, but rather speak about the entire thing as if she's not there—that the wedding night will *hurt*. As if it were factual. As if sex hurts for people. As if sex should ever hurt. Aliyah didn't move; she just ate her food like it was normal dinner conversation. With every passing day, Elliot's struggle not to say something grows. He wants to shout across the dining hall, follow her into the hallway, chase her down in the woods and beg for forgiveness. Tell her that he thinks she's sunshine, that he loves her.

He sighs, putting the broom away. Everything is clean, everything is tidy. Right on time.

He looks out the window and sees as Aliyah runs on the other side of gardens. He watches her duck under the plum tree that he was supposed to prune last week, and he realizes he doesn't have time to change. He should have done it earlier. Oh well. He hangs up his apron at least, and then he runs.

The evening sun streams through the tree canopy, and Aliyah dodges a high root with ease. Her heart thumps and her chest burns as she runs through the path she's worn down through the forest. It does nothing to quiet her mind, though. Not enough.

The words of her mother seep into her bones as she rounds the corner. Is Aliyah truly foolish to want to want to marry someone she likes? Perhaps. Seeing as it took her twenty-four years and an attempted murder to find someone she liked enough to picture a life with them. She might be about to throw the entire kingdom to the wolves, it's true. If she does not take up the crown, then it will fall to Lucian's family anyway. And if she doesn't marry one of them, then the kingdom will be at its highest risk for invasion. The people of Iledale—her people—don't deserve years of war just because she wants to be happy. She'd lose everything in the process, of course. Her life would probably be the first to go.

But does she want to live her entire life with either Lucian or Dorian? No. Could she run the kingdom with them by her side? Or would they try and take over? The former is unlikely. Would they have her killed within days of the marriage? Definitely.

Aliyah shakes the thoughts of marriage out of her mind. She tries to rid the idea of a wedding night from her brain. She's not entirely sure why it would be necessary. They'd never let her get a divorce, even if the marriage wasn't "legal." She tries to avoid the thought as she leaps over a fallen tree trunk, because the idea that she'd have a choice in her wedding night is laughable. Every time there's a difficult conversation at the dinner table, Aliyah looks at Elliot. As if there's anything he could do. She thinks she's just checking there's a side of him that cares for her. Somewhere. He might not want her, but he cares enough to look upset when it is suggested she should be anything other than happy. It's the only thing that gets her through the days most of the time.

His face, the way he taps on his thighs, the way he rolls his eyes when her mother says... anything, really. How he hasn't been discovered yet, she doesn't know. The way he runs in Wellington boots next to her. The squeak of—*wait*. Elliot's next to her. Running in his Wellingtons. Aliyah frowns as his feet make a silly noise with every step they take. Ridiculous man. He doesn't say anything, though with the sound of his rigid breathing, she's not sure he could if he wanted to.

Aliyah spends the next lap wondering why he's there. But her thoughts change from despair to the thought of him. The way his brow is going to furrow later when he gets back to his room and realize he has blisters because running in Wellingtons—especially wet ones—is strongly discouraged. The way he wipes the sweat from his face every four seconds. The way he's there, with her.

He almost trips—*almost*—but catches himself, his arms flailing in front of him. Aliyah stifles a laugh. It's the first time in so long that a smile has come to her face. It's for him. Of course, it has been every time, but this time, she doesn't try and wipe it off all that soon. Elliot is frowning at the ground, probably cursing the fact that there was a vine in the middle of the forest, but when he looks over at her, his entire face lights up. Aliyah blinks rapidly, screwing up her nose as she wills her face to calm. Elliot looks like he's caught the sun.

They don't talk. She doesn't tell him she misses him, but she does slow her pace. He doesn't say he's hopelessly in love with her, as she was hoping, but he stays with her all the same. Maybe he'll forgive her for everything if she apologizes properly? She hasn't gone to see him. She has no idea what he did with her letter. She explained herself better there than she ever could in person, but he's never mentioned it. He's never waved it at her in the dining hall. Aliyah has never even held a man's hand before; she has no idea what she's supposed to do in this situation. The only person she wants to ask is Elliot, but he's standing doubled over outside his dorm room, watching her leave.

She feels his eyes on her until she gets into her bedroom. As she stands in the shower, she feels the way he used to look at her and puts her head fully under the stream for the first time since the dungeons because she's thinking about him. The way his hands gripped the reins when they were riding, the way his thighs tense when he squats down to look at a plant. The images linger in her mind as she sinks into bed, letting her hand wander down her body. Aliyah wonders if Elliot would be slow if his lips were to replace her hand.

She thinks about him, him, him.

CHAPTER TWENTY

THE NEXT DAY, THANKFULLY, Elliot's feet aren't too bad. The walk back to his dorm from the forest path was the worst. He was practically crawling, but with a smile on his face, because he got her on her own again. He was supposed to speak to her. He was supposed to tell her he was sorry. He was supposed to say anything, really, but he couldn't breathe. Swimming and running are *not* the same thing. But he did hear her laugh when he almost tripped on vines, and he thought he saw God.

She didn't stay to talk to him when they got to his dorms, but he did watch her walk away, and that's the first time he's managed it in weeks. He's still frightfully aware that he's doing the chasing, that if she wanted to see him—properly see him—she would. But he knows her. Knows how hard her childhood has been, knows that she never feels wanted, and he never wants her to think that with him. Now, obviously, he needs to run with her again. So, despite Melody's coach arriving in an hour, he throws on three pairs of socks with his boots and dashes to town to find a pair of running trainers. He grabs some snacks, a silly postcard for Melody, and some chocolates for his mom.

By the time Elliot is back and waiting in the western gardens, he's simultaneously buzzing, practically jumping up and down, and terrified. Melody is close. She keeps sending him updates about getting through security and all the places she wants to see that she can't find online. Elliot tried to tell her he could sneak her into some places but not *all* of them, because how many people with auburn red hair, hanging in loose waves, down to their mid-back stroll around the castle?

So, he waits for her to arrive, surrounded by a large group of people also waiting for their family. Elliot only recognizes a handful of them. Even though he's in the common room more frequently, most of the other people are guards, and they've been here long enough to think they're better than everyone else. He thought he could make friends regardless so long as he avoided the locker-room talk about the Princess's looks, but he almost took out an entire football team's worth of guys because they spoke about her lips and what she'd look like on her knees. Still, as he looks around, he waves at some people, and he wonders if everyone else here with his skin color came on the same apprenticeship.

The sounds of people trekking along the stones shake the thoughts from his mind. Excitement buzzes through his veins. He loves his sister, and he misses her greatly. This is probably the longest they've been apart since she went away for college. (He barely forgave her at the time, but he did get on the six-hour train almost every other week anyway.) This time, it might be his fault. There's no rule against leaving castle grounds at the weekend (it's more difficult during the week because people can smuggle things in and out, but he still managed to get a saw over the wall), but he's been so busy moping around and stalking dungeons that he hasn't found the time to go home.

Elliot is also nervous. Just a little. Because Melody can tell from a mile away when something is wrong. She already knows he's hung up on someone. She already knows he's fucked it up. Elliot went to great lengths to not say she was a woman, because his dating record in college showed that anyone with an attractive face was fair game. He thinks if he neglects to tell her anything about his crush, the love of his life, his dream girl, then she won't figure out who he's talking about. It's not like Melody is going to meet Aliyah, probably ever. Even if Aliyah did let him kiss her in a darkened room at some point, she was never going to want to meet his family.

Besides, Melody has already expressed her disappointment at not getting to meet her. She's done her research, and the Princess has never been at one of these events. Elliot wonders if it's her choice, or if it's something to do with her disappearing from the limelight. (Finally admitting he needed some information from Melody turned into him learning almost everything about Aliyah. Elliot did stop Melody if it got to something he wasn't sure Aliyah would tell him. He wants her to have secrets to share, should she ever want to.)

"Oh, hey!" Melody shouts as she turns the corner. Everyone turns to look at her, various levels of disgust on their face, but she doesn't bat an eye. Mel looks a bit like him, or so everyone says, but he doesn't see it. Her features are rounder, and her gaze is always razor sharp, but he supposes he can see a slight similarity.

"Hey, girlfriend!" Elliot shouts back, his hand in the air with a click. It makes everyone stare harder, but it still makes Melody laugh, like it did in high school.

"I can't believe how much I missed your ugly ass," she says, throwing her arms around his neck. Melody isn't quite as tall as him, but there's not much in it. Her hair is red, as promised, bouncy, and curled down her back.

"I missed you too," he sighs.

Pulling back, she pushes her sunglasses on top of her head. "No comeback? You're still hung up on that girl, aren't you?"

Elliot rolls his eyes. "How heteronormative of you."

"Oh, shut up," she replies, hitting him on the arm. "Eeesh, it's pretty here. I can't believe you've been stingy with the photos! What are you showing me first?"

Elliot lets out a breath. "What do you want to see? And are you hungry? I think lunch is on soon."

"Always, but let's look first, then we can avoid the crowds."

"Alright. What about—"

There's a commotion, people gasping and squealing. Elliot looks around, but there is nothing in the sky. He watches the visitors gather like a gaggle of ducks, all following one person. Swarms of people move; he could have sworn there weren't this many visitors before just now.

He frowns. "What's going on?"

"Oh my fucking *God*," Melody replies, her jaw dropped. How can she see better than him? He's taller than her! She hits him on the arm a couple of times, and he frowns. "She's here!"

"Who?!" Elliot follows the eyeline of everyone moving, hearing whispers of dresses and sun-kissed and things that make no sense to him. "Why is everyone talking in riddles, for fuck's sake?"

He jumps, ready to see beyond this group to see why they're so excited, and then he sees her. Aliyah, in her crown and all. Her hair looks different from how he saw it yesterday. He'll ask Melody what they're called when she stops screeching.

Lia's hair is twisted through the sides of her crown, and she looks ethereal. Like she belongs in a fantasy land. Her light-blue dress is bright against her skin. Elliot's not sure he's ever seen the entirety of her arms before, but now, he's appreciative of a sleeveless dress. He feels like a high-schooler who has just seen a girl's shoulders for the first time. There's a large necklace hanging from her neck with gems that he wouldn't be able to name in a million years. He's seen Aliyah in various dresses since he started working in the palace, but this one is more extravagant than the others, and he can tell by the pull of her neck that she hates it, but she's in it all the same.

"She's here," he whispers.

"Yeah, no shit! I'm not properly dressed!"

Elliot laughs. As if Aliyah would ever care what people were wearing.

"Oh my God!" Melody squeals, somewhat under her breath. "How is she flawless in real life?"

"I—"

"I don't wanna hear it, Ellie! Keep your negativity to yourself while she's out here looking like that." Melody whistles. "Do you think she'll want to read my scholarship proposal?"

"Yeah," he replies. "She will."

"Good thing I have it in my bag," she says, rubbing her hands together. Melody is nervous so infrequently that Elliot forgets it ever happens.

"She's going to love you." His eyes drift back to Aliyah. She's shaking hands and taking photos, and he wonders if this will be the only time he might be able to touch her in public.

"Elliot?"

"Er, yeah?" Elliot says, turning to look at Melody. The look on her face suggests she's been trying, unsuccessfully, to get his attention.

"I was going to ask how you would possibly know anything about her, but that look in your eye..."

He huffs. "What look? You're insane." But his eyes drift back to Aliyah all the same. If there's one thing Elliot is bad at, beyond football, sleeping eight hours a night, and not being hopelessly hung up on the Princess, it's lying. Melody looks from him to Aliyah and back again.

"It's her?!" she whispers.

"No," he lies. "Shh."

Melody bounces on the balls of her feet. "*Elliot.*"

"It's complicated, Mel." He sighs, rubbing his hand over his face.

"Yeah, go figure! Why did you hurt her? She looks like a cartoon lamb, you asshole."

Elliot chuckles, pulling Melody away from the line of people. "Can you quieten down?"

"She's not going to come over here, now, is she? Oh, I'll never forgive you, you little shit!" Melody groans, turning to watch the queue of people getting ever so slowly shorter. Elliot knows Aliyah will come and see her, even if she has to ignore him completely.

He laughs. "I'm telling Mom if you don't stop swearing at me. And yes, she'll come over."

Melody squints at him, pulling her top down slightly. "She will? Even though she hates you?"

He sighs. "She will. Even though she hates me."

"I thought you were going to make up?" Melody frowns.

"I don't know how," he replies, running his hand over the back of his neck while he keeps half an eye on Aliyah. "I'm at dinner, like you suggested, but it's not like I can just talk to her. I am putting myself everywhere I can, I'm just... waiting for her. I don't think she wants to be friends."

"Well, she might not have told you that directly, but she's here for you, you idiot."

Elliot's jaw drops. His sister is never wrong, but right now, she's having an absolute nightmare. "What? No, she's not. It's an event," he replies, pointing at the tens of people here. There would have been hundreds if anyone knew she would have been here.

"That she's never been at before!" Melody stresses, her voice as low as he thinks she can get it, which isn't that low. "You think if I thought there was a chance she'd come to say hi, I would be in trainers right now?"

Elliot ponders the thought. The open day has barely been discussed at breakfast. A passing comment made by the Queen that the fountains needed to be cleaned before people came to look around. Aliyah wasn't threatened about talking out of turn. She didn't say anything. Was she planning on coming at all?

"You think?"

"Dude," Melody says with a laugh. "Did you tell her I like her?"

"Yeah," he replies, though he leaves out how often he followed up on those comments with the fact that *he* didn't like her. "Of course."

"So, technically, she's here to see me." Melody flips her hair off her shoulder. Elliot wouldn't be surprised if Aliyah really was there to see her. He told her Melody had missed the proposal deadline. Maybe she is here to ask about that. But there's a glimmer of hope that starts in his toes.

"You really think she's here for me?" Elliot asks, his brow furrowed enough for Melody not to make that much of a joke.

"God knows how you managed to get her to like you, but all of this," she says pointing at the cameras and the gown, "it's for you."

Elliot ruminates over her words. He did tell Lia that Melody was a fan, and that she was coming to visit. But if she's here for him specifically, he might just pass away.

Melody keeps hitting him when he fidgets like a child waiting to go on the fairground rides. "Be cool," she chastises. Aliyah is only one person away from them. Well, technically, she's at the end of the queue of people, because Elliot and Melody never actually entered the line. "I can't believe you're in love with a princess," Melody stage-whispers. "You little hypocrite."

"Shhh."

"Wait." Melody speaks with no amount of cool in her voice at all. "We're not even in the queue! She's going to think we don't want to meet her."

"Chill out," he says under his breath.

"Ellie—"

"Mel, just—"

Aliyah walks over, and they both stand straight, the slap of their feet turning to face the front lingering as he looks at her. She's smiling, a faint thing as she walks over the grass. He wonders if she's wearing heels. She's taller than usual. They should have stayed on the path. She stands in front of them, and Elliot is expecting Melody to say something—anything—because he can't get his body to react at all. He's back in ninth grade when a pretty girl asked if he wanted to go to the dance and he stood there in silence until she left.

Melody is also no use. Elliot can feel the nerves radiating from her. She's starstruck.

The Princess laughs lightly, flipping her hair over her shoulder. "Hello."

Elliot blinks, and she tilts her face, an amused look plastered over it. Elliot bows, his arm stretched out, and he hears Melody's gasp and subsequent curtsey. When he raises his head, he sees the aftermath of Aliyah's eye roll.

He smiles. "Hi."

"Hi," she replies.

"Hi!"

Aliyah jumps slightly at Melody's voice. Elliot smiles.

Melody pulls it back, holding her hand out. "Hi. It's a pleasure to meet you, Your Highness. I didn't know you were going to be here," Melody says, shaking her hand, "or I would have worn something else."

Elliot almost laughs. Melody is *so* nervous, and for no reason at all. He's already anticipating the slew of texts he'll get later about how she wasn't cool, and how Aliyah would never like her now. Then he'll get more explaining how she never cared anyway.

"Princess, this is my sister," Elliot says, gesturing to Melody, who is still shaking Aliyah's hand.

"Melody, right?"

Melody squeaks, and Elliot laughs loud enough that the birds in the nearby tree take flight. Melody frowns at him, finally dropping Lia's hand.

"I am the better Harper twin, yes," she replies, then says, "You know Ellie, right?" There's a look in her eye that suggests he's going to regret laughing at her.

Elliot swallows, widening his eyes as Melody smiles. "*Don't.*"

Aliyah frowns, looking between them both. "What?"

"My brother fancies the pants off you."

Elliot groans, closing his eyes. "Melody, I swear to God."

Aliyah's eyes widen, but she stifles a smile. She doesn't look mortified at Melody's outburst—that he *will* call her out for later—she just looks shocked. Like she has no idea how gone for her Elliot is. He frowns. Maybe she's shocked Melody knows about her at all. Maybe she's so wide-eyed because she thought he'd keep her a secret. Maybe all the fears she has about everything being told to the press are playing on her mind.

"What?" Melody asks, though Elliot can tell she's embarrassed by her actions. "She has eyes, she can see you fawning over her from across the courtyard."

Lia looks around, pulling her lower lip between her teeth. God, it must be awful to be talked about—like she's not a person too.

"*She* has a name," he stage-whispers, and it finally gets Melody to calm down.

"Sorry," Melody says, looking at Elliot, then back to Lia. "Sorry, Princess. I—having a brother is a lot, especially when he's the *worst*, and I'm not used to being so nervous."

"It is quite alright," the Princess says with a smile. "My name is Aliyah. You do not have to call me Princess. You are not my mother," she says with a smile. Then she looks right at him. "Elliot calls me Lia."

Elliot sighs. He hasn't called her Lia in so long. He hasn't spoken to her properly in so long. He's been hanging on by fumes. The glances he gets over the dining table, the run he's waiting to go on this evening. But it's not enough. He needs mornings, and talks, and knowing that she's alright beyond simply knowing she's alive.

"Your hair is everything," Melody says, like she couldn't possibly keep it in any longer.

It's true, of course. Aliyah's hair has been done in the few days since he's seen her. The box braids are gone, but she has twists in—at least, that's what he thinks Melody just called them in her squealing compliments.

"Thank you," Aliyah says with a light laugh. "I adore the color of yours." Melody giggles, flipping her dark auburn hair over her shoulder a few times.

"Let me know if you ever want a silk press, or bright hair. My girl Laurel will hook you up."

Lia leans closer and whispers, "I am sure that will go down well with the aristocracy."

"How do you deal with those pasty old white men?" Melody scoffs. "I think they would have kicked me out of the palace years ago."

Aliyah laughs. "Believe me, they have tried."

Elliot wants to ask something—anything—to get her to stay. Aliyah has only spent a handful of moments with each group so far, and he can tell by the way her jaw clenches that his time might be up.

Lia looks around. The day is bright; a perfect, slightly warm summer's day. "Elliot tells me you run a nonprofit?" she says.

Melody's entire body comes alive. Even if she is the most nervous she's ever been, talking about the company she birthed from the ground up is something she can do in her sleep.

"Yes." Elliot's thoughts leave the statistics Melody is mentioning, not because he doesn't care, but because he's heard it all before. Last night, to be precise, when he listened to her seventeen-minute-long voice note. Instead, he focuses on Aliyah, because, let's be honest, when isn't he? She seems genuinely interested in the things Melody talks about. She's not just nodding along when there's a pause; she asks questions that Melody wouldn't have been asked before. She cares.

"The cycling initiative, that is what you require the funding for?"

"Exactly." Melody sighs. "It's difficult to get anyone to read a proposal past the introduction. People like to care when they are seen to save us, but it's harder to get funding for fun, you know? Little Brown kids deserve fun too."

"Do you have a costed maintenance plan?" Aliyah asks, and Elliot winces. Thanks to her voice note, he already knows Melody has been waiting for her finance officer to finish. Elliot also knows that he's useless, but one of Melody's oldest friends. (Elliot never liked him.) Melody is weighing up the pros and cons of firing him. A con to firing him would be not having a plan when the richest person in the land asks her for one. Then again, she hasn't fired him yet, and that's the situation they are in now.

"It's in the final stages," Melody says. "I am expecting it by the end of day Friday."

"This late into the financial year?" Aliyah asks. It's not unkind, and Melody doesn't falter at all, but Elliot feels protective over things he has no idea about.

Melody sighs. "The finance officer is my friend. I think, anyway."

"What do you mean, you think?" Elliot asks. Marcus has been her friend since the fourth grade. He came to family events; he was practically a staple at Elliot's swim meets.

"I saw a meeting invitation for an interview."

"Going for a new job does not require him to be an enemy," Aliyah says. "But letting it be detrimental to your business without letting you know is not particular friendly."

"I know," she says, with a small smile. There's something else—something that Melody isn't telling them. Telling him. "But there's not much I can do about it. The company will survive until next year," she says with a sigh. "Can I see something pretty now? Other than you, of course, Princess."

Aliyah laughs. "You are welcome to see what you like." She takes a deep breath, and Elliot wonders if the flash of sadness is all in his mind. "And when your friend is finished with the plan, give it to Elliot, okay?"

Melody frowns. "Ellie isn't great with math." Elliot scoffs, turning to her to tell her she's a big liar, but he can't dispute the fact. Aliyah laughs again, wiping down the front of her dress. She keeps looking around, clearly uncomfortable with how people have been staring at her this entire time. Elliot hadn't noticed; he'd been too focused on her. But he's seen the tension in her neck, and the way her shoulders barely move at all.

"There are some beautiful tulips over here. I haven't seen them at the palace before this year. Shall we wander while we talk?"

"Please, Princess, lead the way." Melody gestures for Lia to proceed. Elliot goes to walk with her, but Melody throws out an arm to hold him back, waiting until she is five steps ahead to follow.

"You know," Lia says, "Elliot once he told me he could catch at least five fish, and yet, there were less than five at the end, were there not?" She looks at him, a delightful smile on her face. It would be truly awful to lean forward and press his lips to hers. It would probably get him thrown out of here so fast he wouldn't know what hit him, but God, does he want to.

Melody gasps. "You went fishing?!"

Lia smiles. "We did. I caught four," she stage-whispers. Elliot realizes she's not lying; she did catch four fish. And Melody knew nothing about it. Not from him, anyway. Aliyah is casually talking about him to a member of the public (his sister, but it *counts*) about being with him privately. Also, she knows he's not great at math, even if her reasoning is flawed. It's not a fair trial when he had someone that looked like her next to him being utterly charming. But, if she knows he doesn't need to look over Melody's proposal, then she wants it for another reason.

She wants it to look at it. His knees shake.

"Oh my God." Melody laughs. "I can't believe Father taught you all those tricks just for you to be rendered useless because you think Aliyah is too pretty."

"You can stop talking at any time, you know," Elliot replies, leaning forward until they're almost face to face.

Melody rolls her eyes. "How boring." She pulls out her phone to take some photos of the tulips.

"You have to be nice to me, or I'm not giving Lia your proposal."

"I do not—wait," she says, turning back to the Princess. "What?"

Aliyah smiles, her eyes flitting between him and Melody like she's enjoying a tennis match. "I shall look at it, when it is ready."

"You will?"

"I will."

"You are my favorite person my brother has ever spoken to."

Aliyah laughs again. "Why, thank you. I think."

If Melody weren't being embarrassing on purpose, he'd be over the moon with how this afternoon is going. Elliot has never introduced a love interest to his family. Melody is protective, even if she needn't be, and his mom is terrifying to everyone around her. But Melody is the hard one to please. If she's winding people up, she likes them. Melody pulls a metallic stick out of her bag; he wonders how she got through security with something that resembles a weapon. Elliot realizes, then, that Aliyah's guards are nowhere to be seen.

Aliyah gasps, her eyes wide. "Is that *the* lipstick?"

Melody smiles so brightly Elliot thinks she might split her cheeks. She holds it out, spinning the case in her palm. "Yeah! You like it?"

Aliyah nods, inspecting the lipstick as though it's a precious gem like the ones around her neck, albeit one she dare not touch. "They are beautiful. I wanted to try the red, but I cannot get a hold of it. They say the color is not 'sophisticated' enough for the palace. It looks flawless on you, though," she says with a light groan.

Melody smiles. "You can have it!"

"Oh, no..." Aliyah holds her hands high like she's forcing candy off a baby.

"You may as well save yourself the time and take it," Elliot replies, crossing his arms over his chest. Aliyah looks over at him, and he wishes she'd never stop. "She won't give up until you do."

She takes it from Melody with a small smile and slips it into a discrete pocket in the side of her dress. Melody misses the movement because she's immediately back to taking a photo of

PERFECTLY CANDID

the flowers, but if she'd seen the move, she would have lost her mind at this dress having pockets.

"Would you like me to take a photo of the two of you?" Aliyah asks, as Melody moves to take a selfie that includes the roses climbing the stones beside her.

"Lia loves a candid," Elliot says, without really thinking. He knows it to be true. Aliyah looks at him like she had no idea he remembered anything about her. As if he doesn't have a notebook full of information about her just waiting to be used. As if he's not wearing this long-sleeved top even though it's hot out because her eyes linger on his shoulders whenever he wears it.

In an instant, Melody has her phone up, capturing photos of the way Aliyah frowns at him, the way he gazes at her. Then, quickly, he moves to stand in front of her.

"You can't just take photos of the Princess, Mel," Elliot hisses. He's not even technically sure if she's not allowed; there's probably protocols in place, though. What he does know is that Aliyah doesn't like it. She likes to be asked things before people take a piece of her.

Melody shoves her phone down by her side. "Sorry! I thought you meant you wanted one." Aliyah just laughs, a light sound that works its way into his mind.

"It is alright. You can take a photo if you like." She shrugs. "I think everyone else has already. I am sure you will be much more flattering than they were."

Melody throws her head back in disbelief. "You've never taken a bad photo in your life. The media will try because they are truly the worst and they dislike any confident woman, but you don't have a bad angle, Princess." Aliyah smiles, a light blush over her cheeks as she tucks her hair behind her ear. "Let's take one together?" Melody asks.

"Sure."

"Can we recreate your infamous 'the Princess hates us' photo?" Elliot smiles, and Aliyah laughs, a true laugh that settles the thumping of Elliot's heart. He's not sure what Melody is referring to. Maybe he should have gotten a better education from Melody the other day. Then Aliyah stands next to his sister, and they throw peace signs in the air, Melody pouts, and Aliyah smiles so wide she looks like a Cheshire cat. Elliot takes a photo of them taking a photo.

"I thought we weren't allowed to take photos!" Melody shouts. Welp. Caught in the act.

"I said *you* weren't!" he replies, backing up as Melody stalks toward him and snatches his phone. Aliyah follows behind. Melody gasps, and he regrets getting his phone out at all.

"How many photos of Lia do you have, Ellie?"

Elliot swallows, watching as Aliyah tilts her head to the side. Melody stops her advance, but Aliyah takes over, her eyes narrowing as she backs him up against a tree. It's not too close that anyone would think she was about to touch him, but naturally, that's all he's thinking about. She's probably close enough that if anyone got a photo from the right angle, they could spin it. It wouldn't be that much of a stretch to say that a palace gardener was fawning over the Princess, though.

"You have photographs of me?"

She must know that he does. She was there at the lake. But he supposes he does have others.

"Uh..."

"Elliot," she says, with a hint of amusement on her face. He looks down at her. "How many?"

"A few. You look really beautiful today."

She blushes, and he can't be the first person to have mentioned it. "You think so?"

"More precious than those jewels on your neck." Aliyah's eyes drop to his lips, and then she blinks, backing up slightly.

"I should go," she says quickly.

"Lia."

"I have already pushed the boundaries today," she replies, throwing a smile on the end of her sentence. "It was lovely to meet you, Melody."

Melody thanks her, but Elliot can't concentrate on what she's saying. Is Aliyah going to get in trouble for coming to see them? Before he can figure out a way to ask her, she's walking across the grass, back toward the palace. He watches her, of course, as he always will. Maybe tomorrow, she'll look at him.

"Why didn't you tell her you love her?!"

"It's not something you shout, Mel. Not when she's the Princess." He sighs. "I need—God, I just need to see her alone." Elliot thinks he might never get the chance. He's going to be resigned to watching her leave, watching her eat, watching her, and never being with her. Her hair blows in the light wind, and she waves to the groups of people that have been ogling her this entire time, and he misses her already.

And then the unspeakable happens. She turns back and looks directly at him. Melody will say she's looking at both of them, but he knows that's not true, because the smile she only ever gives him is plastered over her face. It distracts him long enough that he doesn't notice Melody racing across the gardens.

Aliyah walks away, enjoying the warmth of the sun on her shoulders. She doesn't want to leave, but she's already done enough damage by being here at all. She prepares herself for the cell in the dungeons that awaits her this evening. Hopefully it's just a small crime—being out when her parents have not allowed it. Being out in public this close to her birthday without a man on her arm.

"Your Highness," Melody calls out. It's not a shout—she's not that far away because these heels are making it far too difficult to walk through the grass with any decorum or dignity. When Aliyah turns, Melody is almost over to her, her panting suggesting she ran.

"Is everything alright?" Lia looks for Elliot, but he's standing under the tree, a frown on his face like Melody didn't tell him she was leaving.

"Ellie is getting lunch," Melody says, her hand on her chest. "Well, he's supposed to be, but he's probably still standing stock-still under that tree."

"He is, yes. Is he okay?"

"You and Ellie are friends, right?" Melody asks, like she already knows the answer. As if this isn't the actual question she's asking. "Because he likes this girl he won't tell me about—someone from the palace—and I'm wondering if maybe you will spill?" Aliyah blinks, but she has no time to respond before Melody is talking again. "Because he told me once that he went to touch her—like her hand or something, I do *not* need to hear about any other touching." She shudders. Aliyah flinches at the thought of him touching someone. "Anyway, he went to touch her, and she flinched." Melody looks at her. Aliyah can't remember a time when she didn't want Elliot to touch her, but she supposes she could have flinched, right at the start.

"So, if the person he likes liked him back, they might need to make a move. If you knew who she was, maybe you could…"

Aliyah looks over at him. He stands there, his arms crossed against his chest, and Aliyah wants to tell him she never meant to give him the idea that she didn't want his touch. She runs her hand over her arm, chasing the feel of his fingertips as if he's ever touched her at all.

"He's always looking at you," Melody says, apparently deciding to drop the "other girl" act. Aliyah wonders how much he has told her. "Not in a princess way. Just in a 'he has no other choice' kind of way. You are there, so why wouldn't he be looking at you?"

Aliyah blinks, taken aback. Should she tell Melody she's in love with her brother and they have barely spoken beyond today? Should she tell her she's been waiting for him to say *anything*? *Sorry. I miss you. I love you.*

"He didn't tell me anything," Melody says, a small smile on her face. "He told me he likes a girl. Well, actually, he told me he likes a *person*. He was very specific in not giving any facts away, but I knew it was you the moment you turned up. His entire face changed; his body pulls to you. I know he can be difficult…" Aliyah frowns. She's never thought he was difficult. "Believe me, I shared a room with him growing up. And I know he fucked up. I know you probably both did a little bit, if you don't mind me saying so, Your Highness, even though I don't have any idea what went down. But you are impossible to see if you don't want to be, Princess, and even harder to talk to, and I know he's putting himself anywhere he can where you might see him. So, maybe, if you miss him as much as he misses you, you could see him at the greenhouse tonight? Around eight. If you want, that is..."

"The greenhouse," she whispers, her brows furrowed.

"Only if you wanted." Melody shrugs. "I am going to go back and probably be chastised, but it was truly lovely to meet you."

"It was lovely to meet you as well," Aliyah replies, letting Melody's words spin around in her mind. She knew he must have been on the run with her yesterday for a reason, but then, he never said what the reason was. Is he working in the dining hall just to see her? Melody curtseys and spins.

"I mean it," Aliyah says, finally remembering how her voice works. "Irrespective of what happens with Elliot, I would like to see your plan."

"You got it, Your Highness."

CHAPTER TWENTY-ONE

ALIYAH DOESN'T REGRET GOING to the open day. She doesn't regret shaking hands and smiling at people she doesn't know. She doesn't regret the dress she wore, even if she did change the moment she got to her room. She doesn't regret any of it. Even as the thick towel is laid over her face, the sarcastic remark she had on the tip of her tongue nowhere to be seen as the water is poured over and over. It's time to fight back in a whole different way. She's not sure who's holding her down this time. The last guard wasn't strong enough or fast enough to dodge her flailing legs. She caught him in the groin as she was choking on the freezing-cold water.

Now, it's someone else. Someone from the old guard, probably. Someone she's known from childhood perhaps. Maybe they're pouring the water. She can't think because she's drowning. She's so sure she's drowning today. She was *about to drown* when the towel is pulled away and Aliyah is able to turn her head to the side. She coughs up an endless stream of water, bile, and something that resembles the last of any happiness she may have left.

It's been hours. For a while, she thought she'd gotten away with only having to endure the makeshift torture chamber. She thought there was a chance she would just sit here in her pajamas and try not to freeze to death. God, what she'd give for a little hindsight. No one ever knocked on her bedroom door, not without the birds flying away and the guards disappearing at the sounds of her mother's heels clicking on the tiles. Maybe she should have put up a fight. A guard might have seen her then. That wouldn't matter, not if history is anything to go by, but the sounds of a screaming princess would be hot gossip, and Elliot would know about it soon. Lia's not sure what he would do, if anything, but she'd feel less alone if he knew.

Now, the tank top and shorts she'd been wearing in her room were well and truly soaked, and she can't even be embarrassed about how much of her body is on show to men she never wanted to see her. Not now, as she heaves in a rabid breath. Her eyes, throat, and nose burn with the violent irritation. But then her head is shoved back, and the towel is over her face all over again.

The scream is lodged in her throat, being forced back by the onslaught of water that just won't stop. They hadn't even bothered to say anything that time. Maybe eight rounds ago, they said something about marriage. Something about a ball. *Something*.

It feels endless. The stopping and starting and the pleading that she never manages to get out. Aliyah survived it once. She's survived it all before—the water, the aftermath, the torment—but every new trip under the flow of never-ending water has her convinced she may not survive this time.

The only thing that flows through her mind is Elliot. Is he okay? How will he find out? Will it be in the common room on the television? Will he wait for her in the dining hall, only to find she never shows? Is he waiting for her now? God, of all the ways they could have her killed, Aliyah is sure drowning would be the most miserable. It will be planned, of course. Take something she loves and turn it into her nightmare. If she makes it out of here, she'll never see the lake again, let alone swim in it. Her hair will also stay straight for longer, because the last time they did this, she couldn't stand under the shower properly for weeks.

She's choking again, just about ready to give it all up, when the hands on her are gone. The jug of water falls, hitting the table next to her head, then toppling to the floor. Aliyah wonders if someone's there to save her, but she should have known better. Her hands are cuffed behind her, so she has to force herself onto her side and use that momentum to rid her face of the towel, choking, choking, *choking* all the while.

Her chest burns, her nose drips, and her heart aches as she looks over at her mother.

"You *will* marry him. And you still stay away from that boy, or I will have him killed."

CHAPTER TWENTY-TWO

THE QUEEN'S THREAT ROLLS around in her mind far longer than the fear of water does. Aliyah managed to wash her face in only forty-five minutes today, all the while thinking, does her mother know about Elliot? When she made it back to her bedroom the other night (thankfully, there is a hidden passageway no one but her knows about, so her dripping frame wasn't seen by anyone), Aliyah thought she was bluffing. How would she know? Apart from the boat rides on the lake, and the secret picnics under the trees, and the way Aliyah looks at him every time she has a chance. There's still no concrete proof that she knows who he is. That there is a *him*.

And then Aliyah went to breakfast, Lucian sitting a seat closer to her, and Elliot was nowhere to be seen. A fluke, possibly. He was not present at lunch either, and Aliyah's stomach hit the floor. So, she went to the greenhouse—the place she was supposed to be at eight o'clock a few nights ago—but he wasn't there. She ran and she ran, but he is nowhere. Not the dungeons, not the trees, not the lake, and it's been *days* and she can't focus. So, she does the only other thing she can think of. She visits Anna.

"Here, sweetie," Anna says, placing the tea in front of her.

"Thank you," Aliyah replies. She doesn't like the sound of her own voice, so she shakes her head, willing the heartbreak to leave through any means necessary.

"Still not fixed it, huh?" Anna asks, sitting down on an armchair.

It takes Aliyah longer than it should to sit down. Every time Aliyah turns up here, she's pulled in two different directions. One, this place is her home. The small cottage on the very edge of the castle grounds, surrounded by tall walls that Anna has lined with trailing flowers. She's lived here for years. Longer than she would have if Aliyah wasn't here. Longer than she would have if Aliyah had anyone else at all. But the other part knows Aliyah needs to let her go. The only reason Anna stayed here is for her. But Anna's nearing retirement, and Aliyah knows she's desperate to go to the beach, to see sights she hasn't seen in years.

"I am not sure it can be fixed."

"You love him?" Anna asks. Aliyah has spent the last few weeks trying not to think about the word *love*. She's been away from him for longer than she was ever with him, and she's not sure she's ever actually with him at all. How can she say she cares for someone this much when she never gave her entire self to them? It's funny, in a messed-up, life-altering way, that he knows her better than anyone else. Better than Anna, even if she practically raised her.

"I miss him," she whispers. "I miss him like I would miss a limb. I feel it in my bones." She huffs. It's embarrassing to admit how badly she wants him, but she knows Anna would never judge her for it.

"And does he miss you too?"

She thinks about it. They haven't spoken in weeks. The most they have spoken was at the open day. He did ask to see her—well, Melody set it up—but naturally, life had other plans. He watches her at breakfast, and he makes her food she'll eat at dinner, and he's always there. For her. He misses her too. Except, suddenly, he's not. And now, all she really knows is that she can't drag him into this life. He doesn't know what he would be getting into. At best, her mother is bluffing, and Aliyah will see Elliot at dinner tonight. At worst is a fate she can't fathom.

So, this is all they can be. That will have to do. She will have to survive on the small interactions they have. When she runs around the gardens, hopefully, he will still look at her. He's always looking at her. When she sleeps, he's always in her dreams. When she wants to throw herself from the castle roof, he's the only thing that stops her.

And he'll get over her when he leaves in a few months anyway.

"Speak to him," Anna begs. Lia looks over at her, cradling her teacup between her hands. "He can't come to you. You are the Princess."

"That is the problem," she mutters. Anna scowls at her.

"You will always be a princess."

"Well—"

"Don't even think about it," Anna stresses. Aliyah doesn't talk about abdication all that often, and especially not with Anna. "You are a princess whether you like it or not. Abdication won't stop that. It will only stop the changes you are so capable of making."

Aliyah swallows a sip of tea that's slightly too hot. The burn helps.

"But Elliot can't just stroll up to you," Anna says, her eyes kind as Aliyah looks at her, begging her for an answer. "Sweetie, look what happened last time. If you want him to talk to you, you need to give him the option."

"It is not that. I could do all of that again," she whispers. "If it meant talking to him, I would—I could do it, but I think mother knows, and I—I do not know how to save him from her."

"What does that devil-dragon know?"

Aliyah has to be careful with her words. Anna found out she was in the dungeons once and had a heart attack, so she's not about to tell her she almost drowned last night.

"She threatened him, but—I do not know how she knows who he is."

"Did she name him?"

Aliyah shakes her head. "But he was not at breakfast, or lunch. He is nowhere. I think she is bluffing, but I cannot risk it."

"What is your goal?" Anna asks, placing her teacup on the side of the armchair. Aliyah used to think it was so dangerous, the threat of tea falling over the linen cushions. She knows now there are worse things that can happen.

"What do you mean?"

"In life. If you tell Elliot he might be hunted by the grackles that are your parents, what do you want him to do? Stay? And if he stays, are you going to stop talking? Are you going to get married? Will he be King?"

"Elliot would not marry me," Lia replies, the heartbreak evident on her face, if the way Anna's expression softens is anything to go by.

"So, are you hoping to keep him here, secretly? Or..."

The tears do not fall—she makes sure of it—but her throat burns, and her heart feels like it's wrapped in barbed wire. "Oh my God."

"Sweetheart," Anna says, her voice full of motherly warmth, yet it's not the one she wants.

"I have to let him go."

"You are the strongest person I know," Anna replies, a hand warmed by tea against hers. Aliyah wonders if that's true. She wonders how many more jugs of water it will take for her to do what they ask. "You will get through heartbreak."

Aliyah sighs. She doesn't want to cry today. She'll get over him, embarrassingly slowly and probably not all the way, but that's alright. He'll be safe, fine, somewhere away from her. He'll have a family and Christmases and matching pajamas. He'll be happy.

Sometimes, in her bedroom, she pictures him as an old man, swinging on a rocking chair in the gardens, looking right at her. But she doesn't want this life for him. She doesn't want him to have to sit around, watching her get hurt when there's nothing he can do about it. She doesn't want him to have to hide with her. She wants him to be loved out loud, the only way he would ever deserve.

Aliyah clears her throat and changes the subject. "There is a ball."

"Oh, goody," Anna replies, with all the sarcasm she can muster. It's quite a lot. "Who for this time?"

Aliyah rolls her eyes, the ache behind them almost making her wince. "Lucian."

"For fuck's sake," Anna groans, and it always makes Aliyah laugh when she swears. "That man is old enough to by *my* husband. How your parents even entertain the idea of you marrying him, I will never know."

Aliyah hums. "He came last night. His delightful presence is here for a fortnight."

PERFECTLY CANDID

Anna sighs. "Forever wouldn't be enough time to find something about him to love."

Aliyah wonders if that's true. If she's forced to marry him, will she truly never find something to like? Something to entertain herself?

"You are not to marry him," Anna says, leaning forward. Her hair is whiter than it is brown now, curling above her ears in a way only old white ladies manage. She'll give it three years before she has a blue rinse.

Her parents could force her to marry Lucian or Dorian by sheer force of will, but legally, she could marry whomever she wanted. An idea that has been playing at the back of her mind ever since she saw Elliot under the plum tree. It would never work; she knows that. Fairy tales don't happen in real life. She lives in a tower like a princess. She feels alone like a princess. But she was never going to be saved like a princess. She doesn't need him. She would never need him. She didn't want him to save her, but she does *want* him. The thought of abdication has never weighed on her mind as much as it has these past few weeks.

"I do not think I have that much of a choice," she says with a sigh. She won't find comfort with Lucian, that much she knows. But if it were all different, if she was free to love Elliot in public, he wouldn't marry her. His thoughts on the monarchy are clear. They always have been. Besides, yes, he looks sad at dinner, but he hasn't told her he loves her either way. She supposes he might not. Just because she fell in love beneath the plum trees in an embarrassingly short amount of time doesn't mean he did. Aliyah has read that being hit with a barge pole is less painful than heartache, but here she is, heartbroken, and it feels like she's been hit by a barge pole all the same.

"Besides, he is bringing Dorian."

Anna scoffs. "That cockroach." Her concern is evident between her eyebrows, even if she tries to act nonchalant for Aliyah's sake. Dorian has always been the cruelest person Aliyah knows—even crueler than his father—but he's never physically hurt her. She knows he's been waiting for the green light, a light which is now permanently on. She wonders if they'll kill her before her birthday and come up with a suitable alternative. Aliyah assumes the only reason she's made it this far is because they haven't figured out a replacement for her yet.

Aliyah looks out the window at the clear skies so she won't have to look at the hurt on Anna's face.

"I had better go," Aliyah says, taking hers and Anna's teacups to the sink. "While it is not raining."

"Talk to him," Anna says, following her to the front door. "To Elliot."

"What good would that do?" Aliyah asks. How is she supposed to look him in the eye and tell him she loves him but she needs him to leave? She knows him well enough now to know he never would.

Anna rests her hand against Aliyah's forearm. "Please. For me."

"I am already sponsoring a bloat of hippopotamuses for you," Aliyah says with a smile. It will never be enough; she knows that. Anna gave up her entire life to ensure Aliyah wasn't here alone, over nothing but a hairstyle.

"He deserves to know, even if you want him gone."

"He will get over me fast enough that he will not even remember what I say."

"Lia."

She sighs. "I will try. I promise."

"Good," Anna replies, all but shoving her out the door. "Wear something scandalous to the ball."

Aliyah rolls her eyes with a laugh. She waves to Anna and ignores the way her heart aches as the door closes before she's at the gate. It's ridiculous how safe Elliot made her feel. It's not as though anything would happen between the stone patio steps in Anna's lawn and the heavy wooden gate; she would have told Anna to go inside before she let all the heat out anyway. Just another way Elliot has solidified himself in her life, and he probably doesn't even know it.

Her fingers linger against the flowers that have bloomed while she sat in her room. The roses are budding, the foxgloves deepening in color, and she's missed so much on her runs. She's never focused on anything other than ridding herself of the thoughts in her head. The flower beds in front of her bedroom are still her favorites, after all this time. Cosmos and nigella bloom so beautifully, and she's lucky they are so abundant this year.

The weather is about to turn again, so she runs. Aliyah always enjoys running with her cloak on because she feels like a character from a book with the way it flows out behind her. She just forgets how long they are, and how muddy the bottom is going to be by the time she makes it home. Aliyah's shoes pound against the limestone path, the light color turning dark with small splatters of rain as she comes up to a blockage. It's been raining for *weeks*. It's the wettest month Aliyah can remember, which is why she should have remembered that this path back to the castle always becomes waterlogged.

"Bugger," she mutters, when she sees the large puddle gathered in the dip in the path. Every year, when it rains for more than four seconds, the puddle stretches to either side of the path, creating a meter-long pile of water. Sometimes, when the children are here, she lets them jump in it during lunch. Lia could turn around and go the other way, but that would take too long, and she thinks it's about to start raining properly again. She avoided the rain this morning, and now, as the first drop hits her skin, it feels too much like water. Too much like she can't get out of it. Too much like she's being held down.

If she had thought about it for longer than three seconds, she would have run the other way—the quicker way—but she was hoping to see Elliot. She's not sure she would be able to speak to him properly right now, not with the threat of the ball or the leftover water lingering in her throat. Not now she has to tell him to please leave. There's something about his face that makes her want to tell him everything and anything. But she can't. She won't put that on him. She won't tell him he's in danger, just that he needs to leave.

But merely seeing a glimpse of his face would have been enough to see her through until tomorrow. She just wants to know that he's safe. That he's alive. That he's here. Alas, he wasn't there, and now, she's heading toward a muddy puddle the size of a small lake. Could she leap it? Maybe. She stops just in front of it, staring at herself in the reflection. Her face looks weird to her, and it has nothing to do with the ripples on the surface. The raindrops fall, blurring her reflection, and she sighs. At least she isn't quite wet yet. She's about to bend, pick the back of her cloak up, and risk the shoes, but before she can, she feels a slight pull. When she looks down, Elliot has gathered the material in his hand.

"Allow me," he says, his chest heaving like he ran to her. Though she guesses she's out of breath by his mere presence, so she can't call him out on it.

He stands in the puddle, the bridge of his foot sticking out of the water just slightly. He's wearing Wellingtons, which is a *much* better idea than her shoes. He holds out his hand, and she takes it without having to think. He hasn't got gloves on, and the heat from his fingers makes her heart stutter. Or maybe it's the way he's looking at her. Maybe it's the sound of his voice. Maybe it's everything.

He looks tired. Still unfairly beautiful, but as tired as she feels. Like it's under his skin. She wonders if his insomnia is playing up. She wonders if her mother has gotten to him. She wonders if he'd tell her if she asked. She wonders what he'd do if she told him she missed him. His hand is softer than it looks, and she's greedy with it, rubbing her thumb over the back of his knuckles. She steps on his foot, a simple movement that gets her to the other side completely dry, even as the rain falls around them.

Everything in her settles, just for a moment, as she looks at him. His eyes are trained on hers, yet she feels like he's cataloging every minuscule movement she makes.

"Elliot," she whispers.

He bows his head as her hand lingers against his. "Your Highness."

"Thank you," she replies. She wants to pull him with her, to take him to her room. To keep him in her life. But he's stopped walking like this is as far as he goes. Still, he doesn't let go. His arm stretches out in front of her, hers behind, and she holds onto his fingers for as long as she can. The stretch of her arm feels like the pull of her heart, like everything is going to snap if he dares to drop her hand. She can feel her brow is furrowed, her jaw slack. She'd be surprised if there's a single person in this kingdom that would look at her now and not know she's in the worst pain of her life.

"Are you hurt?" she asks. The next raindrop hits her when his hand falls away, and she wonders if it's reasonable for the weather to be out to get her too. The rain comes thick and fast, a downpour that feels fitting for life right now.

"What?" he replies, his voice barely louder than the rain, even though she can tell he's shouting. "I can't—Lia, I can't hear you."

"Elliot?" Her voice is frantic. She can barely see him through the sudden torrential downpour. The panic of not being able to get the water off her face works its way up her spine. She needs to tell him to be careful, she needs to tell him to go but she—she can't—she—*the water is on her face.* It's on her face and she can't breathe. Oh no. She needs to get out of here, with him. She needs to talk to him. Her hands move before she can think about it, before she can overthink it. She tries to hold onto his arm. "Elliot."

"Princess," he replies, and she spins, her hair sticking to the side of her face. He steps closer to her, like he has no issue seeing through the rain—like his mind isn't as messed up as hers. Because he's not terrified of water. Not yet. His hand is light against her forearm.

"Please," he shouts, taking a small step forward. His eyes travel across her entire face, and she feels like he's taking something—she doesn't know what it is, but she'd give it to him anyway. She takes a breath. *Hurt him to save him.*

"Can we—"

"I do not wish to see you anymore," she shouts over the downpour. She wants to ask him if he read the letter. If he forgives her. If he'll forgive her for this next part. But her hands shake as the water forces its way into her eyes, and she can't breathe, so she doesn't.

His face and his hand drop. "What?"

"I am over this," she replies, clenching her hands into fists to stop them from shaking. "I am over you." Then she turns, runs up the stairs she ruined everything on last time, and flees into the palace.

CHAPTER TWENTY-THREE

The hot water from the shower runs down his body, and Elliot does everything he can not to imagine it's her touch. Ever since Elliot has been here, Lia has been on his mind. From dirty thoughts of her when he's in the shower, to wondering how her day is when he's working. And he's missed her tremendously. The one moment he got to see her alone wasn't enough. He fears it will never be enough. Yet, it's done what he wanted; it's settled his heart for just a moment. She's okay. She looks tired, and maybe like she's getting over an illness, but she's alive, and he's seen her, and that's all he needed. So, yes, even as he fights it, the way the water warms him does nothing to keep her from his mind as much as he wants it to.

For the past few weeks, when he's desperately missed her, all his thoughts were on if she was okay. He can barely get the thought of her in the dungeons out of his mind long enough to sleep. If he'd known who she was... he couldn't have stopped it, but he could have been there for her. He could have made her feel less alone. Instead, he's spent the entire time he's known her making sure she knows how much he dislikes her. Even if every fiber of his being wants her closer; wants her to know that she never faltered.

He left his room earlier in the hopes of seeing her outside of dinner, and then he did, and he panicked. She didn't turn up to the greenhouse last night. She doesn't want to see him. Melody the meddler said she had been so clear with her intentions, that if she wanted anything to do with him, she would have been there. But she wasn't, and he wasn't able to get out of bed at all. He didn't go to dinner, and he avoided breakfast like the plague.

Then, he convinced himself he could see her just to say thank you for the open day. But, as he saw her standing by the puddle, his thoughts turned to telling her he missed her. He found himself wanting to ask her to come back. But she never wanted that, and it's taking him an upsetting amount of time to realize it. So, all he did was stand there, feeling the weight of her hand in his. If he knew all it took to touch her, to feel her pulse beneath his fingers, was a puddle, he would have thrown bucket after bucket of water outside her bedroom the moment he arrived, then stood outside, desperately waiting for her to search for his hand. He wishes he had longer to hold her earlier, that the rain hadn't washed away everything he wanted to say, but she looked sad. Too sad. Too tired, too different to how he's seen her before. She's already told him how she feels by not turning up yesterday, and again today. That doesn't mean it's not hard for her. He needs to remember this is what she wanted.

Now, it's five past six the next evening, and Elliot's thinking about Lia. He's always waiting for a time to be thinking about her. He sits at his bedroom window, waiting to see if she'll run past again. Even though he knows the likelihood is small, he'll spend most of his time waiting to see her walk across the courtyard. There's not much more he can do now. Maybe it's not in the stars for them to be anything other than people who knew each other once upon a time. Maybe she's supposed to linger in the back of his mind for the rest of his life.

Elliot wipes the dust from his bedroom windowsill, and he throws his laundry in the hamper. It's taken him weeks to clean his room, and he'll ignore the judgment for his lack of ability to be a functioning member of society. He goes to work, waits under the plum trees, goes to grab dinner, traces the layout to the palace, and eavesdrops on Lucian's plans, then he lays in bed until two a.m., when he goes to check the dungeons. She hasn't been there, thank God. It's a weird feeling, though—every night he hopes she's not there, and yet his chest sinks when he crawls on the floor to check, because he hasn't seen her at all. He would never want her to be hurt, but he doesn't know how she is, and it's slowly killing him.

PERFECTLY CANDID

He sighs, buttoning the bottom of his duvet cover. Melody had a go at him when she called him last night. She thinks the stack of dirty dishes, the unopened letters, and the general mess are because he's disgusting, and she told him she was always the one who did the majority of cleaning when they shared a bedroom. He didn't have the heart to tell her he's not sure how he's supposed to function when Aliyah could be anywhere. She could be hurt, she could be sad, she could be *anything*.

He didn't have it in him to tell her he's heartbroken. So, he cleaned as Melody talked to him and told him that her proposal is finished and she fired Marcus. He smiled as she said she was emailing it to him and asked if he could give it to Aliyah. Maybe he could sneak it to her at the ball tomorrow? She doesn't want to see him again, but she did say she'd look at Mel's proposal just the other day. If she doesn't have him thrown out for simply turning up.

But then Mel had to go—she had another work proposal to get through before she took time off to go to the beach with his mom—and now, the stack of letters judge him from their place on his nightstand. Elliot always thought getting letters was the most exciting thing when he was seven and got a notice from the opticians that he needed an eye test. Now he's older, he knows nothing good ever comes from a white letter with his name written on the front.

He sighs, opening the first and immediately discarding it because he's not sure how telemarketing manages to get through palace security, but you can never underestimate the power of a large corporation and their need to send someone a fifty-cents-off-cupcakes coupon. When he gets down to the last one, he's over it, but he twists it in his hands all the same.

The envelope is different, weighty, with a velvet-like texture. There's a wax stamp on the back, and he runs his finger over it. A welcome letter from the palace, perhaps? He vaguely remembers getting this weeks ago, and he thought it was hilarious that they'd send a welcome letter the same day someone tried to throw him in the dungeons for daring to talk to Lia. The seal suggests it's from the Princess, but he would expect her to welcome those on the scholarship she started. Elliot's not sure he can read it without a minor breakdown. He's not sure how to read something everyone else also gets from her, not when he's been so spoiled before.

Curiosity and the way he misses her words get to him in the end, and he carefully breaks the seal, placing the orange wax with an "A" perfectly etched into it on his nightstand next to her knife. He takes a deep breath and smells a sweet, floral scent. The paper opens, and a flattened, browned daisy chain falls out. The letter is handwritten, the daisies dead.

Elliot,

It is Lia.

Elliot's hand shakes, and his throat burns, and he thinks he might pass out. How long has he had this? Her handwriting is beyond fancy, yet it feels entirely like her. He wants to show her his, how he really does write her name in a heart on the pages of his notebook.

He blinks the tears from his eyes. He needs to know what she needed to tell him. Perhaps it is asking him to stay away, perhaps not. But she deserves to have all her thoughts out in the open. Elliot clears his throat, steadies himself, and reads.

I suppose I should start with my reasoning for this letter. I hope it finds you well, by the way. I always hope you are well.

My full name is Aliyah Giorgia Juliet Panimiro. The Princess of Iledale, I suppose is the long title.

Please, do not throw this letter away just yet. I am sorry I did not tell you sooner. I thought that I might lose you, and I suppose that should have always been your choice. I was selfish with the information because I did not want you to go. I realize now that is not up to me. Life does not always turn out the way one had hoped, but still, I am hoping for you.

I am not here to give you my best qualities, nor tell you why you should not hate the monarchy. Those are your thoughts, and I will respect them however this may end. You will receive no backlash from me. I will leave you be.

What I will do is tell you why I took so long to tell you. Why I am telling you in this letter, as opposed to telling you under the plum trees we were sitting under just earlier tonight. If this letter finds your room, I was supposed to tell you on our ride, and I have not. Maybe your face distracted me, or maybe I was just too scared.

He's had this letter since they went riding? That was before he even saw her as a princess for the first time. God, it was before the greenhouse. Elliot squeezes his eyes closed until they are fuzzy with stars, then he reads again.

I have been here since I was four. I think. The dates are a little blurry. Life has always been a little difficult, but I coped, as one does in a palace with anything they needed at their disposal. In all the time I was here, I did not realize how my loneliness has become a part of who I am. It has altered me as a person down to my bones. It was never something I could pinpoint, never something I remember happening, and yet, it follows me like a shadow. And then you came along, my darling, and everything changed.

I suppose it makes more sense to talk about what I do know. For the entirety of my life that I can remember, I have been here, and no time has come close to how happy I am right now. With you. You make me feel alive and safe and like I can be myself. As though I could tell you the darkest parts of my mind, and you would be there anyway. As though I could tell you my worst traits, and you would never use them against me.

Elliot jolts, the tears tracking down his face. She trusted him, and moments later, he did exactly what she was so sure he never would. He hurt her, like everyone else. He looks away, just for a moment, to see the rain against his window. It's slowing. He wonders if she's running tonight. He wonders if she's running because of him. He deserves the pain that comes from this letter. She poured all her thoughts onto paper for him, and she thinks he's ignored it entirely.

Even if you may feel like you do not know me at all, I am sorry. I am so sorry I did not tell you right away. I should have, and there is no excuse for how long I kept it from you. I hope you can come to understand why it took me so long, and why I was cowardly enough to put it on paper instead of saying it in person. I am not sure what I would do if I had to see the way you may hate me over the face that brings me such joy.

J.S. JASPER

I have never wanted to talk about my being a princess as little as I do in this letter, because I am terrified. If life were fair, my royal standing would not matter, but I suppose worse things have broken a heart before. I know that you do not care for the monarchy. I know you do not feel like you ever could, and I am here anyway, asking if you would consider making an exception... for me.

If you cannot, I do not blame you. If you have to leave anyway, know that I have never had a bad thought about you. You have always been the sunshine on my darkest days, and I will adore you until the end of time.

To be perfectly candid, you are my favorite thing; the absolute best of all things. The most wonderful person I know.

I hope to see you soon, and if not, please know you are the loss of my life.

All my love, as always.

Lia

(PS: I know the daisy chain probably feels like a bribe. That is because it is.)

CHAPTER TWENTY-FOUR

YESTERDAY EVENING, AFTER THE rain, the sun had a warmth to it that it hadn't had for some time. Aliyah was a fool and convinced herself it meant summer was truly on the way. Instead, this afternoon, her curtains blow with strong winds. Aliyah has spent the day camped out in the shelter of her bedroom. The wind was too strong to sit on the balcony and watch Elliot working. He's doing something to the flower beds closest to her room, but she can't shout and ask him what it is. Does he need help? Does he want a drink? No, she made sure he knew she didn't want him; she can't backtrack on it now. It wouldn't be fair.

Aliyah has never wanted to go to a ball less than she does right now, and she's not sure if it's because of who is attending, or the fact that he is not. The orange curtains blow more furiously, and she wonders if she's due a change of color. For a moment, she's nervous she missed Elliot leaving. She's supposed to be going down to the dressing room, but she's waiting to get a glimpse of him. He might work late tonight. He might leave tomorrow. She wonders if her saying she doesn't want him anymore has any actual effect on his life. If he thinks, fine, he'll work here until his contract is up anyway.

Aliyah is not sure what she is supposed to do when he leaves. When she wakes up and doesn't see him below her. It's a fate that doesn't bear thinking about, even if she knows it's best for him. The same creak of the greenhouse doors seeps into her mind, pushing out any other thoughts. She rushes over, peering from behind her curtains. He's there, locking the doors under the heavy battering of rain. She wants to invite him in, to run him a warm bath, to make sure he's getting enough sleep, but she cannot.

She sighs, watching him go, then groans, knowing she, too, must leave. The walk to the dressing room is not long, but it is lonely all the same. There are tuts and scornful looks when she arrives. She thinks it's fair, but still, rude.

"Is there an issue, ladies?" Aliyah asks, sitting in the chair and crossing her legs. She pulls at the cuffs of her sweater.

"No, Your Highness," they respond, a bow following their words. Lia smiles, but it's fake. They might know that, but she is beyond caring what people in this palace think of her. She rolls her neck, avoiding her reflection in the mirror. She has spent an upsetting amount of her life making sure she liked what was in the mirror. Now, she's terrified to look. It's not the under-eye bags; it's not the way her hair needed doing days ago but she can't face standing under the shower; it's not even the way she's been pulling at her lips. She thinks if she looks in the mirror, she'll see just how heartbroken she is. How the effects of not having Elliot in her life have been seared into her skin.

So, she asks the makeup ladies to move the mirror, saying she wants a dramatic reveal at the end. They giggle with glee, taking photos and videos of the transformation.

Aliyah spins the ring on her pinkie finger until the skin is raw, but it does the trick. By the time her finger is aching, her makeup is on, her hair has been twisted back into place, and Aliyah slips into the black silk dress her mother picked out for her with ease. She always thought she would have to be beaten down; that wearing gowns and jewelry to a ridiculously over-the-top ball with people who don't even talk to her would only happen if she couldn't bear to fight anymore. It never occurred to her that her mind would be preoccupied with something else. Some*one* else. The dress is trivial now. It deserves no space in her mind, not when she could be thinking about him.

She tries to ignore how revealing the dress is. How it sits across her chest, the arms tight against her upper arm, her entire décolletage on show. It's not for her. It's all for the gaze of men she will never want. Her stomach turns knowing that Dorian is here. She

PERFECTLY CANDID

shakes her head and thanks the seamstress for buttoning her up. Aliyah wonders if she'll always be afforded this kind of grace with the clothing she wears.

In the time it takes to apply her mascara, the weather turns from unpleasant to catastrophic, with deep gray skies and rain so heavy it sounds like the windows are about to shatter. She leaves the bottom half of her braids down today. It's been so long since she's worn her hair up, but she needs the security they give her. Besides, she knows her mother will hate it, and it brings her some comfort. If they help to hide the possible bruises she thinks she has on her shoulder blades, that's just good planning.

The walk down to the ballroom feels like she's walking through a cave, the walls getting closer and closer until she's not going to be able to breathe, yet the corridor is almost twenty feet wide. There are people behind her, her train is being held, her bag is in someone else's hands, and yet, she's never felt so alone in all her life. She takes in a breath, waiting for her announcement at an event she doesn't want to go to. The sound of rain on the large stained-glass windows makes her breath choppier than she wants.

There's no time to turn around. There's no time to run away. This night is the beginning of the rest of her life, and she can't breathe. They're going to announce her, she's going to walk in, and no one is going to talk to her. She's going to be stared at, and spoken about, and she'll be alone. And for the first time, she'll care. Elliot's presence makes her care. It is all his fault.

Aliyah knows Lucian is in there. He's her father's lifelong friend, which should tell everyone in the palace that he's decades too old for her. (And that's not even the number-one reason she doesn't want to be around him—it barely makes the top five.) Alas, King Stephen has been pushing Lord Feathermore to become King since her sister died. But there has always been a backup. A worse fate than to lie next to someone you despise. He comes in the form of Dorian.

Aliyah knows Lucian is the better option, and that's by a minimal margin. She might stay alive for a few years rather than days. She might outlive him. The only solace Aliyah has right now is that *they* cannot choose. Lucian thought he would be fine having his son as the King, but now he's had that power put into his mind, he wants it for himself. Marrying Lucian won't go over well with the public, but the palace could bring that under control. Dorian, however, is barely her senior. He's an attractive man, an easier sell than anything else. He keeps his hatred for her and people who look like her away from the cameras, even though it is ingrained into him, passed through the generations to the point it's practically in his blood. Aliyah has spent her life saying no to these men, but she's not sure how long she has left.

For now, she has a part to play. So, she stands straight, shoving the panic to her feet as the doors open.

Usually, Aliyah would walk in, shake some hands, and admire the sight in front of her. The flowers, the lights, the band. It's usually the best part of a ball. It's harder tonight. With the onslaught of eyes from *his* party. With the unsettling gaze of Dorian on her at every turn, as though he was imagining her with nothing on at all. Of course, Aliyah has been made aware of the physical requirements of any marriage her parents would attempt to throw her into. Dorian reminds her of his rights every time he is close by. His hand lingers against her waist, and she says nothing, because there would be nothing she could do anyway. Not here. Not in front of anyone.

Aliyah looks around, thankful Lucian and Dorian haven't come up to her yet. The word on the grapevine is that they're going to try and "woo" her, the thought of which sends shivers down her spine. The candles are lit, the alcohol flowing, and Elliot stands to the side.

Aliyah clenches her jaw. He's not looking at her. He's talking to someone, another worker. They're smiling, and she thinks, *good*. That's what she wanted. What she needed. And then the girl leaves, and Elliot faces forward. He knows she's here. Everyone knows she's here—she was just announced. But still, he does not look at her. It's exactly what she asked for, yet she feels her heart break in two.

PERFECTLY CANDID

Elliot's knuckles feel bruised with how hard he is squeezing his hands together behind his back. He can't look at her. He can't make this harder for her than it already is. Elliot has replayed her words over and over. *I am over this.* But she must forget he knows her. He knows when she's lying, when she's hiding something from him, when she's hurt. So, she doesn't want him, for reasons he might never know, and he'll do that, for her. He would have walked to the ends of the earth for her. He'll leave her alone if that is what she wants. If that's what she needs. There are plans in place to protect her, whether she likes him or not. His heart can shatter—he'll survive it, he's sure—as long as she's okay. As long as she's happy. He'll do whatever she asks.

Aliyah stands unnaturally still, her champagne glass between her slender fingers. It's entirely possible it will go flat before she moves a muscle. He knows she's looking at him, and his heart is clawing its way out of his chest to get to her. Instead, Elliot does a sterling job of standing on the sidelines while she waits by the dance floor, surrounded by people he's never heard of. Elliot knew from dorm-room discussions that balls are really nothing more than men trying their luck with the Princess. That she'll dance and entertain people who would never deserve her. But now, her jaw holds all her tension, and not a single person has asked for her hand.

And still, Elliot doesn't move when he feels her eyes on him like she is just waiting for him to look back at her. It's an unnatural feeling, to know Lia is around and not be looking at her. Looking for her. Waiting for a time to be looking at her. He must fight every instinct to keep away, like his body gravitates to her.

She looks away, and Elliot almost breaks when her eyebrows tilt inwards like she's about to cry. He's about to walk over, tell her to get her stuff and they'll go to the lake, to his home, to Jupiter, but then someone walks over to her, and he remains stock-still. He wonders if she knows that she could have asked him to be here, to watch her marry either of the two men who stand so oppressively at the edge of the hall, watching her like predators, and he would have stayed. She could tell him she'd only see him at night, that he'd have to climb into her room up the rose trellises, and he would have. She could have told him to wait, and he'd stand like a statue until he turned to stone and crumbled to the earth.

Elliot doesn't move when he hears Dorian mocking her. How he's told everyone here not to ask her to dance so that when he does, she'll be *grateful*. Ever since Elliot found out Aliyah was a princess, he's been practicing. He can't go feral every time someone is rude to her. It would do more harm than good, and Aliyah can defend herself. There's no way she'd ever care what Dorian said about her. It's been a struggle, but usually, he gets through it by looking right at her. Watching her roll her eyes without a care in the world. Now, he can't check that she's okay. Now, he can't distract himself from the violent thoughts in his mind with the blush on her cheeks.

Even without her presence, Elliot has always known he needs something for if she's ever hurt beyond sharp words and aggressive stares. If anyone ever tried to touch her in a way she didn't want, he knew he needed more than his fists and the ability to knock someone out, because it would never be just him and someone else. There's no one in this palace that ever does anything like trying to scare a woman on their own. But he has plans now. He's spent weeks making sure he could protect her. That he'd survive doing so. Now, every room he walks into, he figures out the exits, he knows the secret passageways, and he knows how to get her out without everyone seeing. He knows how to keep her safe.

So, when he hears Dorian talking about how he'll have her on her knees, Elliot almost pops a knuckle, but he does not react, because he knows it will never happen. Aliyah will be safe, and she'll get on her knees if she *wants* to. She'll only ever do what she wants to do. There are more important things to defend her from than the words of callous men.

"Make him." Lucian sniggers, gesturing his head to the bar. "Imagine the headlines—*Princess shunned by all but her staff.* That should bring her down a peg or two."

"You, boy," Dorian calls out to him. Elliot turns his head. "Dance with her."

"Who, sir?" he asks, and they laugh, but the jokes on them.

"The Princess. Ask her to dance."

Elliot nods his head. "Sir."

Elliot walks over, his eyes on Aliyah. She blinks rapidly, looking away like he doesn't know she's been watching him this entire time.

"Your Highness," he says with a bow. When he stands up straight, her brow is furrowed. "May I have this dance?"

She looks around, glancing over at her parents. She can't know that she won't be hurt for this, that it was all preplanned. It takes her a moment, his hand out in front of him, and he thinks she might say no. That she might leave. But she slides her gloved fingers over his palm, and he walks her between people to the middle of the dance floor.

Elliot places his hand against her back, pulling her flush against him. He never thought he'd have her this close, and he wishes it were under different circumstances. He wants her to know how badly he wants her this close all the time, because he wants her. Because he needs her. Because she wants it too. But she doesn't; she's made it clear. There's never a time he wants her to think he's like those men.

"I was told to dance with you," he says, his voice low as people twirl next to him. Her face drops, and he regrets his words.

Her hands loop around his neck, her fingertips hovering like touching his skin will burn her. "Oh."

"Aliyah," he whispers, but she shakes her head, a practiced smile on her face. "You know I would die to dance with you. I just—I don't want you to think I'm ignoring you. You told me you didn't want me, and I will respect that."

She smiles still, but it doesn't reach her eyes. "Okay."

"You look beautiful," he says, and she looks up at him, her big, brown eyes telling him so much more than he thinks she'd planned for him to know. "You are beautiful."

Lia watches him for a moment, then clears her throat. "Thank you."

Elliot hums, pulling her a tad closer. Now might be the only time he gets to speak to her beyond her forcing him to leave, so, just like the first day under the plum trees, he takes a chance again.

"I only just saw your letter," he says. "I'm sorry I was so late. I didn't know it was from you, and I've had a hard time doing anything at all lately." Her hands finally rest against his neck, and he tries to avoid twisting so they're left touching his skin, not lingering against the ridiculous collar of his suit.

"I did not send you a letter."

"Lia."

She swallows, and he feels it in his toes. "I am not interested."

Elliot sighs, and Aliyah's finger traces down the side of his throat. He wonders if she knows. "You know, if you want me to leave you so badly, you could be a little better at hiding the fact you're lying."

"I am not," she whispers quickly, but she won't look at him.

"You have spent the entire time lying to me," he says, his voice low, and he waits until she's looking up at him before he speaks again. "But you weren't lying in your letter."

"Elliot," she whispers, her eyes asking with him more than her words. "*Please.*"

"You forget that I know you, Lia. You let me get to know you. So I know what you look like when you're lying. Please, just tell me. Tell me what's going on."

"Master Harper," she replies, but it sounds more like a plea. "There is nothing I wish to discuss with you. I do not even know why you are here."

"You said *yours*, Lia. So please forgive me if I thought there might be a time when you wanted to be mine, as I am yours."

Lia grinds her teeth. "And in what way were you mine?"

"In every way," he says. She pulls a little closer, and he feels her eyelashes against his skin. "I am yours in every way."

"You are here, in your server uniform, because I am yours?"

Elliot works his jaw. She's infuriating, yet still the best thing in his life. And even if she weren't, she'd deserve to be happy. To be safe.

"There were extra shifts available due to the number of guests." It's not a lie. He signed up for it before she said she was over him, and he couldn't get out of it because the security list was updated, his name added to the list of waitstaff. He couldn't tell them it was in error without blowing his cover.

Aliyah pulls back, and he almost sighs with how much he's missed her frowning at him, though he doesn't think she means for him to see it. "Do you need money?"

"No."

Her frown deepens. "Then why are you working so many extra shifts?"

He wants to laugh. He's not even supposed to be there. "I'm not working."

"Excuse me?" she asks, her eyes wide in panic. Her palms are flat against his neck, her thumbs under his jaw to tilt his face to hers. She doesn't need to use force, he's always willing to be looking at her. "What... who is making you do that, El? You—you do not have to just be here because someone is forcing you to be."

"I'm not being forced."

"Are you being paid?" she asks, and he sighs. She's going to make him stop.

"Well, I am tonight."

"Elliot," she begs. Lia looks around the room quickly, then her hands drop to his shoulders. "What about everything else? You are there morning, noon, and night. I will fix it, just... can you tell me?"

"Lia—"

"Darling, please. I will fix it."

His hands tighten against her waist. How is she expecting him to stop talking to her when she slips up so easily? How is it that she doesn't falter under the scrutiny of nations, but one possible unpaid shift for him and she looks at him like that. The music changes, and he should leave, but her hand slides down his arm, her palm resting in his, and he takes the lead.

"I'm not supposed to be there." Aliyah frowns at him again, and God, there's going to be a day when she stops. "In the dining hall. Anywhere but the greenhouse, really. I'm only there for you."

Her hand rests at the bottom of his neck, the other tangled with his. "Pardon?"

"I didn't know you were over me." He sighs, and her lip quivers, but she clenches her jaw. "I didn't know you were over it—over us, and I'm not... I'm not over you."

Her eyes well, but she blinks them dry before his hand touches her face.

"I don't see how I ever will be, and I missed you. You stopped coming, and I—I missed you."

She swallows, a small sigh escaping her lips. "Elliot, you *must* stop."

Elliot sighs, resting his cheek against her forehead, moving her around the floor with ease. The chandeliers are nothing like the dreams he's had of him and her on the dance floor. The lights are dimmer, the music shriller, the atmosphere colder. The only thing that trumps the late-night thoughts he has is the feel of her in his arms. The way her cheek rests against his shoulder, even though they're dancing around a crowded room. The way her thumb rubs across his hand.

"In another life, I would show you the music I grew up with," Elliot whispers, and her hand tightens in his. "The music my mom would play every Sunday while she'd cook and I'd sweep the house. I'd show you around my hometown, and we'd get ice cream at the parlor Mel used to work at. The owner's daughter fancied me so bad I never paid." Lia sucks in a breath, but he continues. "I'd buy yours, though, and I'd let you eat mine too. I'd take you to this cute café on the coast, and we'd drive—"

"What would you get?" she asks, her voice low. "At the café."

"Mac and cheese," he says, sounding dazed. "I always get mac and cheese."

Aliyah hums, and he wants to pull her closer, but the music requires a spin, so he lets her go, but only because he knows she'll come right back. His eyes stay on hers, even as she spins under his arm.

"You'd never be alone. You'd never need to be alone."

She's back in his arms before too long, and she's looking at his lips, and he's about to make a life-ending decision. But before he can so much as flex a muscle, she's pulled back. She swallows, blinking violently as she looks around the room. Elliot readies himself for an attack. Not from the men leering, but from her. He thinks the only way she knows how to be cruel, is how she's read about in books. It's not in her nature, so she can't figure it out for herself. If he were a betting man, he'd have thought she would already have said he's not good enough for her. (It's true, of course, but he never thought she'd say it.)

"I suppose this all worked out rather well for you, did it not?" she asks, but her heart isn't in it. Part of him wants to walk away, if only to make this easier on her. He wonders if he would do it if she weren't in danger.

"And how's that, Your Highness?"

"The mean princess who led you on. You have always been waiting for a justification for the way you felt about me. About my family."

Elliot scoffs, his hand against her back as they settle into the next movement. "You didn't lead me on, Lia, and I never needed justification for your family. Tell me you're comfortable here. Tell me they're not trying to get you to marry two of the world's most despicable men when you clearly don't want to. Tell me how I would ever need justification for the way I loathe your family."

Aliyah swallows, though he thinks she might pull herself a little closer. She's already touching him from chest to his feet as they glide around the ballroom, but he wants more. He needs more.

"Tell me," he whispers, his fingers light against the bare skin of her back, "why you are bruised."

Her eyes widen as she looks at him, but she forces them back down. "I am fine."

Elliot hums, his fingers stroking over her skin. He's covered by her hair, he thinks, so he's a little freer with it.

"Would you tell me if you weren't?"

"Yes," she replies.

"Have you told me anything true?" he asks, and she looks up at him, blinking too fast. She spins away, but his hold on her fingers makes her come back to him. He thanks the band for the dance that means she stays with him and no one else, even if she doesn't reply.

"I am sorry," he says, and she looks up at him, frowning. He wants to press his lips to the scrunch between her brows. "For what I said that night."

"I do not care," she says, shaking her head and looking away. "It is fine."

"Lia."

"I do not care, Elliot. There are more important things to me than what you think," she snaps, but he knows she's trying to hide her true emotions. Sometimes, he wishes he did not know her all that well.

"You let me fall in love with you, knowing full well you were never going to keep me," he says. "At least let me apologize so I can clear my conscience before I never talk to you again."

She sighs spinning away from him. "Elliot." She'll come back, just this once.

"Please," he says, his hand reaching for hers again. "Please. I am so sorry."

Aliyah looks at him—truly looks at him—and he sees something switch, though he's sure if he asked her, she'd lie about it. He can see on her face that she already regrets snapping at him, but he wants her to know he'd let her shout at him for the rest of time if only he was also able to tell her how lovely she was after.

"I'm sorry," he replies. He'd be surprised if he's not about to be hauled off the floor. There's no way people can't see how in love with her he is. Elliot moves closer than he was a moment ago, and the movement makes her tilt her head to look up at him.

"Eli," she sighs looking around the room.

"Princess, please." She huffs, looking back at him, but he takes it as a sign to continue. "I realized too late that I didn't need you alone with flowers and all the time in the world to ask for your forgiveness. All I needed to do was tell you how much I regret what I said. It doesn't matter if you forgive me or not. It doesn't matter if I'll never know if you have the desire to know what I had for breakfast as much as I want to know how you slept. I just need you to know I have no bad thoughts about you. None at all. I never have. That's why I so cruelly said what you kindly told me. I have nothing else in my mind surrounding you that isn't unabashedly positive."

"You hate me," she says, and it slices through him like a hot knife through butter. Her chest shudders, and he feels it against his ribcage. "Even if you like the person you met under the trees, you hate *me*, and there is nothing I can do about it."

"My love," he whispers, his fingers tight against her back. "I could never hate you."

"I have never had a bad thought about you," she says, her eyes flicking over his face. "You cannot say the same about me."

"I think about you all of the time," he replies. "Every moment of the day since I met you, I have thought about you. And not even one of them has been bad. God, Lia," he stresses, his hands clasped in hers as they come together, then move apart. "Hatred is nowhere in my vocabulary for you. Not for a moment."

"I have never," she whispers quickly, as if she knows time is running out. As if she knows soon, she'll go back to telling him to go. "I have never known someone like you. I did not know what to do. Not with you. And I know I should have told you who I was, but I wanted you so badly. I wanted you. And you hated me before you had even met me, and I had no idea what I was supposed to do."

He sighs, his hand sliding higher up her back until his fingers trace the back of her neck. "I was hurt. I was blindsided, and I'm not even sure how. It is so completely obvious that you are a princess," he says, looking around at the ballroom in which they dance. "I just... I was hurt, and when I'm hurt, I'm a bit of a prick. I had nothing to say to you that would cause you any of the hurt I thought I was going through; nothing in my mind at all about you that doesn't sound like someone who has devoted their life to writing poetry in your honor."

"I am still a royal," she whispers. "I cannot change that. The way I—the way I need, the way I want you..."

"Lia," he whispers, moving closer to her. She looks away, but she doesn't move. She doesn't flinch.

"It does not change that."

"Is that what this is about? Lia, I don't want you to change anything," he says, his eyes frantic as he looks at her. "I can't sleep. I can't eat. I can't *breathe* without you." Lia swallows, her breath coming in short bursts that don't match the slow rhythm of the song. "I have thought about nothing else since our argument. Believe me, I have gone over every scenario in my head, and it all ends with you. *You* holding my hand as we sneak walks through the forest. *You* showing up in the greenhouse. Always you. I miss you in a way that lives under my skin. It just stays there. I'll sit at dinner, and I'm wondering if you'd like it, if you'd sit next to me if you could, if you'd steal fries from my plate. I lie down and can't sleep because all I think about is you. I'm right here, and I am sorry for what I said and how I acted, and *you*," he stresses, "God, if you don't want anything to do with me, if you don't trust me, if you don't want this, then we don't have to be friends, but please, please tell me that you're okay, because I can't walk away without knowing. It is killing me, my love."

Aliyah looks at him, and then she looks away, and her face falls. Elliot tries to turn, to see what has her eyes wide, but her hand rests against his neck. He thinks maybe she's going to kiss him—the way her eyes dip to his lips, the way her breath is choppy, the way she leans toward him. But it's foolish to think he'd ever get another moment with her.

She takes a step back and curtseys, and Elliot follows suit. "Thank you for the dance," she says. "Please believe me when I say I do not want to see you again."

Elliot is unsure how he gets off the dance floor in one piece. It shouldn't be surprising; she's told him in more ways than one that she doesn't want him anymore. That his friendship is not something she wants to pursue. She told him that at the start, and yet, he feels hollow all the same. He stands back in his place, watching her from afar. It's how it was always going to end.

Dorian walks over, the savior to her mortifying dance with the help. She smiles, and Lucian curses on the sidelines. As if Elliot would ever think that was a real expression. Elliot finds something to watch—anything to look at other than Aliyah floating around the ballroom with a man who isn't worthy of kissing the ground she walks on.

Then the song abruptly changes, and the dance floor is crowded again. Elliot frowns, finding it difficult to spot Aliyah in the crowd, but he does, and Dorian's close. His nose is almost against hers, but he's snarling. His face is utterly livid, masqueraded badly as a smile. Elliot tilts his head, trying to get a view of what's going on. He knows now that the extra dancers are a ploy, a distraction. As if anyone else in this room would help her when she needed it.

Elliot moves through the crowd of people surrounding the dance floor. He can't hear from over here, and he needs to know what's happening, and what scenario he needs to implement to get the terrified look off her face.

Dorian's voice is low, but Elliot hears him. "Am I hurting you, Princess?"

Aliyah scoffs, but Elliot hears the pain in her tone. "You could not snap my wrist if your life depended on it." God, Elliot loves her, but the way Dorian's face contorts into anger, like he's forgotten the part he has to play, makes him wish she hadn't said anything at all.

"I could fuck you right here," he snarls, as Elliot dips through the crowd. "And no one would bat an eye. No one would help you."

"Why would I need help, Dorian? Can you not get a girl off?"

Dorian growls. "I wonder if you'll be saying that when I let my men have at you, when the water starts, when—"

Elliot pulls on the fire alarm hidden behind a thick curtain and waits half a second for the high-pitched sound to blare out from around the room. Dancers bend their knees, throwing their hands over their ears to get away from the noise. The sprinklers turn on moments later, and Elliot watches as Dorian runs through the crowd, pushing people out of the way, leaving Aliyah alone. Elliot doesn't go over. Even as he watches her hold her wrist, he doesn't go over. But he does watch her direct the crowd out of the room with a practiced ease, and when she finally leaves, Elliot allows himself to go.

CHAPTER TWENTY-FIVE

ALIYAH STALKS DOWN THE corridor, her hand gripping the wrist Dorian tried so hard to snap. She knows better than to wind him up but sometimes forgets that she needs to be careful, because she's spent so long thinking about someone who makes her feel safe. Someone who would never dream of touching her in a way she did not crave. Elliot flashes through her mind, but he's on it so much she's surprised when she has a thought without him. Even as she knows she must make Elliot leave, she thinks about what he'll be doing when he's fifty-five. Will he have children? What does he want to call them? Would he be happy? Lia can't have that with him, and yet, she wants nothing but to run to him. To tell him that she desperately wants the musical mornings and the lazy Sundays. She wants to tell him everything if only to give him all the facts. The reasons she needs him to leave have nothing to do with the way she loves him. Elliot doesn't even need to fix it, because it's her lot in life to be miserable. But he'd help. He'd hold her and he'd tell her it would be okay, even if he didn't mean it. She'd spend twenty-four hours a day in the dungeons, growing closer and closer to death, if it only meant she had a moment with him.

But now, she's made sure he's not here—a frightening insight to the rest of her life—and she's storming down the hallway, alone, with a wrist that's not quite fractured. The words she uttered to annoy Dorian take up no space in her mind. There is only Elliot. It would have been silly, and inconsequential to anyone else, but Dorian is always waiting for a moment to hate her publicly. So,

J.S. JASPER

Lia is running to her safe place, with the sound of the fire alarm ringing in her ears. How glad she was to feel the first smatterings of water, even if it terrifies her still.

Aliyah ducks through the stone doorway, then makes her way up the narrow stairway. There's a tower here that's rarely used for anything other than her lookout, and it takes her to a section of roof no one else ever goes to. No one knows it exists. She only found it once when she was trying to escape the dungeons and fell upon a loose metal drain in the floor. Thankfully, this stairway is cleaner, and she takes the steps two at a time, willing the pain in her arm to fade. Lia takes a deep breath, pushes the door open, and prepares herself for the chill of the night air.

And when she looks up, Elliot looks back at her.

Fuck. *Fuck*.

How is Elliot always around to see her at her worst? When all she needs is him, and she can't have him. She almost walks over, almost throws her arms around his neck, but she doesn't. Aliyah can't keep him here. She's spoken to him all of twice in the past days, and already, he's hiding from someone. From something. She realizes that he does not move to come to her, not that she would expect him to. She is bad news. It was practically written on her birth certificate. She knew that, at some point, she'd have to let him go for real, and if his words earlier were anything to go by, he knew it too. She should never have seen him again after the first near-death encounter. She knew then that he would change her life, and now, she has to make him leave, and it might kill her. But despite everything, despite her smart mind and her inner strength, her fingers creep closer to him, as though she can pull him closer through sheer will. She clamps her hands behind her back, throwing on her best nonchalant face.

"Why are you here?"

Elliot frowns, his face pained as he leans against the wall. "I was here first."

Aliyah swallows, crossing her arms. It's cold up here. It's probably going to rain again, because of course it will rain. Her wrist hurts, but it's nothing like the ache in her chest.

"Are you injured?" Elliot asks.

"I am fine."

Elliot nods like he doesn't believe her, but he doesn't force her to tell him the truth. Aliyah wonders if he's planning on staying here. If he likes the job he has, he's going to stay regardless of if they speak. She would be able to cope with that, possibly. She *would* deal with it either way if the threat to his life wasn't so high.

"I think it would be best if you seek employment elsewhere."

Elliot scoffs, his hands in his pockets as he looks at the floor. She watches as the rain starts, hitting his suit. Was he there just because she asked for him to be? Was he there because he was forced to be? Will she ever know either way? The rain marks the roof, turning it from pale to dark. She watches until it's illuminated with the reflections of the stars.

Elliot moves closer, but Lia daren't look at him. The rain soaks through her dress quickly enough, the cold water making it hard to breathe. How cruel, for her to be scared of nature. At least the panic in her spine is a reminder of how she couldn't get any air. How she had to fight the hands of men who were supposed to help her. At least the rain makes her remember what she's doing this for. They won't be so kind to him.

Her body shakes as the rain drips down her neck, her hair sticking against her face.

"Let's go in," Elliot says, but she shakes her head. "Lia."

"I do not want"—she forces a breath, and her jaw almost locks with how hard she's grinding her teeth—"to leave with you. I am *over* this. I am bored of this. I am bored of you."

"Look at me," he says, and she swallows, her jaw clenched so hard her teeth might shatter. When he speaks again, his voice is softer. "Lia, please. Look at me." She does, even if she tries not to. Aliyah pulls her bottom lip between her teeth, her best nonchalant face on even as her heart flips back and forth.

"Tell me to go," he whispers. "Tell me to go, and I will. If that is what you want, I will leave you alone. I promise I will, but please don't try and make me leave you here in the dark. I can't do it. I don't want to do it. Please."

She sniffs. "I am fine."

"I know," he replies, taking a step closer. His hands flail for a moment, the war on his face obvious with his want to touch her. He's never done it because he wanted to, she knows that much. He was there to help her over the water, and he was forced to hold her at the ball, but he's never—God, he's never even touched her. She swallows, and he takes his chance. His hands are light against her jaw, and she lets her eyes flutter closed, the smallest sound leaving her mouth. His hands cradle her shivering face, and she wants him to take care of her. She wants to let him.

A small sob escapes, but she says, "I am fine."

"I know that you are. You always will be." Her jaw clenches beneath his palm. "But I need to know that *beyond* you just saying it. It is killing me, my love, not knowing how you are." There are three tense seconds when Aliyah thinks she's about to give in. To tell him everything as his thumb rubs against her throat. But she *can't*. She loves him, and he really might love her, and he'll stay. For her. Like Anna did. At best, he'll resent her. At worst, he'll no longer be breathing.

So, she takes a deep breath, flinches, and says, "Do not touch me."

Elliot recoils as if he has been burned. He steps back, his entire face folded in pain.

"I'm sorry, Princess."

She knows there's only one way he'll ever leave her. "You scare me," she says, immediately biting the inside of her cheek so hard she might bleed, but she needed to get ahead of the way his expression would fall, of how she'd break in half when his jaw dropped. It's worse than she thought it would be, but she does not move.

His voice is rough when he asks, "What?"

Aliyah swallows. She will keep him safe. "You scare me. I would like for you to leave. The palace, and the grounds when your scholarship expires. All of it."

Elliot blinks rapidly, and she can see the hurt on his face, even with the dark night. His hair blends into the inky black sky. There is no moon tonight, and she's glad that his furrowed brow isn't illuminated. The rain feels like it's permeating into her skin, turning her blood ice cold. She shivers, the action so violent she almost falls to the ground. Elliot unbuttons his jacket, though he doesn't move to put it over her shoulders.

"Like," he starts, his voice stuttering over how he licks his lips like a wounded animal. "Like I am scaring you now, or—or I scare you all the time?" He holds his jacket out, his arm stretched as far as it will go so he doesn't step closer to her.

"Lately," she replies. She looks anywhere but at him. He'll see right through her if she dares to look him in the face. "You are always around, and I did not ask for you to be." It's a lie. She never knocked on his door and begged him to follow her through the forest, but she did it every other way. She was always in his eyeline, always putting herself there. There are dinners she barely takes her eyes off him. She's made this worse, and now she's dealing with the consequences.

"Oh," he whispers, his hand still outstretched. "Well, that is—that's. Well. The worst thing I've ever heard."

Aliyah hums, a pained noise she tries to turn into something else. "Like right now. Why are you even here, if not to stalk me in the dark?"

He frowns. "Don't do that."

"Do what, Master Harper?"

Elliot huffs out a laugh, his tongue running between his teeth and his lip. "Take the jacket, Princess."

She does, but only because his face is so pained at the sight of her. She's already hurting him; she doesn't want to make it worse. Her fingers touch his, and she jolts. When she places the jacket around her, it's heavy and wet, but it smells like him, and she does her best to ignore the way it makes her feel better.

Elliot paces around the roof, looking at her with a frown every few seconds. She watches the way his shirt soaks in the rain, the material sticking to his chest.

"How was I stalking—you know what, no. I'm not having this argument with you." He spins and walks toward the edge of the roof. Aliyah wanted to show him this place. This roof holds a special part of her life. No one else ever comes up here. She wants to follow him, to look at what he's looking at when he leans his hands against the top of the wall. But then she hears a sniff. It's minute, barely audible over the sound of the rain, but she knows it's him all the same.

He turns back, and she's not sure how good she is at hiding the destroyed look on her face.

"Sweetheart, why are you doing this?"

"How do you even know this place exists?" she asks, desperate to get ahead of anything else he might say, but the rain is coming thick and fast, and she needs to calm down. She needs it to settle. "It does not—" She closes her eyes. It's not being poured; it's just raining. She can still breathe. "No one knows it is here."

Elliot runs his hand over his face, and she's hurting him. She's making sure there's no way he'd ever want to talk to her again. That he'd ever think about her again. Every thought he's ever had about the monarchy, about the way they treat people, will have been correct.

"Do you spy on me in my room?" she asks, avoiding his face when he frowns. "What, I do not want to touch you in real life because you are just..."

"Just what?" he challenges.

The love of my life.

"Just a gardener," she breathes out, though he makes no outward suggestion that he's shocked by her words. "And I am a princess, so you, what, watch me when I am in my room?"

Elliot places his hands in his pockets, his jaw up slightly, like he's waiting for another attack. Aliyah wonders if he'll tell Melody about tonight. If his entire family will hate her before dawn. She's never wanted strangers to like her more than she wants his family to.

"How do you know this place exists?" she begs.

He takes a deep breath. "I know every single route in this palace that leads me to the dungeons."

Aliyah's heart drops to her feet. He's already been there. She's too late. "Have you—oh God, you have been there? What have they done to you?" She dashes across the roof, her hands against his face for the first time, and she can't even enjoy it because she's searching for injuries. "Where were you hurt?" Elliot's face drops, and she wonders how she's still standing. "Darling, please. What happened?"

She spins him, and he turns with ease until he's back in front of her. His shirt is stuck to his skin, and she selfishly spent the entire time on the roof tracing his skin through the rain running down his chest, not trying to spot injuries. His brows are furrowed like they were when they argued in the greenhouse. The water hits her face here on the roof, and in the dungeons, and none of it means anything. He was hurt anyway. She's been cruel to him all evening, and it's too late. They already got to him.

Her breathing stutters, and she tries to blink the raindrops from her eyes, but it feels too much like she's failing. Too much like she's drowning. She doesn't know how to save herself. Not anymore.

"El, *please*. Please," she mutters.

"I'm not hurt," Elliot whispers. His hand lingers against hers where it lies on his shoulder. He twists their fingers together, and she lets him, because she's selfish and needs him. "Sweetheart, I have not been in a cell. I'm not hurt."

"No?" she asks, but the panic sits at the back of her throat. "Are you sure?"

Elliot carefully lifts her injured wrist, the sleeve of his jacket drops to her elbow as he removes her glove, and she feels completely bare, but there's never been a place or time where she's felt safer. He presses his lips against where her wrist is bruising. Over and over, his lips touch her skin, until eventually, he holds it close to his chest.

"You are the only one being hurt, my love."

Aliyah feels his heartbeat thump against her fingers. She wonders if she cracked her chest open, would they find she beats in the same rhythm. Elliot pulls her closer, his free hand wrapping around her, his hand tight against the back of her neck. How is she supposed to leave now she knows her cheek rests against his shoulder so perfectly? How is it reasonable that she has to ask for him to go when she knows what his breath feels like against the top of her head? Aliyah isn't sure how long they stay there, how long he lets himself freeze in the rain as he runs his thumb against the back of her neck.

"You were there," he whispers.

"Pardon?"

"You were there," he repeats. "In the dungeons. The night we met in the greenhouse, you had just come from there, and I swore I'd never leave you there again."

She almost recoils, but she stays against his chest instead. "That is not your job."

"I'm not foolish enough to think I could just stroll up and get you out if I found you there, so I found every way possible to get you out—of the dungeons and the palace. That's why I know this roof exists."

"How did you do that?" she asks.

With a shrug, he replies, "The palace is quiet at night."

He's tired because he's sneaking about the palace at night to make sure she's okay. Aliyah might be sick. He's going to get caught, and he's going to get killed. She'll have killed him. Aliyah wonders if they'd tell her over breakfast like it's barely news. She wonders if she'd have to tell Melody and his mom, or if they'd never find out the truth. She wonders how the earth is supposed to go on spinning when Elliot is gone.

"You have to go," she says. There's no heat behind her words. No conviction, no truth. Nothing. She barely attempts to pull back from his chest. His grip doesn't need to be strong to keep her here. She is flailing, with nothing to keep her above water. It's possible being waterboarded is preferable to having this conversation, but at least it will be her and not him.

"I can help you," he begs. He says it like he believes it. Like he wouldn't get killed for something as minuscule as defending her at dinner. Like he isn't supposed to be frolicking through the palace gardens rather than spending his evenings finding tunnels to get her away. He deserves more than this. More than her.

"If you could help me," she starts, her voice low as she thinks about whether she can hurt him like this. She pulls away, clenching her jaw. "Then why are you telling me you know every which way to the dungeons, yet I was there the other day, and you were nowhere to be seen."

His hand flies to his chest, his eyes looking wet, even in the pouring rain. "What?"

"What is the purpose of this? To taunt me? To tell me you knew I was there, being tortured, and you did not care?"

Elliot pulls a notepad out of his pocket, flipping through pages frantically. "No, no, no. When? I checked—I was there, but you—Aliyah when?"

"They held me down and poured water over my face time and time again, and you did what? Stood around with your hands in your pockets?"

Elliot's face loses all color. Aliyah has never seen someone look like they might die right where they stand. He shakes his head, his hand trembling with his pen. He hums, his fist against his mouth, and she thinks he might be sick, that he might throw up right here and now and it's her fault.

"When?" he asks, wiping at his eyes before returning his pen to his page full of numbers. "Lia, please. When was it?"

"It does not matter."

"It doesn't matter?" he asks, blinking violently. "It doesn't—Lia. I need to know. Please."

She shakes her head, and he looks furious.

"Why would you bring it up if you were not going to let me help you?" he asks, shoving his notepad back in his pocket. "Do you want me to go so badly that you want me to die? Do you want me to throw myself off the roof? Is that what you want? Why else would you tell me you're being fucking *tortured* and—I can't do this. I can't watch you get hurt, and you won't let me in. I can't." Good. That is what she's been aiming for, so why does it feel like she's about to pass away?

"You would not be able to save me," she says, her throat burning with the reality of her words. Elliot would die trying, and still, it would not work.

He scoffs. "And how did you get out of Dorian trying to break your wrist?"

Aliyah frowns. "The fire alarm went off."

"Convenient."

She panics. He can't be trying to get a fast one over Lucian and Dorian; they won't stop until he's dead. "Eli, what did you do?"

"That night you were supposed to go to the museum opening, but you had an escort instead? That's because I knew they were planning to hurt you in the car," he says, his neck tense, and she frowns. "I know everything because I have plans for this, Lia. Well, not this part, but I can protect you anyway. Even if you hate me, I can keep you safe. Why won't you let me?"

How does he know that? He's putting himself in danger for her, she knows it. He's going to get himself killed, and she won't know how to live anymore. Not knowing that he no longer exists.

She shakes her head. "I do not want you. One day, you will make someone very happy, Elliot, but you are simply not good enough..." she says, her voice breaking. "...for me."

Elliot rolls his eyes, like he was just waiting for her to say so as he paces the rooftop, running his hand through his hair.

"If you want me to go, that's fine. I mean, I accepted the position beyond six months," he says with a huff. The agony of his words—that he would have stayed with her even though she's been avoiding him—plucks at each of her rib bones until it feels like her chest will cave in.

"I'll leave," he replies, wiping his face clean. He gives her a small smile, and her stomach flips at the way it doesn't reach his eyes. At the way he's trying to keep himself small. Less threatening. As if he'd ever been anything other than the safest space for her. "I will be gone by tomorrow. I promise. I will go."

Aliyah bites her lip, willing the way her heart falls to the floor to make no noise, though she'll be surprised if he can hear anything other than the pained gasps he makes.

"But you'll never convince me you're anything like your parents," he says, and Aliyah's jaw falls. "You can say whatever you like, Lia. I won't hate you. You can't make me hate you."

God, she's not going to be able to let him go. She doesn't want to let him go.

He walks slowly closer, and she knows she has just one chance. So, when he's almost at her, when she can feel the warmth of his skin even though he must be cold to the bone like she is, she flinches. Her eyes are wide as she takes a step back, her hands protecting her from barreling into the wall. She's forgotten that she was hurt in any way other than her heart, and she lets out a pained breath as her wrist hits the brick. It wasn't intentional, but Elliot looks like he's going to pass out.

"I'm sorry," he says, his hands high. He sighs, dropping his chin to the floor, then looks back at her. "Even if I was just a phase in your life—a person to get you through the boring days—you are the light of mine."

Aliyah whimpers, swallowing so hard she thinks her throat might snap.

"God, you're everywhere." Elliot sighs, his voice completely shattered. "You're in the golden leaves on the trees, the way I listen for birdsong, the light glinting off the lake. You are everywhere, and I am not leaving you here, in the dark, soaking wet, while some men are trying their best to hurt you."

Aliyah shakes her head. He doesn't care for her; he can't care for her. "You do not care for me. You can't. Why would you?" she asks, though it sounds too much like begging. Too much like she needs him. She swallows. "And why would you think I would ever – care for you. I am a princess, and I was bored, and now, I would like you to leave."

"You're lying," he responds, with a slight shake of his head, though he doesn't force her to admit it. "You are lying, and you're breaking my heart, my love. I thought you wanted me to fight for you. I thought maybe you were pushing me away to make sure I stayed, and I have been. I will, if you only hint that that is what you want, but I am playing a game I don't have the rules for, Lia, and you won't tell me how to win, and I—" He rubs his hand over his face again. "God, you're breaking my heart."

She blinks back her emotions and focuses on anything that isn't him. The shake of her freezing body. The sounds of the rustle of the leaves of the trees they used to sit under. The sounds of running water on the lake he took her out onto. Anything, *anything* but him, but he gets through. Everything in her mind is always focused on him.

"I can't hurt you," he says. "I don't want to hurt you. And if I find out this whole time you wanted me to go—that everything you're saying is true, even if there's no part of me that believes it—I won't make it. So, if you ask me to go, I will go. Tomorrow. Tonight, I am not leaving you here. I will escort you back to wherever you need to be."

"Elliot—"

He shakes his head. "You can say what you like, Lia. You can tell me in every single way that you hate me—" His voice breaks, but he swallows and continues. "You can tell me there's not a single life where you would ever look at me twice." She looks up at him, and he knows. He knows she's lying, that she's just trying to hurt him. He *knows*.

"And still, I am not leaving you here. You are being hunted in broad daylight by men who would never deserve you. I know that you must know I know that. But you won't tell me anything. You'd rather get rid of me, and I can't understand why. I would tell you anything, but I've been in love with you since I met you, so maybe you don't understand. Maybe I've been wrong this entire time. Maybe you never wanted to bring me sandwiches and watch the stars on your balcony.

"Maybe you do want me to leave. I'll never know if you're telling the truth. You always lie to me," he says, his voice strained. "And still." He clears his throat. "I am not leaving you here, in the dark, in the rain. So, you can vent. Shout at me, scream at me, tell me you hate me and how you'll never love me. Tell me how you think I could *ever* hate you, and I will wait, and I'll show you how it's not true because I am not leaving you here. So, we can stand here until morning light, or you can walk ahead, and I'll be like everyone else, walking five steps behind."

"Eli," she whispers.

His voice is firm, the most livid she's ever heard him. "I am not leaving you here."

"You should," she starts, but she doesn't know what else she can say before she collapses to the ground. He knows she's lying. He knows she's just trying to hurt him, and it's working. "This is all your fault."

"Then tell me how to fix it," he begs.

Her face is frantic, her eyes wide as she pleads with him. She won't make it if he gets hurt, if he ceases to exist. "You cannot. You have to leave, Elliot."

"I am not leaving you here."

She sighs, her hand against her mouth. Aliyah was expecting it to be hard, but she wasn't expecting this. Losing the only man she's ever loved, and she has to gut him in the process.

"If we leave together, you will be gone by morning?" she asks.

He wipes his face again, his jaw working overtime. "Yes."

"Then let us go," Aliyah says, and turns to walk away. Elliot walks behind her, and she's never hated anyone more than she hates herself right now.

She clicks the door open, and Elliot says nothing at all. She wonders if he knows this way as well—if he truly knows the palace that well. She wants to know how many sleepless nights he's had trying to make sure she was safe. How he found secret passages that the guards don't even know exist. His footsteps are light behind her, and she thinks he might be stepping that way on purpose. It doesn't take long to get to the corridor outside her bedroom. He'll let her go here, she's sure.

Aliyah turns to look at him, his hands shoved in his pockets. "Do you know your way from here?" she asks.

Elliot smiles, and it takes her breath away. She's never going to see him again. Her body shakes, and her knees almost buckle. She held up better with the waterboarding. She's about to cave just from the look on his face.

"I do." He bows, his hand stretched out to the side. "Your Highness."

It takes her too long to turn back around and open the door she's had her hand on for a minute now. He'll have seen the way her entire face broke, the way her lips trembled, the way her eyes watered. But he'll leave anyway. She made sure of it. It's what she had to do. He'll be happier, safer, able to live the life he wants, away from here.

"Lia," he whispers, when she does nothing but look at him. Her eyes drop to his lips, and she almost whimpers at the sight.

He's never even been able to touch her just because he wanted to, because he needed to. "Don't," he whispers, closer than she realized. "Don't do this to me."

He could mean any number of things. *Don't kiss me. Don't break my heart. Don't leave me. Don't love me.*

"How am I supposed to watch you set up your new initiatives from outside?" he asks, his voice low. "How am I supposed to know if you ever stopped eating cereal when all I'll hear about you is in the newspaper? Lia, how am I supposed to leave knowing that you are here without me? I don't know how to do this without you anymore."

"Sorry," she mutters, squeezing her eyes closed. "I am sorry." She feels his body near hers, and she drops her hold on the doorknob. His nose brushes hers, just barely, and she wets her lips in anticipation. "Please," she whispers.

He backs away faster than she can lift her hands to keep him there. She means for him to lean closer, but she can't blame him for thinking she meant something else. Not with her words this evening. He sighs, the war of the words he wants to say to her all over his face. *Please*, she thinks, *don't say it*. He raises his hand and wipes at his face roughly.

"The greatest pleasure of my life," he says, blowing out a breath and resting his hand against his chest, "was meeting you."

She takes in a shuddering breath. He backs up, his hands back in his pockets, and she wonders if he wants to touch her as badly as she wants to be touched. He smiles, a soft, sad thing that settles behind her ribcage. "You are the loss of my life also, Princess."

Lia barely hides a sob behind her palm. She feels the prick of tears. He bows, and her chest fissures.

"Goodbye, Aliyah," he whispers.

She watches him walk away. Just before he's out of sight, she whispers, "Goodbye, Elliot."

She barely waits until he's no longer in view before her legs give out. Before her heart falls onto the floor and she follows it. Her knees hit the stone, and she thinks she might never get up again.

CHAPTER TWENTY-SIX

ELLIOT DOESN'T STAND UNDER the stream of hot water long enough to let his thoughts fall on Aliyah. He's desperately trying not to think about her, because he's not sure how he's supposed to leave. How on earth is he supposed to leave her here? As he turns the shower off, he wonders if he should—if he should fight her on it. But how many times can he chase after her, only for her to tell him to leave, before he does? If he knew—truly knew—that this was all a ploy, he'd stay. But as he folds his sweaters into neat piles—things he'd like to take home, and things he wants to leave for her—he doesn't believe anything that flies around his mind. He doesn't know how to trust anything she says. Does he just want for her to care about him?

Lia doesn't *hate* him. He knows that. He thinks. But she needs him to go, and he said he'd leave, if that was what she wanted. And now, he knows there's people just waiting for a time to try and drown her, and he wonders what they'll try next. He sits on the bed she never saw, the bed he did a great many things on while thinking about her. He touched himself thinking about her on this bed. He memorized the next two weeks' schedules for Lucian and Dorian on this bed. He came to the realization that he would kill for her on this bed. And now, on this bed, he looks through the photographs of her he had printed. The ones where he wrote things on the back. The ones he was going to give her, at some point.

The photo of her on the lake with the caption *to the moon and back*. The blurry photo that's mainly sunshine, and she creeps into the corner, her smile wide, with the caption *my heart is outside of my body*. Photograph after photograph that takes him to his knees. His favorite, possibly, is the one he took when she turned to face him as she showed him the lake for the first time. She's flawless, because of course she is. He captioned it, *I wonder if you would marry me*.

In that moment, he realizes she might have said no, and it would have hurt, but he wouldn't have died. She might die. There is a strong chance she might die here, and it doesn't matter if she wants him, it doesn't matter if she loves him. She'll be dead all the same.

Elliot throws his sweats on, grabs a jumper, and puts on some shoes. She can fight him all she likes, but he'll keep her safe. He doesn't need her hand in his, or for her to smile at him, to do that. He only needs for her to be alive. He needs her to know he's got a plan for her, and she can be happy. She needs to know she deserves to be happy.

He grabs his backpack, tossing the photographs on his bed, but the rest of what he needs is already in there—his daily tools for every imaginable scenario he's conjured up. And then he runs.

Straight into Aliyah, who is standing outside his door, dripping wet, with his suit jacket still in her hand.

"Lia?" She blinks, looking around, and he ushers her in. "Are you okay? What's going on?"

She moves quickly, but she doesn't speak. He takes the jacket, tossing it into the bathroom, and when he turns to face her, she's still standing there, a vacant look in her eye, her entire body shaking.

"Princess," he says, his fingers tensed against his thighs so he doesn't reach out and touch her, and she looks up at him. "Please. Tell me something." Her face crumples under the weight of whatever she's supposed to be saying. He wants to go to her, to hold her, but he can't.

"I am—" She stutters with the force of her entire body shaking. "I... um..."

Elliot looks her over, looking for any injuries, any blood.

"What happened?"

"I just needed to say that..." She blinks slowly, and she can tell him she hates him later.

"Are you hurt?"

"I—I need to tell you—"

"Aliyah," he says, his voice firm, and she swallows as she looks up at him. "Are you hurt?"

She blinks, then shakes her head. "Just, just my wrist, nothing else."

Elliot looks her over once, and he thinks she's telling the truth, because she's never been particularly good at lying to him. Even if she tried her hardest on the roof.

"Can I talk?" Elliot asks, and she never stopped looking at him, but her eyes are wetter than before. He wonders if she's been crying since he walked away from her.

Her voice is quiet. "Sure."

"I cannot, in good conscience, leave you here," he says. There's no leeway in his tone. She's not going to convince him otherwise. Her lip wobbles, and he tenses his hands by his thighs. "I know I promised you I would, and you can hate me for that. But I can't, Lia. I can't. You are in danger, and I can help you. So you can hate me, and I'll take it. You can do whatever you want—ignore me, banish me when you're queen, have me killed. But I *will not* leave you here alone."

Lia looks at him for one terrifying moment, and then she rests her forehead against his chest.

"Touch me," she whispers. "*Please*. Please touch me."

Elliot mutters a prayer, pulling her against him with so much force he almost topples over.

"I am sorry," she says with a gasp. "I am so sorry. I am selfish—I am. I am supposed to let you go and I—oh God, the thought of you leaving without knowing how much I—"

"My love," he says, then, "take a breath. A deep breath, okay? Can you do that for me?"

She hums, nodding her head, but it does nothing to calm the way her chest heaves, the way her body still trembles. The way he wants to hold her closer, the way he wants to love her.

"I am so selfish," she says again, pulling away, but he moves his hands to the back of her head. Her eyes are wide, full of tears, and he lifts his thumb to wipe them dry, but it's not use.

"You couldn't be selfish if you tried, Aliyah."

"I am," she repeats. "I do not know how to do any of this without you."

Elliot wants to tell her she needn't worry he'll be there no matter what, but he gives her a moment to talk.

"I did not even know how lonely I was." Lia takes a deep, shuddering breath. "I did not know I missed knowing what other people liked, what they thought about, what made them laugh. Then you came along. God, it is all your fault."

"Lia," he whispers.

"And I know the people need me," she says, wiping the tears from her face. Her hand brushes his, and she clasps their fingers together. "I know they do, because the other option does not bear thinking about, but I cannot do it alone. I am not allowed to do it alone, and I—I know they need me, and yet, every morning I wake thinking that I could just run away with you. I cannot think of anything other than how cruel life would be without you in it." She looks up at him, her red eyes so wide, holding so much hope and pain.

"No one has ever loved me before," she says, taking a deep breath, like the weight of those words has been weighing on her. It takes Elliot's breath away, the way she clearly never expected him to say it. How is it that she knows diplomatic law but doesn't know he'd have married her the day he met her?

"No one," she repeats, then says, "and I still need you to leave."

"Lia," he begs. "Do you understand what you're asking me to do? You want me to just leave you here? Aliyah, you were hurt in a room full of people. I can't just—leaving you here would kill me. It *will* kill me."

She leans back, and Elliot moves her wet hair from her face as she blinks rapidly. "Take me with you."

Elliot laughs lightly. As if that hasn't been on his mind since he saw her under the plum trees that first day. "Lia, if I thought you wanted to go, we would already be on our way."

Her bottom lip pops out, and he thinks she's the sweetest thing in the world. "I want you."

"Good," he replies. "Because I'm not leaving."

Her eyes widen, and true terror floats over her face. "No. No, you cannot stay. You are in danger here."

"From whom?"

"Everyone," she says, her voice in panic. "They all know about you."

Elliot scoffs. He knows all their game plans, and he is not one of them. "No, they don't."

"They do. My mother—"

"Lia," Elliot says, and she frowns. He wonders if she feels as happy as he does right now, even given the circumstances, simply because they're together. "God, you're so cute." Her mouth pops open in a small o, and then, the best thing he's ever seen happens. She smiles. Just a little, but it's there all the same. She slowly moves her arms from where they're folded between them, and she hugs him back. He can feel how cold she is through his jumper.

"I'll tell you all my super-secret spy information *after* you get warm," he says.

She laughs lightly, and he feels it against his heart. Everything from tonight, her words and Dorian's scowl, was worth it to hear her laugh. "Super-secret spy?"

Elliot hums. "Let's go."

She holds onto him tighter. "I cannot. You are holding me hostage."

He laughs, loving seeing the more playful side of her again. Elliot has never witnessed it physically before. He smooths the hair from her face and then goes to move. "Shower time."

She jolts back, her eyes wide. "No. No, no, *no*," she squeals, shuffling back until she hits the wall with a thud. Her face contorts in pain as she moves her wrist lightly. He needs to wrap it.

Elliot holds his hands high. "Okay. Alright." Still, her breathing doesn't settle. "Lia," he whispers, his hands still up. "I won't make you do anything you don't want to do. I swear. Can you take another breath for me, my love?"

She does, mimicking his actions when he breathes in and out.

"Okay," he says, letting his last breath out. He stands, feeling the useless panic he felt watching her linger in his fingers. She reaches out for him, and he pulls her closer, holding her against his body.

"What if we just change into dry clothes? Okay?"

She blinks, and then nods.

"Okay," he replies, relieved. He runs to grab a sweater and some sweatpants from the pile on his bed he was going to leave for her. He hands them to her, and her eyes are locked on his suitcase. Can he tell her now he was never going to go? Or will she fight him on it later?

"You can change in the bathroom, or here, and I'll go in the bathroom."

Aliyah bites on her lip, nervously looking around.

"Can you tell me what you're thinking?" he asks.

"I have to wash my hair," she whispers, then, "because I am getting my hair done tomorrow. I am supposed to have my twists taken out and—uhm, they change them. I think I am getting braids, but I cannot remember." Elliot lets her ramble, because he's missed her voice so badly, and because he wants to help.

"I have a photoshoot and the event for the new Giorgia Gardening Center, so my hair needs to be done, and I think I might die."

"Can we postpone the event?" Elliot asks, and she shakes her head.

"They have flown in. The children are already there, and if the event is postponed, so is the funding."

"Okay, so we leave the hair?" he asks. It's not even grown out. He's pretty sure she only just had it done when Melody visited. If she was a regular girl walking down the street, no one would bat an eye that she had the same hairstyle twice.

"I think I would get more dungeon time," she says with a huff. "I am usually pretty good at it, you know, but lately, I can...uh, it is too much."

Elliot swallows bile as he remembers what she told him.

"So, we do it now?" Elliot asks, then, as she looks up at him. "We take the hair out, and wash it, right? That's it?" She nods. "Do you trust me?"

Her answer is immediate, even as her brows fall before she answers. "Yes."

"So let me do it."

"Okay," she whispers. "Thank you."

Elliot's bathroom smells like lemons and his aftershave, and it helps. *He* helps. Lia stands with her hands against the sink, her head bowed as she waits for Elliot to find a safety pin to help her out of these ridiculously small buttons. Occasionally, she watches him in the mirror, and he's about to touch her, maybe place his hand on her waist or his fingers on her back, but he stops himself, and it's her fault. She is selfish, even if he tries to tell her she isn't. There's a part of him that thinks he might be scary. That he would ever terrify her, and as her throat burns, she knows she needs to fix it.

"Elliot," she whispers, and he turns to face her, the safety pin in his hands. It's a little ridiculous how good he looks without his top on, and she wonders how she even has the brain capacity to think about it right now. How her thoughts are on whether or not she can touch him now. How even though the ball was terrible and her wrist aches, all her thoughts were on how sexy he looked in that ridiculous navy suit.

"What's up, Princess?"

She swallows and his face softens. "You have never scared me." Elliot lets out a breath, his entire body sagging. "I have never felt safer than when you are near." Elliot places the safety pin on the counter, pressing his body against hers. His fingers travel to her temple.

"Can I kiss you here?"

"Yes."

He's immediate with it, his hands against her waist as he presses his lips against her skin. She wants to tell him she loves him, but only a gasp comes out. She trusts him, significantly more than he could ever trust her, so, even as her fingers shake with the need to get him out of here, she'll let him in. She'll trust him that he isn't at risk.

"Ready?" he asks, his hands moving to her back, and she nods. Aliyah has been undressed by a handful of people before. It's never bothered her. When she was younger, she used to be nervous, but it wasn't in the good way she is now. She's never cared before if people like what they see. There was always a "you look nice, but..." and she'd roll her eyes and ignore them. But now, Elliot's fingers ghost down her shoulders so carefully, his eyes focused on her, and she wants him to like what he sees. Her thighs shake slightly as Elliot's fingers skim across her skin, moving her hair out of the way. He's careful with it. With her.

He starts, and she feels the goosebumps on her skin as it hits the air, but it has nothing to do with the chill and everything to do with him. He swallows, and she catches his frown in the mirror, then he traces her shoulder blades.

"Can I kiss you here?" he asks, his fingertips light against the bruises on her skin.

Her breath is shaky when she replies. "Yes."

He does, and she feels like it's healed a part of her she never knew was broken. She sighs, rolling her neck as his lips warm her skin.

"Here?" he asks, his fingers light against her waist. Aliyah's answer remains the same, but he asks her every time anyway. When he gets to the end of the buttons, just above her bum, her wet dress sticks to her front. His fingers trail up her spine, and she lets out a deep breath, closing her eyes. Aliyah's about to shake her dress off, but Elliot's hands glide along her body until he tucks his fingers into the front. Aliyah's breathing is heavy, like she's done anything other than stand here, as he peels her dress off from her shoulders down to her waist.

"Fucking hell, Lia," he says, a half-bitten moan following his words. "Is all your underwear like this?" he asks, his voice tight.

He bends down, and she feels his lips near her hips, her heart racing like she's run a marathon. She lifts her feet when the dress hits them. She opens her eyes, and he's still on his knees, watching her. Her underwear is strapless, black, and lacey. Slightly see-through, but nothing special. Nothing compared to what she usually wears. "Are you telling me you're always just walking around looking like this under that cloak?" he asks, his thumb under the strap of her thong.

She shrugs, but the way he looks at her has her feeling on top of the world. "Some of them are bodysuits."

He groans, resting his forehead against the tail of her spine. Aliyah's body has been spoken about more than she would ever like, and yet, she's still managed to not hate what she sees in the mirror. Since she was a teenager, she knew she'd never care what anyone else thought, but now she knows that's not true. She wants Elliot to like what he sees. She'd never change for him, not even if he asked her with his handsome smile, but she wants him to like her all the same.

"You're flawless," he mutters, looking like a man possessed. "You look like people would dedicate their lives to trying to paint you, and they would never be successful. Can I touch you here?" he asks, his fingertips light against her hips.

"Always."

Elliot's hands glide over her skin, and she rolls her neck as he reaches her shoulders. His fingers rest against her neck, and when she opens her eyes, he's looking right at her. "You are unreasonably glorious, and you're going to need a robe."

Aliyah frowns. "Why?"

"Because you will get cold," he replies, "and because I am a gentleman, and you don't want to feel my dick against your ass the entire time."

She laughs, and Elliot pulls her into a hug. His bare arms match her body, she thinks. Like a watercolor painting. He kisses her temple again, and then he pulls his robe around her and lifts her onto the sink. His hands touch her back, and he slips her strapless bra off with ease. She helps him out with her panties, and she lifts her hips, wondering if his hands could have been heavier against her bum. She widens her legs a little, and Elliot slots between them.

"Ready?"

She hums and watches him as he starts unraveling her braids with care. Like this task is important to him. Like it matters if it goes well. He's doing it for her, despite how cruel she's been this evening. How mean she's been for days. Her eyes well up.

"We can stop," he says, taking his fingers out of her hair slowly. "Don't panic, sweetheart. I am done." He holds his hands up for the hundredth time this evening, and it just makes her want to sob harder.

"It is not," she says, wiping her face with her hand. God, she must look a mess. "I trust you. I trust you more than I trust myself. I would not have dreamed of being this close to the idea of water on my own, but it does not seem like such a big deal with you." Elliot frowns, the panic on his face lessening. "I trust you, and you cannot trust me back, and I am so sorry."

"Lia," he chuckles, moving closer, but she's already started talking again.

"And I know it is all my fault, but I could—I will prove to you that you can trust me."

He places his hands on her face, pushing her cheeks together just slightly. He laughs at the expression, and she wonders if he's as happy that they can touch now as she is. Even if he keeps hovering.

"Look at me," he says, his hand under her jaw. "Don't make me kiss you."

She frowns. "I would not mind."

Elliot laughs, groaning as he pushes her legs further apart, pulling her closer to him. "I don't want our first kiss to be because you have a guilt complex, and I need you to just *shhh* your pretty face for a second so I can tell you that I do, in fact, trust you with my life."

"But you..." She hesitates. Will it sound like she's forcing him to touch her?

"But I what?" he asks, his thumb stroking along her jaw.

She swallows. "You keep going to touch me, and then you stop, and if that is because you do not want to, that is obviously fine. But if it is because I said..." Her bottom lip quivers again.

"I hesitate because I don't want to overwhelm you. I have spent weeks thinking about touching you. Innocently and not," he says, and she feels her cheeks heat. Elliot doesn't mention it. "But I am aware of your distressingly difficult week, and you don't like physical touch, and I just—I don't want you to ever feel bad if you think you have to always say no to me."

She frowns. "What do you mean?"

He sighs, dropping his hands until he's leaning entirely on the sink. It brings him closer, and she wonders if she's ever wanted to kiss him more. "If I could, I would always be touching you. Somewhere. A hand on your ankle, or our thighs would touch while we sat together. But I know you don't like that."

"How? Is this what Melody was talking about?"

"Mel?"

"She mentioned you said someone—not even me, some other girl—flinched once, and—"

"She's a snake," he says with a laugh, running his hand over his face. "I didn't tell her anything about you, she just figured it out."

"I know." Aliyah smiles. "She told me."

"She tells you everything, apparently."

"El," she mutters, and he rests his forehead against her sternum. She runs her fingers along the back of his neck. "You can always touch me. Whether I like physical contact with people or not is irrelevant when it comes to you. You are different to everyone else."

He hums, pressing his lips to her collarbone, and then he's gone, but when she sees his face again, he's smiling. He starts unbraiding her hair again, and she resumes starting them off. She wants to get the wash over with, and she wants to lie on his bed with him if he lets her. Hopefully, he won't mind if she stays.

Aliyah gives it at least thirty seconds before she asks, "What do you want our first kiss to be?" she asks, the guilt still there but not her number-one priority. He is.

Elliot laughs a little as his face moves closer. He presses his lips to her temple, her jaw, and her nose. "Whatever you want it to be," he whispers. "And nothing at all to do with anyone else but us."

"Okay," she says, with a small smile. He picks up the braid again, and she wonders if she wishes he did just kiss her.

"I just want you to know," he says, almost through with the braid he started on minutes ago, but she kept distracting him. "I always want to kiss you. Me not kissing you then means nothing. The thought of kissing you comes as easy as breathing to me."

She groans. "It does not."

"It does too." He laughs, then says, "I think, where is Lia? I want to kiss her. What's Lia up to? I want to kiss her. Why's the Princess frowning at me? I want to kiss her."

"*Shhh.*"

"It's going to change my life," he whispers.

Lia pulls her lip between her teeth. Does he know she's the most inexperienced person alive? That the only thing she's ever learned is how to moan his name while she finds her own release?

"I have never..." she starts, playing with the drawstring on his sweats. "...I have never kissed anyone. I have never even touched anyone, Eli. I do not think I am going to change your life."

"Oh, my love," he says, his voice deliciously low. "That kiss is going to change my life."

"Elliot," she whispers, but he just dips his head, his lips against her ear.

"Your lips, your tongue, your sound," he mutters, his hand heavy against her waist. She's not sure when he slipped under her robe, but she wants it to fall undone with the tone of his voice. "Are going to change my life." And then he's gone, back to unbraiding her hair like her clit isn't pulsing, like there's not an ache between her legs she's not going to be able to quell. She wants to get him back—to play this game with him—but she's not sure she'd be any good at it. It's a terrifying thought, trying to be sexy and ending up, well, not.

"I want to kiss you as well," she whispers.

Elliot smirks. "I know."

She groans, this time with good-humored frustration. "You do not!"

He rolls his eyes, placing his hand on the sink.

"You know when you tried to slice my throat?" Elliot asks, and she rolls her eyes back at him. "You kept looking at my lips because you think I'm stupid pretty and all I thought was, damn, the prettiest girl in the world is going to kiss me. No thoughts about death. Just, *are my knees going to give out if this dreamboat gets any closer?*"

"Dreamboat?"

"I know," he says with a shrug, working on the next braid. "Austen ain't got nothing on me."

CHAPTER TWENTY-SEVEN

ELLIOT IS PUTTING OFF the inevitable. The last braid is undone; he's really just messing around with her hair now. It's cute, the bouncy curls that fall to the middle of her back. Everything about her turns him on, and she might know it. He can't think of another reason she's run her fingers along his abs every twenty seconds for the past hour. He thought he might burst into flame, but with every step he gets closer to washing her hair, the more his hands shake, and he can't think of anything other than the fear on her face when he mentioned the shower. He needs a moment to not think about how the love of his life was hurt when she should never have been. He just needs that.

"What's your favorite song?" Elliot asks.

Aliyah hums, her fingers playing with the tie on his sweatpants. "Something with bass, or something... unhinged."

"Unhinged?" Elliot asks with a laugh.

"Yeah. Like embarrassing lyrics that you belt from an open car window. Ooh, or a ballad."

Elliot hums, thinking as he goes to grab the hair products that he spent an unreasonable amount of time finding in the shop. He probably should have looked up a routine too. He used to do his mom's hair over the sink when he was younger after she got too stiff to do it herself, but their hair patterns aren't the same.

"Like, this?" He starts humming the tune, occasionally badly singing some words that he remembers from his family's Saturday cleaning days at home. He clicks his fingers, and he sways his hips and he dances, bending over so their eyeline is the same, if only to see her eyes sparkle in the florescent lights. His hips sway, and Lia covers her mouth with her hands, but it doesn't matter—he sees the smile either way.

"Are you not going to sing with me?" he asks, spinning on the spot.

"Absolutely not," she says with a laugh, wiping the tears from her face. What a beautiful sight. He pauses in front of her, holding his hand out.

"How about a dance?"

Aliyah smiles, a blindingly bright thing he wishes he had his camera for, then hops off the bathroom counter. Elliot wastes no time in bringing her close. He hums the melody as she breathes against him. They sway under the bathroom light, and he wonders if any dance has ever been more important. Elliot feels her lips against his throat, the light puffs of breath warming his skin as they move slowly.

"Elliot?"

"You can do whatever you want, Lia," he replies, and she laughs, but then she kisses the side of his neck.

"I can do it," she whispers. "If this is too hard for you, I understand. I can do it."

He kisses the top of her head. "No, we'll do it together, just promise me you'll stop me if it gets too much. I don't care if it takes us all night, I only want you to be as okay as you can be."

"Okay."

"Okay," he breathes, grabbing the supplies. Aliyah takes a deep breath, and he sees her knees shaking as she bends over the sink.

"What about if you lie down," he says, trying to figure out the best way to pour water over her head without having to imagine her having water poured over her head.

"I do not think there is space."

"Would that be better?" he asks, then, "Because whatever way it would be better, Lia, I'll make it work."

She swallows, her hair folded over her head. Her knees shake, and he can see the white of her knuckles. "I would like to see you."

Elliot wastes no time moving things around until Lia can lie down, her head hanging over the sink as she looks up at the ceiling. Her eyes are wet, she's shaking, and clearly terrified, and Elliot might kill everyone in the palace tomorrow whether they were there or not. Although, he supposes he should be killed too. She's right. He did leave her there. Why didn't he check? He thought somewhere in the back of his mind she'd be punished for attending the open day, but the thought of it being during daylight hours never crossed his mind.

"I am sorry," she says, her hands tight against the towel she has under her neck as he turns the tap on.

"You're not allowed to be sorry," he whispers. "Not right now."

She flicks her eyes to him, then back to the spot on the ceiling she's stared at for the last five minutes. "I did not mean to tell you about it like that."

"Lia."

She shakes her head, squeezing her eyes closed. "It was cruel, and I am *so* sorry. I would take the words back if I could."

"It's alright," he says, his voice low. He bends to press his lips to her hairline. "I forgive you. I will always forgive you. We're gonna wash it all away, okay? Anything that happened before right now, apart from the way you laughed when you tricked me at the lake," he says, and she laughs just slightly, "or the way you look in the morning sun. The way you frown when you're trying not to smile at me, and the way you make my heart stutter. Everything but you, we're washing away."

"You are my favorite thing," she says, her voice watery. "Do not wash that away."

The exhaustion hits Aliyah like a freight train the moment she sits on Elliot's bed. She feels like she's lived eight lives in the span of one evening. She holds the pajamas he gave her in her hand, and she feels her eyelids getting heavy,

"Can I help?" Elliot asks, and he's closer than she was expecting, but she doesn't flinch. Not anymore. She feels him sit on the bed next to her, and her breath is too choppy to answer him, so she just drops her hands. Elliot's fingers pull at the dressing gown without touching her skin at all, and the exhaustion leaves her so fast she almost gets whiplash. Aliyah almost leans back into his touch, her body thrumming with the need to feel his fingers on her again. She rolls her neck instead of curving her back into him as his hands reach toward her waist. The movement moves her hair over her shoulder.

"Sorry," she says quickly, but Elliot's already gathering her curls in his palm. She sees his hand come over her shoulder, tangled in her hair. Aliyah takes a deep breath.

"Arms up," he whispers, and she maneuvers until her arms are through the sleeves, and she lets him pull the front of the top down. She feels the warmth of his skin against her ribcage, but nothing ever touches her. Nothing ever lingers. "Jumper too?" he asks. Aliyah wonders if the scent on his jumper will send her over the edge. She's already dangerously close to burying her nose in the shirt, even though he's right behind her.

"No. You might get cold."

"I'll be fine. I want you to be comfortable," he replies, grabbing a sweater too. When he pulls her hair out of the way, she sees all his stuff in piles.

"I did not want to break your heart," she says with a sniff. Aliyah's not sure if she'll ever stop crying.

Elliot kisses her temple again. "I was never going to leave, and you can break it as many times as you want, as long as you keep it."

"I do not want to," she whispers. "Hurt you, I mean. I want... I do want to keep you."

Elliot gasps as he sinks to the floor, his tracksuit bottoms in his hand. "You want to keep me?"

Lia lets him move her feet through the legs, and she lifts her hips when he drags the material past her thighs. "Please," she whispers, her breath catching when he looks at her. "I missed you. I missed you so much. Please do not leave."

He's on his knees in front of her, and she knows as he looks up at her face she must look utterly wrecked. Her skin is on fire, and the soft lighting in his room will do nothing to stop him from seeing it. His hands are over his tracksuit, heavy against her waist, and she could reach out and touch him from here. She moves to touch him, to kiss him, to do something, but she leans on the wrist she forgot was aching, and her face collapses.

"Ow."

His face drops, his eyes immediately wet, and she gasps, holding his face in her hands.

"Darling," she whispers, but it does nothing to stop the sob that racks through his body. "I am *fine*."

"I missed you," he says, his eyes closing as he turns his face to kiss her palm. "Fuck, I'm there every fucking night, and I missed you there. I left you alone."

"Look at me. Elliot, do not make me kiss you."

He laughs, and it sounds like sunshine after months of rain. "Sorry."

She wipes his cheeks dry. "You did not leave me there," she begs. "And I will never forgive myself for how I told you, but please, please... You are already saving me. You have already saved me. We washed it away."

"I don't know how to do this," he whispers, and Lia closes her eyes, taking a deep breath because he's about to tell her he can't be around her and she's only been touching him for five seconds. "I want to protect you, and I'm not allowed near you—you won't let me anywhere near you. I need you to tell me you won't push me away. I need you to trust me, to listen to my plans and just—please, don't ask me to leave again. No matter what."

"I will not ask you to leave," she whispers, running her thumb over his lip. "But God, Elliot, I do not want you to feel helpless. What are you going to do when someone screams at me, when—when someone tries to touch me?"

"Lia," he says, lying on the bed and pulling her against him. "You can handle yourself when someone screams at you. I know you can, so all I will do it make sure *I* never scream at you. I have plans in place for everything else, okay? From Lucian trying to throw something at you in the dining hall, to a full invasion."

"Elliot."

He laughs. "I'm serious. I will take you through it all tomorrow. I don't have to share you until tomorrow. Tonight, it is just you and I. But I have spent the last few weeks making sure you are safe, and I plan to do it for the rest of my life."

"I do not want you to feel like you cannot control your life."

"I knew that was a risk when I met you under the plum trees, Lia. I would have done anything for you. I would do anything for you. Everything I have control over is already yours."

"You are ridiculous," she mutters, tracing her name over his heart. Sometimes with the word Harper after.

Elliot laughs, threading his fingers through hers. "I knew there was a risk with this life, and I fell in love with you anyway."

Lia swallows. It's not the first time tonight that Elliot has said he loves her, but it's the first time she's allowing herself to really listen.

"You love me?"

He nods. "Yes. But I have a plan and a better first-time story, so *shhh*, pretend you didn't hear me."

Aliyah laughs, a wet sound that claws up her throat, battling the happiness to see what comes out first. "I do not need a better first time."

"Nope," he replies, pulling her even closer. She tucks her head into the crook of his neck.

"Elliot."

"*Shhh*."

CHAPTER TWENTY-EIGHT

The sky is so bright that Elliot has to squint, even though he's not looking directly at it. The rays reflect off the fountains, the tiny spades on the lawn, and the windows in the greenhouse. Elliot can't get away from the sunshine. It's a nice feeling after weeks of rain, and he wonders if the weather has decided to play ball for her. Elliot knows Aliyah is on the lawn, overseeing one of the many gardening initiatives she's set up. He knows she's avoided it so far this season, but now, she's back. She's happier, and the sun is shining.

Elliot is blindingly happy, and he's managing to only feel thirty to forty-percent guilty about it. He woke up this morning next to Aliyah. Encased by the warmth of her skin, and the curls against his face that escaped the braid he made for her. He kissed the back of her neck, and she smiled at him like she'd been waiting for him to come home for the past eight months and he finally walked through the door. A life with her is all he wants, so having a slice of it this morning made him incredibly happy.

The rest—the nervousness, the terror, the determination to take down the monarchy—seep through his bones without a moment's notice. When Lia changed into some clean clothes of his, and the bruises on her shoulder blades hadn't gone, even if her wrist had looked dramatically better in the morning light. She moved it with ease, and his heart settled every time she did so without a wince of pain. When he sees a guard walking through the gardens, unaware if he's someone who held her down in the dungeons, or if he's someone Elliot could get onside. Elliot's not foolish enough to think the struggle is over now just because they're talking again. It doesn't mean they don't have a monarchy to take down. He used to feel ridiculous, writing schedules in his notebook and maps on the back of his hand while he sat cramped in a makeshift tunnel. Now, he's armed with plans that will keep her safe. Equipment that a child would use, but he's just smart enough to use them differently.

They need to discuss everything properly, but he'll let it go for one more day, because what he really needs to know is what is Aliyah's end goal? Does she want to rule alone, or will she surprise him and say she's marrying Lucian after all, and he'll have to figure out how to keep her safe while his heart plummets off a cliff? Just because he told her he loved her—she didn't say it back, but he wasn't expecting her to—doesn't mean her endgame is him. He knows she cares about him, she might even love him, and maybe one day, she'll tell him. For right now, he's content to watch her blush when he says she's pretty, screw up her nose when he says she's lovely, and kiss his nose when he says he loves her.

The thought of being King has weighed heavily on Elliot's mind ever since he found out who she was. He's not naive enough to think she would fall for him and immediately want to spend her life with him, but sometimes, she says things out loud that he thinks she's supposed to keep to herself, and it gives him a glimmer of hope.

Elliot never wanted to be King. It's not something he thought about when he was a child. It's not something he ever dreamed of. When he found out she was the Princess, he spent more of his time figuring out how to get her to stop. Would she run away with him? And then he realized *who* she was as a princess. How kind she was, how fair. How she would turn this kingdom around so fast if she was given the proper opportunity. If she wasn't tripped up at every possible occasion. If only she had people on her side. Elliot started speaking to guardsmen in the common room, landscapers in the gardens, and house staff over breakfast, and found that despite the palace's image and the media portrayal, the kingdom is waiting for *her*. They're ready for her. He could never ask her to leave.

So, his thoughts turned to wondering, could he be King? Probably. It doesn't look that hard. The worst thing about it is that he would become everything he ever hated. But now, he knows that's not true. He's never hated Lia. So the question is, is there a world in which Aliyah would ever want him next to her? Does she think of her life with him, or does she think of him for just some time? Just until the wedding. Just until the next person. Just until. He wants to ask her, but right now, they have a plan to put in place. And he doesn't want her to feel pressured. If she laughed in his face at the concept, would she be worried he'd leave her alone right now? He never would. If she asked him to, he'd walk to the ends of the earth for her.

But right now, they need a game plan. And he has all the facts and ideas, and she has the ability to pull them off. So, he sits in the greenhouse, just waiting to see if she'll come and talk to him, because it's been at least six hours and he *misses* her.

The sunshine is blazing overhead, and Aliyah feels a headache blooming from how she keeps frowning under the bright sky. But she's tired, she had a late night and an early headache-filled morning. That, along with the worst few weeks, and the fact she set up the umbrellas for the children to ensure they had shade (she sat down before she realized she didn't have one herself) means she's frowning.

"Lia, Lia," Jamie says, running over with a tiny bent spade in his hand. "It broke."

"Oh, no!" she says, taking it from him as he pouts. "The roots were too big?"

"Yeah," he whispers, his head low, and his hands in front of him like he's done anything wrong. "I'm sorry, Princess Lia."

"Did you do it on purpose?" she asks, and he shakes his head. "Well, then, there is nothing to be sorry for, is there?" She feels her frown lessen when he looks up and smiles at her. "Sometimes Superman is just *too* strong."

Jamie giggles, bending forward like children do when they can't control themselves. He's adorable. "Can I ask Mr. Harper for a new one?"

And the answer is yes, of course. His spade snapped, and he needs a new one, and Elliot would definitely have one. So, yes, he could ask him for one. The only issue is that would deny Aliyah a reason to go and see him beyond the fact that she just wants to. It was different before, when she could pretend she just liked to sit under the plum tree and he happened to stroll past. He never knew she was sitting there for hours at a time waiting for him. But everything feels a little different now, more monumental. Like she can't just walk over and see him. Not now he's seen her at her most vulnerable—the parts she hides from people. She's not sure she wants to anymore. Not with him. That doesn't mean she's particularly good at this. She spent the night with him, he told her he loved her, and now she's too scared to go and see him because she only saw him this morning, and is that too soon? Will she be coming on too strong? Does he know how she wants to keep him forever if only he looks at her the way he has been?

But now, finally, there's a reason to go and see him. And she doesn't mind stealing that from a child.

"I can go, J. You work on separating the dahlias, okay?"

"Okay, Princess Lia," he replies with a smile, running back to the group. "Thank you."

She almost feels guilty. When she gets to the doors, she swallows. She hasn't been here since their fight—a fight that lingers in the back of her mind every now and then. Elliot may love her, but he still despises everything else. The palace, the lifestyle, royalty. There's no way she could ever keep him here. He may love her now—an idea that she hasn't fully come around to—but he might still leave in a month or two.

She shakes her head and knocks. Jamie needs a spade, and Aliyah needs to see Elliot's face.

"It's open."

Aliyah walks in, the creak of the door settling her jittery heart.

"Hi."

Elliot spins, his eyebrows high as he smiles. "Hi, my love!" He walks over, and she wants to hug him. Can she, even though she spent the entirety of the night clinging to him?

She takes a step back, holding her hands behind her. Elliot squints, but he stops too, a few steps away. The door is closed now, but if she gets used to touching him in broad daylight, she'll be thrown to the bottom of the lake with a boulder tied to her feet.

"You know you don't have to knock, right?" Elliot asks. It almost makes her take another step back. Does he think she can just go wherever she likes simply because she's royalty? Or is it a simple question? He cocks his head, presumably because she hasn't replied at all.

"Lia," he says softly, and she looks up at him. "Not because I think you will just barge in here with your royal procession floating behind you." She rolls her eyes, and he laughs. It's not lost on her that he figured out what was wrong without her having to say so. "You don't have to knock because it's you."

Lia hums, rolling her lips. "May I have another small spade, please? Jamie's is bent."

Elliot squints again, but she sees the playfulness on his face, and she's in trouble. She'll fall for his boyish charm every time.

He walks closer, and she takes a step back until she hits the workbench. Elliot doesn't stop, his body against hers as she looks up at him. Her eyes fall to his lips, because when don't they? She knows he's waiting for her, that he'll stay doing whatever they're doing without so much as a peck if she doesn't initiate. What she wants is for him to claim her, wrap his hands through her hair and kiss her like it's the only thing he ever thinks about. Every time he's in her eyeline, she's thinking about him. What his lips would feel like against hers. If he'd use his tongue on other parts of her body. If he thinks about what she'd feel like when she comes.

Her breath is ragged, and her body is hot, thrumming with need as he reaches his hand up. Maybe it's now. Maybe now he'll tug on her hair until she's in the perfect position for his teeth to pull on her lip. Maybe it'll be soft, his nose brushing hers until she's a panting mess.

"Elliot," she whispers, as his nose does, in fact, touch hers.

"Yes, Your Highness?" he whispers. His hand falls, and she closes her eyes, waiting for the impact. If he'll hold the back of her head, or if his hand will fall to her waist. Instead, she feels something hard against her stomach. She blinks her eyes open, and he's smirking, that stupid attractive look he has on his face whenever he's being the worst person she knows.

Aliyah fumbles for his hand, but that's not what she her fingers fall on.

"A spade for you," he mutters, and she wants to bite him. Just a little. Elliot moves away, and there's an ache between her legs that will stay until she touches herself later, she just knows it.

"Thank you," she replies, her chest heaving as if she's done anything other than look at his face.

"You're welcome."

He potters around like he's completely unaffected by her presence. Like his entire body isn't sparking because they dared to be close. She wants him to react, wants him to come completely undone just by her words and the mere promise of their skin touching. But she's never tried before. There's never been a time when she wanted to turn someone on. There's never been a time she wanted someone to fall apart beneath her hands. There's never been him.

Aliyah pulls her lip between her teeth. She could leave now. There's no reason for her to be here. Still, she asks. "Would you have said yes if it were for me?" The words leave her mouth before she can think about the implications of that question. Her fists tighten beside her as she comes to the horrifying realization that she cares what his answer will be. He'll say yes. She's so sure he'll say yes, and yet, she's not sure what to do when he does.

Elliot smiles, his tongue running behind his bottom lip, and her heart skips a beat. It's becoming a regular occurrence, a borderline nuisance if she could think about anything other than the shape of his mouth. Aliyah wonders how many times it has to happen before that's just the way her heart beats now.

"I would expect a curtsey, Your Highness."

Aliyah laughs—an undignified sound that takes her by surprise, as it always does. She's used to being in control of her actions. There hasn't been a time since she was a child that she's laughed out of turn. That her smile hasn't been practiced beyond criticism. And yet, one moment with him, and the sound flutters around her ribcage before it explodes in his face. He looks just as shocked as she feels, but his smile widens all the same. He walks closer to her again, and she steadies herself. She's in control this time. She's thought about him in her bedroom enough to know that sometimes, she can be in control.

"Would you?" he asks, placing his hands on either side of her on the workbench. She looks up at him, her tongue peeking out to moisten her lips. She smiles just slightly when his pupils dilate and his arms tense.

"Would I what, Elliot?" she asks, her voice low, and he pulls himself closer. She dips her mouth to his ear as she asks, "Would I curtsey for you?" Elliot clenches his jaw, and she feels it under her lips as she runs her fingers along his side. "Or do you want something else?"

"I want whatever you want to give me," he mutters, his voice strained. Aliyah hums, and she prays that she sounds more confident than her shaky fingers suggest.

"What if I were to get on my knees?" she asks, and Elliot's hands tighten against her waist as he groans. She smiles, pulling her lip between her teeth as his breath becomes heavy.

"Go outside."

Lia gasps. "How rude," she says, putting a hand to her chest in mock outrage.

He lifts his head, pulling her fully against him with his palm flat against her back. She gasps for real when she feels him against her. Elliot brushes his nose against hers, and for a fleeting moment, she thinks she might have sex for the first time in the middle of the greenhouse, in the middle of the day. She doesn't think she'd mind at all.

"*Please*. Go outside. Princess."

She kisses his cheek, and then she pulls back. "Bye."

Elliot chases her lips, but he lets her go with a huff.

"Lia," he says, and she turns before she opens the door. "Just so you know... I think you're delightful."

Lia is frowning again, but she might be the happiest she's ever been. Sure, the threat of imminent death is close, but it has been the entire time she's been here. But Elliot distracted her enough that on her stroll back to the gardens, she handed Jamie his spade and forgot all about the umbrella. Now, she thinks if she moves to get it, she'll go back to him, and she hasn't done enough research on what to do if she *was* on her knees, so she stays seated. The clouds pass over the sun, and Lia spends at least ten seconds trying to get her eyebrows to go back to their normal position before she realizes it's not cloudy at all.

"Hi, Princess."

She turns her head, frowning again, but Elliot just laughs, tightening the umbrella in place. He sits down, but he's not close to her. He's about as far away as any normal guard would be, but she feels the pull in her chest. She spins, her knees tilted toward him so she's a little more comfortable, and maybe because she likes his face. Even with the space between them, she feels the warmth coming from him. How she never wants to sleep again without him right there. The only reason she's allowing herself to be in public with him at all is because Elliot swears they have no idea who he is. That he knows they are scrambling to scare her. It makes sense, seeing as her mother hasn't mentioned it since.

Aliyah smiles. "Hi."

"I thought you might want some help."

"I am literally doing nothing," she replies, resting her elbow on her knee and her head in her hand.

He hums. "But that group of boys over there are about to ask you to help them with their trellis."

"Are you sure you did not just miss me?"

Elliot laughs, but then the boys walk over, and Lia screws up her nose. Damn.

"Miss Princess, please can you tie the rope for us?"

"Of course," she replies, holding her hands out, and they start placing string and random bits of stick in her hands, and then they're gone.

"See," Elliot says triumphantly. "I am here to rescue you."

"It is just a trellis," she says, holding her materials hostage. Elliot moves to sit on the grass in front of her.

"It's an obelisk."

"Same thing."

He squints. "Is it, though?" he asks, and she sighs, handing the sticks over. His fingers graze along her palms and she swallows thickly.

"This program is great," Elliot says, easily screwing the wood together to make a shape she never would have thought of. "The children love it."

Aliyah hums. "I am trying to replicate it in Loven, and—"

Elliot's eyes widen. "Yeah?"

"Yes," she replies.

"Loven's my home," he says with a smile. "I would have killed for a program like this."

"It is just some basic gardening skills," she says, looking around.

"Don't do that. You don't have to do that." She looks at him. "You know, put your ideas down."

"I know" she replies. But she doesn't, not really. Every idea she's ever had has been scrutinized. Watered down until she was able to get it past her parents. Lia is not used to people saying nice things to her, not about things she cares about.

"You're doing a great job," he says, twisting the rope around the wood. He'll be done soon, and she's looking around for anything that might make him stay. "Even if this is what you did with all the power in the world and a family that deserves to be near you, it would still be amazing. You're doing amazing things, Lia."

She clears her throat, blinking away tears. "Thank you."

"You're welcome, my love," he says, admiring the obelisk in front of him that would have taken her too long. Well, time's up.

"You see the roses outside my room?" Lia says, pointing to the trellis that arches over her balcony. He nods that he does. "Would you be able to trim them back for me?"

"Sure." He shrugs. "I will need permission to do it during the day."

"You have it," she replies.

"I do?" he says with a gasp. He lowers his voice, leaning a little closer as if they are not five feet apart. "Does knowing the Princess come with perks?"

Aliyah rolls her eyes, holding the ball of string as he ties it around the small makeshift *not* trellis. "You can have anything you want."

He looks at her for a moment, saying nothing at all. She wonders if he's about to pounce on her or if it's just wishful thinking. Then he settles, rolling his shoulders.

"I can't believe there's nothing else to build," he groans, then adds, "because I did, in fact, just come out because I miss you."

Aliyah smiles. "You did?"

"Mm-hmm. Even though you were being a temptress," he says, looking around, then, with his voice low, he says, "and you're clearly desperate for me to come in my pants. I missed you."

Lia laughs, her palms pressed into the raised bed she sits on. "Am I not tempting now?"

"Don't start," Elliot whispers. Then he takes a deep breath, his playful glare disappearing. "We need to talk about our game plan. Do you want to do that now, or later?"

"Later," she replies. "Although, I suppose I do have dinner tonight."

"Ew," Elliot says, his attempt at being jokey when he's clearly planning Lucian and Dorian's demise. His eyes linger on her wrist.

"It is better," she replies, flexing it a little. It's not fractured; it was barely even strained. The ache has pretty much disappeared. "I promise."

"Okay," he replies. "Okay."

"So," Lia starts. She trusts Elliot, so she'll do whatever he thinks is right, whether that means stabbing them at dinner or smothering them to death in their sleep. She'll do whatever it is he thinks is right.

"I need you to be nice to them."

Well, fuck.

CHAPTER TWENTY-NINE

Elliot paces around the greenhouse, waiting for Aliyah's arrival. They agreed that he shouldn't go to dinner. That his presence at all events may be too obvious. Even with the number of Black people Aliyah has made sure are hired by the palace, he is still outnumbered. He is still easy to pick out of a lineup. He said okay at the time, but now, he's sweating. The dungeons were clear when he checked earlier. Just once. Elliot also looked through the dining hall windows *just* once. Lia was fine, a small smile on her face as Lucian laughed. Not at her, he hopes, but he wouldn't know because he's not there.

It made sense—it made so much sense—but he's not sure how he's supposed to survive while she's there. So, he's pacing. It was stupid, thoughtless, to leave her alone. He could—he would—he can—

"Hi."

Elliot spins, and she's there. In the safety of the greenhouse. His eyes flick over her body as he walks toward her.

"Are you alright?" he asks, wrapping his arms around her. He pulls her close, frowning just a little when she hesitates. Her hands are against his waist, but as he pulls back, she hugs him properly, and he feels a bag hit him in the back.

"Yeah."

"Lia," he says, pressing his lips to her temple. "This only works if you're honest with me. Are you okay?"

She smiles as he leans back, her hands still clasped behind his back. "I am fine. I just... Dinner is weird when you are not there."

He lets out a deep breath. "Well, we're about to go over our game plan, and I don't know if I can *not* be with you when they're around. If I can be, without it being detrimental, or you know if you don't want that too, that's fine. Whatever you want."

"Eli." She laughs. "It is fine. You can be there."

He smiles, even if she doesn't tell him she wants him there. He doesn't push her because—well, she might not. Elliot walks over to his workbench, his plans laid out like he's trying to take down an entire nation and not an old man and his son.

"What is all this?" Lia asks.

"Um," he says, a nervous laugh against the still night air. He flicks the fan on. "This is my plan."

"Elliot," she replies, her fingers against the hand-drawn maps and the detailed itinerary. "How long have you been planning this?"

"Since I found out who you were," he says with a shrug.

"Since the greenhouse?" she asks, her head tilting.

"No, before that. The evening after the canopy."

"But you did not know I had been hurt then."

He shrugs. "At first, I was looking Lucian up because I was jealous and wanted to know anything bad about him so I'd feel better." He lets out a self-deprecating laugh. "It sounds lame out loud. Then it was just too easy to find out evil stuff about him. I—well, at first I thought I was just going to give you the information and let you figure out if you wanted to marry him, and then I realized you didn't want to, and by the time I knew about the dungeons," he says with a wince, "I was already deep into figuring out how to get him gone."

"You love me," she whispers, her eyes still on the table in front of her.

"I do."

Aliyah hums, wiping her face with the back of her hand. "When do you plan on telling me properly?"

Elliot laughs, his head tilting back. "Mind your business!" He has a plan that he thinks she'll love, and it's almost killing him not to tell her right now.

"What is step one?" Lia asks, sitting on the bench he made for her. She places the bag on the table. "Oh, and I brought you dinner."

Elliot gasps. "Oh, you really want me to tell you, huh?"

Lia frowns at him, screwing her nose up, and he thinks he's never been more in love in his life.

"I could banish you."

"I know." He smiles, opening the bag. "But I love you, so please don't."

His plan is still in motion, but he doesn't feel any less for telling her now, not with how her smile lights up the greenhouse.

"Did you know that whenever you tell me something—anything about you, really, or if you suggest you might like being around me," Elliot says, fingers fiddling with a tray on the side, "that you disappear for days?"

"Pardon?" Aliyah asks nervously. She wonders if he's upset she hasn't said she loves him. She does, of course, she even thinks he might know that. But she's terrified to say it out loud.

He shrugs. "It's not a big deal. It was more before. You know I'd just walk around the forest waiting for you, but you were somewhere hiding from me, and now—now you don't tell me much."

"What do you mean?"

"Nothing bad," he replies. "I just—I would like to know if you miss me, and maybe that's silly because I'm not giving you enough time to miss me. I don't know. It's not a big deal, okay. I just miss you all the time. That's all."

"I am here," she whispers, looking at her fingers. Can he not tell every fiber of her being wants to be wherever he is? That she *always* wants to touch him, and she spent twenty-four years avoiding anyone's hand? Sometimes she's not sure how to tell him anything useful. She's so used to people not wanting to talk to her that she forgets she can tell him silly things, important things. Like she wants to wake up next to him, or she wants to know if he had nicknames when he was a child, and ask if his sister is coming to visit again.

Elliot's smiling at her when she looks up. "I know. I know." He turns away. He's probably doing something useful while she sits here and wonders how she's supposed to tell him she cares what he thinks, and that she wants to hold his hand, and that she's so stupidly, embarrassingly, ridiculously in love with him that she barely knows how to function when he's not around. Aliyah has never been one for emotional displays. She vaguely remembers crying at a charity dinner, and then her mother chastised her about it because they had to make a bigger donation than they wanted. Still. Elliot was brave enough to tell her about his feelings. She'll be brave enough to act on them. He's moving seed trays around, and she can't see him at all, which is better, she thinks, for what she's about to try and do.

Aliyah swallows, blinking rapidly. She counts to five, then...

"You look handsome today." *Nailed it.*

Elliot laughs. Loudly. The sound floats through the air, tousling her braids and settling behind her ribcage. She still hasn't figured out how to make it her alarm clock. (As if she's woken up later than him a single day since he arrived.) When he spins back to face her, he's still laughing, though it's not unkind, so the frown she wears is mainly for show.

"God," he groans, his head thrown back. She's suddenly aware she hasn't been spending enough time thinking about the thick cords of his neck. "You're so fucking cute."

Aliyah hasn't been called cute by anyone but Elliot since she was about eight years old and thrown into some ugly thick white socks and plastered across the front page of the tabloid papers. The moment she turned ten, the adjectives used to describe her changed for the worse, though she was never supposed to see them anyway.

Elliot runs his fingertips over the back of her hand, and she almost misses his question. Aliyah knows they've touched now. They danced together, and then they slept side by side, but there was a reason behind it. He was forced to dance, and he was comforting her last night. She's not used to the feeling of touching someone just because she *wants* to.

"Have you been practicing that while I potted up the lupines?"

It takes her a moment to remember how to talk, shove the blush from her cheeks, and act like she's always been taught.

"Of course not." *Yes.* "I always think you are handsome."

Elliot smiles—charming, mischievous, and everything she fell asleep thinking about last night. And every night since she met him, if she had to be honest... which she does not, so she refuses to say it out loud.

"I think you are the most glorious person every second of the day," he says with a wild smile. She knows he's being an ass, but she can feel the blush on her cheeks all the same.

"You are not allowed to piggyback on my compliment."

"My sincerest apologies, Your Highness," he replies, with a deep bow. He drops her hand, and she barely resists the plea for him to put it back. She can sense his smirk, even though she can only see the top of his head.

She sighs. "Tomorrow, I am having you banished."

"Can't wait," he says, his palms against the workbench as he swings a little closer to her. She's looking at his lips when he turns away, and she's sure he knows it. He doesn't act on it, though—he just goes about with his tasks. He takes the flowers out of their cells, finding new pots to put them in. He brings one closer to her.

"Aren't they adorable?" he says, cradling the lupine seedling in his palms. They are cute, with their mismatched leaves. Aliyah tilts her head to get a better look, but really, she just wants him to stay. Her hand hovers just underneath his, and she counts to two in her head before she presses her skin against his. She hears his intake of breath and looks up at him.

"Yes," she replies. Her thumb rubs against his knuckles. "Very cute."

Elliot hums, moving away and placing it into another pot. She watches him wash his hands. She wants to help him. Something he could do himself, but she wants to do it because she cares. Because she loves him. She doesn't, though, she just sits on the workbench and wonders if she should leave. It's dark, and according to the plans in Elliot's mind and all over his workbench, they're trying to take down a monarchy from tomorrow. By the time she suggests calling it a night, she's touched him three times. And it's not enough. Elliot walks her to the door, and she wishes she wasn't under constant scrutiny so he could walk her home.

"You do not have to watch me," she says with a laugh.

Elliot smiles. "I know."

Aliyah rolls her eyes, heaving the door open just a crack. She has one foot on the gravel path before she turns back. He frowns, clearly about to ask if she's alright, but she talks before he has a chance.

"I used to be a night owl."

"Oh, yeah?" Elliot teases, though he's smiling like even if this is the most information she's willing to give him, he'll take it with open arms. "I despised waking up early because there was no point to it. I would just be lonely earlier in the day. I think being lonely at nighttime is different. You can convince yourself everyone is lonely when it is dark. And then you happened," she says, her fingers knotting together. "And now I cannot wait for morning."

Elliot smiles at her, his fingers brushing her arm just slightly, and it's still not enough. Her arms loop around his neck, and she rests her chin against his shoulder. His arms wrap around her so quickly it takes her by surprise, even if she knew he'd hug her back. He sighs, one hand tight against her ribs, one holding her head close with his thumb rubbing beneath her ear and she honestly, truly, never wants to leave.

He whispers. "You are, without a doubt, the best part of my life."

"See you tomorrow," she replies, letting her hands run down his chest as she moves back.

"Good night, Your Highness."

He smiles at her, and she thinks if she doesn't kiss him right now, she really might cease to exist. So, she leans forward, just slightly—enough so he can move away if he wants, but he doesn't. He doesn't lean forward either, but she doesn't mind, not when it's so obvious in the way he breathes and the way his muscles tense that he's been thinking about kissing her as long as she has him. So, she moves first. Her nose brushes against his, and for a moment, they breathe together and it's enough. She could move back, and it would be enough for now. But she's always wanted as much of Elliot as she can have. So, she presses her lips to his, her hands fisted in his shirt. It's slow, short—everything she meant for it to be—but she wants more. She's just not sure how to get it. But Elliot helps with his hand back against her neck, holding her close.

His lips brush hers again. "Can I—"

"*Yes.*"

His lips are dizzying against hers, and she stumbles back into the greenhouse. Her hands are rampant with need, touching his chest, his arms, anywhere she can reach to make him closer. They move together like a practiced dance until he backs her against the workbench.

"Do you want to sit up here?" Elliot asks, his breath coming thick and fast. Aliyah nods, not trusting her voice. He moves everything—pots falling to the floor, soil scattering the ground—and Lia would laugh if she could get enough air into her lungs. Elliot looks at her, his hair wild from her hands, and he smiles as his arm sweeps out to the side and he bows deeply. She'd roll her eyes at him if she could concentrate on anything but the muscles of his back. "Your Highness."

"You are insufferable," she says with a sigh, though she moves closer to the workbench all the same. She wonders if it's a little high for her to jump onto with any decorum. There's an eighty-percent chance she'll snap her wrist, even if it is mainly healed, but at least then she won't have to go to the dance this Friday. There's barely a moment to genuinely consider the offer before Elliot's hands are against her waist, lifting her through the air. It happens so slowly she's sure she can see the specks of dust in the air, the slight movement of Elliot's arms, the way her stomach drops to her feet.

"Are you alright, Princess?"

Aliyah looks at him. It's supposed to be a kiss only, but she can't bring herself to look away from his face. She knows him; he lets her know him. She knows every angle of his body, even if this is the first time she's touching this part of him. She knows if she slides her hand down his back, there will be a sliver of skin, because his top is never fully tucked in. She knows he wants her as badly as she wants him, and it makes her feel feral.

"You stopped breathing," Elliot whispers. She runs her finger along his top lip.

"Careful," Elliot warns. His hair brushes against her cheekbone, invading her personal space. She wants him to move closer. "I will come entirely undone with the brush of your thumb and the wit of your mouth."

"Can I tell you something?"

"Anything," he replies, his hand resting against her thigh, the other against her jaw. She accommodates him, opening her legs. He stands between them, and she thinks it will be a miracle if he hears her question over the thumping of her heart.

"I had never kissed anyone before," she whispers as his thumb brushes over her bottom lip. "And yet I think I am going crazy with how badly I want your lips on me."

His grasp on her jaw tightens. Her eyes are trained on his lips, but she catches the way his eyes close.

"Lia," he mutters.

She leans forward again, her lips parted just a little, but it's enough. Elliot wraps his arm around her back, pulling her closer. He kisses her like she is about to vanish, like she will disappear into thin air. His lips are persistent, dizzying, but calm as she figures out how to kiss him back. She's supposed to be leaving it here, but she can't help herself, and she kisses him again and again until his hands are under her thighs, pulling her closer. One of his hands drops to the workbench, and one lands on her waist, and she thinks she might burst into flames.

"I have been thinking about this kiss since I was sixteen," Elliot mutters.

"You did not know me when you were sixteen."

"So?" He shrugs, pulling her closer still. "I missed you anyway, and I thought about a kiss like this. It was always going to be you."

His thumb rests against her chin and she lets him maneuver her mouth until his tongue touches her. When he nips at her lower lip, she lets out a little sound—a sort of desperate moan. She spreads her legs wider, even though there is no point between them where they're not touching. She feels him harden against her, and she wants to move. She *needs* to move. Her body feels warm, even with the cold evening. A lick full of lust crawls up her throat as he tugs at her hair. She moans, her hand fisting against his top to pull him closer as she rocks her hips just once—barely a movement at all—but he ducks, his forehead coming to rest against her shoulder.

"So... sorry," she pants, dropping her hold on him. She can barely breathe, let alone think up an appropriate apology for the pain he appears to be in. He groans, his hand heavy against her lower back holding her flush to him.

"Don't."

Aliyah places her hands against the workbench. Feeling the grains on the wood helps to ground her. Her head is somewhere in the clouds, yet all she can see, all she can think about, is Elliot. The hot breath he pants against her collarbone. The ache between her legs. His hand slides up her back, and when his fingertips touch her bare skin, she realizes she's covered in a light sheen of sweat. She hasn't done anything, apart from being taken completely apart by Elliot's mouth. His other hand finds hers gripping the counter edge, and he places it back against his chest.

"Never be sorry," Elliot whispers, his lips against her jaw. "You drive me crazy."

"Why did you stop?"

Elliot chuckles, his forehead against her shoulder. "Because you are entirely captivating, and I don't want to come in my trousers."

Aliyah maneuvers him until his lips are touching hers again.

"Stay with me," she says. "Tonight. Stay with me."

CHAPTER THIRTY

THE LATE-NIGHT BREEZE DOES nothing to stop the light sheen of sweat that rolls down Elliot's neck. He's had sex before. He's not even sure sex is on the cards tonight, seeing as they kissed for the first time half an hour ago, but he has had sex before. Yet, every time he's around her, he feels like he's about to blow. She says something, anything, and he's hard. She looks at him with her wide eyes, like she has no idea he's burning from the inside out. And yet, as he stands nervously on her balcony, it's not that that makes his hands shake. He's about to see her room for the first time.

Elliot knows the differences between them. He's been researching it for weeks. He's known since the moment he met her that they're opposites, yet he's about to go in a room that's bigger than his entire house, full of things he could never afford. Aliyah has never made their differences an issue—she's never seemed like she cared at all—but it weighs on his mind as he waits for her to slide the doors open.

"You do not have to knock," she says, and he hears her before he sees her. But then she opens the curtain, and he's breathless. Her face is clean, no makeup left over from dinner. Her hair hangs loosely, cascading over her shoulders, and she's so beautiful. It does nothing to calm his nerves.

"Come," she says, ushering him in. He thinks he will, probably too quickly, and if she has her way (which she always will), in his pants. "I made tea."

"I don't want to get your stuff dirty," he says, standing as still as possible in her room. She frowns more at her things than him as she hands him a cup.

"You look clean. Besides, I do not mind a little mess."

She gestures for him to sit on her bed, and he toes off his shoes, leaning them up beside the window. He's imagined this room so many times. The thoughts of her dancing to bassy songs, doing her hair, touching herself. And yet, it's not what he expected, and somehow exactly what he would think her room would be like. It's more subtle than the rest of the palace, with subdued, neutral colors on the wall. It looks like someone lives here. Like someone is happy here. Lia sits next to him, and the duvet swallows most of her bottom half which is good because she's only in his sweater and a ridiculously small pair of shorts. He smiles at her, his heart thumping too loudly for how quiet the room is, and spins to place his tea on the saucer so he can get it out of his shaky hands, but he knocks over some trinkets while he moves.

"Fuck. I'm—shit."

"It is okay," Aliyah says with a laugh, moving over toward him to see the damage. He can't look at whatever fell on the floor, because she just placed her hand on his thigh, her fingertips brushing the inside of his leg as her entire body leans over his. His head feels fuzzy with her this close, in this position, in this room. But he steadies her body with a hand against her waist anyway. Just so she doesn't fall over the edge.

"It is just some books," she says. "No big deal."

"I think I'm too clumsy to be here," he replies, huffing out a laugh. Lia moves back, no longer hovering over his lap, but she's closer than she was before.

"They are just things, Elliot."

"What if it was important? Or expensive? I..." He wants to tell her he wouldn't be able to replace it, but she knows that. He's not entirely sure he could afford anything in this room. He definitely doesn't have anything worth giving her.

"You are more important than the things I own," she whispers, her fingers playing with the edge of his top. "I know I am not particularly good with words, but you know that, right? You know

I think the world of you, and that I think you are stupid pretty. Right?" And he does. He does know that. Aliyah sneaks out of her house, past guards and a villainess mother just to come and see him. She brings him dinner, and she watches him working from her balcony. He does know that.

He kisses her once as he lies back on her bed.

"I do know that." She follows him, and her eyebrows raise when he gasps at the ceiling. It's covered in pastel watercolor paints: the depiction of a sunrise from corner to corner.

"Is that hand painted?"

"Yes," she replies, pulling her lip between her teeth. "I did not do it. But it is pretty, is it not?"

He looks at her, tucking a braid behind her ear. (She said they were called goddess braids, and he joked that every braid she has is a goddess braid.) "So pretty."

Lia rolls her eyes, but she lets her nose brush his.

"I do not suppose you want to wait at the ball at the weekend?" she asks, and he spins and buries his face in a ridiculously soft pillow so he doesn't have to see her expression, because if she pouts at him, it's game over.

"*Lia.*"

"If you do not wish to, that would be fine. They are just so boring, and—"

"And I just make your life better, right?" he asks, a smirk across his face he hopes she hears even though she can't see him. He doesn't know why. He's definitely going to say yes. "Would I have to wear one of those ridiculous suits again?" he huffs, and he can practically hear her smile.

"Yes," she whispers, her fingers ghosting over the back of his neck, and *fuck*. "But you look so handsome in a bow tie."

"Princess," he groans.

"Yes?" She laughs. "Will you do it? Tell me."

"You can't make me," he replies, burying his face further into the pillow, and it smells so much like her he almost moans.

"I would never make you do anything," she says. Jokes on her, he'd do anything she asked.

J.S. JASPER

He can feel her moving across the mattress, and he's nervous and excited for the fact she might touch him again. But he's entirely unprepared for her leaping onto his back, her fingers digging into his sides. "You did not answer my question!" she says with a laugh.

"Ali!"

"I am the Princess, am I not? Those are the rules."

"Those are not the—*Lia*," he gasps, his laughs getting swallowed by the feather-down pillow. He lets her fingers roam his body as he shakes against the mattress, and he only realizes why that's an issue when he flips them so she's underneath him, and she gasps as he leans against her.

He wasn't supposed to do anything. He wants her to know he wants to see her all the time, whether they kiss or not, and yet here he is, in bed with her, his dick prodding against her stomach. As his arms shake, he gulps willing his brain to restart so he can fling himself from the window. But then her hands move to his neck, and her eyes flick all over his face, and she's breathing so heavy her chest brushes his with every breath she takes.

"Elliot," she whispers, and he thinks it's a warning, even with her gaze locked on his lips. He'll be killed if anyone found them here—if he even thinks about kissing her in the ways he's dreamt of since he started here. But the moonlight trickles down her neck and across the swell of her breast, and he can imagine a different life for them. And he thinks if he's going to die, it would be worth it to know what she feels like, what she tastes like. So, he's foolish once more, dropping his head to touch his lips against her neck just once. He goes to move back, to move her, but then she holds his head to her throat, and he feels the vibration of her moan against her skin. He sucks lightly just below her jawline—not hard enough to mark, but enough that she'll feel it.

"Oh my God."

Aliyah's voice is deeper now, and Elliot feels it in every nerve ending on his body. She tilts her neck, and he doesn't need further prompting—he licks the juncture of her throat, sucking lightly as she pulls him closer. Her fingers tighten in his curls.

"Aliyah," he moans. It's half a warning, but he'll do whatever she wants. He moves his hand from the pillow to her shoulder and down. His fingers are light, ghosting over her arm until his hand is snug around her ribs. She rocks her hips like she did in the greenhouse, and his jaw is clenched so hard he might pass out. Lia presses against his chest, and he can't take it anymore. He spins until he's on his back, but she follows him, straddling his waist. Her hair hangs by her face, and her lips are slightly puffy, and he thinks she's utterly glorious.

She moves a little, blinking as she rests against him. Elliot doesn't want to pressure her, and he also doesn't want her to feel like she's alone in this, so he rests his hands against her hips.

"Okay?" he asks.

"Yes," she replies, her lips parted. "I did not – I do." She laughs a little. "I had no intentions of progressing further than a kiss, but I – I would like to try something."

"Whatever you want, I'm here." He rises to press his lips to her throat before he says, "Promise me something."

"Anything."

"You'll tell me to stop," Elliot insists.

"Okay."

"Promise?"

She nods, leaning down to kiss him just once. "I promise."

He runs his thumb against her chest, just on the side, so light he can barely feel past the material of her top. When his thumb traces over her nipple, she gasps, rocking her hips shallowly. His lips brush hers, but it doesn't count. Her mouth is open, her pants clear as day as he moves slowly. He's harder than he thinks he's been before, and he wants to cum so badly he feels like his toes are on fire. He slows down, just enough to stop the stars in his vision.

"Elliot," she whispers, her voice sounding like that's not what she wants. But he'll wait. "Can I—"

"Yes."

She laughs, and the curls that have fallen over her shoulder brush his chest. "You do not know what you are saying yes to." But she spreads her knees until she rests against him, her eyes closing as she makes contact, and he knows *exactly* what he's saying yes to.

"You're the prettiest thing that exists," he whispers, his hand against her face. He was supposed to move her hair, but he lets it hang as he brushes his fingers against her mouth. Elliot's just exploring. He's done this before, but never with someone as important to him as her. Never with someone that has not done this before, whatever *this* may be.

To his surprise, she licks over his thumb, edging it into her mouth. Elliot groans as her teeth graze over his knuckle, just on the softer side of hard. It makes his dick pulse, and he pulls her closer to him with her jaw in his hand.

"I want to be in control," she says around his thumb.

"You always are, my love," he replies. He watches her—the determination in her eyes, the nerves she holds in her shoulders—as if she's not the sexiest person he's ever seen in his entire life.

"You are glorious, and I've thought about this moment every day since I met you, and it's already better than my wildest dreams. So, don't overthink it," he whispers. "I will help you."

"Oh, you will help me?" she asks, dropping down until she rests her forearms on either side of his head. Elliot thought he was getting used to the effect Aliyah has on him, but he dangerously underestimated her like this. She's confident and sexy normally. That's just how she carries herself, with a beautiful fury and grace. Now, he gets to see her come alive, and it's possible coming will be something that happens embarrassingly fast.

Her teeth graze his ear, her fingers scratch at his scalp, and her voice is unfairly rough. "And how will you help me?"

Elliot closes his eyes, laughing through a clenched jaw. "*Fuck you.*"

"You want to, right?" she asks, rocking her hips slightly. Just enough that he knows she has all the power. Just enough to almost send him over the edge. "That is why you cannot breathe right now?"

"You have no idea," he says through gritted teeth.

She slides her hand between their bodies, her palm resting against his aching dick, and he's not sure how he's gotten this lucky. That she wants to touch him—that she wants to be with him like this.

"I have some idea," she whispers. He runs his fingers across her back, under her T-shirt. When he lets his fingers trail up the dip of her spine, he finds she has no bra on. He knew, of course, but the confirmation makes his stomach taut. "Do you want to hear what I do in my bedroom?"

Elliot groans, thrusting against her hand. "Yes. Tell me."

"I think about you," she whispers, her nose against his collarbone, and he thinks he might burst into flames. "Any time I touch myself, I am thinking about you."

"What do you think about?" he asks. He misses her face, but he's not about to tell her to stop. Her hand is still between them, and he's desperate to feel her touch on him, for her to slip her hand under his sweats, but he'll wait for whatever twisted game she has planned. She licks from the base of his neck to his ear, moving her hand in the same pattern along his dick.

"*Lia.*"

He throws his head back, and she bites along the chords of his neck. He uses the momentum of her movement to get her where he wants her, his hand heavy against her jaw. She slides her tongue against his like this is what they were made to do. Elliot has always liked kissing—he thinks it's unappreciated when sex is talked about—but he's never been kissed like this. Like all she can think about is him; like she needs *more*.

"You think about me, right?" she asks, her tone seductive, but he hears the undercurrent of nerves. As if he's thought about a single thing other than her since he met her. He was thinking about her long before he even knew who she was. She moves back, panting against his mouth.

"Yes," he replies. "I think about you, always. That's why I've been permanently horny since I moved here."

Aliyah giggles, kissing him again, and he feels lightheaded.

"What do you think about?" she asks, and he's well aware she didn't answer his question, but he'll let her off, because she keeps moving her hips against him and he loves her.

He hums, pushing her hair from her face with one hand, the other against her hip, moving her a little harder, a little faster.

"What you'd sound like," he mutters, rocking his hips harder, and the universe simply *loves* him, and she moans. It's quiet, caught behind her teeth, but his thighs tense all the same. Lia rolls her neck, and his hand falls to her chest. He's being patient—he wants to see her like this in so many ways—but he's hypnotized by the way her breasts move under her top as she grinds against him.

"What you'd taste like," he says.

She places her hands against his chest, the soft pants coming harder and faster as she moves. He watches her thighs tense with every movement and he's hypnotized. Her face is flushed, and Elliot knows his isn't much better. He lets her chase her high, her hips moving against his as he fights off his own orgasm. He squeezes her nipple through her shirt, his thumb flicking back and forth.

"Elliot," she whines, her hand against his jaw. He bites at the tips of her fingers, and she slides two into his mouth. He sucks on them, but she doesn't appear to care what he does right now. Her hips jerk, quickly, with no sense of rhythm.

"*Elliot.*"

He takes her hint, his hands grabbing fistfuls of her ass as he moves her with move vigor, grinding against her.

"Yes," she pants, "yes, Elliot, there. It—" She moans, a half-bitten thing that leaves him breathless, until she collapses until his chest. He comes as she shakes on top of him, and it's so strong he swears he almost blacks out.

"God, you're so fucking hot," he says, his chest tight as he holds her against him until his dick stops pulsing. She collapses her arms so her forehead rests in the crook of his neck.

She laughs, her hand against his chest. "Sorry that it was—"

Elliot frowns, rising to sit, and she follows, sitting on his thighs. "What?"

"Like, over clothes," she says. The confident woman who practically made him beg to come has disappeared into her pajamas.

"It's like a teenage rite of passage," Elliot replies with a smile. "Criminally underrated if you ask me."

She smiles. "We are not teens."

"No," he whispers, falling back to the mattress, closing his eyes as he links his fingers with hers. "But you were never allowed a teenage life, so we're allowed some do-overs."

"You do not mind if it takes a while until..." she starts, unreasonably nervous for someone who is still panting from their first orgasm with someone.

"Oh, my love, I would be just fine if we never touched again."

She lies on top of him, and he thinks he really could stay here forever. "Is that right?" she says.

Elliot hums. "Believe me, if you ever wanted to do anything else, I am game. So game it's embarrassing. But if you decide you didn't like it, then we'd cuddle and watch a film and I'd jerk off in the shower."

Lia laughs loudly, pulling their joined hands to her mouth. "You are ridiculous."

He shrugs. "Perhaps."

"I do want to do it again," she whispers. "I had fun."

"I had fun too," he mutters as he pulls her closer. "Lia?" She hums, her fingers tracing patterns against his stomach. "I *am* going to get you back."

Elliot leaves it five minutes before he groans and pulls Lia off the bed to wash up. They just use the sink, and she lets him be extra close because she's tired, and he never wants to be without her again.

"Eli," she says, as she slides into bed. He's waiting, because he's not sure what side she sleeps on, or if she wants him to actually stay. Then she frowns at him, looking between him and the bed, and he rests next to her with a laugh.

"What's up, Princess?"

"I think we need to add to our gameplan that we should always spend the night together."

"Alright, but you have to sleep like this," he jokes, wrapping his legs around her waist. Lia laughs, her face buried against his neck as he struggles to stay balanced with his entire body encasing hers.

"Elliot," she giggles, though she just places her arms around him too.

"Closer," he groans, pulling her tighter to him.

Aliyah laughs, shuffling until she slots against him. She sighs, her warm breath against his neck. "I have a photoshoot in a few days," she says, her voice low. "For my birthday portraits."

"Do you want me to come?"

She shakes her head. "You have the program all week, and you are desperate to spy on Lucian and Dorian."

"Those kids are at least six; they'll be fine unsupervised."

She groans. "You are so—"

"Funny? The love of your life? The hottest guy you've ever seen?"

Lia laughs, and as he feels her lashes stop moving against his neck, he wonders if she'll beat him to sleep. His eyes are heavy, and she's soft, and he thinks he might win.

Especially when she whispers, "*Yes*."

CHAPTER THIRTY-ONE

THE SPOON CLINKS AGAINST the china, and Aliyah smiles as Anna passes her a tea. Decaf, hopefully, because it's late, and she has a photoshoot she doesn't want to go to tomorrow.

"I don't suppose this Elliot wants to marry you," Anna huffs, perched on her armchair.

Aliyah told her of their plans. It's simply, really—engaging both Lucian and Dorian until the last moment, and then announcing on live television that she's going to be queen *without* a husband. It's the only way to get away with not marrying either of them, beyond them both dying in the next week. (Something Elliot assures her can still happen, but Aliyah's never been that lucky, and she'd never want Elliot to hurt anyone.) It will go over horrendously with her parents, but it will already be out. If they backtrack, the public retaliation will be hard and swift, and the Panimiros will never recover. Aliyah knows her mother says that if she does not marry either Lucian or Dorian, they will rule anyway, but Aliyah sees the fear in her eyes. It would tarnish their legacy, and she'd rather die than let that happen.

Anna thought it was a smart plan—the only plan—but she worries about how things will be alone. Anna knows as well as Aliyah does that the law allows her to marry whomever she chooses... but Lia happens to have fallen for someone who would never want to be part of her family.

"You would know if he did," she replies, pushing her hair off her shoulder with a sigh.

"And how?"

"I would have already asked him."

Anna sighs, a kind smile on her face. "And have you?" she asks.

Aliyah frowns. She just said she hadn't.

"I don't mean proposed," Anna continues. "I just mean have you asked him if that would be something he wanted in the future?"

"I do not know what I would do if he said no. And it is not fair to ask, anyway, because I would not say yes if he asked me to leave with him."

Anna looks at her with a knowing eye. "Wouldn't you?"

Lia huffs. He hasn't asked her, so she's not sure what she would say. Sure, if she married Lucian or Dorian, she'd probably spend all her days refusing to let any of their heinous bills pass, until they killed her. And if they manage to pull this off, the assassination attempts will be rife, even with the guards Elliot has managed to get on her side. She wonders what she would say if Elliot wanted to run off to some beach town. She hasn't thought about it, because he hasn't asked.

"I do not want to trap him here," she whispers. "Not like I did with you."

"Aliyah," Anna scolds. "You did not."

Lia knows that she did, but Anna would never admit it. It's why she's here, telling her of a plan that will allow Aliyah to live her life—a life she doesn't need protecting from—so that Anna can go. She can be free.

"If I become queen, will you go?"

"Lia," Anna sighs.

"Please. I will be free to leave. I will come and visit, I swear. Please, for me, will you leave?"

Anna places her teacup down, reaching for her hand. "*When* you become queen, I will leave."

Aliyah smiles, rubbing the back of Anna's hand with her thumbs. "You will?"

Anna laughs. "As if you won't banish me the moment that crown sits on your head."

Aliyah laughs back. "Maybe," she replies, looking at the time. "I should go. I have my birthday portraits tomorrow."

"Oooh," Anna replies with a shimmy. "I can't believe you're all grown up." Her eyes well. "Go, before I cry."

Aliyah laughs, reaching for her hand, then stands up and walks to the door. She hesitates. She never thought she'd have a guy she ever wanted to introduce to anyone, but she knows Elliot is waiting for her, and she wants him meet to Anna at least once.

She turns, her hand against the front door. "Do you want to meet him?"

"When?" Anna asks, her eyes bright.

"Uh... now? He is outside, waiting to take me home."

Anna jumps up, quickly wiping crumbs from the coffee table and putting dirty teacups in the sink as Aliyah laughs. When she's finished smoothing her hair, Aliyah opens the door.

"Eli?" she calls, and he stands up from the chair he's resting in. She hopes he hasn't been waiting long.

"Hi, my love. You ready?" he asks, walking closer. She bites on her lip, going out to meet him.

"Do you want to meet Anna?" she asks quietly.

"You want to take me home to meet your family?" he says, a sparkle in his eye as he wraps his arms around her waist.

She screws up her nose. "I changed my mind," she groans.

"Too bad. She's right behind you. Let's hope she likes me."

Anna laughs a little like Lia. It takes her a moment, and then her head is thrown back, and she holds onto her stomach. Elliot loves finding out more about Lia. Where she got her mannerisms from, and her childhood stories. (For the rest of time, he's going to tease her about talking to herself as a child.)

"I do not have a favorite color," Aliyah exclaims, as Anna assures her she used to be obsessed with pink. "Well, I do not have one now."

Elliot scoffs. "Yes, you do. It's orange."

Lia scowls at him, and he smiles. "And how would you know if I have never told you?"

"Everything you like is orange." He shrugs. She told him under trees that she didn't have a favorite color, but she's a dirty liar. "Every flower you point out on our walks is orange, the foxgloves you love at the lakeside are orange, your curtains are orange. You're definitely going to pick the crown with sapphires, because," he says, tapping his finger against her nose, and Anna laughs. "You love orange."

Aliyah's jaw drops open just slightly.

"Why do you think everything I have in the greenhouse is orange?" he says.

"What?" Aliyah laughs in surprise, and Elliot watches Anna smiling, like she knows how gone for her he is better than Lia does. She probably knows he'd marry her tomorrow.

"My notepad," he says, listing things off on his fingers. "The crates, the bench I made for you, the flowers that I regrow every few weeks because they *should* be outside. I'm not obsessed with orange, but you are, and I'm obsessed with you."

Elliot unwraps another hard sweet, popping it into his mouth as Lia leans over the counter to kiss him hard on the cheek.

"You are extraordinary."

He holds up the orange wrapper so she can see it. "See, I pied-pipered you. *Obsessed.*"

Anna laughs, Lia frowns, and Elliot thinks he's the luckiest guy alive.

"We are going now," Lia says, pretending to be grumpy.

Anna hops up from her seat and rubs Lia's shoulder. Elliot wonders if she lets anyone else properly touch her. It makes his heart beat too quickly.

"Pleasure to meet you," Elliot says, pulling Anna into a tight hug.

She hugs him back, whispering. "Do you have a ring?"

Well, he's the least subtle man alive.

"Yes," he whispers back, a knowing glance between them as Aliyah holds her hand out for him at the front door.

"Bye, lovebirds," Anna sing-songs, and Lia groans as Elliot bows as though Anna, too, were royalty.

The door closes, and the night air is chilly, but it's not too bad. As she storms down the path, Elliot wonders if Aliyah is truly upset with how the evening went. Her hand barely holds onto his as she tugs him out of the garden. He thought it went well, but he supposes if she's never had family members meet before, she might not understand the banter—she might take it the wrong way.

"Lia," he says chasing after her, but he needn't have, because a few steps later, she turns, pushing him against a tree, and her mouth is on his—urgent, insistent—and he'll let her do whatever she wants for the rest of time. He moans as she tugs at his lip, and he pulls her closer when she tries to retreat.

"If I put my hands down your trousers, are your boxers going to be orange?" she pants.

Elliot lets out a half-bitten moan. "You can find out."

She works her fingers into his trousers.

"Nuh-uh," he replies, holding her hand, then says, "It is my turn." Lia pouts, and he kisses her hard. "Bedroom. Now."

Elliot beats Aliyah to her room, because that sucker had to take the stairs and he climbed the trellis. Thankfully, she left the door unlocked. Or he did when he left this evening after sneaking in here. He forgot when she kissed him that he had slumber-party plans. That there is pizza, and snacks, and ridiculous activities that don't involve her hands on his dick, and he wants to throw it all away. But then the door unlocks, and she's there, pushing it closed again. She's panting, and he doesn't know if it's leftover from their need to kiss at every turn in the path, the way she rode his thigh for a moment, or her running up the stairs just now. He doesn't mind which.

When she spins, she comes straight at him and then stops, her eyes floating around her room. The fairy lights he's tacked to her four-poster bed. The bowls of sweets he set up.

"What... when did you... Eli?"

He huffs out a laugh. "I set it up while you were with Anna, and then promptly forgot when you kissed me. I was supposed to explain."

"What is this?" she asks, moving to lightly touch the basket of supplies he has on her bed. It's mainly eight types of face masks and hand creams. He had no idea what to get beyond trashy magazines and chocolate, but he didn't get the magazines, because they were all about her. But he does have plans to prank call Melody later, and he does have tweezers in case she wants to do something with his eyebrows, and he has his laptop full of rom-coms.

"It's a slumber party."

"For me?"

Elliot nods, watching her eyes light up when she sees the pajamas. They're matching because he's lame, but he doesn't mind when she throws herself at him.

"Why are you so cute?" she asks. "I love the pajamas."

"I know," he whispers, kissing her quickly. "They're orange."

She pouts at him, but it doesn't last long. "Can we start?"

"Of course." Elliot moves and hands her the pajamas and some sheets.

"Why do these smell so good?" she asks, sniffing the shorts with oranges on. The top says *orange you glad to see me*, and he has his phone ready for when she reads it.

"I washed them. I'm not a savage, Your Highness."

Lia pushes him away, but then she drags him to the bathroom.

"What are the sheets for?" she asks as she takes her socks off. Elliot is suddenly very aware he's going to see her without her top on for the first time. Properly. Obviously, when he helped her undress after their fight, he saw her then, but it doesn't count. He feels like he might giggle with glee.

"We need to build a fort," he replies, tugging his sweatshirt off. "Maybe we should just hang them from the corner of your bed because I forgot to bring anything for the floor."

"I have some air mattresses," she says as she pulls her T-shirt off. Elliot is supposed to ask her why she has those, but she's wearing a jewel-green bra—a tiny, sheer thing that distracts him entirely.

PERFECTLY CANDID

Elliot would still be in love with her if she didn't look like someone people painstakingly carved into marble, but she does. He has tried not to comment on her body because he knows others often do, and he never wants her to think he wouldn't be besotted with her no matter what she looks like, but it's a struggle as she slides her trousers down. The matching underwear might take him out. The way the green sits against her skin, the curve of her hips. His gaze glides from her hips, to her waist, to her chest.

"Eli?" she asks, with a light frown. "Are you alright?"

He huffs, scrubbing his hand over his face. "Yes. Sorry. Why do you have air mattresses?"

Her frown deepens, and she looks down, her arms coming across her toned stomach as she avoids his gaze. He realizes this is the first time he's seen her, and the first time she's shown him.

"Lia," he whispers, and she blinks rapidly, her hands searching for pajamas to put on. "Lia."

She swallows. "Yes?"

He grabs her shirt, pulling her toward him. His hands rest against her neck.

"You are the hottest woman alive—truly and unfairly the most glorious thing I have ever seen. I'm trying to be a gentleman," he whispers, and she looks up at him. His hand slides down her back, across her hip, and he grabs a handful of her ass. "But you are going to kill me."

"Do not... be a gentleman."

Elliot kisses her, one hand sliding to her waist, tugging her closer, and the other against the back of her neck. Lia licks her tongue into his mouth as they move together.

"How free is the palace with money?" he asks, as he lifts her with his hands heavy under her thighs, placing her on the ornate vanity. "Because I *need* a marble statue of you."

"You are a ridiculous man," she replies, her hands moving down his body.

"Maybe." His lips trace kisses against the line of her jaw. He runs his thumb over the material of her bra. Aliyah rolls her neck, but doesn't move against him, so he stops the motion, and he waits for her to decide what she wants. He kisses her neck, her jaw, and her nose before she moves her hands from his stomach to his chest.

"Are you okay?" he asks, his chest heaving.

"Yes," she replies, but it's too quick. His heart sinks—not because he thinks she's changed her mind, but because she's not telling him that. He can't—he won't—touch her if there's a hint of uncertainty.

"Elliot."

"What's up, Lia?" he asks, pushing her hair from her face. He tilts her face with his hand under her jaw. Her eyes are wide, something in them that looks too nervous, too unsure.

"I want you to think I am attractive," she says.

Elliot's eyes bulge. "Lia—" But she waves him off.

"I think you do; I did not mean that. I just—I want you to want to touch me, and I want you to tell me that." She swallows, and he moves closer. "I always want that. You make me feel... I do not even know how to describe how you make me feel when you look at me. But I want to kiss you."

He frowns, confused. "Okay," he replies.

"I *just* want to kiss you," she says. "For now. Not always. But right now, I just want to kiss you."

Elliot sighs with relief, kissing her quickly. "Okay."

"I know at the tree, I said—"

"Lia," he says, interrupting her, and she frowns. "You can always change your mind. We could be doing anything, at any time, and you can change your mind, and I will stop. I will always stop."

"And you will still kiss me?" she asks, the vulnerability in her tone making his chest tight. "Even dressed like this?"

"I will still kiss you," he replies, leaning forward. "Even more so when you are dressed like this. Unless you tell me not to."

She smiles, sitting up straight, pulling him closer. His dick is hard under his boxers, and it rests against her stomach.

"Um," he starts, feeling like a teenager for the first time. "I'm still going to be hard, because you look like a goddess and you kiss me like you want me and it drives me insane, but you never have to do anything about it."

Aliyah giggles, bringing his lips back to hers. It's slow, building toward nothing but a kiss, and it's the best moment of his life.

"Can we make a fort and put face masks on now?"

"Yes."

In the end, Lia puts a mask on him (she can't have one because she has a photo shoot tomorrow and she doesn't want to risk breaking out), she paints his toenails (orange), and he eats an upsetting amount of pizza. Lia eats two slices and a donut and says she's going to throw him into the lake if she bloats tomorrow, but she makes him promise to bring her some on the weekend. She gave them away by giggling when they prank called Melody, and now she has to invite her to her inauguration (but she said she was sending a car for her and his mom anyway). They kiss under the makeshift fort until she's panting, and he finds out she bought four different air mattresses for him to try (and kissed him quiet when he pointed out that three were orange).

It's the best slumber party of his life.

CHAPTER THIRTY-TWO

Disgusting. That's all Aliyah hears when she stomps across the field, her picnic basket in hand. It's a lovely day, weather wise, and she wants to go to the lake and be alone. She wants to throw things against the smooth water and watch them ripple and disappear. On days like today, where she's spent the morning getting ready for a photoshoot she never wanted to be in only to be berated for hours, she likes to imagine every stone she throws is her thoughts. Every time her shoulder aches from trying to reach the other side, the hurt that Graham thinks she looks too "urban" disappears. The fight she has every time about them wanting to straighten her hair, or about the fact they think she looks fat today, disappears completely as the pebble sinks in the water. Every single time, they disappear when she sits at the lake. Usually after a few hours and a book, but it's the only place apart from her bedroom where she can be truly alone, and she doesn't like to sully her bedroom with negative thoughts.

Somehow, she ends up outside the greenhouse. Aliyah waits for a moment to decide whether she even meant to come here. She didn't anticipate him coming with her—she's not even sure she packed enough food—but the children have gone home, so she supposes he could come, if he wanted. Does she want to show Elliot the hidden lake? Yes, probably. So she knocks.

"Hi," he shouts from somewhere deep, probably head-deep in compost because it's the middle of the afternoon and most people have things to do beyond strolling around the castle grounds. "I'm busy. What's up?"

"Oh," she says. Mainly to herself. She goes to walk away, to go to the lake by herself. She hasn't brought her swimsuit because she's not sure she wants to be in the water right now. Not by herself, anyway. She misses the days she'd get up at six a.m. just to swim.

"Lia?" he asks. She smiles because he sounds delighted that it might be her. It takes the sting out of the morning.

"Uh..." She starts talking to the door. "Yes, but do not fret. I can go."

"Wait, please," he replies, and she hears him jogging toward the door. She'd be able to see him if these windows weren't frosty with years of use. Maybe she'll clean them. But then the door swings open, and he's already smiling at her when she gets to look at him.

"Hi!"

"Hi," she smiles, the basket digging into her hip.

"Fuck, you look incredible," he says, looking her up and down. She took the ridiculous outfit off, but her makeup is still done. Elliot takes a quick look around, and before she has a moment to follow his eyeline, his lips are on hers. It's quick and dangerous and does everything to make her bad mood disappear. She pushes him into the greenhouse, and he lets her, reaching over her shoulder to close the door. He takes the basket from her, placing it on the side, and she kisses him again, just as quick, but no less heart racing.

"Sorry," she says, taking a step back. She wonders how long it will be before the warmth stops flooding through her body with every press of his lips. "I forgot people had jobs."

Aliyah never wants to remind Elliot who she is beyond her name, because there's no way he's forgotten how much he's never liked her family. Even if most of their conversations are surrounding how she's going to be queen by herself, sometimes she likes him just to think of her as Lia. He frowns, and she looks at the plants growing on the hanging shelf instead.

"Aren't you in the middle of designing the winter program?" he asks.

"Yes, but—"

"No buts," he interrupts, and her nose crinkles. "You have an important job, Lia."

She knows that. Sort of.

"Did you bring me lunch?" he asks, wiggling his eyebrows. And she guesses she did. She always packs a blanket and some snacks when she spends the day at the lake, but if she looked in the basket, she'd see two of everything, one of them bigger than the other. So, she nods.

"Is everything alright?" he asks, and she hates the way her throat burns. "Lia, are you hurt?"

"No," she says, shaking her head. Her voice is wetter than she would like, but it's fine. It's just Elliot. "Just a photo shoot with people who hate my face," she says with a huff.

"My love," he mutters, moving her hair from her face. "Did you want to stay? I'll tell you how beautiful you are every minute." Lia laughs. The greenhouse is nice. She feels safe here, so she sits on the bench Elliot made for her. She lasts five seconds.

"Actually," she says with a swallow, "I was going to the lake. Do you want to meet me later?"

"We can go now." He shrugs, removing his gloves.

"I thought you were busy," she says, frowning as he dips his head to kiss her.

He jogs to wash his hands. "Never too busy for you."

"Are you sure?"

"Uh, lady, I got an order from the Princess that I need to go to a lake. The rest will have to wait," he replies, pushing her out the back door as she laughs.

It's pretty out here. She always forgets how pretty. The trees are a lush green, and there's a new abundance of flowers. Oh, how she'd love to walk through the castle grounds showing Elliot anything and everything without the fear of repercussions.

She waits for him to lock up, her picnic basket in his hand. "I want to show you Lake Dalinko," she says.

Elliot gasps, spinning to face her as he turns the key. "Your secret hiding spot?"

Lia rolls her eyes, but she doesn't try and hide her smile from him. Not when they're finally on a path so hidden she knows no one will see them and she can think about holding his hand. It's silly, she knows, to still be nervous about initiating touching him first when she rode him yesterday with no issues. There's something in the way he looks at her that unleashes something. She wants to be sexy for him. He makes her feel like she's the most precious thing in the world.

They turn a corner, and she takes a deep breath. She chances a look at him, and he's already looking right at her. She screws up her nose, and he laughs, reaching for her hand. Their fingers glide over each other for a moment, but she secures them, squeezing their palms together. He lets out a happy sigh, and she thinks if she doesn't kiss him right now, she might explode.

"You can kiss me, you know," Elliot says, smug as anything, and her cheeks turn pink. "You don't have to think about it."

"Shhh," she groans, though she eyes the large tree coming up.

Elliot laughs lightly, but he beats her to it, dropping the picnic basket and pushing her against the tree trunk. His hands are soft against her waist, and she places hers against his chest. He doesn't kiss her in the way she's hoping for, and the panic rises in her chest. But she can be honest with him; that much she knows.

"I do not know how to do this," she whispers, her eyes on his lips. "I have only ever known love that you are supposed to think is there, even if you never see it. Even if it's never shown." She looks up at him, smiling as he looks down at her. "So please forgive me if it takes me some time to get used to the fact that you want me as I want you."

"I'm sorry, my love," he whispers, his fingers light against her hairline. He takes a deep breath. "I always feel so venomous when you speak about how people view you as if you should ever be anything other than joyfully happy."

"It is okay," she shrugs. "I have you."

"You do," he says, pressing his lips to her nose. "You do, and truly I would do anything for you. If you want me to cut my heart out and give it to you, I'd ask for a knife and—"

"Why would you need to?" she asks, standing on her tiptoes to kiss him for real. "You still have mine, do you not?"

Elliot laughs. His hands encase her body, and he lifts her just slightly as she strokes her tongue into his mouth.

"I love you," he whispers. "I love you. *I love you.* I am sorry for messing with you. It wasn't my intention."

PERFECTLY CANDID

"Was it not?" she asks, wondering if she's supposed to be able to stay standing when he tells her he loves her so casually.

"Maybe," he jokes, placing her back on the floor. He kisses her again, then bends to get the basket. "But I didn't know how you felt. I will stop."

"I do not mind when you mess with me," she says, reaching for his hand. He gives it to her easily.

"No?" he asks, and she shakes her head, pulling him closer so she can place her other hand against his bicep.

"But you might need to take the lead."

"Is that an order from the Princess?" He gasps, and she pushes him away.

"No, just me."

Lake Dalinko looks like it came out of a painting. The colors are so vibrant, and yet so pastel-like that Elliot thinks it's fake. The banks at the side of the lake are full of flowers that he will spend an unreasonable amount of time trying to decipher. A small waterfall splits the banks in two. There's a possibility that Lia lured him here for *something*. That he's actually in virtual reality. It would make any of this make sense. It would give a reason for the woman standing next to him, looking at him like he hung the sun for her.

"Pretty, right?"

Elliot scoffs, feeling emotional that he gets to see places like this with her. That she wanted to show him this area that is just for her. It's a smaller lake than the one they fished on, but it's infinitely more beautiful. The foxgloves sitting under the trees on the other side of the lake. The bluebells and the marigolds around the edge of the water.

"Thank you for bringing me here," he whispers.

Lia hums, resting her head against his shoulder, and he wonders if he should just tell her that he wants to stay here forever. That he'd want to be here next to her even if the lands were gray and barren. That there's nothing in his heart that doesn't yearn for her. That it has nothing to do with her being a princess; it's because everything he has and everything he is, is hers. She can have whatever she wants from him.

He presses his lips to the top of her head softly, and she tilts until her lips meet his. He gives her a moment to get used to it before she entirely intoxicates him, and then his hands are buried in her hair, and he's spinning them to back her against the nearest tree. There are few books on how to kiss, and even those he's sure aren't allowed in the palace, yet even though Lia has never kissed anyone but him, her lips on his are the best feeling in the world. Still, he opens her mouth slightly with his thumb, sliding his tongue against hers, and he can't hold back his growl when she moans lightly against him. Elliot slides his hand down her waist to under her bum, and she accommodates him by hiking her leg against his hip.

"I love this dress," he mutters against her lips as his hand slides past the short material. He waits, his palm against her thigh instead of gripping a handful of her ass like his dick is begging for.

"I only wore it for you."

Elliot groans, resting his forehead against hers. He pants, and he feels her thumbs stroking against his jaw. He kisses her cheek. His plan to tell her he loves her is right now. He was going to do it this evening, but now they're here, and he can't think of a better location. (Also, he told her he loved her three times like a second ago, so he's desperately running out of time.)

"Let's sit."

"I could kill them, you know," Elliot says with a shrug. "I have numerous ways to make it look like an accident."

"You had better be joking," Lia replies, though she's not sure he is. Well, she knows he won't kill Graham because he wanted her to be more sexual in her photos, but the thought that he knows how to kill now is something that weighs heavy on her heart. It will be for her, she knows that. Soon, there will be no threats. They only need to make it through one more ball, and they will be free.

"I will not slice his throat," he jokes with his hands in the air. "Though I think it's hypocritical, because you—"

"I did not," she says with a laugh, pushing him away, and he falls to the blanket. She follows him, smiling when he immediately opens his arms for her.

"Are they always like that?" Elliot asks. "I'm surprised they don't just ask to sleep with you when it's so clearly what they want."

"I have been pressured before, but—" She feels Elliot's hand tense behind her, and she wants to tell him he's ridiculous and cute and her favorite thing in the world. Instead, she rests her forearm on his chest and looks at him. "Nothing has ever happened. It is difficult to want to do anything like that when you know it can be plastered over tabloid news. I do not want to show someone my body and then read every critical thought someone has about it. It is bad enough when this afternoon happens. I cannot bear it if it were someone I cared about."

"Well, if you ever see someone you might want to trust, let me know."

"It is already you," she whispers. She trusts him, of course, and she knows he knows that. Elliot looks at her, moving her hair from her face with his fingertips.

"Is that right?"

She shrugs, letting her face fall against his chest again. "Do not be weird about it."

He laughs. "I've never been weird about anything in all my life."

Lia hums, watching the ripples on the lake and playing with Elliot's fingers. It does the same as if she were able to throw stones into the water. Her anger and her heartache sink to the bottom. The only thoughts she has left are of Elliot, the sunlight, and the slight embarrassing want for him to tell her she's pretty. It's ridiculous. Lia is almost twenty-five, and her stomach aches at the need for a guy to tell her she has a nice face. She'll allow herself the thoughts, though—she'll just keep them to herself.

"What are you thinking about?" Elliot asks.

Lia frowns. "I miss swimming."

"Did you bring a bathing suit?"

"No," she replies. "I was planning to come on my own, and I am not sure I could do it yet."

"Oh," he says, looking down at her. "Did I gatecrash? I can leave."

Lia holds onto his arm before he thinks he's funny and starts to get up. "I came to get you," she says with a laugh. "I just—I did not know until I got to the greenhouse that I wanted you to be there. I am used to being by myself, but it is nice to want to do nothing with someone else."

Elliot tips her chin up with his fingers, kissing her once. "Can I show you something?"

When Lia nods, Elliot pulls some envelopes out of his backpack. She wonders if he wrote her a letter back, but then she opens it, and there are photographs. They cascade out of the envelope, and as she tries to catch them, she realizes they're of her.

"I've been conducting my own photoshoot," he says when she picks one up. It's her, but she doesn't remember him taking it. She was expecting to see the lake—he never did show her those photos—but she's in the forest, frowning at him. The photo is at a strange angle, as if he had the camera down by his hip, but she still thinks it's nice. The trees are bright, and there's strong blades of sunshine above her. She smiles, slightly aghast as she looks at Elliot, and he turns it over.

Prettiest would-be murderer of all time.

Lia laughs and places the photo carefully back in the envelope. She picks another one. It's them on the lake. He's smiling at the camera, all wide and beautiful, even if half of his face is missing from the shot. Lia is in the middle in the sweater she never gave back to him, and she's looking right at him. She takes a deep breath, turning it over.

The moon and stars ain't got nothing on you.

"You wrote things about me on all of them?" she asks, her waterline filling with unshed tears.

"Yeah." He shrugs.

She looks at the photographs in front of her. There must be fifty at least.

"How did you think of so many?" she says, with a wet laugh. She looks at another. Her hair is flying around her face, her eyes obscured from the shot, so she can forgive herself for not realizing he had a camera.

Your rebellion is stunning.

She takes a deep breath. The things he's written are lovelier than anything she could think to say about him, even if she feels them down to her bones.

"It's not hard," he says, with a laugh that she thinks might be nervous. Maybe it's terrifying to have so much of yourself on show to someone. She wouldn't know. She's never been brave enough to say her thoughts out loud. "I could write a sonnet about the way your hair moves in a slight breeze."

There he goes again, saying life-shattering things like it's nothing.

"Shakespeare, are you?" she asks, looking over at him. His hand rests against her chin, and he wipes her cheek dry.

"My love," he whispers. "If Shakespeare could hear the way I think about you, he'd be quaking in his boots."

Lia gasps because how is he allowed to be so romantic? She flips over another photo. She's not even sure what she looks like in it, she only wants to see his words.

Perfectly candid.

"Elliot," she says with a soft sob. She lifts the next one, and she's not in it—no one is. It's a cherry blossom tree she's seen in the newspapers before. She told Elliot she missed being out in the real world, that she wanted to see this tree for real. She takes a deep breath, flipping it over.

I tried to cut a branch, but it's a busy street. I'll go back after dark. (I thought about kissing you here for an embarrassingly long time. I miss you.)

"We can go," she whispers, wiping the stray tears from her face. "When I am queen. We can go." She picks up another. It's from their impromptu sleepover. Lia is smiling despite the carrots and hummus being in shot. She doesn't even remember Elliot being particularly funny. But then she sees the angle, from when he pretend-fainted to the floor. God, she loves him. She might have loved him then. She turns it over.

The night I realized you were the love of my life.

"Oh my God." She looks up at him then back to the photo. "I love you."

Elliot moves quickly, up to his knees before she can think about it. His hands are against her face, his eyes frantic.

"Say that again."

Lia laughs and lets out a soft hiccup before she can speak. "I love you. I am in love with you."

Elliot laughs, kissing her once. "You love me?"

"To the moon and back."

Elliot gasps, spinning them until she's on her back and his leg is between hers. "Stealing my quotes, is it?"

Lia doesn't reply; she just brings his face to hers. His hand slides along her body, resting at her waist. Is it reckless to want him to touch her here? Perhaps. Does she think she's going to ask him to anyway? Yes.

"I can't believe you stole my first-time story," he whispers, his lips against her collarbone. His hands smooth over her ribs, pushing her arms above her head. He's close—somehow closer than they were the other day—and she loves it.

"You told me you loved me this morning," she says with a laugh, gasping as he licks down her chest.

"Semantics, sweetheart," he says. His voice is low as his finger traces along her bra strap. She looks down, and her sundress has fallen open just slightly. "This is pretty. Did you wear this for me?"

Lia shrugs. "I have always liked pretty underwear," she says, lying her hand against his and pushing it down until her dress moves out of the way. His hand lingers against her chest. No, she doesn't wear the underwear for him, but with the way his pupils blow, she's not mad that he sees them.

Elliot lightly traces the pattern in the lace, occasionally running over her nipple, and she doesn't try to hide how he affects her. He leans closer, his teeth pulling at her neck, down to her collarbone.

"Okay?" he asks as his lips touch the swell of her breast.

"Yeah, yes," she says, her hands in his hair. Her hips jolt when his tongue traces the same lines his fingers just took. When he moves the cup of her bra, exposing her to the air, she drops a hand to the picnic blanket.

"God, you're phenomenal," he mutters, before taking her nipple into his mouth. Lia gasps, her hand tightening on the blanket. She knew she would like to be touched here, but it feels more incredible than she thought.

"Elliot," she whines softly.

He chuckles, his tongue flicking over her as his hand descends to the waistband of her panties. "I fucking love this dress."

Lia bucks her hips, and he dips his fingers past the waistline in a torturously slow movement.

"Are you sure?" he asks, and she swallows. It will only hurt for a moment, and Elliot will make sure she's alright after.

"Ye—yes."

"Lia," he says. When she opens her eyes, his face is full of understanding. "What are you thinking?"

"Is—how long will it hurt?" she asks, and he frowns.

"It won't hurt."

"Are you sure?"

He pulls his fingers from her underwear, and she almost whines at the lack of contact that she's never even had.

"It won't hurt. We won't start until you are ready."

"But how will you know? I am ready now. I want you to touch me."

He kisses her. "I know. I know you do, and it's driving me crazy, but I need you to relax. I need you to trust me when I say it won't hurt. I don't want you going into this nervous."

She swallows, nodding. "I have done it myself," she says, and he groans, resting his forehead against his shoulder. "But your hands are bigger than mine."

"I'll make sure you're ready, my love," he says, kissing her shoulder. "But we can wait."

Aliyah doesn't want to wait. She wants him right now, and she knows he wants to touch her because she can feel him against her hip. So, she pulls him to her, his nose brushing hers.

"Touch me."

And he does. His fingers slide straight to her clit, and she barely stifles down a moan. No one has come to this lake before, but she doesn't want to call them over. Elliot's tongue is stiff against hers, and she thrusts her hips to meet the slow circling of his fingers.

"I've been thinking about this forever," he mutters against her lips. He rubs faster, harder, and when she's about to beg him, she feels him at her entrance.

"Breathe," he whispers, and she does. Her body slacks, and he pushes in slowly. She was expecting resistance, but he slides right in, and it takes her breath away. It doesn't hurt—not at all—but she can feel him. She takes a moment, and he doesn't move until she kisses him. It's slow, too slow, just the right amount of slow, until she's ready for more. She doesn't need to tell him, he just knows, and he bends his finger, and her back arches almost painfully.

"Oh my God," she moans. Her toes curl, and her fingers ache with how hard she's gripping the blanket as she tries to rock her hips against his hand—not that it's any use, his arm is holding her down. He moves his fingers deeper, and she'd be embarrassed by the whine she let out if she was capable of thinking about anything other than how good he makes her feel.

"Good?" he asks, then he lifts his head from where he was pulling her nipple with his teeth. "Lia."

"Good," she pants. She pulls him back to her chest, and he moans against her. His thumb strokes against her clit, and she needs him. She *desperately* needs him. She already has him, but she needs him to anchor her down, so she looks for his hand, and when she finds it, she twists their fingers together. He kisses up her throat until his lips hover against hers.

"Hi," he says casually, like he's not taking her apart, but his face was all she needed, and she tries to reply, but her orgasm barrels through her. Her back arches, and her toes curl, and she's never felt so electric in all her life.

"Holy fuck," she gasps, letting herself just breathe. Elliot pulls his fingers out slowly, but it still makes her frown a little. Somehow, it feels more intrusive than going in. Maybe she just wants him to stay. He pulls back, his face bright with a smile that she sees when she unscrews her eyes.

"What?" she asks, her fingers loosening in his hair as he presses his lips to hers.

"I have never heard you swear," he teases. Aliyah feels herself blush more than she already is.

"It is not very becoming of a princess to cuss." Elliot licks his fingers clean, and she's shocked, and maybe a little turned on. Then he whispers against her lips, "You will always be a princess to me, filthy mouth or not."

She laughs, pulling him into a hug. "I love you."

Elliot hums, spinning them over so she's on top of him. He fixes her bra for her, buttoning up her dress. "I love *you*. That was the best thing that's ever happened to me."

"You did not get anything out of it," she replies with a frown.

"Sweetheart, I got everything I could possibly need from that. Being able to touch you," he says, moving her dress until it sits properly. "Hearing your moans, knowing that I'm allowed to make you feel that way? It's the best thing that's ever happened to anyone."

"You are ridiculous," she says, leaning down to kiss him.

"So you've said, my love."

"It is sexy though," she whispers against his lips. "That you like it that much."

"I would give you everything I have to go down on you, and it's embarrassing how little I'm joking."

She laughs, sitting against his hips. She knows he's not lying because he's been hard against her bum this entire time. Lia thinks they should leave soon—being wet isn't something she finds comfortable for all that long—but before they do, she thinks she might go crazy if she doesn't touch him. She thinks she might understand what he means, because the thought of turning him on, of touching him, of making me come, makes her feel ecstatic. Besides, she already wants to give him everything she has, so she might as well get something out of it. He hasn't hinted. He'd probably be fine if she never touched him. It makes her want to even more.

She leans down, and he smiles, moving her hair.

"Hi."

"Hi," she replies. "Can I...?"

"Can you what, my love?" he asks, his eyes dark. She flicks her eyes over his face.

"I want to blow you."

Elliot chokes, his grip on the back of her neck heavier than before.

"Lia," he warns. She panics, just slightly.

"I know I have not done it before, but I have researched a bit, and—well, if you do not want me to, then—"

"Lia," he repeats, and she pouts as she looks at him. "You can do whatever you want to me for the rest of time."

"I can?"

Elliot huffs. "Yeah. I mean, I love you, I trust you, and you have lips like this," he says, his voice low as he runs his thumb over her bottom lip. She sucks his thumb into her mouth, and his eyes roll to the back of his head. "And when words like that come out of them... You said you were never going to kill me in the forest, and yet, it looks like you may try."

Lia bites at his thumb as she moves to undo his belt.

There's the snap of a twig somewhere in the forest, and she jolts. It'll be a squirrel. At worse, a deer. But then she hears laughter, and Elliot is moving before she can figure anything out.

"My love," he says, pulling her dress down, wiping the lipstick from her chin and making sure she's presentable. "Stay here."

"What?" she asks, her head spinning as the footsteps get closer. Two men? Maybe three? Are they here for her? Or worse, Elliot.

"There is too much to pack up," he says, looking at the food, the blankets, and the photos. "So, just pretend you were here as always, okay? Make them leave. Be all royal about it."

"Where are you going?" she asks. There's nowhere to hide. A tree trunk at best, but Elliot's shoulders are wider.

"I'm good at hiding."

PERFECTLY CANDID

Lia's heart breaks. She wants to shout from the rooftops that she's in love with him. "I do not want to hide you," she begs.

"Lia," he says frantically. "I love you. I love you, and I need you to stay safe, okay? So, right now, my love, we can't."

She knows he's right, and she wipes her face as he runs. One day soon, it won't matter if they're caught here, but for right now, they need to hide. She thinks he's going to take off around a corner, but he dives into the lake.

Lia settles down against the blanket, pulling Elliot's notepad out of his bag. She could be reading. They won't know her clit is still pulsing. So, she waits, and she puts on an air of disinterest. She's ready to tell them to get back to work, even though she has no idea what they are supposed to be doing. It's entirely plausible that they're guards sent by her parents and she's about to end up in the dungeons. Or, perhaps, she'll join Elliot in the water, but with a boulder attached to her feet. Lia doesn't care what they do to her, she just needs Elliot out of the lake.

But the footsteps become more distant. The path they followed didn't lead to the lake. Aliyah thinks it's worse that no one came around. No one would have seen them together, and yet she remains dry, and he's soaking and sad submerged under the shimmering surface. It makes her stomach flip with disgust. She waits three long seconds until she can no longer hear footsteps, and then she moves.

"I am so sorry," she exclaims, her eyebrows knitted together so closely she thinks she might get a headache. "Elliot." He's not there. Aliyah trips and stumbles over the tree roots to see the other side of the lake. "El, darling," she says, the panic settling in her bones. He'll be fine. He's a self-proclaimed amazing swimmer, and this lake is barely seven feet deep. "Elliot, I *swear* I will banish you."

He comes out from around a boulder, a smirk across his face as he swims toward her.

"Oh, you are a—"

"But you love me," he sing-songs, the water cascading over his shoulders as he swims closer. He's right, even if he's the worst person she knows from here to infinity. He holds his hand out, and she steadies herself, ready to help pull him out. His wet hand grabs hers, and his eyebrow rises.

"You miss swimming, right?"

"Elliot," she warns, but there's no heat in it.

"Princess."

She laughs, and his arm tenses. "Do. Not."

He tugs just lightly—not enough to move her, but enough to show her a life she could have. A life free from terror. A life with him. A life she'll have soon. She doesn't pull him back, and because she knows him oh so well, her eyes are closed by the time he pulls her in.

The water is freezing, even though the sun is hot, and she clings to Elliot as she waits to resurface. When she breaches the top of the lake, she takes a deep breath. There's no panic in her body; no lingering thought she won't survive this. He's smiling when she opens her eyes, and she's not sure how she ever made it this far without him. She missed him, and she didn't even know him, didn't even know what she wanted. And now here he is, and she won't make it if he goes.

"I do not know how to do any of this without you," she whispers, as he moves them around the lake. "You make everything better, Elliot. You make this bearable. You make it all worthwhile, and I cannot lose you. I will not make it." Elliot frowns, but she continues. "I know it is difficult, and I know it should be different. It *will* be different. But for right now—and I know I am being selfish with asking you to hide your emotions and keep us in the dark, but please," she begs, her hands on his face. "Please, just stay here with me."

"I won't leave you," he replies. "I am right here."

"Okay. Okay," she says with a light sigh. She rests her chin over his shoulder as he moves. She squeals as he dips them under the water, twisting them around like they could live under the surface for the rest of time. When they come back up, Lia is laughing.

Elliot smiles, moving her hair from her face. "Even if we're never destined to be more than this," he whispers against her lips. "Even if we're only allowed to be two people in the dark, hiding in the lake. If I have to watch you fall in love with some arch-nemesis

Neanderthal," he laughs, though she can tell there's no heat behind it. He reaches out, and Aliyah thinks he might twist a rogue curl around his finger, or tuck her hair behind her ear, but he pulls her closer with his hand on the back of her neck. Elliot's nose brushes hers, and she'll never tire of the way it sets her heart racing. "You'll always be the best part of my life."

She wants to ask him to marry her, but she won't, because she's not insane.

"You know," he starts, tipping his head back until he rewets his hair in the water. The lake ripples around him, the gold and yellow glint of the sun almost making her squint, but she powers through so she doesn't miss a moment of his smile. "I've been thinking about my life. How it ends, and what happens after, and yada yada."

"Naturally," Aliyah says with a laugh, as if the thought of the end of Elliot's life doesn't make her want to vomit.

"And in every version, it ends with you."

"Excuse me?"

"It's you." He shrugs, pulling her a little closer. Aliyah shivers as his hands slide up her back and the warmth of his skin is replaced by the chill of the lake. "When I think about being eighty-five, in a rocking chair, looking at the plants in our front garden, you're right next to me. And when my mind wanders and I think I'll croak at thirty, you're right there. I'm not sure if it's because I love you so, or because it's true, but I can't fathom a life without you."

"Eli," she whispers.

He shrugs but smiles all the same. "So, no, I don't mind hiding in the water because we can't be seen together. And I won't mind serving you champagne as you desperately try not to look at me for the thousandth time over dinner," he jokes.

"*Alright.*"

"As long as you're right there, the list of things I'd do for you is everlasting."

"Even my hair?" she jokes.

Elliot doesn't take the bait. "I will be here any way you want me to be. I will stand by your side if you want to abdicate and we will run away to my mother's spare room, and it will be amazing because I'll have your hand in mine. Or you can marry Lord

Fuckwad tomorrow, and I will still be here. I will stand in that hall with you, and then I will climb into your room every single night. I will be there for every meal if only to be the first person you search for in a room."

"Elliot," she whispers.

He kisses her quiet, and she lets him. "I'm right here. Where I want to be, with you, in any way that you'll have me."

"Every way," she replies. "I want you every way."

Elliot wiggles his eyebrows. "Princess," he murmurs, letting his hand fall from her waist. "How scandalous."

Lia rolls her eyes. "You are my boyfriend. That should not be a surprise."

"Am I?" he asks, his eyes wide, and Aliyah panics. She supposes not—she's never asked him, and he's never asked her. That's what normal people do, right? She's spent her entire life waiting for someone to declare themselves hers; she forgot it wasn't something she could just decide herself.

"Um..."

"Do you want me to be?" he asks, his hands lightly against her waist. "Because I would very much like to."

"You do?"

"Aliyah." He laughs, then says, "If I had thought that's what you wanted, I would have asked you the moment you held a knife to my throat."

"Let it go already." She laughs, then rests her forehead against his. "What else do you think about?"

Elliot hums, moving them to a sunnier patch of water. "You. My *girlfriend*. If you would like Melody's banana bread. Whether our children would know how to put two words together, or if they'd hit their second birthday and start by saying 'I need milk, do I not, Mommy?'" he asks, his voice posher than she's ever heard it.

"You think about our children?"

"Yeah," he replies, completely unphased. Like of course, he's thought about it. "Just, you know, pillow thoughts. If you didn't want children, I'd be fine with that too."

"You think about children but had no idea I would want you to be my boyfriend?" Lia asks with a laugh, and Elliot groans, swimming away. She misses his touch even tho he's barely three meters away.

"You're not allowed to call me out on my ridiculous thoughts."

She pouts, but then his hands come up, his phone between them, and she knows there will be another quote that will take her down by the knees.

"Are you not going to break that?" Her chin dips below the water but she manages to smile for him either way.

Elliot rolls his eyes, swimming back. "You're so old. Phones are waterproof now."

"Since when?" she asks.

"Such a grandma," he says with a shake of his head. He's next to her now, and he pulls her closer. "Do you want to know what I'm going to write on this one?"

She links her hands behind his neck. "Yes."

"There is no end without you," he whispers. "There is no comfort in knowing tomorrow exists if you are not by my side."

"Would you like to marry me?" she asks, the question out before she can think about it. Before she can figure out if this would feel like a trick because now he'd have to either say yes or tell her he didn't mean what he said.

"Yes."

"Sorry," she says quickly. "I know you hate the monarchy. That was—I should not have. I just do not know how to do this all without you, and I have been trained for it my entire life."

"Lia." She looks up at him, his smile rivaling the sun. "I said yes."

"Excuse me?"

Elliot laughs, kissing her hard, and the water rises to her cheeks, but she doesn't mind. "Yes, I want to marry you."

She kisses him back. "You do?"

"Ever since you tried to kill me under the plum trees."

Aliyah tries to frown, but it's no use. Her smile burst out of her regardless. "Are you sure?"

"You never needed to ask," he whispers. "I have always been yours."

"You hate the monarchy."

Elliot rolls his eyes. "I love *you*. I don't hate you. I could never hate anything you did, and you are the future of the monarchy, are you not?"

She smiles, her jaw aching with the suddenness of it. "*We* will be the future of the monarchy."

"I can't believe you proposed to me while I'm wearing dungarees and soaking wet," he says, his hand heavy against the back of her neck before she can call him out on it. Aliyah leans into the kiss.

"I did not," she mutters, but it's no use. He heard her.

Elliot gasps, pulling her bottom lip between his teeth. "Do you not want to marry me?" he jokes.

She dunks him under the water.

CHAPTER THIRTY-THREE

Elliot throws things into his bag, desperate to get to Aliyah's room. He had to come back to his dorm and change, because one, they were dripping wet from the lake (mostly dried by the time they got back to the main path), but then they realized Aliyah had to make it back to her room unseen. The gardens were full of people because it was the first hot, sunny day in a while, which brings the second point up. Elliot *fell* into the water fountain. A full, shin-hit-the-marble-side, flip over into the fountain fall. But it did what it was supposed to. The people gathered, mostly laughing, some dragging him out, and all the focus was on him, not on the Princess as she ran across the gardens.

Now, he's dry, and the need to see her again is settling into his bones. Otherwise, he'll call Melody and his mom and scream that he's engaged. Melody won't be shocked. Nor will his mom, seeing as she asked him the other day if he wanted her ring anytime soon. She claimed she figured it out with his posts on social media, (even after he said he didn't have a girlfriend because he *didn't*. Lia wasn't talking to him then) and he didn't want to ask her how because he was mortified. He's never posted a picture of her, not even her hands or hair. She's known worldwide, and he would never want to get her in trouble. It's mainly photos of places she's been. Places he wants to show her. God, he's a middle-aged white woman wrapped up in a twenty-something Black man in love.

As he zips his bag up, his phone rings, and he groans. He could ignore it. The last couple of times it's been cold callers. But as he watches the screen light up, he sees his mom's name.

He never ignores his mom.

"Hi," he says, sitting on the bed and setting up his phone so she'll be able to see him. When she comes on-screen, he can see her ear.

"Mom, you video-called," he says with a laugh. It takes her a moment to figure out what he means, and she scowls as she gets the phone into position. She's *so* close to the screen.

"The television won't work." She humphs, and Elliot groans, wiping his hand over his face. He sends a text to Melody. Trying to tell his mom how to use anything technological over the phone is the closest he's ever come to a mental breakdown.

"Mel's on her way, Mom," he replies, but he has missed her. "How's the knitting going?"

"Oh, you know," she says, peering down her nose at him. "I finished a blanket for you."

"Thanks! I'll come home soon. Or you can visit, if you like." He shrugs. "I'll get you train tickets." His mom hates the train, but she doesn't drive, and he can't think of another way to get her here if it's not an open day. Maybe Lia will let him borrow a car. Or a horse. Preferably the car.

"I made one for your girlfriend too," she replies, ignoring him entirely.

"Oh," he replies. "Ah…"

"Melody told me you told her nothing when she visited," his mother says. "And since when do you tell her nothing? Both my children, whom I birthed and raised, lying to me."

"*Mom,*" he replies with a light laugh. "It's complicated."

"Mm. I told you the grass was greener. Bring her when you come home," she says. Elliot wants to tell her the grass would be greener wherever Lia went because she spent so long nurturing it. And maybe he'd follow her anywhere even if the grass never grew. "Does she like tagine?"

"Ma," he starts, but there's a knock at his door, and he groans. "One sec, Mom." He flings the door open, and Aliyah stands there, smiling at him. He tilts his head, and she shrugs, the nerves still clear on her face.

"I just… I like your room." She *missed* him. She *loves* him.

PERFECTLY CANDID

"Come in," he says, pulling her into a hug. She goes to kiss him, and he can't believe the first time she initiates, he has to pull back. She frowns but doesn't say anything.

"My mom is on video call," he whispers.

"Oh. Do you want me to come back?"

Elliot chews on his lip. They're getting married. She'll have to meet his mom at some point. He just doesn't want to force it on her with no warning.

"Do... do you wanna meet her?" he asks, and her eyes go wide.

"Yes."

"Yes?" Elliot says, his eyebrows high, and Lia huffs.

"Do you not want me to?"

"Elliot, what is happening?" his mother calls out, and Lia jumps.

"I would love you too, I just—"

"Then I want to," Lia replies with a smile. She walks over, waiting for Elliot to sit first. "Wait." He hovers next to her, his leg in the video frame. "Does she hate me?"

Elliot frowns. "Why would she hate you?"

Lia looks around uncomfortably. "Because you did, and I—I just like to know beforehand if I need to make up for something."

Elliot's heart breaks as she plays with her fingers. This is his fault, and he'll be dealing with the consequences for as long as it takes for her to feel completely comfortable. When he's sure they're out of frame, he kisses her quickly.

"She's going to love you."

Aliyah takes a deep breath and sits next to him. Elliot's not sure his mother will, but she won't *dislike* her because of who she is. His mom just doesn't like many people. Elliot only ever introduced her to one girl, after they sat together on the bus home, and that girl never spoke to him again. His mom isn't rude; she's just not outwardly friendly. Those aren't mutually exclusive things.

"Mom, meet Lia. Lia, this is my mom, Tinisha."

"It is a pleasure to meet you, Mrs. Harper," Lia says, spinning her ring. Elliot pulls her hand between his.

"You can call her Tinisha."

Lia scoffs. "As if."

"Lia?" his mom asks. "Isn't that the Princess?"

"Er, well, yes." Elliot prepares himself.

"Thank you," his mom replies calmly. "Mellie's scheme is going to start next month, and she's been ecstatic."

Elliot frowns. He'd forgotten to give Lia the proposal. *Fuck*. He's the worst brother in all the land.

Lia, the ever-professional, smiles. "Oh, that is fantastic. Is she doing a launch?"

"I think so. It's the best program she's been able to pull off, and it's all thanks to your funding."

"You gave it to her without seeing the plans?" Elliot asks, and Lia shrugs.

"She is your sister."

Elliot's hands fly to her face, pulling her into a kiss. He almost slides his tongue into her mouth when he hears a throat clear.

"Elliot," his mother scorns. "I am right here."

He thinks he might blush for the first time.

"Sorry."

His mom tsks. "I am going, anyway. *Murder She Wrote* is on... or it will be, as soon as Mellie arrives to fix this darn television. Come home soon. Bring Lia, or don't come at all."

"Mom." Elliot frowns, but she doesn't say she's joking.

Lia laughs, running her hand over his before she asks, "Mrs. Harper, would you tell Melody that if she wants me to go to the launch, to let me know?"

His mom shrieks, the phone wobbling, and with the shaking fingers that appear on-screen, Elliot knows his mom is trying to call Melody at the same time. He waits for it, and then it happens—the call disconnects. She's probably unaware that they've even gone, but he'll text Melody later.

"Why are you the best thing that's ever happened to anyone?" Elliot asks, and Lia blushes.

"I think she liked me, right?"

"Sweetheart," he says with a light laugh. "She's already replacing my baby photos with pictures of you that she'll cut from the newspaper. You're the golden child now."

"You think?"

Elliot hums, kissing her deeply. She falls back onto his mattress, and he maneuvers them until he's between her legs. "She made you a blanket, and that was before she'd even seen you."

"*What?*"

Elliot pulls on her lip with his teeth. "I haven't told her about you, but apparently it's obvious I'm crazy in love from the way I talk," he mutters against her mouth. His hands grasp at the sweater she's wearing—his sweater—and he feels so possessive over her. Her happiness, her calm, her life. Lia's hand goes to his neck, and she takes control of the kiss, and he lets her, as he always will.

"I can't believe you sorted Mel's proposal out. I didn't even give it to you."

"I looked her up. It's a great program," Lia says, pulling his lip between her teeth. "But even if were not, I would have done it. I only did it for you, anyway. Melody being great is a bonus."

She tugs at his top, and he realizes wearing a shirt was a stupid idea. Lia sits up, pushing him until he's sitting on his heels, and she starts undoing his buttons. Her fingers are a little shaky, but he doesn't mention it, not when she licks over his throat.

"Elliot," she whispers.

"Yes. Whatever you want."

"You do not know what I am going to ask," she replies, pulling his earlobe between her teeth.

"Anything. Anything I have is yours."

She falls back to the mattress, and he stays where he is. She traces down his abs with her fingers, lingering against his waistband.

"I want to have sex."

Elliot's mind goes blank. It's not a shock. He thought they might have sex, but the fact she wants him in any way near like how he wants her? Well, it blows his mind.

Aliyah wants to laugh. Her chest is so full of love for him—the crease furrowing his brow, the way his thumb rubs along her cheekbone. It's entirely too cute how nervous he looks—as if she wasn't ready to give him everything the day she met him.

"Are you sure?" he asks, his eyes wide and his lips parted.

"Yes," she whispers, leaning up to pull him back to her with his lip between her teeth. "I never thought I would be able to make the decision myself, but I want it to be you. I will always want it to be you."

Thankfully, he takes that as a cue to take the lead, his hands deep in her hair as he pushes his tongue into her mouth. She's gotten used to kissing him (she knows how to flick her tongue to make him gasp now) but when they're like this, with him moving against her as well, it's all suddenly very new. She tightens her grip on his shirt, pulling up slightly. Aliyah has never undressed anyone before, but she's pretty sure this is okay. Besides, she's seen him without his top on, and she thinks he should be topless all the time.

"All the time?" he asks, a small smirk on his face as she feels her face heat up with the knowledge she spoke out loud. But she loves Elliot. She wants to do and try everything with him, so she shoves the embarrassment back down her throat as she locks eyes with him.

"All the time," she repeats, undoing the fiddly buttons on his shirt. She frowns. He was coming to see her. Why is he in a shirt?

"Is that an order, Princess?" he jokes, pulling the shirt from her hands and tearing it from his body. It's unreasonably attractive, and she feels herself clench as he throws it across the room.

"Yes," she replies, her fingers against his abs. "It is an order."

He smiles at her, her favorite smile—the one that threatens to split his face in half.

"I would do anything for you," he whispers against her lips, and she just wants him to take her clothes off. So, she finds his hands, and she moves them slowly over her chest and down to the hem of her sweater. Elliot's pupils blow, and most of her nerves fall to the floor when he drags it up with his teeth.

Aliyah's touched herself before. She told Elliot about it days ago when she was teasing him. She knows what she likes, and she knows Elliot will give it to her. There's just the small niggling in the back of her mind that he's done this before, and she has no idea what to do, not with him. She's tried to read all the books and she's researched so much recently, and there's nothing that suggests she should be good at it first time around, but she doesn't want to be *bad*.

"What's wrong?" he asks, slowing down his kisses against the column of her neck.

"Nothing," she replies, pulling his face back to hers. She gets lost in the feel of his lips, the way his hands move under her back, pulling her toward him. He tightens his grip around her as she moans against his tongue, and she feels far too hot when he pulls her lip with his teeth. Elliot pulls back, and when she opens her eyes, she finds him sitting on his heels on the floor between her legs. She should be embarrassed that she didn't even notice them moving around, and now she's perched on the edge of his bed, looking down at him.

"Hi," she says, her fingers playing with the edge of his duvet.

"Hi, my love," he replies, his hands lingering around her ankles. "Will you tell me what is wrong?"

"Nothing," she says instinctively. She wants to do this with him, and she doesn't want him to change his mind when he realizes she has no idea what to do. But she knows him, she trusts him and he's the best person she knows, so she knows he would never judge her for it. So, she laughs slightly, tucking her hair behind her ear as he looks at her in a way that makes her heart sing.

"I have not done this before," she whispers. "And I know you know that. But I also know you have done it before, and I do not want you to be let down."

Elliot frowns. "You could never let me down. We could stay like this forever, never going further than kissing each other, and you would still never let me down. I only want what you want to give me. I will only ever want what you want."

"I want to give you everything," she says, the hunger building in her chest.

"We can wait," he replies, his fingers tight against her legs. He's looking at her like he wants to devour her but is trying *really* hard to pretend he doesn't, and it makes her feel insane. So she leans to kiss him hard, pulling him until he's up on his knees, his hands sliding up her legs under her thighs.

"I want you now," she murmurs against his lips, spreading her legs when he tucks his fingers into her waistband. She lets him move her until her sweatpants are on the floor and her legs are wrapped around him. Aliyah feels her head hit his pillow, the smell of him all around her as his hands expertly move to rid her of her sweater.

The nerves turn to excitement. Excitement to know what he feels like, excitement to learn what she likes, excitement to be this close to him. Elliot is a fast learner, because every time he ghosts his hands over her chest, Lia can't help the breathy moan that escapes her lips, so he does it again. And again.

"Eli," she gasps, her hands gripping the sheets as he continues to touch her but never quite enough. She figures he's doing it on purpose, because he's the *worst*.

"Touch me."

"I am touching you," he teases, though he makes quick work of removing her shirt. She pouts at him—he's a menace—but it melts into a smile when he swears under his breath.

"Lia," he groans. "*Come on.*"

He tosses the top to the floor, and she watches him watch her. His eyes glide over every inch of her body, and she doesn't feel self-conscious at all. She may have never felt more beautiful than when Elliot smooths his hands over the bodysuit she has on. It's sheer, with embroidered flowers on it, and she loves it. Maybe even more when he licks over her nipple. His hands linger against the top of her hips, where the material meets her skin.

"Is this okay?" he asks, his hands moving around her thighs, and she lets out a shaky breath. She wants to feel his tongue, and she wants to know what he sounds like—if he will truly like getting her off. She wants everything with him, as long as he's naked as well.

"Can you take your trousers off?"

He's back between her legs before long, and she can see his toned ass from this angle, and she thinks that's *much* better. But then he moves the bottom of her underwear to the side and runs his forefingers lightly along her, spreading her lips. Lia swallows.

"Can I take this off?" Elliot asks, his voice rough. "It's pretty, and I don't want to tear it."

Aliyah huffs. "Yeah, yes." Elliot unbuttons her, and she sits up as he pulls the material from her body.

"Hi," he says, when they're face to face. "You're magnificent."

"Hi, darling," she replies, and she misses his smile because he kisses her too fast, laying her back down on the bed. He moves down her body, and she's lost to the feeling of him, the way his tongue claims different parts of her. The way his hands linger against her curves. The way he's careful with her. She becomes aware of herself when he settles between her legs, his hands hooked over the top of her thighs.

"Okay?" he asks, pressing his lips to her inner thigh. She nods, and he raises his eyebrows.

"Tell me," he demands, and a thrill rushes through her. Lia hates to be told what to do because she never has a chance to say no. Elliot would listen to her every thought, of that she's sure. He would never push her, and he'd be so unfalteringly kind about it that it makes her want to do whatever he asks.

"Yes, Elliot," she replies. "I want you to."

He smiles, ducking his head. She takes a deep breath and throws her head back against the pillow as he licks a stripe up her slit.

"Oh my God," she gasps, her fingers gripping his sheets tightly. She wants to thread her hands in his hair, and she probably will when she can think about anything other than how insane his tongue feels. He moans around her as he changes the pressure until he figures out what she likes. Aliyah grinds her hips against his face, chasing the feel of his tongue instead of overthinking her movements. He rewards her bravery by slowly dipping a finger into her cunt.

"Breathe," he whispers. "Remember what I taught you." She does, and when she relaxes, he pumps his finger lightly until she can barely think, the only thoughts she has centered around him.

"God, you're so fucking wet," he moans. "I'm never leaving here, by the way. I live here now."

"Shhh." She laughs, though it turns to a moan when he slowly moves his fingers again. Aliyah knows that sometimes a second orgasm can take longer, but with the way Elliot's tongue moves, she doesn't think it will take long. She holds onto his hair, thrusting her hips to meet his tongue.

"I need you to relax again," he mutters against her, and she does, but he removes his finger, and she almost pouts. Before she can tell her brain to move her muscles, he's back. It's tighter this time, and her back arches.

"Just breathe, sweetheart. I won't move." It's not painful, as he promised, but she can feel him *everywhere*. Her nerve endings are on fire, but she breathes like he said.

"Good girl," he whispers and she clenches around his fingers. Still, he doesn't move his hand, he just slows his tongue until her body is slack again. His movements are slow, and calculated, and when she misses him, she looks down, and he's looking right at her. She feels the tingles in her spine, her toes curling as her heels dig into his back. Her back arches as she feels herself teetering on the edge, but she needs something else. She just doesn't know what.

"Elliot," she whines.

"Just let go, my love," he murmurs against her, gripping her thighs, and the way his voice vibrates against her is enough. Her body shakes as she grinds her hips against his face, his fingers filling her, his mouth and hand cresting her higher until she finds her release. He licks her through her come down as she gasps for breath, and she hopes the sensation never leaves. Already, she can't wait to do it again.

"Fuck, Eli," she wheezes.

"You are perfect," he moans, crawling up her body. "So perfect."

Aliyah pulls his face to hers, slipping her tongue into his mouth the second she can. She's missed him. She frowns. "You taste like me," she whispers. "It is strange but I am alright with it."

Elliot hums happily. "Was that okay?"

She groans, but she'll indulge him anyway. "I think you know it was. It was *perfect*."

"*You* are perfect," he repeats, and she rolls her eyes.

He kisses her slowly, his tongue teasing hers as she feels his cock against her. He rocks against her, his tip jolting against her clit, and he moans when she grasps at his hair.

"Elliot, I want..." Their mouths are so close, but they aren't touching. "I want you. *All* of you."

"Are you sure?" he asks, grinding against her, and he'll be able to feel how wet she is for him, but she doesn't think he's teasing her this time.

"Yes." She moves up on her elbows so she can watch him roll a condom on, and she gulps. She's seen him through his sweats, through his dungarees, but she's never seen him like this. She's so sure it's longer than her fucking arm.

Elliot looks at her. "Lia. It'll fit."

Lia huffs. He leans down, and she feels him resting against her. "It will, and it won't hurt, but we can stop. We can always stop."

"I trust you."

"I know," he replies, then says, "but we still don't have to do anything."

Lia watches him—the small smile on his face, the blush on his dark skin, the way he blinks every time his dick pulses against her. She wraps her hand around him, and he's heavier, thicker than she thought. Somehow, she thought it might deflate a little, like the air bed she has sitting in her room.

She shuffles her hips, smiling wildly when Elliot groans as she pumps her fist. She could get him off like this, but she wants him—she *needs* him—so she lines him up. She thinks that she might have positioned him against her inner thigh, but she forgives herself, because she's swollen and going in blind.

"Darling," she whispers when his nose brushes hers. "Fuck me, please."

Elliot huffs, kissing her hard until he pulls back and she watches him line up, feeling his tip against her. It's not going to fit. But she trusts him, so she nods, and he pushes in slowly, the feeling more intense than his fingers but not unwelcome—it's just a lot.

"*Breathe*, Lia," he says, sounding a little like he needs to take his own advice.

"Yeah, okay," she replies, inhaling, then letting out a deep breath as he looks at her. He pushes in slowly, more and more each time, and she's unsure exactly how far he has left to go, but she feels like she can feel him in her chest. But then he stops with a groan.

"Are you comfortable?" he asks, his face flushed and his body tensed. It's a little unreasonable how attractive she finds him.

"Yeah," she replies, blowing out a deep breath to relax her body. It doesn't do as much as she's hoping, but it still doesn't hurt. "Are you?"

"Great," he says, looking strained, his neck taut. "You feel—*fuck*—amazing. You are amazing." His words are tight, but his face is as electric as she feels. She's not been waiting for this, but now she's here, she can't believe they've waited this long at all.

"You want a pillow?"

"Hmm?" she asks, wiggling her hips slightly to get the pressure off her back. Elliot grunts, and his hands grip the pillow next to her.

"Sorry," she winces but her body somehow relaxes all the same.

Elliot lets out a strained laugh and presses his lips to her forehead. "I am not in pain, my love. It has just never felt like this."

"Because I have not had sex before?"

"No," Elliot says with a tight laugh. She traces the muscles in his shoulder. "Because it is with you."

She grumbles, pulling him down into a kiss. "I am only letting you get away with that because I am happy right now."

"Okay, my love." He laughs, letting some more of his weight rest on her. Lia doesn't mind, because from here she can wrap her arms around his shoulders, and as she shifts her hips down slightly, it all fits better.

"Fuck, you are gripping me so tight. If I come before I've even moved know that it is entirely your fault. Your face," he says with a strained voice. "Your body. Your mind. God, it is all your fault."

"You can move," she whispers, as he presses his lips to her neck. It's slow at first, the pressure lessening slightly with every long, deep thrust he makes. It's not painful, she just feels full. She takes deep breaths when he moves, her body softening from her shoulders to her toes. It's a lot, until it's not. The movement settles into a pleasant, overwhelming feeling as she wraps her legs around his waist, her back arching as she slowly meets his thrusts.

"Faster, you can—yeah, like that," she gasps, holding him tight around his shoulders. "So good, Eli. You are so good."

"Not bad for a gardener, huh?" he says, his thrusts harder.

"There is nothing wrong"—she gasps—"with being a gardener. And you are so much more than that."

"Well, you are the future queen. I will listen to you," he moans, one hand heavy on her hip as the other guides her mouth to his, their lips barely connecting at all. He lets his hand settle behind her neck.

"It's okay?" he asks, and she nods. He presses his lips to hers, the slow movement of their tongues different from the frantic way his hips pulse.

"Can you touch yourself for me?" he asks, pulling back at the right time to see her shocked expression. Elliot laughs, kissing her quickly. "You don't have to."

"I would do anything for you," she whispers, repeating his words from earlier. She watches him watch her move her hand between their bodies, her fingers finding her clit with ease. It's better. It was already insane, but now there are shockwaves running through her body, and she hears Elliot moan every time she clenches, and she wasn't even sure she was going to come again. She didn't feel the need too, but she's already so close.

"Sweetheart," he starts, his chest flushed, and it should be embarrassing how she really only needs his voice to set her over the edge, but her body is tingling as her orgasm washes over her, so she really doesn't care at all.

"Fuck, Lia." Elliot groans, thrusting harder, faster, until he stills above her. Lia feels him pulse inside her, and she wishes they could do this without a condom, but she's already playing fast and loose with being banished, and having a child out of wedlock with a gardener is not going to do her any favors.

He kisses her on the temple as he pulls out. She winces, but it's not from pain. She didn't know she'd miss him when he was gone.

Elliot takes off the condom, and then he's back. He leans his forehead against her collarbone and pants, his hot breath against her chest.

"God, you're everything," he says. She can't help the giggle that escapes her throat as she runs her hands through his hair. They can do this whenever they like. There's one ball, and a few days until they're free.

"What?" he says with a laugh, his lips against her neck.

"Nothing. I am just happy."

"Yeah?" he asks, pulling back, smoothing her hair from his face.

"Yes. You make me so happy."

CHAPTER THIRTY-FOUR

ALIYAH'S GOT A STRIKE of nervousness sitting at the base of her spine. It thrums every time someone talks to her, making her fingers shake just a little. It has something to do with tonight being the end of it all. Probably. Maybe.

It also might be because she catches Elliot's gaze every now and then and it transports her back to this afternoon. He'd left a note and some tulips on her balcony.

Your most Royal Highness,
I know you're going to come and watch me work because you're a stalker and you think I'm stupid pretty, but at least you'll find this note. Please don't slice my throat for asking, but would you wear the green dress tonight? I had a dream and now it's imperative that I see you in it immediately. My life is on the line, Lia.
You look beautiful by the way. I haven't seen you in hours (a tragedy, please check I haven't died from lack of your face at once. You can send a hero on horseback, but I'd much rather see you). But you always look beautiful.
Please, if you have the time, meet me on the roof at five. Or four-thirty. Or six. Whatever time works for you, I will be there.
Yours,
Forever and always, until the end of time, for as long as I breathe, to the moon and back (you can pick one, but really, it's all of them)
Elliot
(Your future husband, sucker)
I love you.

J.S. JASPER

Aliyah all but ran to the roof the moment she was ready. The green silk flowing behind her as she ascended the stairs. And when she got there, there he was. Suit and all, flowers surrounding him, looking entirely like the only man she ever wants to look at for the rest of her life.

Her eyes watered and she did her best to blink them away. Not for fear she'd ruin her makeup, but because she didn't want to miss a moment of him.

"May I have this dance?"

Maybe it's the way he held her hand is his which means her breathing is choppy now she's standing holding a warm glass of champagne. Maybe it's the way he kissed her neck which is the reason she feels herself blushing whenever her hair touches her there. Maybe it's the way he pinned her front to the wall because she wouldn't stop trying to kiss him, and he didn't want to mess her lipstick up. Maybe it's the way his hand slid up her dress with the promise of *later*.

Maybe she's not nervous at all. Maybe it's just Elliot.

Elliot thinks it was a mistake to ask Aliyah to wear the green dress to the ball. Now she looks heartbreakingly beautiful while she laughs with men he wants to kill. Every time Dorian's hand lingers on her lower back, or he watches her flinch when Lucian whispers in her ear, he regrets every moment in his life that didn't lead to him being a lord. Especially when he can't even get close. Elliot isn't usually a jealous guy. He's always been of the idea that if you're in love, you only need to trust your partner. He does, he trusts Aliyah with his life. And yet, his spine thrums with a need to tell her she looks beautiful. That these men aren't worthy of the air they breathe. That he will keep her safe. That there's a permanent pulse in his fingers that's aching to hold her hand.

PERFECTLY CANDID

Aliyah doesn't belong to anyone. Even if Elliot *was* a lord, Aliyah would never be his. Yet the searing jealousy that runs through his veins when he has to watch from the sidelines as she's leered at and as people accost her as if they would be worthy of her time almost kills him off. Elliot hasn't felt this stressed since they put their plan into action. Every dinner and breakfast is relatively chill. Aliyah laughs, she lets her hand linger, and nothing has happened. When Elliot eavesdrops, he hears Lucian think she'll pick him, and he hears Dorian discussing the way he's going to change the palace colors when he's king. Neither of them seem aware that it's all going to be pulled out from under them.

Tonight feels different. Maybe because they're *so* close. It's her birthday in two days. They just need to make it forty-eight hours, and it seems like the world knows that and is testing his very existence.

It's better when he catches her looking at him. Every now and then, he stops circulating with his tray of champagne, and he looks over, and she's already looking at him. There's a possessive side of him that likes that she's wearing that dress for him because he asked her to. She's not trying to impress anyone here but him, and it settles the furious want to behead Lucian where he stands.

Aliyah either isn't as stressed out as him, or she's trying to calm him down, because she winks at him when his gaze drifts down her body. She flips her hair over her shoulder when she catches him staring. She runs her tongue over her lip when she finishes drinking and he's looking right at her.

He takes his chance, walking across the room with a tray of champagne that tastes like bathwater (not that it stopped him downing a few in the cellar when he needed a moment to calm down), and he stops in front of her. She ignores him entirely, barely acknowledging his existence until his head is bowed, and he watches her reach out for the tray. It was worth it, though, especially when she whispers to him. "The night is winding down, and no one has tried to kill me. So, meet me upstairs? I will be there as soon as I can." Then she places the empty glass down, and she's gone.

J.S. JASPER

Elliot wanders through the palace halls, smiling. The stained-glass windows look so decadent at nighttime, when the chandeliers flicker off them, leaving a rainbow glow on the limestone floor. He wonders if Lia will want to change anything. If she wants to redecorate the whole place, or if she thinks that would be a waste of money. He supposes they could redecorate a wing that's just theirs. He hopes she wants to stay in the same room she's in now. He likes the views over the gardens, and it reminds him of everything they've accomplished together.

He sighs. It's been hours since Lia whispered for him to meet her, and the ball has raged on this whole time. He waited in her room, then he waited in the greenhouse, and now, he misses her. It's almost three a.m., and he walks back to the ballroom. If she can't come to him, then he'll go back to her.

Waiters scuffle past him, whispering. He thinks nothing of it until he sees groups of people gossiping. Something happened. He looks around for anyone he can ask, but he comes up short. He walks toward a nearby group, hoping to eavesdrop. His money is on the Queen slapping a member of staff.

"I can't believe they pulled that card this close." A guard laughs. "Did you see her face?" The way they speak is vile, the hatred in their words is palpable. Elliot looks up, and the guards are old—they've probably been here longer than he's been alive—and he realizes they're talking about Aliyah. They have to be.

His heart drops, and he picks up his pace. When he gets to the ballroom, it's empty, though the band plays anyway. Where *is* she? He knew that the atmosphere was off tonight. That the Queen was practically giddy in her throne, and he's seen her stoney-faced at her own birthday party. He should have known they'd try something tonight. Some last-ditch attempt to coerce her into marrying either of those vile men.

Elliot takes a deep breath. Just because she's missing doesn't mean she's down *there*. But he runs either way.

The grass is damp with dew, and his stupid shoes slip every three seconds, but he pulls himself back up and follows the outside route. He doesn't need his notepad with the maps; he's got them memorized. It takes him too long to get there, between slowing down when guards walk past him and not being able to see in the dark, but he sees the faint change in the brick pattern.

The iron bars are hard to see in the darkness, but he'd find her anywhere, which only makes crawling onto the floor all that easier. The wet grass turns to mud the moment his hands hit the ground, but he pulls himself lower all the same. Elliot's quiet, just in case. It might not be her; she might be somewhere else. It could be someone else in there. It's a hope that makes him feel a bit sick. He doesn't want anyone to be hurt, but he'd throw a bus full of people off a cliff for her.

Elliot has never been angrier than he is now. His entire body vibrates, the ground beneath him threatening to topple. She can't be there. He's become distraught and delusional in the past five minutes. That's all. He's jumping to all sorts of conclusions. There's a logical reasoning behind why he hasn't seen her. Their paths crossed moments too late. She was by the lake while he wasted time by the greenhouse. Though, even as he says it to himself, he doesn't believe it. Elliot didn't believe in soulmates before Aliyah. But now that he knows her, how could he not? The love he has for her feels destined. Like even if he fought it, he'd never stand a chance of not being frightfully in love with her.

He creeps toward the bars, and it takes a moment for his eyes to adjust, but he knows in his bones it's her he can hear. Moments later, his heart falls out of his throat and into the dark, cold, stone dungeons she sits in.

"Lia," he whispers, but she doesn't hear him. He'd be surprised if she could hear anything over the sound of her teeth gnashing together. It's beyond cold tonight—almost freezing—and they've left her here in nothing but her ballgown. Her knees are pulled to her chest, her cheek against them. She looks so fucking sad.

Elliot swallows, the need to be rational taking over the animalistic side that wants to take down every single person in the palace as she wipes away a tear.

"Aliyah," he says louder. It startles her, and she all but jumps out of her skin. Her eyes are frantic as she wipes her face clean. Her expression is bored now, even though he can see the tension in her neck from here. She rubs at her wrist, and he wonders if she's preempting something. Elliot can't tell from here if she's been hurt, but the way she moves suggests she has, and his anger is barely contained.

"Lia," he says, his voice almost breaking at how terrified she looks. "Sweetheart."

"El?" she asks, standing up quickly, but she jolts, her body collapsing as she falls back to the ground. Elliot almost growls—he almost screams—because she is *chained to the fucking wall.*

"Lia, up here. Please. I am here."

Aliyah spins, her eyes frantically searching for him. A whimper penetrates the damp air when her eyes land on him.

"Hi," she chokes out. Her lower lip trembles, even as she holds her jaw tight. "Hi."

"I'm going to get you out of here, okay?"

Elliot is expecting a fight, and he's got a thousand reasons why she just needs to listen to him, but he doesn't need them. She nods and sits back on the floor.

Elliot riffles through his pockets. He's prepared—he's always prepared—but his hands are shaky because he's never seen her here. He never imagined it would be this hard. He tries to focus. The chain is the only thing that's different. The drain that leads to the stream is still there, so he can get her out that way if this iron bar doesn't shift.

"Darling," she whispers, and he looks over at her. "You need to breathe."

"Lia."

"Breathe, Elliot. Please."

He takes three deep breaths, and when he opens his eyes, she's still tied to a wall, and the bile rises in his throat.

"I am not hurt," she replies. "I am not hurt, but they will come back, so I need—*please*, take a breath."

She's right, as always, and he takes another breath.

"I love you," she says, and he chokes out a sob.

"Lia," he begs, wiping his face with the back of his hand. He looks for the lockpick that he's practiced on this window numerous times.

"Take a photo."

"What?" he asks, willing his fingers to stop shaking so he can make this work.

"Having proof is good, is it not?"

Elliot blinks rapidly. She's right. He grabs his phone, taking photos and a quick video where she says her name, and he wants to never see it again. He shoves the pin into the lock. Hopefully he can use the same one for her. Every time he's been here to scout the dungeons, the chains haven't been here, but he should have known. He was prepared for handcuffs, not chains.

There's a clang, and then footsteps coming toward her cell. Her face loses all color, and his hands shake as he tries to just get the fucking grate open already. Elliot has been so preoccupied with it being over, of keeping Lucian and Dorian away from her, of just getting to her birthday, that he forgot there was a chance they'd never make it there at all.

"Elliot," she says, her voice panicked as she looks at the door. "You need to go."

"No."

"You will get killed. Please, go."

"I am not leaving you here," he says, making sure each word is clear. "I will be here. If you are here, then I am here."

"Eli." She sobs. "*Please.*"

He sighs. He at least needs to hide if he is still to have a hope in hell of getting her out. So, he tucks himself to the side, but he leaves his phone propped up and recording. He can see through his phone screen as the door slams open. She doesn't jump, she doesn't flinch. She barely reacts at all.

The Queen walks in, and Elliot frowns. He was so sure this was Dorian or Lucian's doing.

"Hello, Mother," Aliyah says with a sweet smile.

"Princess," she replies. "I am sure you are upset."

"Why would I be upset? Because *you* changed the laws so that I cannot rule alone mere days before my twenty-fifth birthday?"

Elliot frowns. That's the notice he missed at the ball. It's nothing they spoke about before, but he supposes he did stop stalking them as much the past few days.

"Do not be childish, Princess," her mother says. "You and I both know that you were playing both of them. You had no intentions of marrying either one."

Lia frowns. "So what was the purpose of changing the law?"

The Queen hums. "Distraction. How was I to get you so upset you would not notice being stalked down a corridor? Besides, the law changes *after* your birthday, but I will make it so you marry a lord either way. So, pick."

"Pick what?"

"Lucian or Dorian. Pick one."

"I will not marry either."

Her mother hums like she was expecting that answer. "I tried to make this easier for you, dear." She sighs. "But you leave me no choice. You will marry whomever you have a child with."

Lia frowns, and Elliot's heart hits the bottom of his stomach. There's a reason she's chained to the wall this time. He moves slowly, his fingers back against the lock because he needs to get her out. He cannot leave her here. He cannot watch what she's suggesting is going to happen. He needs to get her out.

Aliyah scoffs. "Mother, if you think I will sleep with either of those two men—"

"And how will you stop them?" Lia's jaw drops. "You can still pick. Lucian can barely move his leg, so that might be preferable. Dorian is younger, a little more feisty."

"Mom," Lia begs, pulling at the chain attached to her arm. "Do not. I will—I will marry one of them. I will, I promise. Please."

The Queen sighs. "You have done nothing but let me down, Princess. You will not talk your way out of it this time. The time for decisions is over. You can have them at the same time," her mother says, like she's discussing pudding. "I am sure they would *love* that."

Aliyah yanks at the chain on the wall, and Elliot fiddles with the lock, but it doesn't move.

"No, mother, you cannot do this," Lia begs. "Mom, please. *Please*. I am your daughter."

The Queen looks at her. "You are no daughter of mine."

Lia doesn't bother looking shocked—she spends her energy trying to wriggle her wrist out of the cuff, but Elliot hears the heartbreak in her sob. It's too tight. It's not going to work. She contorts until she can stand on her wrist and Elliot moves back, resisting the urge to throw up as he looks through the supplies he has in his jacket pocket.

"You cannot do this to me!" she screams.

"Oh, but she can," Lucian says. Elliot hears Dorian laugh, and moments later, the cell door closes.

"Go away," Aliyah says, and it's the first time Elliot has heard true fear in her voice.

Lucian snarls, his hand quickly wrapping around Aliyah's braids as he yanks her hair back. "These will be the first to go." Elliot's going to kill him.

"Get off of me," she replies, her voice as calm as Elliot thinks she can make it. He's not as good as her though, he's not calm and his hands are shakey as he searches his pockets but he grabs what he's looking for, then throws them—the childish smoke bombs he got from the dollar store.

"I think I'll use your mouth first," Dorian says, his hand tight against Lia's jaw as she winces in pain.

"Please, go," she cries, and the men snicker. "You can go." But she wasn't talking to them.

Elliot barely waits the horrific two seconds it takes for the smoke bombs to take action, and then he runs to the nearest door into the palace—thankfully a rarely used staff corridor. Elliot stalks down the corridor, pocketknife in hand as he follows the directions he's spent weeks memorizing. His hands aren't shaking now, the need to protect her has taken over all other thoughts. The smoke starts spilling into the corridor, so he knows when he's close. The cell door is closed, so there's a chance both men are still in there, but he pushes it open with a creak. The realization sinks into him again. He is just a gardener who fell in love with a woman, and he will kill these men if he has to.

It's quiet, too quiet, and he can't see a thing because the smoke works better than he thought. He gets on his knees, trying to find a pocket of air that he can see in. Thankfully he can still breathe. He feels around, looking for her. His hand lands on the chain, and she whimpers. Elliot follows it until he touches a hand, and she kicks him in the chest. That's his girl.

"Lia?" he wheezes. "It's me."

"Oh my God." She sobs, pulling him into a hug. "You are here. I am so sorry. Are you hurt?"

"You're not allowed to be chained to a wall and ask me if I'm hurt," he says with a huff, pressing his lips to her temple. "I'm so sorry I'm late." He knows he needs to get her out of here, but the thought of letting go of her now makes no sense in his heart.

"It is alright. I knew you would come."

"Always," he says. "I'll always come for you."

He takes a deep breath and pulls against the chains. He pulls from the wall until he thinks his teeth might shatter, but it doesn't move. He tries to pull it apart at her wrist, but there's no use. He's sweating immediately, saliva dripping from his mouth with how hard he's straining, and it doesn't budge a bit.

"I could not get it off," she says with a sniff. "I think—um, I think we need to break my wrist, or my thumb. I tried, but—"

Elliot gags at the thought, and he shoves his hand into his pocket until he feels a set of keys—handcuff master keys he found on the internet. "Let's try this first." He traces her wrist until he finds the keyhole and shoves one in. It doesn't work.

When the fourth key doesn't work, Elliot starts to panic. The smoke is lifting, and they'll be back soon. He'll kill them, that's not the issue; the issue is the guards that will keep coming. At some point, he needs to get her out.

"Elliot," she says, then, "I think it is time—"

"I can't do it, Lia," he begs. "I can't break your wrist. I *can't*."

She holds his face in her hands, and he lets his nose brush hers in the dark.

"Please," he cries.

"It will not hurt," she whispers. "Not if it is you. And it is far better than what they have in store for me."

"Oh my God." He sobs, wiping his face. He's out of keys. He holds her hand in his, his thumb lightly against hers, and she's shaking, and he can't. "Lia."

"Eli," she begs. "I cannot stay here. If they... I will not make it. I know it should not be you, but it is. *Please*. Get me out of here."

Elliot bites on his cheek so hard it bleeds. He can do this. He can. He swore he'd be the only person who would never hurt her, but he has to. The smoke clears, and he sees her face for the first time. She's hauntingly beautiful, and she's looking right at him. There's no fear, there's nothing but acceptance.

"It is okay," she says with a sniff. "I love you."

His thumb lingers against her shaking hand, and he presses down just slightly, and she takes a deep breath and he still *can't*.

"It is okay, Elliot. It is okay. There is—there is money in an account you can access," Lia says, and Elliot frowns as he looks around the room, desperate for something—anything—that might help. "The numbers are under my mattress, okay? Elliot, darling, tell me you are listening."

And he scampers off the floor when he remembers he left his phone recording.

"Lia, stop," he says, blindly feeling his way across the room. The smoke is lifting, but not enough.

"You need to get Anna out for me," she says, ignoring him completely. "Get her and, uh—there are accounts for her, and you, and Mel and your mom, so just—"

"*Aliyah*. We are getting out of here," he says, his voice breaking as he grabs his phone, and the pins he was using to try and open the window. Of course she'd think about everyone else when she's the one chained to a wall. When he kneels in front of her, her hand smooths over the back of his neck. She presses her lips to his sweaty temple.

"I love you."

"Lia," he begs.
"You know that, right?"
"Lia, *please* stop saying goodbye."

She lets out a sob that breaks his heart in two, but as he inserts another pick and wriggles it furiously, the chain loosens. It doesn't open, but it might be enough.

"Okay," he says, holding her wrist gently. "I will pull it apart as far as I can, and you pull your wrist out."

Aliyah nods, quickly licking the skin on her hand to help make it slippery, and he pulls so hard the blood from his cheek spills out of his mouth. Aliyah gasps in pain, and he pulls harder. They're making too much noise; he knows that when he hears footsteps. He spins to face the door. "Fuck."

Aliyah whimpers, and Elliot places his foot against the wall for leverage. He strains his arms in the process, but the cuff snaps.

"Oh my God!" She lets out a sob of relief.

"Let's go," he says, pulling her toward the drain. "It's clean." He lifts the drain cover, and she hesitates, looking down at the dark, flowing water. It's pitch black, the water higher than he's ever seen it, but he knows that tunnel like the back of his hand.

"Sweetheart, I will be right there with you. Please, please go."

Aliyah's knees shake, but she moves, and he hates this. He hates how terrified she is, but the footsteps get closer. He'll get her in here if he has to pull her in screaming.

"Look at me," he says, and she does. "I will not leave you here, so if they catch us, they'll kill me."

Lia blinks, and then she moves, shuffling down his body and into the frigid water. He follows her, lowering the drain cover as quietly as he can as he hears the door slam open.

"Where the fuck is she?!" he hears Lucian growl. "Find her!"

Elliot's hold on Aliyah is strong, and he takes a moment to catch his breath. To know that she's safe, in his arms.

"I love you," he mutters against her hairline.

Elliot has walked this path numerous times, though the water has never been this high before. He didn't have time to do it at high tide. But he knows where the boulders are, and, more importantly, he knows where the exit is. The water reaches their chins, but she doesn't shake.

"Lia, I need to swim us out. I need you to get on my back and hold on. Okay?"

"I can swim," she says, her teeth chattering.

"I know. I know. But I won't know where you are, and I am two seconds away from a meltdown. I need to feel you on me."

She kisses him once. "Okay."

"We need to go. Trust me?" he asks, and she nods again, moving to his back and wrapping her arms around his neck. He hooks her thighs around his waist, then dives below the water.

CHAPTER THIRTY-FIVE

Aliyah knows she's in Elliot's room. She knows he's trying to talk to her, but she can't get her brain to function. She wants him to do whatever he has to—she trusts him—but she can't get the words out.

"We need to get you warm," he says, his voice low. "Lia." She looks at him, her eyes flicking over the panicked look in his eyes. "Do you need to do it?" he asks. "Or can I?"

Elliot looks worried, and she wants to snap out of it, if only to lessen the fear on his face. But all she can do is look at him. Her eyes flicking between the crease in his brow and the way he worries his lip with his teeth. His fingers brush her jaw and her eyes flutter closed. Somehow, with the terror still thrumming through her veins, battling the cold for what's going to make her panic most, all she needs, is his touch. Elliot leads her gently into the bathroom. Aliyah needs to shower, she knows that, so she lets him strip off her dress and absentmindedly thinks about how she wore it for him. How she was always anticipating him being the one to take it off. His hands move with care like she knew they would. His throat bobs like she knew it would. But this is never how she thought the night would end up. She walks to the shower, and Elliot holds her wrist gently.

"I can do it at the sink if the shower is too much."

Lia just shakes her head. She steps into the shower, then holds her hand out for him. Elliot joins her, holding the showerhead in his hand as he turns the water on. She doesn't flinch. She's not scared of him, she's just tired. So tired. So, she sits down, resting her back against the cool tiled wall. Elliot hangs the shower head up, the hot water hitting her skin, and then sits next to her. He doesn't touch her, just sits close. Aliyah takes some deep breaths, letting the warm water soothe her cold joints. She watches as the water runs clean. The blood from her wrist, from Elliot's mouth, circling the drain. The sting of the temperature change lessens and all she's left with is the way her mother left her there. The way Lucian pulled at her hair. The way Dorian grabbed her jaw.

Lia feels the pit of despair in her chest. The overwhelming need to cry, to scream, to throw something. But she never lets herself. She's been angry and sad for almost twenty-five years, and she's never let herself let go, because she never felt truly safe enough to do so.

She's left with the realization that she has no family. Not really. She was brought here under false pretenses, and it's done nothing but ruin her. She's been here for her whole life and still no one knows Elliot exists because there's no one in her life that thinks she's worthy of loving. Her eyes sting and she twists her ring with her thumb. Lia swallows, nothing good comes from crying and screaming. She knows that. Elliot rolls his neck beside her and she knows he's exhausted. He's had a traumatic evening too. She knows his entire time here at the palace has been plagued by the simple fact that he *knows* her. That he loves her. He should have been making friends, cutting roses, and enjoying his life. Instead, he's here with her. Saving her, time and time again. He's been in dungeons, crawling through tunnels, and listening to the words of men he should never even be in the same room as. He's the only person she has.

She's left with Elliot. And she'll ruin him too.

"Lia." She swallows, her throat burning. "Lia, look at me." She does, and he's already looking at her. His face is kind as he smiles at her. He's always kind.

"I love you. Whatever you're thinking right now. I love you."

"Please," she whispers. "Touch me."

The moment she talks, Elliot's arms are around her, moving her until she's sitting sideways between his legs, both of hers over one of his. She rests against his chest, letting him press kisses to her temple, and she breaks in the safety of his arms. He doesn't tell her everything is okay, he doesn't tell her she's alright. He just holds her.

Aliyah feels more like herself when Elliot carries her out of the shower and wraps her in a robe. Not like she wants to talk, but like she *could* if she wanted to. Like her fear has gone, leaving her in desperate need of rest. But she just watches him—the way he dries her hair, trying to smooth out the braids that have frizzed from the water (if she were a better person, she'd tell him they're getting changed tomorrow). The way he washes her makeup off with the products she knows he went out and bought the moment he thought she might stay here. The way he kisses her nose when he dries her face.

"Stalker," he whispers when she watches him change into sweats. She giggles—a small thing that starts in the center of her heart.

Elliot wraps his arms around her and moves her to his bed. It's almost morning, but she's going to avoid her parents until her birthday anyway, so she doesn't mind if she sleeps all day. Lia wonders if her parents know she's missing. Probably. Lucian and Dorian would have gone straight to their wing when they found the dungeon empty. She wonders what it all means now. If they'll leave before her birthday announcement tomorrow, knowing all is lost. If she'll have to see them at breakfast once again. If the moment she steps onto the lawn, they'll kill her.

"Stop thinking so hard, my love," Elliot whispers as he lays her on his bed. He's right. She's not scared now. The laws don't change until too late. Lucian and Dorian can't find her here. She'll be queen, and she'll have them banished, and everything will be alright. She just needs to get there, and she will, with Elliot.

He puts lotion on her and she wonders if anyone has been this in love in all their life. He pulls fluffy socks onto her feet and changes her into his softest sweats, and then he tucks her into bed, kneeling by her head.

"Hi," he whispers.

"Hi." He smooths the hair from her face, and she smiles. "This is the kindest thing anyone has ever done for me."

Elliot sighs, kissing her softly. "I will be kind to you beyond my last breath."

Lia laughs, but it morphs into a yawn too soon.

"Sleep, my love," Elliot says, his voice low. "I will get you pizza when you awake."

Lia frowns. "Are you not tired?"

"Yeah," he replies. "I will sleep on the floor." Her eyes immediately water, and Elliot rests his hand against her cheek. "I don't want to assume." He sighs again. "You've had a really traumatic fucking night, Lia. I will understand if you don't want to touch me for a while."

She sniffs. "You would not hurt me."

"No, of course not."

"Then come and lie with me, please?"

Elliot slides in next to her, his arms opening immediately as she twists their legs together.

"Thank you for coming for me," she says, her eyes heavy.

"I'm always on your side," he whispers. "I will always be there."

"Tell me you love me."

Elliot laughs, and she feels it in her toes. "I love you. I love you. I love you. You can sleep, my love," he mutters against her hairline. "I am right here."

"Tell me what you did today while I was getting ready," she whispers.

"You're supposed to be sleeping."

Lia grunts, her feet shuffling with minimal effort. "It is an order."

So, Elliot tells her about his day. How he missed her. How he pruned the trees by the lake. All of it, even though she fell asleep before he stopped laughing.

CHAPTER THIRTY-SIX

ALIYAH HAS NEVER BEEN excited for her birthday. Her twenty-fifth has been the most nerve-racking thing for *months*. Years, if she's honest, because she always knew what it meant. There will be a live television broadcast this afteroon, and she'll address the kingdom. They're expecting a husband, and what they'll have is her. Alone. Well, at some point, they'll have Elliot too, but she can't ask him to announce himself on television before he's even told his family they're engaged. So, she'll do it alone, for now, knowing Elliot will be watching from the stands.

Lia will get a fight from her parents, she knows that. There's not much they'll be able to do, though, and she's prepared to threaten them with the evidence Elliot has at his disposal. It will be enough to get them to stop, to get Lucian and Dorian to leave, but it will also be the end of them. Aliyah always wondered what would happen when she became queen. Would she still be fearful of her parents, or would she make them leave, to live the rest of their lives in a stately home and make rare appearances? She wishes she told Elliot who she was on the first day so she could have had it planned out. So she didn't feel so uncertain.

Alas, they had other things to discuss. How to get her out of a marriage she never wanted, among other things. She spent last night curled up against Elliot's chest as he took her braids out and kissed her softly, and she didn't care about anything other than him and the soft thump of his heart under her cheek.

Now, she's walking to breakfast. Possibly the last with her parents, but she wishes it wasn't. She wishes they were already gone, that she didn't have to tell them everything. That it all had worked itself out and she could eat pastries by herself. Elliot would watch her from the sidelines, and she'd be happy. She misses him already, and she's only been gone from him for a few hours as she got her hair done with the vague terror that her mother would stab her with a hairpin. But she wasn't there to wish her a happy birthday. So, Lia went with twists again, because Elliot said she looked like a dreamboat months ago, and it makes her stomach flip whenever she thinks about it.

She sighs as she walks along the corridor. It's just one more bad birthday. Lia doesn't even *care* about birthdays. (Even if she is planning Elliot's four months in advance.)

"Happy Birthday, Your Highness," a guard says, with a deep bow. Aliyah almost trips up. Guards don't talk to her.

"Thank you," she replies, with a light frown. He doesn't see it, of course; he's looking at the floor. The doors to the dining hall open, and she prepares herself for the announcement. The shout. But it never comes. The doors open, and it's blissfully silent. Lia finds out why moments later. No one is here. There are no guards lining the walls; her parents aren't sitting down ignoring her completely. Lucian and Dorian's seats aren't even at the table. But Elliot is.

He smiles at her, blindingly bright, and it's her favorite sight in all the land. Is she dreaming? She walks toward him, almost missing the abundance of decorations that line the hall.

"Elliot," she says, with a wet laugh. There are bouquets of flowers on every surface—light orange foxgloves interwoven with white peonies. There's orange bunting from corner to corner, hanging deep into the room. The table is covered in confetti, and yet, she can't take her eyes off him.

He bows, his arm out to the side. "Happy Birthday, Your Highness."

She can hug him, right? No one else is here. She thinks about it for a moment, but by the time she's figured it out, his hands are against her face, kissing her until she can't think about anything apart from the taste of orange juice on his tongue.

"Have you started breakfast without me?" she jokes.

He laughs, and she feels it against her ribs.

"I was thirsty, Lia," he chastises. "I can't believe you want me to die of thirst, today of all days."

She pushes his chest, but he doesn't move. He kisses her again, softly, until her heart is thumping like she's run a marathon, and then he pulls away. Out of the corner of her eye, she sees a branch from the cherry blossom tree she's dreamt about for years. She gasps. "Did you commit a crime for me?"

He clears his throat. "I have no idea what you're talking about. Are you hungry?" he asks, pulling her chair out. She sits, and he sits down next to her.

"Elliot," she whispers. Their fingers stay entwined as the staff—the *real* staff this time—bring out breakfast, a selection of pastries, and fruit. Elliot peels an orange for her, and he promises the strawberries aren't poisoned. She wants to ask him everything, but she just reaches for his hand instead.

"The children made the bouquets," he says with a smile when he catches her looking at them. "I had to bribe them with *so much* ice cream not to tell you."

Lia gasps. "Is that why Jamie was bouncing off the walls the other day?"

"I will not lie to my queen," Elliot says seriously, even as every part of his face is desperate to smile. "So, I will neither confirm nor deny."

"You are ridiculous."

"So you have said, my love." He pours her a glass of juice, and she laughs as he takes a sip even though he has his own in front of him. She wonders how it is that he's here. Alone. But she daren't ask in case she wakes up from a dream.

Elliot rubs his thumb over her knuckles. "I showed your parents the evidence," he says, and Lia's throat closes. "I also sent a copy for safekeeping, so if anything happens to me, it still exists. They're coming to the announcement, and they want to discuss the future with you later, but Lucian and Dorian have already gone."

Aliyah wonders if she wants to know the answer to her next question, but it's out of her mouth before she can think about the implications.

"Did you kill them?"

Elliot gasps. "On your birthday?" he scoffs. "I would never."

Aliyah's heart flipflops in her chest.

"But," he says, his free hand coming to rest against her face. "If they come back—if they so much as breathe your name." His fingers work their way into her hair, soothing the slight remaining sting from where Lucian grabbed her. "I will not hesitate."

"Elliot," she whispers, though she can't deny the thrill shooting through her that someone *wants* to protect her.

He shakes his head. "I will protect my lady, my heart, my queen." He ducks his head to press his lips to her jaw, and suddenly she wishes the lingering wait staff would run away. Then, with a wry smile. "Besides, you cannot stop me, I am your King."

Aliyah's smile takes over her face, and the terror of what may happen with her parents, the pain of what almost happened in the dungeon falls to the floor as Elliot whispers, "Am I not?"

"I love you," she says. "*I love you.*"

Elliot sighs, a smile on his face as he says wistfully, "The Princess loves me."

She giggles, looking around the room. It's so pretty that she barely wants to look away. But then Elliot rubs his thumb over her knuckles and she remembers she can watch him. In public. Out loud.

Aliyah takes a sip of orange juice. She wants the awful stuff over, then she can think about the rest of her life.

"What did my parents say?"

Elliot shrugs. "For a moment, I thought your mom might try and have her guards kill me."

"Elliot."

"Joking," he says with a smile. "Sort of. I told them we would go to the media if they tried to make you marry either of them. Your father threatened me a little, but he can barely move, so I wasn't afraid. Besides, I had backup."

Lia's fingers tighten around his as he spoons some strawberries onto her plate. "Backup?"

Elliot hums. "You know the guards and the staff I have gotten onside? Well, news spread, and it turns out, my love, that they love you. They are, in fact, ready for you to be queen."

"You think?"

"Mm-hmm. I told them you were planning a systematic overhaul of the political, social, and economic inequalities within your first year of reign, and, well, they thought that was a lot, but they were on board either way."

She rolls her eyes. "It is just three things."

"You're incredible," he says with a longing sigh. "Is it okay that I told your parents? I didn't want you to worry about it."

Lia leans across the table, kissing him hard on the mouth. "It is the best birthday present I have ever gotten."

Elliot scoffs when she leans back in her chair. "Wait until you see my *actual* gifts."

"*Elliot.*"

"What?" he laughs. "You reimbursed me for the hair products—which I did not want—and for the shifts I spent here when I was just staring at you. I had money to spend. Besides, I know the numbers to your accounts now."

She laughs. "They will be our accounts soon."

Elliot hums around his food, taking a sip of his drink. "Good, I still need a marble statue of you." Before she can call him out, he speaks again. "Also... do you want to announce that you're ruling alone because you *want* to rule alone, or because you don't want to pressure me? Because if it's the latter, I have a plan."

"What plan?" she asks, her eyes flicking over his face.

"Answer the question, Princess."

She smiles. "I would have married you the day I met you."

Elliot wrings his fingers together as he hears her footsteps coming along the path. Aliyah made it clear when she proposed that it didn't mean he had to rule with her if he didn't want to. That they could get married whenever he wanted. But he wants her now. He wants her to know that for every tough decision, he'll be by her side. And, more importantly, he wants her to know it's because he wants it, and not the timing of the announcement they made this afternoon. Her mother screamed and her father had a heart attack (he's fine, which is a real shame) but the media and the residents, they're ecstatic.

Elliot was always going to ask Aliyah to marry him. It floated through his mind when he thought death was imminent. He was just waiting for a nice summer evening. Also, for his mother's ring to arrive, and now, as he stands next to the lake during golden hour, he has both.

Elliot's not nervous Aliyah is going to say no. She asked him to marry him once, and he said yes, and he burst out of the public this afternoon to propose to her on national television, and she said yes. So, no, he's not nervous. His hands shake because he's excited at the prospect of getting to spend his life with her. Though, she might think he's utterly bizarre for this, seeing as they've already gotten engaged twice. But he's been planning this for weeks—longer than he even thought it could be something that could happen.

Elliot looks around to check it's perfect. The wind is slightly stronger than he thought, so the marigold petals keep being picked up, but it's alright. The way he's situated the candles means they shouldn't blow out, even if the wind picks up considerably. It's not lost on him that they could be caught here, but he's not hiding. They don't have to hide anymore.

"Eli?"

"Hi, my love," he whispers, stepping out from behind a tree just so he can see the moment her eyes widen slightly when she sees him.

"Hi." She smiles. "What is this?"

He waits until he can pull her into his arms, her hands lacing behind his neck as she kisses him slowly. He threads his hands into her hair, holding her close as he pulls back for air.

"I love you," he whispers, his chest heaving as she rests her forehead against his. "I love you." He strokes his thumb across her cheeks, and her eyes glisten with the candlelight.

"I love you," she replies, smiling at him like she has no idea how gone for her he is. Like she has no idea this is all for her. It will hurt when he thinks back on it—how unaware she is that she deserves the best in life. But for right now, he'll push that to the back of his mind, and he'll let go of her face to hand her a daisy chain. She rolls it onto her wrist.

"What is this for?"

He smiles. "In case I need a bribe."

Elliot gets down on one knee and watches her jaw drop and her eyes widen.

"What are you doing?" she asks, her eyes flicking over his face.

"I love you," he says, his voice wet as the tears pool in the corners of his eyes. He pulls a small wooden box he made weeks ago, now holding his mother's ring, out of his pocket, lifts the lid, and turns it to face her.

"I love you as well," she replies.

Elliot laughs. "I know." The thought is as utterly absurd as it was when he first sat down next to her. There was never a chance he deserved her then, and he doesn't now, but he loves her anyway. "I know technically we've been engaged twice already, but three times sounds so much better, right?"

"Elliot." She laughs, her hand over her mouth, but he can see her smile peeking through her fingers. "You already said yes, did you not?"

"I don't know what you're talking about," he whispers, standing up because he misses the feel of her hands. She doesn't make him wait, her hands pulling his face toward hers, her lips telling him she's saying yes even though he hasn't heard the word yet.

"I cannot believe I love you this much, and yet I am banishing you tomorrow," she says with a laugh, her tongue in his mouth before he can combat her. Their kiss is soft, though he feels her shiver against him. Elliot feels the edges of the ring box in his palm as he spreads his other hand against her back.

"You can't get rid of me, Your Highness," he promises, "especially if you -"

"Yes," she replies instantly.

"Princess," he teases, pressing his lips against hers. "You don't know what you're saying yes to."

"Whatever you may like, it will always be yes," she says, and he feels the smile across her face as she kisses him back.

"Marry me, Lia," he says for the second time. This time just for them. Just for her. Elliot kisses her before she has a chance to answer, but he knows what it will be. He has done ever since she tried to kill him all those months ago.

"I promise to love you forever," he says, his hand finding hers. He slides the ring on her finger, and it fits perfectly, because of course it does. He watches the topaz sparkle in the candlelight, and when he looks back at her, she's already looking at him, her lip caught between her teeth.

"You can ask me for pizza every day, and you can dismantle the monarchy on a Thursday if you like, and you can ask me to run you a bath at four a.m. You can have whatever you want from me. I will love you forever anyway."

"I will love you, as well," she whispers, her eyes wet as she looks at him.

Elliot pulls a photograph out of his pocket. It's her, as it always is, but he's in it too. They're on the lake. He likes to say it's their first date, because Lia *did* tell him he should take her. She's looking at the camera, and he's looking at her, exactly as it always should be. He holds it out for her, turning it over when she looks up at him.

I'm going to ask you to marry me one day.

"Aliyah Giorgia Juliet Panimiro, will you marry me?"

"Yes," she says with a beaming smile, and he lifts her to spin her around because it seems like the right thing to do. And it is. She's magnificent. And best of all, though he'll never say it out loud, she's his.

EPILOGUE

Coronation day is always stressful. Aliyah knows that. She's known it since she was four. The guards are in a panic, the guests try and slide into restricted rooms, and her dress is too tight. But right now, her nerves are nowhere near her. Not as she leans against the bookcase in the library, her leg hiked over Elliot's shoulder. His mouth works her in such a way that it almost makes it impossible for Aliyah to stay still. She needs to be quiet; they could be found so easily. Even though they no longer have to hide, she thinks this is a sight she'd like left out of national newspapers. At the very least, not something her guards should witness.

She looks out of the window. The grounds are perfectly manicured, covered in flowers and decorations. She's had oversight on the plans, ensuring local companies are used and money is saved where possible. They'd wanted to do the coronation at a different time, because currently, there are building works underway for new education centers and a children's home (a massive project, with matching locations set up in Loven), but Aliyah and Elliot realized they didn't mind. It's not about looking perfect all the time; it's about making the biggest difference.

"Stop thinking so hard," Elliot says against her cunt. "I am doing my best work here, am I not?"

Aliyah fights the urge to squirm against him, almost certainly threatening his supply of oxygen when her thighs tremble and clamp down on his face, but that only seems to make him suck harder, his lips around her folds, seeming more determined to lick and flick at her clit with his tongue until she's a trembling mess.

Her dress won't crease, she knows that, but Elliot's hair has already been done, and she needs something to hold onto before she combusts. When she tries to draw away, he seizes her hips, pinning her to his face greedily, at such an angle that pulling away out of some last bid of concern for him only makes her ride his tongue in this seesaw manner, like he's fucking her with his tongue.

"Elliot," she moans. He gives her what he wants—as always—and his finger dips into her with an embarrassing ease. He's barely knuckle deep when her thighs tense, and she comes on his tongue.

"You have been perfect every day of your life," he whispers, kissing the inside of her thigh. Or he's wiping his face clean, either or. She won't mind; there's enough layers on this gown for him to get away with it.

"Butter me up all you like," she pants, and her heart settles when she sees his face again. God, he's stupid pretty. He looks less youthful and more manly, with his dark locs and beard she finally convinced him to grow out. Regal. "I am *still* not blowing you before we go out there."

"Not after last time?" he asks, a smirk on his face. It wasn't even a scandal. A gossip magazine mentioned she spilled wine, and she had to deal with a week of a couple of people trying to say she was a drunk. But she let it go, so they didn't realize what was *actually* on her gown before she spilled the wine to cover it. Or the way her husband was blushing the entire night.

"Shhh." She groans, but Elliot just pulls her into a hug.

"How are you, really?"

Aliyah takes a deep breath. "Nervous, but I do not know why. He is ready."

"That he is, my love," Elliot replies. "But you can be nervous all the same. He is our child."

She hums, pressing her lips to his, just once. Dominik II didn't want a wife nor a husband, and Aliyah and Elliot agreed at the time. He wishes to rule alone. They still agree now, but it makes her stomach flip that he'll stand at the altar by himself. He's told them time and time again that he's perfectly happy, that romance

PERFECTLY CANDID

isn't something he feels, and how can they complain when he's the sweetest soul alive?

"We must go. You know he gets mean when we are late."

Elliot shivers. "Last week he told me my socks were *lame*."

"Well, they were covered in mini oranges, darling, were they not?"

"Yes, but my wife bought them for me," he mumbles against her hair. "And I haven't said no to you for thirty-three years, so why start now?"

ABOUT THE AUTHOR

Can we talk about love? I'm dying to talk about love!
Other books by me:
Storm Cloud
The Last Good Thing
Bite Me Twice
Just a Pretty Face
Season's Hatings

You can find me on socials:
linktr.ee/jsjasper

Love you, bye x

Printed in Great Britain
by Amazon